Giorgio Faletti graduated with a degree in Law and went on to become a singer-songwriter, TV comedian and actor.

I Kill was his first thriller. Published in 2002, it topped the bestseller lists for over a year. The novel has since been translated into more than twenty-five languages, including Chinese, French, German, Japanese, Portuguese, Russian and Spanish.

D0334686

I Am God

Giorgio Faletti

Translated by Howard Curtis

corsair

To Mauro, for the rest of the journey

Constable & Robinson Ltd
3 The Lanchesters
162 Fulham Palace Road
London W6 9ER
www.constablerobinson.com

First published in Italy by Baldini Castoldi Dalai *editore* S.p.A. as
Io Sono Dio in 2009

First published in the UK by Constable,
an imprint of Constable & Robinson Ltd, 2011

A copy of the British Library Cataloguing in
Publication data is available from the British Library

ISBN 978-1-84901-433-5 (B-format)
ISBN 978-1-84901-964-4 (A-format)

Printed and bound in the UK

1 3 5 7 9 10 8 6 4 2

I feel like a hitchhiker caught in a
hailstorm on a Texas highway.
I can't run.
I can't hide.
And I can't make it stop.

Lyndon B. Johnson
President of the United States

EIGHT MINUTES

I start walking.

I walk slowly because I don't need to run. I walk slowly because I don't want to run. Everything is planned, down to the time it'll take me to walk that distance. According to my calculations, I only need eight minutes. I have a cheap watch on my wrist and a weight in the pocket of my jacket. It's a green cotton jacket, and on the little pocket at the front, over the heart, there used to be a sewed-on strip bearing a name and a rank. The memory of the person it belonged to has faded, as if that memory was given to a senile old man for safekeeping. All that remains of that strip is a slightly lighter patch, like a small bruise on the material, which had already survived a thousand washes when someone

who?

why?

tore off that thin strip and transferred the name, first on to a gravestone and then into oblivion.

Now it's a jacket and that's it.

My jacket.

I've decided I'll put it on every time I go out for my little eight-minute walk. My steps will be lost like whispers in the roar of millions of other steps walked every day in this city. The minutes will merge into one another.

I have to walk eight minutes at a regular pace to be sure that the radio signal is sufficiently strong to carry out its task.

I read somewhere that if the sun suddenly went out, its light would continue to reach the earth for another eight minutes before plunging everything into the dark and cold of farewell.

All at once, I remember that and start to laugh. Alone, in the middle of the people and the traffic, my head raised to the sky, my mouth wide open on a New York sidewalk as if surprised by a satellite in space, I start laughing. People move around me and look at this guy laughing like a crazy man.

Some may be thinking I really am crazy.

One joins in with my laughter for a few moments, then realizes he's laughing without knowing why. I laugh until I weep at the incredible, contemptuous meanness of fate. Men have lived to think, and others haven't been able to because they've been forced merely to survive.

And others to die.

An anxiety without remission, a breathless wheezing, a question mark to be carried on their backs like the weight of a cross, because that uphill climb is an illness that never ends. Nobody has found a remedy, for the simple reason that there is no remedy.

Mine is just a suggestion: eight minutes.

None of the human beings bustling around me has any idea when those last eight minutes will begin.

But I do.

I hold the sun in my hands, and I can blot it out whenever I want. I reach the point that, for my steps and my stopwatch, represents the word 'here'. I put my hand in my pocket and my fingers close around a small, solid, familiar object.

My skin on the plastic is a reliable guide, a path to be travelled, an ever-watchful memory.

I find a button and press it gently.

And another.

And then one more.

A moment or a thousand years later, the explosion is like thunder without a storm, the earth greeting the sky, a moment of liberation.

Then the screams and the dust and the sound of cars crashing, and the sirens tell me that for many people behind me the eight minutes are over.

This is my power.

This is my duty.

This is my will.

I am God.

Too Many Years Earlier

CHAPTER 1

The ceiling was white, but for the man lying on the couch it was full of images and mirrors. The images were the same ones that had been haunting him every night for months. The mirrors were those of reality and memory, in which he continued to see his face reflected.

The face he had now, the face he used to have.

Two different faces, the tragic spell of a transformation, two pawns that in their journey had marked the beginning and end of that long parlour game called war. Many people had played that one, too many. Some had had to stay out of the game for one turn, others for ever.

Nobody had won. Nobody, on either side.

But in spite of everything, he had made it back. He had kept his life and the ability to look, but had lost for ever the desire to be looked at. Now, for him, the world didn't go beyond the limits of his own shadow.

Behind him, Colonel Lensky, the army psychiatrist, was seated in a leather armchair, a friendly presence in a defensive position. It had been months, maybe years, in fact centuries, that they had been meeting in this room that couldn't erase from the air the slight smell of rust you always found on military premises. Even though this wasn't a barracks, but a hospital.

The colonel was a man with sparse brown hair and a calm voice. At first sight, you'd think he was a chaplain rather than a soldier. Sometimes he was in uniform, but mostly he wore civilian clothes. Quiet clothes in neutral colours. A nondescript face, one of those people who you meet and immediately forget.

Who want to be immediately forgotten.

But in all that time, he had listened to his voice more than he had looked at his face.

'So, tomorrow you'll be leaving us.'

Those words meant many things: a final discharge, boundless relief, inescapable solitude.

'Yes.'

'Do you feel ready?'

No! he would have liked to scream. *I'm not ready, any more than I was ready when all this started. I'm not ready now and I'll never be ready. Not after seeing what I saw and feeling what I felt, not after my body and face . . .*

'I'm ready.'

His voice had been firm. Or at least it had seemed firm to him as he uttered that sentence that condemned him to the world. And even if it hadn't been, Colonel Lensky clearly preferred to think that it was. As a man and as a doctor, he had chosen to believe that his job was over, rather than admit that he'd failed. That was why he was prepared to lie to him.

'That's good. I've already signed the papers.'

He heard the creak of the armchair and the rustle of cotton pants as the colonel stood up. Corporal Wendell Johnson sat up on the couch and for a moment did not move but looked out through the open window at the grounds, where green treetops framed a patch of blue sky. From that position, he could not see what he would certainly have seen if he had

8

gone to the window. Sitting on benches or propped in the hostile relief of a wheelchair, standing under the trees or attempting those few faltering movements that some called self-sufficiency, were men just like him.

When they had left they were called soldiers.

Now they were veterans.

A word without glory, which attracted not attention but silence.

A word that meant that they had survived, that they had come out alive from the hellish pit of Vietnam, where nobody knew what sin he had to atone for even though everything around him showed him how to atone for it. They were veterans and each of them bore, more or less visibly, the burden of his personal redemption, which began and ended within the confines of a military hospital.

Colonel Lensky waited for him to stand and turn before he approached him. He held out his hand and looked him in the eye. Corporal Johnson sensed the effort the colonel was making to stop his gaze turning away from the scars that disfigured his face.

'Good luck, Wendell.'

It was the first time he had ever addressed him by his first name.

A name doesn't mean a person, he thought.

There were so many names around, carved on white crosses arranged in rows with military precision. That changed nothing. Nothing would help to bring those young men back to life, to remove from their lifeless chests the numbers they kept pinned to them like medals in honour of lost wars. He would always be merely one of the many. He had known lots like him, soldiers who moved and laughed and smoked joints and shot up with heroin to forget that they

9

were constant targets. The only difference between them lay in the fact that he was still alive, even though, to all intents and purposes, he felt as if he was one of those crosses. He was still alive, but the price he had paid for this negligible difference had been a leap into the grotesque void of monstrousness.

'Thank you, sir.'

He turned and walked to the door. He felt the doctor's eyes on the back of his neck. It was some time since he had last been expected to give a military salute. It wasn't required of those who were being reconstructed piece by piece in body and mind with the sole purpose of allowing them to remember for the rest of their lives. And the rest of the mission had been accomplished.

Good luck, Wendell.

Which actually meant: Fuck off, corporal.

He walked along the light green corridor. The dim light that filtered through the small skylight reminded him of rainy days in the forest, when the leaves were so shiny they were like mirrors and the hidden part seemed made of shadow. A shadow from which the barrel of a rifle could emerge at any moment.

He left the building.

Outside was the sun and the blue sky and different trees. Trees easy to accept and forget. They weren't scrub pines or bamboo or mangrove or aquatic stretches of paddy fields.

This wasn't *Dat-nuoc.*

The word echoed in his head, in its correct, slightly guttural pronunciation. In the spoken language of Vietnam it meant country, although the literal translation was land-water, an extremely realistic way to express the essence of the place. It was a happy image for some, provided you didn't have to

10

work there with your back stooped, or walk with a pack on your back and an M16 slung over your shoulder.

Now the vegetation he had around him meant *home*. Although he didn't know exactly what place to call by that name.

The corporal smiled because he could find no other way to express his bitterness. He smiled because smiling didn't hurt any more. The morphine and the needles under the skin were almost faded memories. Not the pain, no, that would remain a yellow stain in his memory every time he undressed in front of a mirror or tried in vain to pass a hand through his hair and found only the rough texture of burn scars.

He set off along the path, hearing the gravel crunch beneath his feet, leaving Colonel Lensky and everything he stood for behind him. He reached the strip of asphalt that was the main thoroughfare and turned left, heading unhurriedly towards one of the white buildings that stood out in the middle of the grounds.

There was all the irony of the beginning and the end, in this place.

The story was coming to an end where it had begun. A few dozen miles from here was Fort Polk, the camp for advanced training before shipping out for Vietnam. When they arrived, they'd been a group of boys that someone had dragged away from their normal lives and claimed to be able to turn into soldiers. Most of them had never left the state they lived in, some not even the county where they were born.

Ask not what your country can do for you . . .

None of them did ask that, but none of them were ready to confront what their country would ask of them.

In the southern part of the fort, a typical Vietnamese village had been reconstructed, down to the last detail. Straw roofs,

11

wood, bamboo reeds, rattan. Strange tools and utensils, oriental-looking instructors who were in fact more American than he was. None of the materials and objects was familiar to them. And yet in these buildings, this idealized version of a place thousands of miles away, there was both a threat and something ordinary, everyday.

This is what Charlie's house looks like, the sergeant had told them.

Charlie was the nickname thay gave the enemy. The training had begun and ended. They had learned everything there was to know. But they had done it in a hurry and without too much conviction, because there wasn't much conviction around in those days. Everyone would have to fend for himself, especially when it came to figuring out, among the many identical faces they saw around them, who was Vietcong and who a friendly South Vietnamese citizen. The smiles on their faces were the same, but what they were carrying might be completely different. A hand grenade, for example.

The black man who was coming toward him, propelling his wheelchair forward with sturdy arms, was a good example of what could happen. Among the veterans admitted to the hospital for reconstruction, he was the only one Wendell had become friendly with.

Jeff B. Anderson, from Atlanta. He had been the victim of a bomb attack as he was leaving a Saigon brothel. Unlike his companions he had survived, but was paralysed from the waist down. No glory, no medal. Just medical care and embarrassment. But in Vietnam glory was a chance occurrence, and medals sometimes weren't worth the metal they were made of.

Jeff brought the wheelchair to a halt by placing his hands

flat on the wheels. 'Hi, corporal,' he said. 'They're saying some strange things about you.'

'In this place, a lot of the things people say turn out to be true.'

'So they're right. You're going home.'

'Yup, I'm going home.'

The next question came after a fraction of a second, a brief but interminable pause: it was surely a question Jeff had asked himself many times.

'Will you make it?'

'How about you?'

They both preferred not to answer that, but to leave it to each other's imagination.

'I don't know if I should envy you or not.'

'For what it's worth, neither do I.'

Jeff's jaw contracted, and his voice emerged as if broken by a belated, pointless anger. 'If only they'd bombed those fucking dikes . . .'

He left the sentence hanging. His words evoked ghosts that they had both tried many times to exorcize in vain.

Corporal Wendell Johnson shook his head.

Despite the massive bombardment to which North Vietnam had been subjected, despite the fact that three times the number of bombs had been dropped than in the Second World War, nobody had ever given the order to hit the dikes on the Red River. Many thought it would have been a decisive move. The water would have flooded the valleys, and the world would have branded as a war crime what in all probability would have been close to genocide. But maybe the conflict would have had a different outcome.

Maybe.

'Hundreds of thousands of people would have died, Jeff.'

Jeff looked up. There was something indefinable in his eyes. Maybe it was an ultimate plea for mercy, a mixture of regret and remorse for what he was thinking. Then he turned his head and looked out at some point beyond the treetops.

'You know,' he said, 'there are times when I get to thinking, and I put my hands on the armrests and try to stand. Then I remember the state I'm in and I curse myself.'

He took a deep breath, as if he needed a lot of air to say what he was about to say.

'I curse myself because I'm like this, but most of all because I'd give the lives of millions of those people just to have my legs back.'

He looked him in the eyes again.

'What happened, Wen? More than that, *why* did it happen?'

'I don't know. I don't think anyone will ever know, not really.'

Jeff placed his hands on the wheels and moved the chair back and forth a little, as if that gesture was enough to remind him that he was still alive. Or maybe it was just a moment of distraction, one of those moments when he thought he could stand up and walk away. He was pursuing his own thoughts and it took a while before they became words.

'They used to say the Communists ate children.'

As he spoke, he looked at Wendell without seeing him, as if he was visualizing the image those words evoked.

'We fought the Communists. Maybe that's why they didn't eat us.'

He paused, and when he spoke again his voice was a whisper.

'Only chewed us up and spat us out.'

He pulled himself together and held out his hand. Wendell shook it: Jeff had a firm grip.

'Good luck, Jeff.'

'Now fuck off, Wen. And go quickly. I hate crying in front of a white man. On my skin, even the tears look black.'

Wendell walked away, with the distinct feeling that he was losing something. That both of them were losing something. He had only taken a few steps when Jeff's voice forced him to stop.

'Hey, Wen.'

He turned and saw him, the silhouette of a man and a machine against the sunset.

'Get laid for me,' Jeff said, making an unambiguous gesture with his hand.

Wendell smiled in reply. 'OK. When I do, it'll be in your name.'

Corporal Wendell Johnson walked away, his eyes fixed straight ahead, his walk still, in spite of himself, a soldier's walk. He reached the accommodation block without greeting or talking to anyone else. He entered his quarters. The bathroom door was closed. He always kept it closed, because the mirror faced the main door and he preferred to avoid his face being the first image to greet him.

He forced himself to remember that from the next day onwards he would have to get used to it. There were no charitable mirrors, only surfaces that reflected exactly what they saw. Without pity, and with the involuntary cruelty of indifference.

He took off his shirt and threw it on a chair, away from the masochistic spell of the other mirror, the one inside the wall closet. He took off his shoes and lay down on the bed with his hands behind his head, rough skin against rough skin, a sensation he was used to.

Through the half-open windows, like an emanation of the

darkening sky, came the rhythmic hammering of a wood-pecker hidden somewhere in the trees.

tupa-tupa-tupa-tupa . . . tupa-tupa-tupa-tupa . . .

Memory turned in its vicious circle, and the sound became the muted splutter of an AK-47 and then a tangle of voices and images.

'Matt, where the fuck are those bastards? Where are they firing from?'

'I don't know. I can't see a thing.'

'Hey, you with the M-79, throw a grenade into those bushes on the right.'

'What happened to Corsini?'

Farrell's voice, stained with earth and fear, came from some point on their right. 'Corsini's gone. Mac, too . . .'

tupa-tupa-tupa-tupa . . .

And Farrell's voice, too, dissolved into the air.

'Come on, Wen, let's get our asses out of here. They're tearing us to pieces.'

tupa-tupa-tupa-tupa . . . tupa-tupa-tupa-tupa . . .

'No, not that way. There's no cover.'

'Holy shit, they're everywhere.'

* * *

He opened his eyes again and let the things around him return. The closet, the chair, the table, the bed, the windows with the unusually clean panes. And here, too, a smell of rust and disinfectant. This room had been his one landmark for months, after all the time spent in a ward, with doctors and nurses bustling around him trying to alleviate the pain of his burns. It was there that he had let his mind, almost intact, back into his ravaged body, and had made himself a promise.

The woodpecker conceded a truce to the tree it had been torturing. It seemed like a good omen, the end of hostilities, a part of the past that he could somehow leave behind him.

That he *had* to leave behind him.

The next day he would be leaving.

He didn't know what kind of world he would find beyond the walls of the hospital, nor did he know how that world would greet him. In fact, neither of those two things mattered. All that mattered was the long journey he had ahead of him, because at the end of that journey an encounter with two men awaited him. They would look at him with eyes full of fear and astonishment. Then he would talk, to that fear and that astonishment.

And finally he would kill them.

A smile, again devoid of pain. Without realizing it, he drifted into sleep. That night, he slept without hearing voices, and for the first time didn't dream about rubber trees.

CHAPTER 2

What surprised him during the journey was the corn.

As he rode north, getting closer and closer to home, stretches of it started to appear at the sides of the road, meek in the shadow of the Greyhound bus. The ripples of the wind and the shadows of the clouds made it come alive. He remembered how resistant it felt when you ran your hand through it. An unexpected travelling companion, the colour of cold beer, the warm shelter of the hayloft.

He knew that sensation.

And he remembered how, with other hands, he had run his fingers through Karen's hair and breathed in her scent, which smelled like nothing else in the world. He had felt it like a painful spasm when he had left after being at home on leave for a month, a fleeting illusion of invulnerability the army granted everyone before they shipped out. They had been offered thirty days of paradise and possible dreams, before the Army Terminal at Oakland became Hawaii and finally turned into Bien-Hoa, the troop selection centre twenty miles from Saigon.

And then Xuan-Loc, the place where everything had started, where he had found his own small plot of hell.

He took his eyes away from the road and lowered the peak of his baseball cap. He wore sunglasses held on with an elastic band because he had practically no ears left to rest the arms of the glasses on. He closed his eyes and hid himself in that tenuous semi-darkness. All he got in return were more images.

There was no corn in Vietnam.

There were no blondes. Just a few nurses at the hospital, but by then he had almost no feeling left in his fingers or any desire to touch their hair. Above all, he was sure no woman would ever again want to be touched by him.

Ever again.

A long-haired young man in a flowered shirt, who had been sleeping across the aisle from him, to his right, woke up. He rubbed his eyes and allowed himself a yawn that smelled of sweat and sleep and pot. He turned and started to look in a canvas bag he had placed on the free seat beside him. He took out a portable radio and switched it on. After some searching he found a station, and the strains of *The Iron Maiden* by Barclay James Harvest joined the noise of the wheels.

Instinctively, the corporal turned to look at him. When the young man, who must have been about his own age, noticed him and saw his face, the reaction was the usual one: the one he saw every time on other people's faces. The young man dived back into his bag, pretending to look for something. Then he turned to sit with his back to him, listening to the music and looking out the window on his side.

The corporal put his head against the window pane.

They passed billboards, some of them advertising products he didn't know. Speeding cars overtook the bus, and some were models he'd never seen. A 66 Ford Fairlane convertible coming in the opposite direction was the one image that was at all familiar. Time, short as it had been, had moved on. And so had life.

Two years had passed. The blinking of an eye, an inde-cipherable tick on the stopwatch of eternity. And yet they had sufficed to wipe out everything. Now, if he looked ahead of him, all he saw was a smooth wall, and only resentment was urging him to climb it. In all those months he had cultivated that resentment, fed it, let it grow until it was pure hate.

And now he was going home.

There would be no open arms, no speeches or fanfares, no hero's welcome. Nobody would ever call him a hero, and anyway everyone thought the hero was dead.

He had left from Louisiana, where an army vehicle had dropped him off unceremoniously outside the bus station. He had found himself alone. Around him he no longer had the anonymous but reassuring walls of the hospital. As he waited in line to get his ticket, he had felt as if this was a casting call for the Tod Browning movie *Freaks*. This thought had made him smile, the only choice he had if he didn't want to do what he had done for nights on end, and what he had sworn never to do again: cry.

Good luck, Wendell . . .

'Sixteen dollars.'

Suddenly Colonel Lensky's words of farewell had become the voice of a clerk putting down the ticket for the first stretch of the journey. Hidden behind his window, the man had not looked at that part of his face that the corporal granted to the world, but instead had showed him the indifference due to any anonymous passenger – which was just what he wanted.

But when he had pushed the banknotes across the counter with a hand covered in a light cotton glove, the clerk, a slight man with not much hair and thin lips and lightless eyes, had looked up. He had lingered for a moment on his face and then lowered his head again.

'Vietnam?'

The corporal had waited a moment before replying. 'Yes.'

The ticket clerk had given him back his money.

He had ignored Wendell's surprise. Maybe he had taken it for granted. He had simply said a few words to smooth things over. Words that, for both of them, said everything there was to say.

'I lost my son there, two years ago tomorrow. You keep that. I think you need it more than the company.'

The corporal had walked away, feeling the same thing he'd felt when he'd turned his back on Jeff Anderson. Two men alone for ever, one in his wheelchair and the other in his ticket office, in a twilight that seemed destined to become endless.

He had stopped in third-class motels, sleeping little and badly, with his teeth clenched and his jaws tensed, dreaming recurring dreams. Post-traumatic stress syndrome, someone had called it. Science always found a way to turn the destruction of a flesh-and-blood person into a statistic. But the corporal had learned the hard way that the body never completely gets used to pain. Only the mind sometimes manages to accustom itself to horror. And soon there would be a way to show certain people exactly what he himself had been through.

Mile after mile, Mississippi had become Tennessee, which had then turned into Kentucky. Soon, he was promised the familiar landscape of Ohio. Around him, and in his mind, the different panoramas fell into place, a succession of strange locations, a line traced by a coloured pencil across the map of an unknown territory. Beside the road ran electricity and telephone wires, carrying energy and words above his head. There were houses and people, and the people were like puppets in a toy theatre, and the wires helped them to move, gave them the illusion of being alive.

From time to time, he had asked himself what energy and what words he needed right now. Maybe, while he was lying on Colonel Lensky's couch, all the words had been said and all the forces evoked and invoked. It had been a surgical liturgy, which his reason had rejected the way a believer rejects a pagan practice. The doctor had celebrated that liturgy in vain, while he, the corporal, had hidden what little faith he had, his faith in nothingness, in a safe place in his mind, a place where nothing could hurt him or destroy him.

What had been couldn't be changed or forgotten.

Only repaid.

The slight lurch forward of the bus as it slowed down brought him back to where he was. The time was *now*, and there was no escaping it. The place, according to a sign, was called Florence. Judging by the outskirts, the town was like a lot of others, and laid no claim to being anything like its Italian namesake. One night, lying with Karen on the bed in his room, he had looked at a travel brochure.

France, Spain, Italy . . .

And it had been Florence, the one in Italy, that had most drawn their attention. Karen had told him things he didn't know about the place and made him dream things he had never imagined he could dream. That was a time when he still believed that hope cost nothing, before he'd learned that it could cost a lot.

It could even cost you your life.

By the inexhaustible irony of existence, he had finally come to a place called Florence. But nothing was the way it should have been. He remembered words he'd heard spoken by Ben, the man who had been closest to a father figure for him.

Time is like a shipwreck and only what really matters stays afloat . . .

His own time had turned out to be a question of clinging to a raft, trying to find a desperate foothold in reality after being cast out of his own private utopia.

The driver drove obediently to the bus station. The bus jolted to a halt next to a rust-eaten shelter covered in faded signs.

He stayed in his seat, waiting for all the other passengers to get off first. Nobody moved to help a Mexican woman who was struggling with a sleeping little girl in her arms and a suitcase in her free hand. The young man across the aisle from the corporal couldn't resist throwing him a last glance as he picked up his bag.

The corporal had decided he wanted to reach Chillicothe around sundown, so it was best to stop here before crossing the state line. Florence was a place like any other, which made it the right place. Any place was the right place, right now. From here, he would try to hitch-hike the rest of the way to his destination, in spite of the complications that choice was likely to involve. He didn't think it was going to be easy to get a ride.

People usually thought physical disfigurement meant a nasty character. It never seemed to occur to them that evil, in order to flourish, had to be seductive. It had to attract the world with a winning smile and the promise of beauty. Whereas he felt like the last sticker needed to complete an album of monsters.

The driver glanced in the mirror to check the inside of the bus. Immediately, he turned his head. The corporal didn't bother to ask himself if the man was urging him to get off or looking to see if the image in the mirror corresponded to the truth. Either way, he had to take the initiative. He stood up and took his bag down from the rack. He loaded it on his shoulder, taking care to hold the canvas strap with his gloved hand in order to avoid abrasions.

As he walked down the aisle, the driver, who bore a curious resemblance to Sandy Koufax, the Dodgers pitcher, seemed all of a sudden to be strangely fascinated by the dashboard.

The corporal descended those few interminable steps and found himself again alone in a small square.

He took a look around.

On the other side of the square, divided in two by the road, was a Gulf service station and a diner with a parking lot that it shared with the Open Inn, a shabby-looking motel promising vacant rooms and golden dreams.

He adjusted his bag on his shoulder and headed in that direction, prepared to buy himself a little hospitality without arguing about the price.

As long as it lasted, he would be a citizen of Florence, Kentucky.

CHAPTER 3

The motel didn't live up to the promise of its sign. It was just the usual cheap and nasty kind of place, where everything was strictly utilitarian and lacking in taste. The receptionist, a short, plump, prematurely bald man who made up for the little hair he had left with a big moustache and long sideburns, hadn't had any visible reaction when asked for a room. Except that he wouldn't hand over the key until the corporal had put the money down on the desk. He wasn't sure if this was normal practice or treatment reserved exclusively for him. He didn't care much, either way.

The room smelled damp, the furniture was nothing special, and the shoddy carpet was stained in several places. The shower he took, hidden from prying eyes behind a plastic curtain, alternated hot and cold unpredictably. The TV set worked intermittently, and he had finally decided to leave it tuned to the local channel, where the images and sound were clearer. They were showing an old episode of *The Green Hornet*.

Now he was lying naked on the bed with his eyes closed. The words of the two masked heroes, fighting crime with their clothes always immaculate, were a distant hum. He had removed the bedspread and put the sheet over him, so he wouldn't have to endure the sight of his own body when he opened his eyes again.

He was always tempted to pull the sheet up all the way over his head, like they did with corpses. He had seen so many corpses lying on the ground like that, with bloodstained sheets thrown over them not out of pity, but to spare the survivors a clear vision of what could happen to any of them at any moment. He had seen so many dead people, and now he was one himself even though he was still alive. The war had taught him to kill, had given him permission to kill, and because he wore a uniform he knew nobody would blame him and he didn't have to feel any guilt. Now all that remained of that uniform was a green cotton jacket at the bottom of a bag.

Without realizing it, the men who had sent him to face the war and its tribal rituals had given him something he'd previously only had the illusion of possessing: freedom.

Including the freedom to kill again.

He smiled at the idea, and lay there for a long time in that bed that had unceremoniously welcomed dozens of bodies. In those sleepless hours he went back in time to when, also at night . . .

. . . he had been sleeping soundly, as only young men do after a day's work. A muffled noise had woken him suddenly, and immediately afterwards the door of the room had burst wide open, and he had felt a draught on his face and seen a light shining straight at him and, through the light, the burnished threat of a gun barrel hovering a few inches from his face. There were shadows behind that light.

One of the shadows had become a voice, harsh and clear.

'Don't move, punk, or it'll be the last thing you do.'

Rough hands had turned him face down on the bed. His arms had been pulled unceremoniously behind his back, and he had heard the metallic click of the handcuffs. From that moment on, his movements and his life had stopped belonging to him.

'You've been in reformatory. You know all that shit about your rights?'

'Yes.'

He had breathed that monosyllable with difficulty, his mouth still furry.

'Then just imagine we read them to you.'

The voice then addressed the other shadow in the room in a commanding tone. 'Take a look around, Will.'

With his face still pressed to the pillow, he heard the sounds of a search. Drawers being opened and closed, objects falling, the rustle of clothes. The few things he had were being handled expertly, but far from gently.

Finally another voice, with a hint of excitement in it. 'Well, well, chief, what do we have here?'

He heard footsteps approaching and the pressure on his back lessened. Then four rough hands pulled him up until he was in a sitting position on the bed. In front of his eyes, the light played over a transparent plastic bag full of grass.

'So, we roll ourselves a little joint from time to time, huh? And maybe we sell this shit, too. Seems to me you're in big trouble, boy.'

At that moment, the light in the room was switched on. There in front of him was Sheriff Duane Westlake. Behind him, gaunt and spindle legged, with a touch of beard on his pockmarked cheeks, was Will Farland, one of his deputies. The mocking smile on his lips was a joyless grimace that underlined the malicious gleam in his eyes.

He managed to stammer only a few perfunctory words, hating himself for it. 'That isn't my stuff.'

The sheriff raised an eyebrow. 'Oh, it isn't yours. Whose is it then? Is this place magic? Does the tooth fairy bring you marijuana?'

He raised his head and looked at them with a resolute air they both took to be defiance. 'You put it there yourselves, you bastards.'

The backhander arrived quickly and violently. The sheriff was big and had a heavy hand. It seemed hardly possible that he could be so fast. He felt the sickly-sweet taste of blood in his mouth. And the corrosive taste of anger. Instinctively, he jerked forward, trying to headbutt the sheriff's stomach. Maybe it was a predictable move, or maybe the sheriff was endowed with an agility unusual for a man of his bulk. He found himself lying on the floor, the frustration of having achieved nothing now adding to his anger.

He heard more words of mockery above him.

'Our young friend here is hot blooded, Will. He wants to play the hero. Maybe he needs a sedative.'

The two pulled him unceremoniously to his feet. Then, while Farland held him still, the sheriff punched him in the stomach. He fell heavily on the dishevelled bed, feeling he'd never be able to breathe again.

The sheriff addressed his deputy in a patronising tone. 'Will, are you sure you found everything there was to find?'

'Maybe not, chief. I'd better take another look at this dump.'

Farland slipped his hand into his jacket and took out an object wrapped in transparent plastic. Not taking his eyes off him, he said to the sheriff, his mocking grin wider than ever, 'Look what I found, chief. Don't you think that looks suspicious?'

'What is it?'

'At first sight I'd say a knife.'

'Let me see.'

The sheriff took a pair of leather gloves from his pocket and put them on. Then he took the object his deputy was holding out and started to unwrap it. The rustle of the plastic gradually revealed the gleam of a long knife with a black plastic handle.

'That's a fucking sword, Will. Reckon a blade like that could have been used on those two fucking hippies, the other night by the river.'

'Yeah. Sure could.'

Lying on the bed, he had started to understand. And he had shivered, as if the temperature in the room had suddenly plunged. As far as his voice, still winded by the punch, would let him, he attempted a feeble protest.

He didn't yet know how pointless that was.

'It isn't mine. I've never seen it.'

The sheriff looked at him with an expression of ostentatious surprise. 'Is that so? Then how come it has your prints all over it?'

The two of them approached and turned him over on his stomach. Holding the knife by the blade, the sheriff forced him to grasp the handle. Duane Westlake's voice was calm as he pronounced sentence.

'I was wrong just now when I told you you're in trouble. Fact is, you're in shit up to your neck, boy.'

A minute or so later, as they dragged him away to their car, he had the distinct feeling that his life, as he had known it up until that moment, was over for good.

'. . . of the Vietnam war. The storm continues over the publication by the *New York Times* of the Pentagon Papers. An appeal to the Supreme Court is planned, to uphold the injunction to cease publication . . .'

The imposing voice of news anchorman, Alfred Lindsay, shook him out of the restless lethargy into which he had slipped.

The corporal knew this story.

The Pentagon Papers were the outcome of a thorough investigation into the causes that had led the United States to become involved in Vietnam, an investigation set up by Defence Secretary McNamara and carried out by a group of thirty-six experts, both civilian and military, on the basis of government documents, some dating as far back as the Truman era. Like a rabbit caught in the journalists' headlights, the Johnson administration had been shown to have consciously lied to the public about the handling of the conflict. A few days earlier the *New York Times*, which had somehow come into possession of the papers, had started publishing them. The consequences had been predictable.

In the end, as always happened, it would just be a battle of words. And words, whether written or spoken, never amounted to very much.

What did these people know about the war? How could they know what it meant to find yourself thousands of miles from home, fighting an invisible and incredibly determined enemy? An enemy nobody had thought would be ready to pay such a high price in return for so little. An enemy everyone in their heart of hearts respected, even though nobody would ever have the guts to admit it.

Even if there were thirty-six thousand experts, civilian or military or whatever, they still wouldn't understand anything, or make their minds up about anything, because they'd never smelled napalm or Agent Orange. They'd never heard the *tac-tac-tac-tac* of machine gun fire, the muffled sound of a bullet piercing a helmet, the screams of pain of the wounded, which were so loud you ought to be able to hear them in Washington but in fact barely reached the stretcher bearers.

Good luck, Wendell . . .

He moved aside the sheet and sat up on the bed.

'Go fuck yourself, Colonel Lensky. You and your fucking syndromes.'

All that was behind him now.

Chillicothe, Karen, the war, the hospital.

The river was following its course, and only its bank preserved the memory of the water that had passed.

He was twenty-four years old and he didn't know if what was in store for him could still be called a future. But for some people that word would soon lose all meaning.

Barefoot, he walked to the TV and switched it off. The anchorman's reassuring face was sucked into the darkness and became a little dot of light in the middle of the screen. Like all illusions, it lasted a few moments before disappearing completely.

CHAPTER 4

'Are you sure you don't want me to take you all the way into town?'

'No, this is fine. Thanks a lot, Mr Terrance.'

He opened the door. The man at the wheel looked at him with a smile on his tanned face. In the light from the dashboard, he suddenly reminded him of a Don Martin character.

'I meant thanks a lot, Lukas.'

The man gave him a thumbs-up sign. 'That's OK.'

They shook hands. Then the corporal removed his bag from the space behind the seats, got out of the car and closed the door. The voice of the man at the wheel reached him through the open window.

'Whatever you're looking for, I hope you find it. Or that it finds you.'

These last words were almost lost in the rumble of the mufflers. In an instant the vehicle in which he had arrived was nothing more than the sound of an engine fading away.

He adjusted his bag on his shoulder and started walking. He felt neither nervousness nor euphoria at this homecoming.

Only determination.

A few hours earlier, in his motel room, he had found an empty shoe box in the closet. The lid bore the trademark of

Famous Flag Shoes, a mail order company. The fact that the box was still there said a lot about the care taken by the motel's cleaners. He had removed the flaps from the lid and written CHILLICOTHE on the white background in capital letters, going over the word several times with a black felt-tip he had in his bag. He had gone down to reception with the bag on his shoulder and the sign in his hand. Behind the desk, a nondescript girl with thin arms and long straight hair and a red headband had replaced the man with the moustache and sideburns. When he had approached her to give back the key, the spaced-out Flower Power look had drained from her face and she had stared at him with a hint of fear in her dark eyes. As if he was coming towards her with the intention of attacking her. He was starting to come to terms with this attitude. And he suspected it was a judgement that would never be challenged.

Here it is, colonel, here's my luck . . .

For a moment, he'd been tempted to scare her to death, to pay her back for that revulsion, that instinctive suspicion she had felt for him. But this wasn't the time or the place to go looking for trouble.

With ostentatious gentleness, he had put the key down on the glass desktop. 'Here's the key. The room was disgusting.'

His calm voice, combined with his words, had startled the girl. She had looked at him in alarm.

Die, bitch.

'I'm sorry.'

He had shaken his head imperceptibly and stared at her, letting her imagine his eyes behind his dark glasses. 'Don't say that. We both know you don't give a shit.'

He had turned his back on her and left the motel.

Beyond the glass-fronted door was the little square. On his

33

right was the service station with the orange and blue Gulf sign. A couple of cars were waiting to go into the car wash, and the pumps were busy enough to arouse hope that he'd get a ride before too long. He had walked towards the diner, over the door of which was a sign presenting it to the world as the Florence Bowl and offering home cooking and all-day breakfast.

He had slipped past the advertisements for Canada Dry and Tab and Bubble Up, and had taken up a position at the exit from the service area, so that he was clearly visible both by the cars leaving the parking lot and by those leaving the pumps after filling up.

He had thrown his bag on the ground, sat down on it, and held out his arm, trying to make sure that it was as conspicuous as possible.

And he had waited.

A few cars had slowed down. One had actually stopped, but when he had stood up to go and the driver had seen his face, he had set off again as if he had seen the devil.

He was still sitting on the bag, holding out his pathetic sign, when a man's shadow fell on the asphalt in front of him. He had looked up to see a guy wearing black coveralls with red inserts. On his chest and his sleeves, he had a sponsor's colourful trademark.

'You think you're going to get all the way to Chillicothe?'

He had attempted a smile. 'If things carry on like this, I guess not.'

The man was tall, about forty, with a slender build and a ginger beard and hair. He had looked at him a moment, then lowered his voice, as if to downplay what he was about to say.

'I don't know who messed you up that way and it's none of my business. I'm going to ask you one thing. And if you don't tell me the truth, I'll know it.'

He had allowed himself a pause. To weigh his words. Or maybe to give them more weight.

'Are you in trouble with the law?'

He had taken off his cap and sunglasses and looked at him. 'No, sir.'

In spite of himself, the tone of that 'No, sir' had identified him beyond any doubt.

'Are you a soldier?'

His expression was confirmation enough. The word Vietnam wasn't spoken, but hovered in the air.

'Drafted?'

He had shaken his head. 'Volunteer.'

Instinctively, he had bowed his head as he uttered this word, almost as if it was something to feel guilty about. And he had immediately regretted it. He had looked up again and looked the other man full in the eyes.

'What's your name, boy?'

The question had caught him off guard.

Noticing his hesitation, the man had shrugged his shoulders. 'One name's as good as another. It's only so I know what to call you. I'm Lukas Terrance.'

He had stood up and shook the hand the man held out to him. 'Wendell Johnson.'

Lukas Terrance had not shown any surprise at the cotton gloves. He had nodded towards a large black and red pick-up. It was standing by a pump behind them, and a attendant was filling it up. Attached to the back of it was a tow-cart carrying a single-seater car for dirt track races. It was a strange vehicle, with open wheels and a driving compartment that looked as if it could barely contain even one man. He had once seen a similar one on the cover of *Hot Rod* magazine.

Terrance had explained his situation.

35

'I'm going north, to the Mid-Ohio Speedway near Cleveland. Chillicothe isn't really on my way, but I guess I can make a little detour. If you don't mind travelling slowly and without air conditioning, I'd be happy to give you a ride.'

He had responded to the offer with a question. 'Are you a racing driver, Mr Terrance?'

The man had started laughing. On his tanned face, a spider's web of lines had formed at the sides of his eyes. 'Oh, no. I'm only a kind of handyman. Jack of all trades. Mechanic, chauffeur, cook.'

He had made a gesture with his hands, a gesture that seemed to say: That's life.

'Jason Bridges, my driver, is travelling all nice and cosy on a plane right now. We mechanics do the work, the drivers get the glory. Though to be honest, there isn't all that much glory. As a driver he's crap. But he keeps going. That's how it is, when you have a father with a fat wallet. Money can buy you cars; it can't buy you balls.'

The attendant had finished filling up the pick-up and turned around to look for the driver. When he spotted him, he had gestured eloquently towards the line of waiting cars. Terrance had clapped his hands, as if to bring their conversation to a conclusion.

'OK, shall we go? If the answer's yes, from now on you can call me Lukas.'

The corporal had picked up the bag from the ground and followed him.

The driver's cab was a chaos of road maps, crossword magazines and issues of *Mad* and *Playboy*. Terrance had made space for him on the passenger seat by shifting a packet of Oreos and an empty can of Wink.

'Sorry about the mess. We don't get many passengers in this old wreck.'

He had calmly left the service station behind him, and then Florence, and finally Kentucky. Soon, those days and those places would be only memories. The good ones, the real ones, the ones that would stay with him all his life, like cats to be taken on his lap and stroked, those he was about to create for himself.

It had been a pleasant journey.

He had listened to Terrance's anecdotes about the racing world and especially about the driver he worked for. Terrance was a good man, a bachelor, practically without fixed abode, who had always been involved with races, though never the really important ones like NASCAR or the Indy. He mentioned the names of famous drivers, people like Richard Petty or Parnelli Jones or A. J. Foyt, as if he knew them personally. Maybe he did. Anyhow, he seemed to enjoy thinking he did. and they were both fine with that.

Not even once had he mentioned the war. Once over the state line, the pick-up with its racing pod in tow, had taken Route 50, which led straight to Chillicothe. Sitting on his seat with the window open, listening to Terrance's stories, he had seen the sunset, with that tenacious, persistent luminosity typical of summer evenings. All at once, the places had become familiar, until at last a sign appeared saying *Welcome to Ross County*.

He was home.

Or rather, he was where he wanted to be.

A couple of miles after Slate Mills, he had asked his surprised companion to stop. He had left him to his bewilderment and the rest of his journey, and now he was walking like a ghost in open country. Only the lights of a group of houses in the distance, which on the maps went by the name of North Folk Village, showed him the way. And every step seemed much more tiring than any he had trodden in the mud of Nam.

He finally reached what had been his goal ever since he had left Louisiana. Just under a mile from the village, he turned left onto a dirt path and after a few hundred yards came to a building surrounded by a metal fence. In the back there was an open space lit by three lampposts where, between stacks of tubes for scaffolding, an eight-wheel tow truck, a Volkswagen van and a Mountaineer dump truck with a snow shovel were parked.

This was where he'd lived. And it would be his base for the last night he would ever spend there.

There was no light inside the building.

Before continuing, he made sure there was nobody around. Then he moved forward, following the fence on his right until he reached the side that was more shadowy. He came to a clump of bushes that hid him from view. He put his bag down and took out a pair of wirecutters he had bought in a general store. He cut the fence just enough to allow him to enter. He imagined the sturdy figure of Ben Shepard standing in front of that breach, heard the sibilant voice he remembered lambasting '*those fucking sons of bitches who don't respect other people's property*'.

As soon as he was inside, he headed straight for a small iron door, next to a blue-painted sliding door that allowed access to vehicles. Above it was a big white sign with blue lettering, telling anyone who was interested that these were the premises of *Ben Shepard – Demolition Renovation Construction*. He didn't have a key any more, but he knew where his former employer kept a spare one.

He opened the glass door that protected the fire extinguisher. Just behind the extinguisher itself was the key he was looking for. With a smile on his tortured lips, he took it out and went and opened the door. It slid inwards without squeaking.

One step and he was inside.

The small amount of light coming in from outside, through the high windows on all four sides, revealed a space full of tools and machinery. Hard hats, coveralls hanging on hooks, two cement mixers of differing capacities. On his left, a long counter filled with tools for use with wood and iron.

The damp heat and the semi-darkness were familiar to him, as were the smells. Iron, cement, wood, lime, plasterboard, lubricant. The vague odour of sweaty bodies from the hanging coveralls. But the taste he had in his mouth was completely new. It was the sour taste of enforced separation, a sudden awareness of all that had been taken away from him. Everyday life, affection, love. The little of it that he had known when Karen had taught him what truly deserved that name.

He advanced in the semi-darkness, taking care where he put his feet, towards the door on the right-hand side. Making an effort not to think about the fact that this place full of rough surfaces and sharp corners had meant everything to him.

Beyond that doorway, clinging to the wall of the building like a mollusc to a rock, there was one large room with a single window protected by an iron grille. A kitchen area and a bathroom on opposite sides completed the layout of his old home.

He reached the door and pushed it.

And stood there, open mouthed in surprise.

Here the shapes were more distinct. The light through the window from the lampposts in the parking lot sent almost all the shadows scuttling into the corners.

The room was perfectly tidy, as if he had left it hours rather than years before. No dust hung in the air, and it was obvious that it had been cleaned often and carefully. Only the bed was covered with a sheet of transparent plastic.

He was about to take another step into his old home when he suddenly felt something knock against him and slide quickly between his legs. Immediately afterwards, a dark shape jumped on the bed, making the plastic rustle.

He closed the door, went to the night table and lit the bedside lamp. In the dim light, the nose of a big black cat emerged, and two huge green eyes looking at him.

'Waltz. Holy Christ, you're still here.'

Without any fear the animal approached, walking slightly lopsidedly, and sniffed him. He reached out his hand to grab it and it let itself be picked up. He sat down on the bed and pulled it on to his knees. He started to scratch it gently under the chin, and the cat immediately started purring, as he knew it would.

'You still like that, huh? You're still as much of an old softie as ever.'

He stroked it with one hand, and with the other reached the place where the right back leg should have been.

'I see it never grew back.'

There was a strange story behind the cat's name. Ben had sent him to do some repairs at the clinic of Dr Peterson, the vet. A couple had showed up carrying a kitten wrapped in a bloodstained blanket. A large cat had come into their garden and bitten their kitten, maybe just to punish it for existing. The kitten had been examined and immediately operated on,

40

but it had not been possible to save its leg. When the vet had come out of the operating room and told the owners, the man and the woman had looked at each other in embarrassment.

Then the woman, asked the vet in an uncertain voice, 'Without a leg, you say?' She had turned to the man beside her for confirmation. 'What do you think, Sam?'

The man had made a vague gesture. 'Well, of course, the poor little beast would suffer, with a leg missing. It would be maimed for life. I wonder if it wouldn't be better to . . .' He had left the sentence hanging.

Dr Peterson had looked at him questioningly, then finished his sentence for him. 'Put him to sleep?'

The two had looked at each other with eyes full of relief. They couldn't believe they had found a way out: they could pass off as a suggestion from an authoritative source what they had in fact already decided.

'I see you agree, doctor. Do it, then. He won't suffer, will he?'

'No, he won't suffer,' the vet replied. Her voice was icy, and so were her blue eyes. But the two were in too much of a hurry to leave to even notice.

They had paid, and gone out the door with more haste than might have been considered necessary in the circumstances. Then the sound of a car starting up outside had confirmed that the final verdict had been pronounced on the poor animal.

He had witnessed the whole scene. But when they had gone he put down the pail in which he was mixing plaster and approached Dr Peterson.

'Don't kill him, doctor. I'll take him.'

She had looked at him without speaking. Her eyes searched his for a long time before replying. Then she had said just two words.

'All right.'

She had turned and gone back into her clinic, leaving him alone as the new owner of a cat with three legs. That was what had given rise to its name. Growing up, its way of walking had reminded him of waltz time: one-two-three, one-two-three, one-two-three . . .

And Waltz it had become.

He was about to move the cat, which was continuing to purr blissfully beside him on the bed, when suddenly the door was kicked open. Waltz took fright, jumped down nimbly on his three paws and hid under the bed. A commanding voice filled the room.

'Whoever you are, you'd better come out with your hands up. Don't make any sudden movements. I have a shotgun and I'm prepared to use it.'

For a moment, he did not move.

Then, without saying a word, he stood up and walked calmly towards the door. Just before placing himself in the doorway, he raised his arms in the air. That was the only movement that still caused him a little pain.

And a flood of memories.

CHAPTER 5

Ben Shepard moved behind one of the cement mixers, trying to find the best position from which to keep the door in his sights. A bead of sweat running down the side of his face reminded him how hot and damp the building was. For a moment he was tempted to wipe it off, but he preferred not to take his hands off his Remington pump-action shotgun. Whoever was in that room, he didn't know how he would react to the order to come out. Above all, he didn't know if he was armed or not. Anyhow, the man had been warned. He was holding a shotgun, and he never said anything he didn't mean. He had fought in Korea. If the guy or guys in there didn't believe he was prepared to use it, they were making a big mistake.

Nothing happened.

He had preferred not to switch on any lights. In the semi-darkness, time seemed like something personal between him and the beating of his heart. He waited for seconds that seemed an eternity.

It was pure chance that he was here at this hour.

He had been on his way back after an evening spent bowling with the team he played for. He was driving along Western Avenue and had just passed North Folk Village when the oil gauge had lit up on the dashboard of his old van.

If he kept going, the engine might seize up. A few dozen yards up ahead was the track that led to the his construction company. Rather than be forced to brake, he had quickly done a wide turn onto the other lane and then onto the track, immediately afterwards switching off the engine and putting it in neutral to take advantage of the momentum and get as far as the gate.

As he approached the building, hearing the loose stones under the tyres roll with an ever deeper sound as he lost speed, he'd had the fleeting impression that there was a dim light visible through the windows.

He had immediately stopped the van, taken the Remington from behind the seats, and checked it was loaded. He had got out without slamming the door and had approached, walking on the grassy verge in order to avoid making a noise with his heavy shoes. When he had gone out, a couple of hours earlier, he might have forgotten to switch off the light.

That must have been it.

But in any case he had preferred to make sure by being at the right end of a shotgun barrel. As his father used to say, nobody had ever died from being too careful.

He had kept on, hugging the fence until he came to the point where it had been cut. Then he noticed that a light was on in the room in back, and saw a silhouette passing the window.

His hands on the grip of the Remington had started to get damper than they should. He had quickly looked around.

He hadn't seen any cars parked in the vicinity, which he found puzzling. The building was full of materials and tools. They weren't worth a great deal, but they might still tempt a thief. They were all quite heavy, though. It seemed strange that someone would come here on foot if they planned to clean him out.

He had gone through the hole in the fence, and reached the door next to the vehicle entrance. When he had pushed the door, he had found it open. Groping with his hands, he had felt the key in the keyhole, and in the dim light from the lampposts reflected off the clear wall he had seen that the little window in front of the fire extinguisher was half open.

Strange. Very strange.

Only he knew of the existence of that spare key.

Curious and cautious in equal measure, he had gone inside, woven in and out of the equipment heaped up there, and kicked the door of the backroom wide open.

Now he was holding his shotgun aimed at the open door.

A man appeared in the doorway with his hands up. He took a couple of steps and stopped. Ben moved accordingly, so that he was still protected by the squat, ungainly mass of the cement mixer. From here, he could keep the man's legs in his sights, and if he made even one abrupt movement he would shorten his height by ten inches.

'Are you alone?'

The answer had come immediately. Calm, steady, apparently genuine. 'Yes.'

'OK, I'm coming out. If you or any friend you have with you are planning any nasty tricks, I'll blow a hole in your stomach as big as a railroad tunnel.'

He waited a moment and then came cautiously out into the open. He held the shotgun at his side, firmly aimed at the man's stomach. He took a couple of steps towards him, until he could see his face clearly.

And what he saw sent a shudder through him. The man's face and head were completely disfigured by what looked like terrible burn scars. From his face, they continued down his neck and disappeared inside the open collar of his shirt.

His right ear was completely missing while all that remained of the other was only a fragment, attached like a joke to the cranium, where coarse healed skin had replaced hair.

Only the area around the eyes was intact. And now those eyes were following him as he approached, more ironic than worried.

'Who the hell are you?'

The man smiled. If what appeared on his face when he moved his mouth could be called a smile.

'Thanks, Ben. At least you didn't ask me what I am.'

Without asking permission, the man lowered his arm. It was only then that Ben realized he was wearing gloves of some light material.

'I know I'm not easy to recognize. I was hoping at least my voice had stayed the same.'

Ben Shepard opened his eyes wide. Involuntarily, he lowered the barrel of his shotgun, as if his arms had suddenly become too flabby to hold it up. Then the words arrived, as if he hadn't had the gift of speech before now.

'Christ almighty, Little Boss. It's you. We all thought you were . . .'

The sentence was left hanging.

The other man made a vague gesture with his hand. 'Dead?' The next sentence came from his lips like a thought spoken aloud and a long-buried hope. 'What makes you think I'm not?'

Ben suddenly felt old. And he realized that the person in front of him felt much older than he. Still confused by this unexpected encounter, without really knowing what to do or say, he went to the wall and reached his hand out to a switch. A dim emergency light came on. When he made to switch on another light, Little Boss stopped him with a gesture.

46

'Let it be. I guarantee I don't look any better in the light.'

Ben realized his eyes were moist. He felt useless and stupid. Finally he did the one thing that instinct dictated. He put the Remington down on a pile of crates, approached this soldier and gently embraced him.

'Hell, Little Boss, it's good to know you're alive.'

He felt the boy's arms go around his shoulders.

'There is no Little Boss any more, Ben. But it's good to be here with you.'

They stood there for a moment, out of an affection that was like that between a father and a son. With the absurd hope that when they separated it would be some ordinary day in the past, with everything normal and Ben Shepard, staying late to give instructions to his worker for the next day.

They separated. Ben made a sign with his head. 'Come this way. There should still be a few beers. If you want one.'

The young man smiled and replied, with some of the old familiarity, 'Never refuse a beer from Ben Shepard. He might get mad. And that sure ain't a pleasant sight.'

They moved into the back room. Little Boss went and sat down on the bed. He called out, and Waltz immediately came out from his hiding place and jumped onto his lap.

'You left everything the way it was. Why?'

Ben walked to the refrigerator, pleased that Little Boss couldn't see his face as he replied. 'Call it a premonition, call it an old man's stubborn hope. Call it what you like.'

He closed the door and turned with two beers in his hand. With the neck of one of the bottles he indicated the cat, which had accepted, with its usual feline sense of entitlement, to be stroked on the head and neck.

'I had your room cleaned occasionally. And every day I fed that critter you have there.'

He handed the young man his beer. Then he went to a chair and sat down, and for a while they drank in silence. Both knew they were full of questions that were going to be difficult to answer.

Ben realized he had to be the first.

Forcing himself not to look away, he asked, 'What happened? Who did that to you?'

The boy took his time before replying. 'It's a long story, Ben. And it's an ugly story. Are you sure you want to hear it?'

Ben leaned back in his chair and tilted it until it rested against the wall.

'I have time. All the time in the world . . .'

'. . . and all the men we need, soldier. Until you and your comrades realize you're going to be defeated in this country.'

He was sitting on the ground, up against a branchless tree stump whose roots clutched uselessly at the ground, hands tied behind his back. In front of him, dawn was rising. Behind him he felt the presence of his buddy, who was similarly immobilized. He hadn't spoken or moved for a while now. Maybe he'd managed to fall asleep. Maybe he was dead. Both theories were plausible. They had been in this place for two days. Two days of not much food, of sleep broken by spasms in his wrists and cramps in his ass. Now he was thirsty and hungry and his clothes were stuck to his skin with sweat and dirt. The man in the red headband leaned over him and dangled their dogtags in front of his face, letting them sway from side to side with an almost hypnotic effect. Then he turned them towards himself, as if he wanted to check their names, even though he remembered them perfectly well.

48

'Wendell Johnson and Matt Corey. What are two nice American boys doing here in the middle of these paddy fields? Didn't you have anything better to do at home?'

Of course I did, you fucking piece of shit.

He screamed those words in his head. He had learned the hard way what these people did when you expressed what you felt.

The guerrilla was a skinny guy, of indefinable age, with deep-set small eyes. Slightly above average height. He spoke good English spoiled only by a guttural accent. Time had passed

how much time?

since his platoon had been wiped out by a sudden Vietcong attack. They had all died, except the two of them. And immediately afterwards, their calvary had started: constantly being moved from place to place, harried by mosquitoes, forced to keep marching, forcing themselves to keep going through sheer will, one more step, one more step, one more step . . .

And getting the crap beaten out of them.

Every now and again they had come across other groups of fighters. Men with identical faces who carried arms and supplies by bicycle along almost invisible paths amid the vegetation.

These had been their only moments of relief

Where are they taking us, Matt?

I don't know.

Any idea where we are?

No, but we'll make it, Wen, don't worry.

and rest.

Water, blessed water, was here a piece of paradise on earth, and their jailers seemed to dispense it with a sadistic pleasure.

His jailer didn't wait for a reply. He knew it wouldn't come. 'I'm really sorry your other comrades died.'

'I don't believe you,' he blurted out, and immediately tensed the muscles of his neck, expecting a slap by way of reply.

Instead of which, a smile appeared on the man's face, a smile made cruel by the sardonic gleam in his eyes. Silently, he lit a cigarette, then replied in a neutral voice that sounded strangely sincere, 'You're wrong. I really would have liked to have you alive. All of you.'

The same tone of voice he'd used after the attack when he'd said

'Don't worry, corporal. We're going to take care of you . . .'

and immediately afterwards had gone up to Sid Margolin, who was lying on the ground complaining of the wound in his shoulder, and blown his brains out.

From somewhere behind him came the caterwauling of a radio. Then another guerrilla, a much younger man, walked up to the commander. The two men exchanged a hasty dialogue, in the incomprehensible language of a country he would never understand.

Then the chief addressed him again.

'This looks like it's turning into quite an amusing day.'

He bent his knees and crouched in front of him, so that he could look at him straight in the face.

'There's going to be an air raid. There are raids every day. But the next one will be in this area.'

That was when he understood. There were men who went to war because they were forced to go. Others who felt they had to go. The man in the red headband was there because he liked it. When the war was over, he would probably invent another one, maybe just for himself, so he could continue to fight.

And to kill.

That thought put an expression on his face that the other man misunderstood. 'What's the matter, soldier? Are you surprised? Didn't you think the yellow monkeys Charlie, as you call us, were capable of mounting intelligence operations?'

He gave him a pat on the cheek with the palm of his hand, all the more mocking in that it was as light as a caress.

'Well, we are. And today you'll get a chance to find out who you're fighting for.'

He leaped to his feet and gave a signal. Immediately, four men armed with AK-47s and rifles came running and surrounded them, weapons aimed straight at them. A fifth man approached and untied their wrists. With an abrupt gesture he motioned them to stand up.

The commander pointed to the path in front of them. 'That way. Quickly and silently, please.'

He pushed them unceremoniously in the direction indicated. After a few minutes' quick march, they emerged onto a vast, sandy clearing, flanked on the right by what looked like a plantation of rubber trees, placed at such regular distances as to seem a perversity of nature amid so much chaotic vegetation.

They were separated and tied to two trunks almost at opposite ends of the clearing, with a line of trees between them. No sooner did he feel the ropes on his wrists than a gag was stretched over his mouth.

The same fate befell his buddy, whose show of resistance was rewarded with a blow with a rifle butt in the small of his back.

The man in the red headband approached with his usual sly air.

'You people who use napalm so easily ought to know what effect it has. My people have known it for some time now . . .'

He indicated a vague point in the sky in front of him.

'The planes will be coming from that direction, American soldier.'

He put the dogtags back around their necks. Then he turned his back on them and left, followed by his men. They were alone now, looking at each other from a distance. Then, from that point beyond the trees, in the sky in front of them, came the noise of an engine. The Cessna L-19 Bird Dog appeared as if by magic over the rim of the vegetation. It was on a reconnaissance mission and was flying low. It had almost passed them when suddenly the pilot made a turn, bringing the plane even lower. So low that they could clearly see the figures of the two men inside the cockpit. Soon afterwards the aircraft returned to the sky from which it had come. Time passed in silence. Then a whirr, and a pair of Phantoms arrived at a speed that in their fear they saw as a series of still images. With them came a roar like thunder. Only after that, by some strange quirk, the lightning flash. He saw that light grow and grow and become a line of fire that advanced on them, like some kind of dance, devouring everything in its path until it reached them and hit . . .

'. . . my buddy full on, Ben. He was incinerated. I was a bit farther away, so I was just hit by a wave of heat that reduced me to this state. I don't know how I survived. And I don't know how long I was there before the rescue team arrived. My memories are very confused. I know I woke up in a hospital, covered in bandages and with needles stuck in my veins. And I think most men would take a lifetime to feel the pain I felt in those few months.'

The boy paused. Ben understood that it was to let him

52

absorb what he had just told him. Or to prepare him for what he said next.

'The Vietcong used us as human shields. And the men on the reconnaissance plane saw us. They knew we were there. And they attacked all the same.'

Ben looked at the tips of his shoes. Anything he said would have been pointless.

He decided to go back to the present, and the suspicion nagging at him. 'What are you planning to do now?'

Little Boss shrugged nonchalantly. 'All I need is some-where to use as a base for a few hours. There's a couple of people I have to see. Then I'll come fetch Waltz and leave.'

The cat, as indifferent as all cats, got up from its owner's knees and arranged its three legs in a more comfortable position on the bed.

Ben moved the chair away from the wall and let it drop to the floor. 'I get the feeling you're going to get in trouble.'

The boy shook his head, hiding behind his non-smile. 'I can't get in trouble.'

He took off his cotton gloves and held his hands out to Ben. They were covered in scars.

'See? No fingerprints. Wiped out. Whatever I touch, I don't leave any trace.'

He seemed to think for a moment, as if he'd finally found the right name for himself.

'I don't exist any more. I'm a ghost.'

He looked at him with eyes that asked a lot even though they were ready to concede little.

'Ben, give me your word you won't tell anyone I was here.'
'Not even—?'

He interrupted him curtly, before he'd even had time to finish the sentence. 'I said nobody. Ever.'

'Or else?'

A moment's silence. Then from his tortured mouth there emerged words as cold as those of the dead.

'I'll kill you.'

Ben Shepard realized that the world didn't exist any more for the young man. A shiver went down his spine. Little Boss had left to fight a war against other men he had been ordered to hate and kill. After what had happened, the roles had been reversed.

He had come home, and now *he* was the enemy.

CHAPTER 6

He was sitting in the dark, waiting.

He had been waiting so long for this moment and now that it had come, he didn't feel any nervousness, any sense of hurry. It seemed to him that his presence in this place was totally normal, planned, thought through.

Resting on his knees was a Colt M1911, the army's regulation weapon. Good old Jeff Anderson, who might have lost his legs but hadn't lost his talent for pulling strings, had got him that pistol, without asking any questions. And, perhaps for the first time in his life, he hadn't asked him for anything in return. He had kept it in his bag, wrapped in a cloth, throughout the journey.

The only light thing he had with him.

The room he was in was a living room with a couch and two armchairs in the middle, arranged in a horseshoe around a TV set against the wall. Clearly a place where one man lived on his own. A few mediocre paintings on the walls, a carpet that didn't look very clean, dirty plates in the sink. And the smell of cigarettes.

In front of him, on the right, the door to the kitchen. On the left, another door leading to a little lobby and then the door out to the garden. Behind him, hidden by part of the wall, the stairs that led to the upper floor. When he had arrived and realized that the house was empty, he had forced the back door and quickly searched the interior.

As he did so, he had the voice of the drill sergeant at Fort Polk in his ears.

Before anything else, reconnoitre the area.

After familiarizing himself with the layout of the rooms, he had chosen to wait in the living room because from there he could keep an eye on both the main door and the back door.

Choose a strategic position.

He had sat down on the couch and released the safety catch on his gun. The click sounded as dry as his throat.

Check the condition of your weapons.

And while he was waiting, his thoughts had returned to Ben.

He could still see his expression when he had threatened him. No trace of fear, only disappointment. He had tried in vain to wipe out the effect of those few words by changing the subject, asking what he actually would have liked to ask from the start.

'How's Karen?'

'Fine. She had the kid. She wrote you about it. Why didn't you get in touch with her?' Ben had paused, and then lowered his voice. 'When they told her you were dead, she cried all the tears she had in her.'

There was a hint of reproach in the words and in the tone of voice.

He had got quickly to his feet, pointing at himself with both hands. 'Do you see me, Ben? You see these scars on my face? They're all over my body.'

'She loved you,' Ben had said, then immediately corrected himself. 'She loves you.'

He had shaken his head, as if to brush away a troublesome

thought. 'She loves a man who doesn't exist any more.'

'I'm sure she—'

He had stopped him with a gesture of his hand. 'Nothing's sure in this world. The few things that are, are all bad.'

He had turned to the window, so that Ben couldn't see his face. But above all so as not to see Ben's face.

'Oh yes, I know what'd happen if I went to see her. She'd throw her arms around me. But for how long?'

He turned again towards Ben. If his first instinct had been to hide, now he knew he had to look reality in the face – and make sure reality looked him in the face.

'Even if all the other problems between us were solved, her father and all the rest, how long would it last? I've been asking myself that over and over since the first time they let me look at myself in a mirror and I saw what I'd become.'

Ben had seen tears welling in his eyes. Diamonds of little price, the only ones he could afford on a soldier's pay. And he realized Little Boss must already have repeated these words in his head hundreds of times.

'Can you imagine what it would be like for her to wake up in the morning and the first thing she sees is my face? How long would it last, Ben? How long?'

He hadn't waited for a reply. Not because he didn't want to know it, but because he already knew it.

They both knew it.

He had changed the subject again. 'Do you know why I volunteered for Vietnam?'

'No. I never figured that out.'

He had sat down again on the bed and stroked Waltz. Then he had told him everything that had happened. Ben had listened in silence. As he spoke, Ben had looked him in the face, letting his eyes move over his tortured skin.

When he had finished, Ben had covered his face with his hands, and his voice had filtered through the bars of his fingers. 'But don't you think Karen—'

Little Boss had stood up again quickly and approached the chair where his old employer was sitting. As if to emphasize his words.

'I thought I made myself clear. She doesn't know I'm alive and she mustn't know.'

At that point Ben had stood up and in silence had hugged him again, more tightly this time. But Little Boss hadn't been able to return the embrace, just stood there with his arms down by his sides.

'There are things that nobody ought to feel in life, son,' Ben had said, finally letting go of him. 'I don't know if I'm doing the right thing. For you, for Karen, for the child. But as far as I'm concerned, I never saw you.'

He had left, and Ben had stood by the door, watching him go. He hadn't asked him where he was going or what he was going to do. But in his eyes there was the bitter conviction that he would know soon enough. And the knowledge that he was his accomplice.

At that moment, there were only two things certain, for both of them.

The first was that Ben wouldn't betray him.

The second was that they would never see each other again.

He had crossed the town on foot towards his destination: the house at the end of Mechanic Street. He preferred to walk a few miles rather than borrow a car from Ben. He wanted to avoid involving him in this nasty business any more than he had to. And he hadn't the slightest intention of getting caught trying to steal a car.

As he walked, Chillicothe had unravelled around him,

58

motionless and as unaware of him as it always had been. It was only an ordinary town, where he'd had to make do with a shred of hope when many young men had moved unconcernedly, surrounded by things they could be sure of.

He had walked down many streets, avoiding people, dodging lights, and every step had been a thought and every thought . . .

The sound of a car coming along the street jolted him out of his momentary distraction. He got up from the couch and went to the window. He moved aside a dusty curtain and looked out. A Plymouth Barracuda had parked, the front of it facing the shutter of the garage. The headlights died on the concrete, and Duane Westlake and Will Farland got out of the car.

They were both in uniform.

The sheriff was a little paunchier than the last time he'd seen him. Too much food and too much beer, maybe. Maybe even more full of shit than before. The deputy was just as thin and lanky and repulsive as he remembered him.

The two men walked to the front door.

He couldn't believe his luck.

He had assumed he would have to pay two visits tonight. Now chance was offering him, on a silver platter, the possibility of avoiding one. And of making sure they both knew . . .

The door opened, and before light filled the room he was able to see the silhouettes of the two men framed in the rectangle of light cast on the floor from outside.

He moved towards the stairs and for a few moments leaned against the wall listening to their voices.

Westlake: 'What did you do with those boys we picked up? Who are they?'

Farland: 'Four vagrants. Usual type. Long hair and guitars. No priors, as far as we know, but we're running checks. Meantime, they can spend tonight in the cooler.'

Pause.

Farland again: 'I told Rabowsky to put them in a cell with some hard guy, if you know what I mean.'

He heard a little laugh that sounded like the squeaking of a mouse, and had surely come from the deputy sheriff's thin lips.

Farland again: 'Tonight, they'll make war, not love.'

Westlake: 'Maybe they'll decide to cut their hair and look for a job.'

In his hiding place, he smiled, though with a nasty taste in his mouth.

A leopard never changes its spots.

Except these guys weren't leopards. They were vultures, of the worst kind.

He leaned out cautiously, protected by the wall. The sheriff went and switched on the TV, threw his hat on the table and sank into an armchair.

There was the sound of a baseball commentary.

'Christ, it's almost over. And we're losing. I knew that playing in California wouldn't work out for us.' He turned to his deputy. 'If you want a beer, there's some in the fridge. Get me one, too, while you're there.'

The sheriff was the boss and he made sure his deputy knew it, even when it came to hospitality. He wondered if he'd have behaved the same way if Judge Swanson had been in the room instead of Deputy Farland.

He decided that now was the moment. He emerged from his hiding place with his gun aimed at the two men.

'The beer can wait. Put your hands up.'

At the sound of his voice Will Farland, gave a start. And when he saw him, he went white in the face.

Westlake had turned his head abruptly. Seeing him, he was stunned for a moment. 'Who the fuck are you?'

Wrong question, sheriff. Are you sure you want to know?

'That doesn't matter right now. Get up and stand in the middle of the room. And you: go stand next to him.'

While the two men moved as he had ordered them, Farland tried to slide his hand down towards his holster.

All very predictable.

He took a couple of rapid steps to the side so as to have Farland completely in his sights and shook his head. 'Don't even think about it. I know how to use this gun. Want to take my word for that, or would you like a demonstration?'

The sheriff had raised his hands in a gesture that was meant to be placatory. 'Listen, friend, let's all try to keep calm. I don't know who you are, but let me remind you, you're committing an offence just being here. Apart from that, you're threatening two law enforcement officers with a firearm. Don't you think your situation is serious enough already? Before you do anything else stupid, I'd advise you—'

'Your advice ain't worth shit, Sheriff Westlake.'

Surprised at hearing his name spoken, the sheriff frowned and tilted his head slightly to the side. 'Do we know each other?'

'Let's leave the introductions till later. Now, Will, sit down on the floor.'

Farland was too surprised to be curious. He turned to his chief, not sure what to do. The voice he heard coming at him wiped out any doubts.

'He doesn't give the orders now, asshole. I do. If you'd rather be lying on the floor dead, I can oblige.'

The deputy bent his long legs and eased himself down, with the help of one hand laid flat on the floor.

Once he was down, their visitor pointed to him with the barrel of his gun and said to the sheriff, 'Now, slowly and without making any sudden movements, take your handcuffs from your belt and tie his hands behind his back.'

Westlake did as he was told, going red in the face with the effort of bending. The sharp click of the handcuffs closing marked the beginning of the Deputy Sheriff captivity.

'Now take yours and put it on your right wrist. Then turn around holding your arms behind your back.'

There was anger in the sheriff's eyes. But there was also a gun in front of his face, so again he did as he was told, and a moment later a confident hand locked the handcuffs on his free wrist.

'Now sit down next to him.'

The sheriff couldn't help himself down with his hands. He bent his knees and dropped clumsily to the floor, his bulk falling heavily against Farland's shoulder. The two of them almost ended up sprawled on the floor.

'Who are you?'

'Names come and go, sheriff. All that's left is memories.'

He disappeared for a moment behind the wall that hid the stairs. When he came back he was holding in his hand a jerrycan full of gasoline. During his inspection of the house he had found it in the garage, next to a lawnmower. This trivial discovery had given him an idea, one that made him very happy.

He slipped his gun in his belt and approached the two men. Calmly, he started pouring the contents of the jerrycan over them. Their clothes were soon covered in dark stains. The oily, acrid smell of the gasoline spread through the room.

Will Farland moved aside instinctively to avoid getting the liquid on his face and accidentally headbutted the sheriff in the temple. Westlake did not even react. The pain had been anaesthetized by the panic that was starting to appear in his eyes.

'What do you want? Money? I don't have a lot in the house, but in the bank—'

'I have money, too,' the deputy interrupted his chief, his voice shrill with fear. 'Almost twenty thousand dollars. You can have it all.'

What are two nice American boys doing here in the middle of all these paddy fields?

As he continued pouring the liquid from the jerrycan over the two men, it pleased him to think that it wasn't only the gasoline fumes that were bringing the tears to their eyes. He spoke in the reassuring tone he'd once been taught.

Don't worry, corporal. We're going to take care of you . . .

'Yes. Maybe we can come to an arrangement.'

A flash of hope appeared on the sheriff's face, and in his words. 'Sure we can. Come with us to the bank tomorrow morning and take whatever you want.'

'Yes, we could do that . . .' His voice changed abruptly. 'But we won't.'

With what was left of the gasoline in the jerrycan, he marked a line on the floor as far as the door. Then he put his hand in his pocket and took out a Zippo. A nauseating odour joined the pungent smell that already filled the room. Farland had relieved himself in his pants.

'No, I beg you, don't do it, don't do it, for—'

'Shut your fucking mouth!'

It was Westlake who had interrupted his deputy's pointless snivelling. The strength of his hate and curiosity had given him back a little pride.

63

'Who are you, scumbag?'

The young man who had been a soldier looked at him for a moment in silence.

The planes will come from that direction . . .

Then he said his name.

The sheriff opened his eyes wide.

'That isn't possible. You're dead.'

He clicked the Zippo. The two men stared at the flame in terror.

He smiled, and for once was pleased that his smile was a grimace. 'No, you sons of bitches. *You're* dead.'

He opened his hand more than necessary and let the Zippo fall to the floor. He didn't know how long the fall of the lighter would last for the two men. But he knew from experience how long such a short journey could be.

No thunder, for them.

Only the metallic noise of the Zippo hitting the floor. Then a hot bright whoosh, followed by a tongue of flame that advanced on them.

He stood listening to them scream and watching them squirm and burn until the smell of roasting flesh spread through the room. He breathed it in, savouring the fact that this time the flesh wasn't his.

Then he opened the door and went out on the street. He started walking, leaving the house behind him, the screams accompanying him like a blessing as he moved away.

Soon afterwards, when the screams stopped, he knew that the captivity of Sheriff Duane Westlake and his deputy Will Farland was over.

Too Many Years Later

CHAPTER 7

Jeremy Cortese watched the dark-coloured BMW move away, and wished it would blow up. He was sure that, apart from the driver, none of the people inside would be much of a loss to the world.

'Go fuck yourselves, assholes.'

Having got that off his chest, he went back into one of the two huts on the site. Actually, they weren't so much huts as sheet-metal boxes mounted on wheels and put there as a barrier to mark off the work area.

He resisted the temptation to light a cigarette.

The technical meeting that had just ended had upset him, aggravating the bad mood that had been dogging him since the beginning of the day.

The previous evening, he had gone to Madison Square Garden to see the Knicks go belly-up, losing to the Dallas Mavericks. He had come out feeling bitter, as he always did – leading him to wonder why he still insisted on going to games.

That old feeling of being part of a crowd, celebrating a shared passion, just wasn't there any more. Whether his team won or lost, he always returned home thinking the same thing.

And alone.

Going in search of memories is never an easy matter.

Whatever you dig up, it never really works. You can't fully recapture the good memories, and you can't kill the bad ones.

But he kept going back, feeding that instinct for self-harm that every human being, to a greater or lesser degree, carries within himself.

Several times during the game he had looked around at the bleachers until he gradually lost interest in what was happening in the game.

With a sad tub of popcorn in his hands, he had seen fathers and sons overjoyed at a slam dunk from Irons or a three-pointer by Jones and screaming in chorus with the rest of the fans, 'Defence! Defence! Defence!' when the other team attacked.

He had done exactly the same in the days when he went to games with his sons and felt that he meant something in their lives. But that had turned out to be an illusion. The truth was, they meant something in his.

When one of the Knicks had put in a three, he, too, had risen to his feet by sheer force of habit, rejoicing with a crowd of perfect strangers and using it as an opportunity to repress the tears rising to his eyes.

Then he had sat down again. On his right was an empty seat and on his left a boy and a girl with eyes for nobody but each other, clearly wondering why they were here instead of in bed, having a lot more fun.

When he'd come here with his sons, he'd always sat between them. John, the younger of the two, usually sat on his right and seemed equally interested in the game and the comings and goings of the people selling drinks, candy floss and all kinds of food. Jeremy had often compared him to a furnace that could burn hot dog and popcorn the way an old steam locomotive burned coal. More than once he had thought that the boy wasn't really interested in basketball and the real reason he liked going to the stadium was his father's generosity when they were there.

Sam, the older one, who was more like him, both physically and in character, and would soon be taller than him, was really fascinated by the game. Although they had never talked about it, he knew that his dream was to be a star of the NBA. Unfortunately, Jeremy was convinced it would remain a dream and nothing more. Sam had inherited his big bones and the kind of build that with time would tend to spread outwards rather than upwards, even though he was in the school team and regularly beat his father when they shot hoops behind the house.

Mortifying as that was, his pride as a parent always made Jeremy happy to be humiliated like that.

Then the things that had happened had happened. Actually, he didn't feel any sense of guilt, and didn't see why he should.

It had simply been a piece of demolition.

He and his wife Jenny had found themselves talking less and less and arguing more and more. Then the arguments had ended and only silence had remained. Without any real reason, they had become strangers. At that point, the demolition was over and they didn't have the strength left to start rebuilding.

After the divorce, Jenny had moved closer to her parents and now lived in Queens with the boys. They had stayed on good terms, and in spite of what the judge had ruled, she allowed him to see his sons whenever he wanted. Except that Jeremy couldn't always get away and before long the boys were seeing less and less of him and were less and less enthusiastic when they did. Their excursions had become less frequent, and going to games had stopped altogether.

It seemed that demolition had become his speciality, both at work and outside.

He shook himself free of these thoughts and tried to get back to the present.

Sonora Inc., the hugely successful construction company he worked for, had acquired two adjoining four-storey buildings on the corner of Third Avenue and 23rd Street, paying a considerable sum to the owners and decent compensation to the few families who still lived in those buildings. In their place there would be a forty-two-storey condominium, with a gym, a roof swimming pool and other facilities.

The new was elbowing aside the old.

They had almost finished the demolition. Jeremy found this part of the process necessary but extremely boring. After months of effort and noise, it was as if the work hadn't even started. He had even felt a touch of sadness as he watched those two old redbrick buildings come down, as if a chunk of history was disappearing with them. But the excitement of construction would soon put paid to that feeling. Before too long, the excavators would carve out sufficient space to throw down foundations appropriate to a building of that kind. And then the creation would begin, the gradual climb upwards, the adding of piece to piece, until the joyful moment when they planted a Stars and Stripes on the roof.

Standing in the doorway of the hut, he saw the workers downing tools one by one and walking towards him.

He looked at his watch. The argument with those assholes had lasted so long, he hadn't realized it was lunchtime. He wasn't hungry, but more than that, he had no desire right now to join in the chatter that always accompanied lunch. He'd always been on cordial, even friendly terms with his men.

They didn't share anything outside work, but work did take up most of their time, after all. And on the sites that he supervised he liked people to work as harmoniously as possible. That was why he had earned the esteem of his bosses and the respect of the workforce, even though they all knew that, when necessary, he was ready to take the gloves off and show an iron fist.

The fact that in his case it wasn't a velvet glove, but a work glove, didn't change anything.

Ronald Freeman, his deputy, came into the hut, making the floor sway slightly as he did so. He was a tall, well-built black man with a passion for beer and spicy food. Both tendencies had left their mark on his face and body. Freeman had married an Indian woman – something spicy to get his teeth into, as he put it. Jeremy had been to dinner at their house once. No sooner had he put in his mouth the first piece of something that had a name like *masala* than he had felt himself burst into flame and had been forced to take an immediate swig of beer. Then he had laughed and asked his host if you needed a firearms licence to serve food like that.

Ron took off his hard hat and went to the corner where he had put the thermal container his wife prepared for him every day. He sat down on the bench that ran along one side of the hut and placed the container on his knees. He saw Jeremy's face and realized it was one of those days.

'Trouble?'

Jeremy shrugged his shoulders, downplaying the situation. 'The usual crap. When an architect and an engineer agree after arguing for hours, you can bet the next thing they'll do is go off in search of a third pain in the ass, so they can put together a kind of Bermuda triangle.'

'And did they find one?'

'You know how it is. It isn't hard to find a ballbuster.'

'The Brokens woman?'

'Yeah.'

'If that woman understood double what she understands now, she'd still understand shit. She must be a sensation in bed, if her husband lets her off the leash like that.'

'Or else she's a stiff in bed, and her husband hopes she'll tire herself out during the day so she won't make any demands on him at night. Imagine what it must be like to have that woman lying beside you and feel her reaching out her hand . . .'

Ron gave a grimace of horror. 'If it was me, they'd have to stick a pack of dogs in my underpants to dig it out.'

At that moment, two men climbed the steps to join them. Ron took advantage of their arrival to open his container. A strong smell of garlic pervaded the hut.

James Ritter, a pleasant-looking young worker, took a step back towards the door he'd just come in through. 'Holy shit, Ron. Does the CIA know you're carrying a weapon of mass destruction around with you? Eat all that stuff, you'll be able to solder metal with your breath.'

Freeman's only response was to ostentatiously lift a forkful of food to his mouth. 'You're an asshole. You deserve that trash you usually eat. You know, Viagra, which by the way I'm sure you're already taking, sure ain't gonna work with that crap inside you.'

Jeremy smiled.

He liked this atmosphere of camaraderie. Experience had taught him that men were better able to do heavy work if things were kept light. That was why he usually prepared something at home and ate his lunch sitting in one of the two huts with his workers.

But when he was in a bad mood, he preferred to be alone. To think about his own business and not weigh things down for others.

He went to the door and stood there for a moment looking out.

'Not eating, boss?'

He shook his head, without turning. 'Nah, I'm going to the deli around the corner. When I get back, I'll count how many victims Ron's food has claimed.'

He descended the steps of the hut, and went back to being an ordinary citizen. He crossed at the crossing and set off along 23rd Street, leaving Third Avenue behind him. The traffic wasn't too heavy at this hour and in this part of the city. The rhythms of New York were very regular, except from time to time when things went crazy.

It was like an endless conjuring trick. In this city everything appeared and disappeared constantly. Cars, people, houses.

He got to the deli at a steady pace, without stopping to look in any windows. Partly because he wasn't interested in what was in those windows, but mainly because he didn't want to see his own reflection. For fear of discovering that he, too, had vanished into thin air.

He pushed open the door of the crowded deli, and the smell of food hit his nostrils. Seeing him come in, the oriental girl behind the cash register found the time to smile at him before turning to the line of people waiting to weigh their food and pay for it.

He went slowly along the long display counter, looking for something that attracted him in the various containers. Assistants, also oriental, replaced them as they emptied. He took a plastic container, served himself a few pieces of stewed chicken that looked acceptable enough, and prepared himself a mixed salad.

In the meantime, the line at the cash desk had grown shorter and a minute or so later he found himself facing the girl who had smiled at him when he had entered. At a first distracted glance, he had judged her to be much younger than she was. Now that he saw her at close quarters, he realized she wasn't young enough to be his daughter after all. She smiled at him as if she might be willing to become something different for him. She probably did that with everyone, Jeremy thought. He weighed his containers, paid the money he was asked to, and left the woman to smile at the next customer in the same way.

He went to the back of the deli and sat down alone at a table for two. The chicken kept its promise – in other words wasn't very good. He almost immediately left it and devoted his attention to the salad, remembering how Jenny had insisted, when they were still together, that he eat more vegetables.

Everything always happens too late . . .

With his tongue, he pursued the fragments of salad that got stuck between his teeth and washed them away with sips of the beer.

His thoughts returned to the morning's meeting with Val Courier, a famous architect of somewhat dubious sexuality, and Fred Wyring, an engineer with equally dubious calculations, who had been joined by the wife of the owner of the company. Mrs Elisabeth Brokens, who looked like a brochure for Botox, having tired of going from one analyst to another, had decided that the best cure for her neuroses would be work. Having no aptitude, no training, and no ideas, she had been forced to turn to her husband. Maybe she had freed herself from her neuroses, but only by passing them on to all the people she came in contact with.

Jeremy Cortese didn't have any qualifications, but had graduated on the job. Day after day, working hard and learning from those who knew more than him. He found arguing with incompetents a waste of time, which he'd eventually have to account for to someone, in this case Mr Brokens in person. Mr Brokens knew his work well but evidently didn't know his wife quite as well, if he let her stick her nose in things like that.

Every time he saw her show up, he was tempted to set the stopwatch, so that he could demonstrate to his boss how much a visit from his wife to the site had cost him. Maybe it would have been better for him to keep paying the analysts' fees.

He was so absorbed in his thoughts that he didn't see Ronald Freeman come in. It wasn't until he was standing right in front of him that he became aware of his presence and looked up from his salad.

'We have a problem.'

Ron paused, then put his hands down on the table and looked him straight in the eyes. The expression on Ron's face was one he'd never seen there before. If such a thing was possible, Jeremy would have said he was pale.

'A big problem.'

That started ringing alarm bells in Jeremy's head. 'What's up?'

Ron made a gesture with his head towards the door. 'It might be better if you came and saw for yourself.'

Without waiting for a reply, he turned and headed for the exit. Jeremy followed him, feeling a mixture of surprise and anxiety. It was quite rare to see his deputy fazed by an emergency of any kind.

They walked along the street side by side. As they approached the site, they saw that the men had left the fenced-off area, a homogenous mass of work jackets and hard hats.

Without realizing it, he had started walking faster.

When they reached the entrance, the workers silently stood aside for them. It was like a scene from an old movie, the kind where the camera tracks along a row of despairing faces standing at the top of a mine shaft where a sudden collapse has trapped some of the miners inside.

What the hell's going on?

They lost no time in putting on their hard hats. Ronald turned right, and Jeremy followed. They walked along the fence, next to what was still standing of a wall, then found themselves descending a staircase that led to the old basement, which was now almost completely open to the sky. As soon as they were at the bottom, Ronald led him towards the opposite side of the excavation. The only wall still partially standing here was the solid one between the two buildings, which was currently being demolished.

They reached the left-hand corner, the furthest from the staircase. Ronald stopped and with an almost choreographed effect, as if raising a curtain, moved aside and left the way free.

Jeremy shuddered, and felt like retching. He was glad he'd only eaten salad.

The demolition work had exposed a cavity wall. Through a gap in it, made by a pneumatic hammer, an arm was visible, dirty with time and dust. Above it, a head, reduced almost to a skull, was resting on what remained of a shoulder and seemed to be looking towards the outside world with all the bitterness of someone who has waited too long to see light and air again.

CHAPTER 8

Vivien Light parked her Volvo XC60, switched off the engine, and waited a moment for the world to catch up with her. All through the journey back from Cresskill, she had had the feeling of being out of sync, of moving in a parallel dimension of her own, where she was faster than everything else. As if leaving in her wake a trail composed of fragments of the past, rapid splinters of coloured time, as visible as the tail of a comet by the cars, houses and people that flashed on the screens of her car windows.

The same thing happened every time she went up to see her sister.

She always felt hope when she set out. There was no reason for it, which made it all the stronger – and made her disappointment all the stronger when she found her sister the same as ever. Still a beautiful woman, as if the months and years were absurdly compensating her by having no effect on her face, but with eyes like blue spots staring into an emptiness that grew more all-encompassing as her illness developed.

That was why the journey back was a kind of leap into hyperspace, from which she emerged somewhere in the middle of reality.

She turned the rear-view mirror so that she could see herself. It wasn't vanity. She just wanted to recognize herself,

77

to make sure she was normal again. She saw the face of a young woman some people had called beautiful and others had brushed past as if she didn't exist. The approval, as always happens, was invariably in inverse proportion to her own interest in that person.

She had short brown hair, rarely smiled, never folded her arms, and only allowed physical contact when she couldn't avoid it. In her clear eyes there seemed to be a constant hint of sternness. And in the glove compartment of her car there was a Glock 23 pistol.

If she had been a normal woman, her approach to life might have been different. So might her appearance. But her hair was short to prevent anyone from grabbing it during a fight, her stern expression told other people to keep their distance, folding her arms could denote insecurity, and touching someone helped to create a sense of safety and trust, useful if you wanted that person to come clean. And the reason she had a pistol was because she was Detective Vivien Light of the New York Police Department, working out of the 13th Precinct on 21st Street. The entrance to her place of work was just behind her, and she would only have to get out of the car and take those few steps to be transformed from a troubled woman into a police officer.

She leaned forward to take the pistol from the glove compartment, slipped it into her jacket pocket and came back to earth.

In the side mirror she saw two uniformed officers come out of the precinct house through the glass-fronted main door, descend the steps, get into a car and drive off at speed, lights flashing and siren wailing. They were answering a call, one of the many they received every day: an emergency, someone in need, a crime. Every day in this city, men, women and children walked in the midst of danger, unable to predict when it would strike, unable to fight it.

That was what they were there for.

Courtesy.

Professionalism.

Respect.

That was written on the doors of the police cars. Unfortunately, courtesy, professionalism and respect weren't always enough to protect all those people from the violence and madness of mankind. Sometimes, in order to fight it, police officers had to allow a little of that madness into themselves. The difficult part was that they had to be aware of it and keep it on a tight leash. That was the difference between them and the people whose violence they were sometimes obliged to meet with violence. And that was why she wore her hair short, rarely smiled, and had a shield in her pocket and a pistol on her belt.

For no particular reason, she thought of an old Indian fable she had once told Sundance, about an old Cherokee sitting watching the sunset with his grandson.

'Grandfather, why do men fight?'

The old man, his eyes turned to the setting sun as the day lost its battle with night, spoke in a calm voice.

'Every man, sooner or later, is called to do so. For every man there's always a battle waiting to be fought, to win or lose. Because the fiercest clash is the one between the two wolves.'

'What wolves, grandfather?'

'The wolves every man carries inside himself.'

The boy didn't understand. He waited for his grandfather to break the silence he had let fall between them, maybe to arouse his curiosity. Finally, the old man, who had the wisdom of time inside him, resumed in his calm tone, 'There are two wolves in each of us. One is bad and lives a life of hate, jealousy, envy, rancour, false pride, lies, and selfishness.'

The old man paused again, this time to allow him to absorb what he had just said.

'And the other?'

'The other is the good wolf. He lives a life of peace, love, hope, generosity, compassion, humility and faith.'

The child thought for a moment about what his grandfather had just told him. Then he expressed what was especially on his mind.

'And which wolf wins?'

The old Cherokee turned to look at him and replied, clear-eyed, 'The one we feed more.'

Vivien opened the door and got out of the car. As soon as she turned on her cellphone, it started ringing.

She lifted it to her ear and instinctively replied as if she was sitting at her desk. 'Detective Light.'

'Bellew here. Where are you?'

'Just outside. I'm coming in.'

'I'll go down. Let's meet in the lobby.'

Vivien climbed the steps, opened the glass-fronted door, and was inside the building.

A black man with his hands cuffed behind his back stood in front of the desk, with a uniformed officer beside him holding him by one arm. One of the officers behind the desk was taking down the details of his arrest.

As Vivien entered, she returned the officer's wave. She turned right and found herself in a large room, painted a nondescript colour, with rows of chairs in the middle and a whiteboard on the wall facing them. Another whiteboard stood on an easel next to a raised desk. This was the room where the officers on duty gathered for roll call, to be given the rundown on the current operations and assigned their tasks for the day.

Captain Alan Bellew, her immediate superior, came in through another door facing the entrance. Seeing her, he came towards her with that rapid walk of his that gave an impression of physical vigour. He was a tall, highly capable man who loved his work and was good at it.

He knew all about Vivien's difficult love life. In spite of that, and her youth, her unquestionable qualities in the job had led him to hold her in high regard. A relationship of mutual respect had sprung up between them, and whenever they had worked together they'd always achieved excellent results. One of Vivien's colleagues had once called her 'the captain's pet', but when Bellew had found out about it he had taken the officer aside and given him a little talk. Nobody knew what he had said, but from that moment on all comments had ceased.

Coming level with her, he did what he always did: he came straight to the point.

'A call just came in. We have a homicide. The body's apparently years old. They found it on a construction site during demolition. It was inside a wall between two basements.' He paused, just long enough to give her time to focus on the situation. 'I'd like you to handle it.'

'Where is it?'

Bellew made a vague gesture with his head. 'Two blocks from here, on 23rd and Third. The crime scene team should be there by now. The ME's on his way, too. I already sent

81

Bowman and Salinas to keep an eye on things until you get there.'

'Isn't this something for Cold Case?'

Cold Case was the squad that dealt with long-unsolved homicides. From what the captain had said, this sounded completely like their thing.

'We're handling it for now. Later, we can consider if it's appropriate to transfer it to them.'

Vivien knew Captain Alan Bellew regarded the 13th Precinct as his personal territory and didn't like anyone who didn't work directly for him muscling in.

Vivien nodded. 'Okay. I'll get right on it.'

Just then, two men came through a door to the right of the desk. One was older, with grey hair and a tanned face.

Sailing, maybe, or golf.

Or maybe both, Vivien thought.

His dark suit, leather briefcase and serious demeanour were like a sign around his neck, marked Lawyer.

The other man was younger, about thirty-five. He was wearing dark glasses, and there was several days' growth of beard on his drawn face. His clothes, distinctly more casual than his companion's, bore traces of the night he had spent in a cell. That wasn't the only thing he bore traces of: he had a cut on his lip and the left shoulder seam of his jacket was torn.

The two men went out without looking around. Vivien and Bellew watched them until they disappeared beyond the swaying of the glass-fronted door.

The captain gave a half smile. 'We had a celebrity guest in the Plaza last night.'

Vivien knew what that meant. Upstairs in the squad room, along with the detectives' desks, which were so close together they made the place look like an office furniture showroom, there was a cell. This was where the arrested were kept, sometimes for a whole night, waiting to be either freed on bail or transferred to the jail in Chinatown. With a sense of irony, given how uncomfortable the long wooden bunks fixed to the walls were, they had dubbed it the Plaza.

'Who is that guy?'

'Russell Wade.'

'*The* Russell Wade? Who won the Pulitzer at the age of twenty-five? And had it taken away from him three months later?'

The captain nodded, the smile fading abruptly from his lips. 'Yeah, that's the guy.'

Vivien knew when there was a touch of bitterness in her chief's voice. And few things made him more bitter than when people deliberately, almost complacently, destroyed themselves. For reasons of her own, it was a situation she was familiar with.

'We picked him up last night in a raid on a gambling joint, blind drunk and resisting arrest. I think he caught a punch from Tyler.'

Bellew immediately filed that brief parenthesis away among the closed files and came back to the matter in hand.

'No offence to the living, but I think you have a dead man to deal with. He's been waiting a long time – best not to keep him waiting any longer.'

'I think he has every right.'

Bellew left her. Vivien went outside again, into the mild air of that late spring afternoon. She descended the short flight of steps, and as she did so she had a fleeting vision of Russell Wade and his lawyer disappearing into a chauffeured limousine, over to her right. The car pulled away from the curb and glided past. The guest who had spent a night in the Plaza had now taken off his dark glasses, and their eyes met through the open window. For a moment, Vivien found herself looking into two intense dark eyes and was astonished by the immense sadness she saw in them. Then the car was past her and that face disappeared behind the screen of the electrically operated window.

The site where they had found the body was so close, it was easier to get there on foot. And in the meantime she was already processing the small amount of information she had in her possession. A construction site was often an ideal place to get rid of an unwanted person for ever. This wasn't the first time, and it wouldn't be the last. A murder, a body buried in concrete, an old story of violence and madness.

Which wolf wins?

Those wolves had been battling it out since the dawn of time. Over the centuries, there had always been some who had fed the wrong wolf. Vivien walked on, feeling the unavoidable excitement she always felt on the verge of a new case. Along with the awareness that, whether she solved it or not, everyone would – as they always did – end up defeated.

CHAPTER 9

To get to the construction site, she had walked up Third Avenue.

She had to emerge from that anonymity that had allowed her to merge into the humanity around her and assume a very specific role. The arrival of a detective on a crime scene was always a special moment, like a curtain rising on an actor. Nobody ever moved a finger before the person in charge of the investigation arrived. She knew the kind of things she was going to feel. And she knew that, as always, she'd have been happy to do without those feelings. The place where a murder had been committed, whether recently or some time in the past, had a certain grisly fascination. Some murder scenes even became tourist attractions. For her, a murder scene was a place where she had to put her emotions to one side and concentrate on her job. Whatever theories she might have constructed in her head during her brief walk were about to be put to the test.

Bowman and Salinas, the two officers sent by Bellew, were nowhere to be seen. They must be inside, putting yellow tape around the area where the body had been found.

The workers had gathered outside the door of one of the huts at one end of the site. Standing slightly apart from them were two other men, a large black man and a white man in a blue cotton work jacket. Everyone seemed extremely nervous. Vivien could understand how they felt. It isn't every day you knock down a wall and find a corpse.

She approached the two men and flashed her shield. 'Hi, I think you're expecting me. I'm Detective Vivien Light.'

If they were surprised to see her arrive on foot, they didn't show it. Their relief that she was here, that they finally had someone they could talk to, overcame any other consideration.

The white man spoke for both of them. 'I'm Jeremy Cortese, the site supervisor. And this is my deputy, Ron Freeman.'

Vivien, sure that the two men couldn't wait to get started, came straight to the point. 'Who found the body?'

Cortese indicated the group of workers behind them. 'Jeff Sefakias over there. He was knocking down a wall and—'

Vivien interrupted him. 'OK. I'll talk to him later. Right now I'd like to take a look at the scene.'

Cortese took a step towards the site entrance. 'This way. I'll take you.'

Freeman didn't move. 'If you don't mind, I'd rather not see that . . . that thing again.'

Vivien made an effort to suppress a sympathetic smile. She was afraid that it might be misunderstood, that the man might think she was making fun of him. There was no reason to humiliate someone she instinctively sensed was a good person. Not for the first time, Vivien reflected on how difficult it was to guess a person's character from his body. The man's huge frame would have struck fear into anyone, and yet he was the one upset by the sight of the corpse.

Just then, a large dark sedan pulled up close to the barriers. The driver quickly got out and opened the door for the passenger in the back seat. A woman emerged from the car. She was tall and blond and must once have been beautiful. Now she was only an advertisement for the futile battle some women waged against the indifference of time. Even though her clothes were casual, they all had designer labels. She reeked of Saks Fifth Avenue, massage sessions at exclusive spas, French perfume, and snobbery. Without so much as a glance at Vivien, she addressed Cortese directly.

'Jeremy, what's going on here?'

'As I told you on the phone, we found a man's body while we were digging.'

'Well, I understand that, but we can't stop work because of it. Do you have any idea how much this site is costing the company per day?'

Cortese shrugged and made an instinctive gesture with his hands in Vivien's direction. 'We were waiting for the police to get here.'

It was only then that the woman seemed to notice her presence. She looked her up and down, with an expression Vivien decided wasn't worth the effort of deciphering. Whatever test she was subjecting her to – clothes, looks or age – she knew she hadn't passed it.

'Officer, I hope we can resolve this regrettable incident as soon as possible.'

Vivien tilted her head slightly to one side and smiled. 'And who do I have the pleasure of . . . ?'

'Elisabeth Brokens,' the woman said in a self-important tone. 'My husband is Charles Brokens, the owner of the company.'

'Well, Mrs Brokens, what I might define as a regrettable incident is the nose your plastic surgeon stuck on your face, for instance. What happened here is something the rest of the

87

world insists on calling homicide. And as I'm sure you know, that's something that tends to be of great interest to the law. Which, if you don't mind my saying so, has priority over your company's balance sheet.' She stopped smiling and abruptly changed her tone. 'And if you don't get out of my way I'll have you arrested for obstructing an investigation by the New York Police Department.'

'How dare you? My husband is a personal friend of the commissioner and—'

'Then I suggest you complain to him, Mrs Brokens. And let me get on with my job.'

She turned her back on the woman, and left her standing there like a block of marble, plotting some retaliation or other. She headed for the opening that she assumed to be the site entrance.

Jeremy Cortese fell into step beside her. There was an incredulous but blissful look on his face. 'Lady, if you ever have a site that needs supervising, I'd be happy to offer my services for free. Mrs Brokens' face after your little speech is going to be one of the happiest memories of my life.'

But Vivien barely heard him, her mind already elsewhere. As they crossed the threshold, she took in the situation at a single glance. Just beyond where they were now, marked out by a protection fence, was a hole in the ground that covered about three quarters of the area of the whole site and was as deep as a cellar. The bottom of the hole was the floor of the two different buildings, divided down the middle by a line. On the other side, part of the street level floor still had to be demolished, but most of the work had been done. At the bottom, the two officers were just finishing cordoning off an area in the left-hand corner. A worker was leaning against a wall behind them, waiting.

Cortese provided her with answers before she had even asked the questions. 'Sonora acquired two old buildings next door to each other. We're demolishing them to build a condominium. As you can see, we're nearly finished.'

Vivien pointed to the floor divided in two. 'What was here before?'

'On this side, an apartment block with a restaurant at street level. Italian, I think. We moved a whole lot of old equipment. On the other side, there was a small garage. I think it was put there after the building was built, because we found signs of renovation.'

'Do you know who the owners were?'

'No. But the company probably has all the papers.'

Cortese moved on, and Vivien followed him. They reached the corner to their right, where a concrete staircase, left over from the old buildings, led down to the lower level. There was a desolate feeling to the deserted site, with pneumatic hammers lying on the ground and a big yellow vehicle with a log drilling tool standing to one side. Everywhere was the grey gloom of destruction, without the colourful promise of rebirth.

As they went down the stairs, two of the crime scene technicians appeared, carrying their instruments. Vivien signalled to them, and they approached.

Vivien and Cortese got to the bottom of the stairs. The two officers were waiting for them there. Cortese stopped a couple of paces from the yellow tape. Officer Victor Salinas, a tall, brown-haired young man who had a crush on Vivien and whose eyes made no secret of the fact, waited for her to reach him then raised the tape to let her through.

'What's the score?' she asked.

'At first sight, I'd say normal and complicated at the same time. Come and see.'

At the far end was a kind of square cavity wall. Vivien turned her head and saw that on the opposite side there was another exactly the same. Most likely, one or more columns, now demolished, had formed a line between them.

In front of her, through a gap in the concrete, she saw a forearm covered in what remained of a cotton jacket. A skull with traces of shrivelled skin and hair could also be glimpsed inside, grinning like a figure from the Day of the Dead. But this was no allegory – this was very real evidence of violent death.

Vivien walked up to the wall. She looked carefully at the arm, the body, the material of the sleeve. She tried to peer inside, seeing what details she could make out. She knew how important first impressions could turn out to be.

She turned and saw that the crime scene officers and a man of about forty in a sportcoat and a pair of jeans were standing just beyond the tape, waiting for instructions. Vivien had never seen the man before but from his vaguely bored air she guessed he was the medical examiner. Vivien walked over to them. 'Okay,' she said. 'Let's try getting him out of there.'

Jeremy Cortese stepped forward and pointed to the worker who had been standing to one side. 'If you like, there's one of my men here who has no problems with dead bodies. In his spare time, he helps his brother-in-law who's an undertaker.'

'Call him over.'

Cortese signalled to the worker, who came towards them. He was in his early thirties, with a boyish face and vaguely oriental features. Shiny dark hair peeped out from under his hard hat. Vivien thought there must be something Asian about him.

Without a word he walked past them, went to the wall and bent down to pick up the pneumatic hammer from the ground.

Vivien went up to him. 'What's your name?'

'Tom. Tom Dickson.'

'All right, Tom, listen. We have a delicate situation here. This has to be done with extreme care. Everything inside that hole could be important. If it's all the same to you, I'd rather you used a hammer and chisel, even if it takes longer.'

'Don't worry. I know what I'm doing. You'll find everything the way you want it.'

Vivien placed a hand on his shoulder. 'I trust you, Tom. Carry on.'

She had to admit the man knew his business. He widened the gap in such a way as to make the inside accessible, making the rubble fall outwards but without moving the position of the body.

Vivien asked Salinas for a torch and went closer to take a look inside the hole. There was still a lot of daylight, but the semi-darkness inside made it difficult to see. She shone the torch at the walls and the dead man. The narrowness of the space had stopped the body from sliding to the ground. The dead man was resting on his left side, his head tilted at an unnatural angle. It was this that had given the impression, when seen from the outside, that his head was resting on his shoulder. The enclosed environment and the lack of humidity had partially mummified him, which was why he was much more intact than would normally have been the case – and which also made it much more difficult to calculate how long he had been hidden here.

Who are you? Who killed you?

Vivien knew that for the families of missing persons, the worst thing was the anguish of not knowing. Someone

one night, one day

left home and never came back. And in the absence of a

91

body, his loved ones spent their whole lives wondering what, where and why. Never giving up a hope that only time could gradually extinguish.

She pulled herself together and resumed her inspection.

When she aimed her torch at the ground she discovered, next to the feet of the corpse, an object covered in dust that looked at first glance like a kind of large wallet. She asked for a pair of latex gloves, slid into the opening, and bent to pick it up. Then she straightened up and signalled to the crime scene team and the medical examiner.

'OK, gentleman, it's your turn.'

As the team got to work, she examined the object she had in her hand.

She blew on it gently to remove the layer of dust. The material was imitation leather, and must once have been black or brown. She could see now that it wasn't in fact a wallet, but a document holder. She opened it carefully. There were two hard plastic sheets inside, stuck together, which made a slight tearing noise as she pulled then apart.

Inside were two photographs.

She parted the plastic and gently slipped her fingers in to extract them without ruining them. She examined them by the light of the torch. In the first, a young man in a helmet and combat uniform was leaning on a tank and looking gravely at the camera. Around him there was vegetation that suggested a tropical country. She turned the photograph over. There was something written on it, faded by time, with some of the letters almost erased, but not enough to make them illegible.

Cu Chi District 1971

The second photograph, which was much better preserved, surprised her. The subject was the same young man who had been looking thoughtfully at the camera in the previous photograph. Here, he was in civilian clothes, a psychedelic T-shirt and work pants. In this image he had long hair and was smiling and holding a big black cat out to the camera. She studied the man and the animal closely. At first she thought it was a deformation caused by the angle, but then she realized that her first impression had been correct.

The cat had only three legs.

There was nothing written on the back of this photograph.

She asked the other officer, Bowman, for two plastic bags, and slipped the document holder and the photographs inside them. She went up to Frank Ritter, the head of the crime-scene team and handed them over to him.

'I'd like you to analyse this material. Look for fingerprints, if there are any. Examine the victim's clothes. Plus, I'd like these photographs to be enlarged.'

'We'll see what we can do. But if I were you I wouldn't hold out too much hope. Everything looks pretty old to me.'

The ME walked around the stretcher and came and joined Vivien. They limited the introductions to the absolute minimum.

'Jack Borman.'

'Vivien Light.'

They both knew who they were, where they were and what they were doing. Right now, any other consideration faded into the background.

'Any idea yet of the cause of death?'

'In layman's terms, I'd hazard a guess, from the position of the head, that someone broke his collar bone. With what I don't know. I'll know more after the post mortem.'

'How long do you think he's been here?'

'From the body's state of preservation, I'd say around

fifteen years. But the state of the hiding place also has to be taken into account. An analysis of the fibres should get us there. And I think forensic tests on the material of the clothes will come in useful, too.'

'Thanks.'

'Don't mention it.'

As the medical examiner walked away, Vivien realized that everything that could be done had been done. She gave the order to remove the body, said goodbye to the men, and left them to their tasks. At this point, she considered it pointless to talk to the worker who had found the body. She had given Bowman the job of taking down the details of all the people who might be useful to their investigation. She would talk to them later, including Mr Charles Brokens, who woke up every morning with that woman in his bed.

In a case of homicide like this, the most important leads usually came from the technical data rather than from witness statements. They'd have to wait for the test results before deciding on a plan of action.

She went back the way she had come, until she reached the site entrance. The workers watched her with a mixture of admiration and awe. She set off for the precinct house to pick up her car. She needed to think.

Bellew hadn't assigned her to an easy case. He presumably considered her capable of solving it, but what he was asking her to do was equivalent to pulling chestnuts from the fire. And from the facts that had emerged so far, these chestnuts had been in the fire for at least fifteen years and had been burned to a cinder.

She passed a bar and instinctively looked through the window. Sitting at a table, talking to a girl with long blond hair, was Richard. The way they were looking at each other suggested they were more than just friends. She felt like a voyeur, and hurried away before he could see her, although he seemed to have eyes only for his companion. She was not surprised to find him there. He lived nearby and they'd been there together several times.

Maybe a few more times would have been better.

She'd had a relationship with Richard that had lasted a year, full of laughter, food and wine, and tender, gentle sex. A relationship that had been one step away from being love.

But, what with her work and the situation of Sundance and her sister, she had found it more and more difficult to devote herself to the two of them. In the end, the affair had ended.

As she walked, she realized that she had the same problem as all the people moving on that street and in that city. They all assumed they would live and knew they would die.

CHAPTER 10

Ziggy Stardust was good at camouflage.

He was capable of being a perfect nobody among the millions of New York nobodies. He was a perfect example of neither-nor: neither tall nor short, neither fat nor thin, neither handsome nor ugly. He was the kind of person you didn't notice, didn't remember, didn't love.

The king of nobodies.

But he had turned being a nobody into an art. In his own way he considered himself an artist. In the same way as he called himself a traveller. On average he rode more miles on the subway every day than most passengers in a week. In Ziggy's opinion, the subway was a place for suckers. Which made it the ideal place for one of his many activities: bag snatching. Another of his activities, more of a fringe activity but no less important, was being the dealer of choice for those who loved white powder but didn't like risks or problems.

With Ziggy, they never had any problems.

He wasn't a big time dealer, but the income, though small, was regular. All these grand ladies and gentlemen had to do was call a safe number and they'd get a home delivery of whatever they needed for their parties or be given an address to go to for fun and games. They had the money – he had what they were willing to pay for. This meshing of supply and demand was so natural, it wiped out any possible scruples – not that Ziggy had ever had any.

Occasionally, when he was able to, he also sold information to anyone who needed it. Sometimes even to the police, who in return for a few useful tip-offs – strictly confidential, of course – turned a blind eye to Ziggy's frequent subway trips.

Obviously, that wasn't his real name. Nobody remembered what his real name was. Even he forgot it sometimes. The nickname had been given him, when someone had remarked on his resemblance to David Bowie at the time the record *Ziggy Stardust and the Spiders from Mars* had come out. He couldn't remember who it had been, but the name had remained.

It was the only thing that removed him a little from the anonymity in which he had always tried to live. He never walked in the middle of the sidewalk, but always hugged the walls and kept to the most shadowy areas. If he could choose, he preferred to be forgotten, rather than remembered. In the evenings he went back to his hole in Brooklyn, watched TV, surfed the internet and only went out to make phone calls. All calls related to work he made from a public phone booth. At home, on a cabinet, he always kept a roll of quarters, for every eventuality. There were a lot of people who hadn't realized there was a good reason cellphones were called cellphones. They were telephones but they were also what landed you in jail. And those who ended up in jail because their calls had been intercepted got what they deserved. Not because they were criminals, but because they were stupid.

Even now, as he descended the stairs to Bleecker Street station, he couldn't help feeling justified in his conviction.

Better to make everyone believe you were a nobody than have someone sooner or later decide that they'd prove it to you.

He reached the platform and got on the green express line going uptown. The opening and closing of the sliding doors, the constant getting on and off of weary passengers who wanted only to be somewhere else, meant a lot of pushing and shoving, the contact of bodies, the smell of sweat. But it also meant wallets and distraction, the two basic elements of his work. There was always a purse slightly open, a pocket not well closed, a bag next to someone immersed in a book so engrossing they forgot everything else.

Of course the good old days were long over. Credit cards were everywhere now, and there was less and less cash in circulation. That was why he had decided to branch out – to diversify his activities.

The door is closing, came the voice of the loudspeaker.

He moved towards the rear of the carriage, where it was more crowded, making his way between hanging elbows and whiffs of garlic. Sitting next to the door was a guy in a green military jacket. He found it hard to judge his age. From where he was standing, he couldn't see him well because the blue hood of a coverall came up from under the jacket to partly hide his face. His head was slightly tilted to the side, and it looked as if the swaying of the carriage had made him doze off. Next to his feet was a dark canvas bag.

Ziggy felt a slight sense of pins and needles in his fingertips. There was part of him that displayed something close to extrasensory perception when he singled out a victim. It was a knack, a gift, which had sometimes given him the idea that he had been born to do this work. Of course, the clothes the man was wearing didn't suggest there might be something of value in that bag. But the hands resting in his lap weren't the hands of a man who did heavy work, and his watch looked like a good one.

In his opinion, there was something here that went beyond the guy's appearance. His instinct had rarely let him down, and over time he had learned to trust it.

He had once removed a wallet from a guy in a jacket and tie only because, in brushing against him, he had felt, by touch alone, a cashmere overcoat that must have been worth more than four thousand dollars. Trusting to nothing but the texture of the material, he had made his move. A few minutes later, going through the guy's wallet, he had found seven dollars, a fake credit card and a subway season ticket.

Cheapskate!

He went closer to the man in the green jacket, although staying on the other side of the door. He waited a couple of stops. The number of passengers was increasing. He moved into the middle and then, as if shifting to leave the door clear, he moved next to him.

The canvas bag was on the floor. It was on his left, close to his feet, the handle in the perfect position to be

grabbed at the right stop

getting out while the other passengers got on. He checked that the man still had his head in the same position. He hadn't moved. Many people dozed off on the trains, especially those who had a long way to go. Ziggy was convinced that this guy belonged to that category of person. He waited until they got to Grand Central, where the number of people getting on and off was usually greater. As soon as the doors opened he grabbed the bag in an extremely rapid but natural movement, and got off. He immediately hid it with his body.

Out of the corner of his eye, as he was trying to melt into

the crowd, he thought he saw a green jacket getting out of the carriage a moment before the train left.

Shit.

Grand Central was always full of cops and if that guy had sussed him, there was the possibility there would be quite a scene. And maybe a few days in the cooler. He passed a couple of police officers, an older man and a black girl, who were chatting just outside the station. Nothing happened. Nobody came running, crying 'Stop thief!' to attract the attention of the two officers. He preferred not to turn around. Better to let the guy who was following him think he hadn't noticed anything.

He came out onto 42nd and immediately turned right and then right again, onto Vanderbilt. There was a stretch where there wasn't much traffic and that was the right place to check if the guy in the military jacket really was following him or not. He went back into the terminal through the side entrance, taking advantage of the opportunity to throw a casual glance to his right. He didn't see anybody come around the corner who looked anything like him. But that still didn't mean anything. If the guy was clever, he knew how to follow someone without being spotted. Just as he himself knew the best way to throw someone who was tailing him. He wondered again how come the guy hadn't told the two cops. If he'd noticed the theft and had followed him to get the bag back personally, that could mean two things.

Firstly: he was running the risk that this was a dangerous guy. Secondly: there might be something valuable in the bag the guy wasn't too eager for the police to clap eyes on. And if this second point turned out to be correct, then Ziggy's interest in the contents grew considerably. But at the same time it made the guy *very* dangerous.

That feeling he'd had that he'd found the right target was turning sour. He went down to the lower level, which was packed with ethnic restaurants. The huge space was full of signs, colours, food smells and a sense of hurry. And it was the last of these things that was communicating itself to him, even though he was forcing himself to walk at a normal pace.

He got to the other side and as he was climbing the stairs again he turned to check out the street behind him. Nobody suspicious. He started to relax. Maybe it had only been an impression. Maybe he was starting to get too old for this work.

He followed the signs and went back into the subway, heading for the purple line, which went north into Queens. He waited until the train arrived and followed the stream of passengers getting on. A necessary precaution. If what he'd been thinking earlier was right, the man in the green jacket, assuming he really was following him, would never try anything against him in a crowded place. He waited nonchalantly until the usual voice announced that the doors were closing.

Only then did he rush out and go back to the bench, like a passenger who suddenly realizes he has got on the wrong carriage. He waited for the clatter of the departing train to fade, then changed back to the green line, which would take him downtown and then on to Brooklyn.

He did the journey in several stages, waiting at each stop for the next train, continuing to glance around him with a nonchalant air.

When he decided that everything was OK, he got on another train and found a place to sit. He made himself comfortable and waited, with the bag in his lap, overcoming the impulse to open it and find out what there was inside.

Better to do that at home, where he'd be able to examine everything calmly and unhurriedly.

Ziggy was good at waiting.

He had done it all his life, ever since he was a boy and had started hustling every which way he could think of to make ends meet. He had carried on in the same way, never making the mistake of getting too greedy, contenting himself with what he had, but always with the unshakeable certainty that one day everything would suddenly change. His life, his home, his name.

Farewell Ziggy Stardust, welcome back *Mister* Zbigniew Malone.

He changed lines again before arriving at a station near home. He lived in Brooklyn, in a neighbourhood with the largest concentration of Haitians in New York, where even the signs on some of the restaurants were in French. A multi-ethnic world – women with huge asses and shrill voices and young guys who shuffled as they walked and wore their caps with the peak turned to the side. Bordering that area, the Jewish neighbourhood, houses with well-tended lawns and Mercedeses in the drives. Silent people, who moved like dark shadows, faces serious beneath their black hats.

But he liked things that way. In expectation of the day when he'd be able to say, That's enough of that, and choose for himself.

On the wall of the building where he lived, the windowless wall facing the street, someone had painted a mural. The artist was nothing special, but the colours, in a place so faded, so washed out, had always cheered him up. He went in through the front door and descended the steps that led to the basement where he lived. A single room with a tiny bathroom, worn, second-rate furniture and the smell of exotic cooking wafting down from the upper floors. The unmade bed was against the wall opposite the door, beneath the high window that let in a dim light. Everything seemed to belong to a bygone time, even the few modern touches: the high-definition TV, the computer and the all-in-one printer/copier, which were covered with a layer of dust.

The only surprising thing was the bookcase against the left-hand wall, filled with volumes neatly arranged in alphabetical order. Others were strewn about the room. There was even a pile of books on the night table to the right of the bed.

Ziggy placed the bag on the table, which was cluttered with old magazines, took off his jacket, and threw it on an armchair. He took the bag and went and sat down on the bed. He opened the bag and started emptying it onto the sheet. There were two newspapers, the *New York Times* and *USA Today*, a blue and yellow plastic box that turned out to be a small toolkit, a roll of copper wire and one of grey adhesive tape, the kind electricians used. Then he pulled out the heaviest thing in the bag, the thing that really weighed it down: a photograph album with a brown leather cover and pages of rough paper of the same colour, full of black and white images of people he didn't know in places he didn't know. All the photographs were quite old. From the clothes, he guessed at the 1970s. He leafed through a few pages. An image caught his attention. He removed it from the adhesive tabs that held it to the page and looked at it closely for a few moments. A young man with long hair and a smile on his lips that didn't quite reach his eyes, holding a big black cat. The snapshot, quite by chance, had managed to capture a strange resemblance, as if those two living beings, although of different species, were mirror images of each other.

He slipped the photograph into his shirt pocket and

continued to explore the contents of the bag. He extracted a black plastic object, rectangular in shape, slightly longer and narrower than a cigarette pack, with adhesive tape around the middle to stop it from opening. At one end was a series of buttons of different colours.

Ziggy looked at it for a moment, bewildered. It was like a home-made remote control. Rudimentary maybe, but that seemed to be what it was. He put it down next to the other things and took the last object out of the bag. It was a large, slightly crumpled brown envelope with a name and address written on it, the words already partly faded. The size of it suggested it had been used to send the photograph album.

He opened it to look inside and there he found sheets of paper covered in rough but fairly legible handwriting. The handwriting of a man who was probably not very used to words, either spoken or written.

Ziggy started reading. The first pages were quite boring, filled with a life story expressed in a crude and sometimes disjointed way. He was a reader of books and knew when he was reading something by someone who had studied and could write. This wasn't it.

But he became aware that the text was not without a certain fascination, even though the prose was certainly not a writer's. It was what it said that mattered, not how it was written. He continued reading with increasing attention, and gradually the attention turned to interest and finally a kind of frenzy. By the time he reached the end of the letter, he couldn't help leaping to his feet. He felt a slight shiver down his spine and the hair on his arms stood on end, as if he'd had an electric shock.

Ziggy couldn't believe his eyes. He sat down again slowly, with his legs open and his eyes fixed on some undefined point. A point in time rather than in space.

The great opportunity had arrived.

What he had in his hands might be worth millions of dollars to the right people. He felt dizzy at the thought of it. The possible advantages for him made him forget the definite consequences for others.

He put the pages down on the bed with exaggerated care, as if they were fragile. Then he started thinking about how to take advantage of this unexpected piece of luck. What to do, how to distil this material in such a way as to arouse the greatest interest and get the greatest advantage.

And above all, who to contact.

All kinds of thoughts moved through his brain at speed.

He switched on the printer/copier and put the sheets of paper on the table next to the computer. The first thing to do was make photocopies. A copy would be enough to arouse someone's interest and that someone would have to be willing to pay a tidy sum just to get hold of the original. Which had to remain in his possession until the deal was done. The original he would put in an envelope and send to an anonymous postal box he sometimes used. There it would stay until someone gave him a reason to go and get it out.

And that reason could only be a substantial sum of money.

He started the copying, placing the original of each page next to the copy as he did so. When it came to work, Ziggy was a meticulous person. And this was the most important work he had ever done in his life.

He placed one of the last sheets of paper on the glass of the scanner, lowered the lid and pressed the *start* button. The scanning light moved through the machine until it had the whole page in its memory. As it was about to print, the sensor warned that there was no more paper and an orange light started flashing on the left-hand side of the machine.

Ziggy went to get some sheets from a ream on a shelf of the bookcase and put it in the tray.

At that moment he heard a noise behind him, a slight metallic click, like a lock snapping. He turned in time to see the door open and a man in a green jacket come in.

No, not now, not now that everything was within reach . . .

But what he saw in front of him was a hand holding a knife.

It was clearly that knife that had been used to force the lousy lock. And from the look in the man's eyes he realized that wouldn't be the only use for it.

He felt his legs give way. He didn't have the strength to say anything. As the man advanced on him, Ziggy Stardust started crying. He cried because he was afraid of pain, and afraid of death.

But more than anything, he cried with disappointment.

CHAPTER 11

The Volvo moved smoothly through the traffic drawing it towards the Bronx. At that hour, going north could be a real journey. But once she left Manhattan, Vivien had found that the traffic was flowing smoothly. Since she had terrible the Triborough Bridge on her right, she had driven the length of the Bruckner Expressway in a relatively short time.

The sun was sinking behind her and the city was getting ready for sunset. The sky had a dark blue luminosity, so clear that it seemed to have been hand painted – the colour that only the New York breeze could offer, when it managed to blow clean that small stretch of infinity that everyone deluded themselves they had above them.

The car phone interrupted the music coming from the radio. She activated the speaker.

'Vivien?'

'Yes.'

'Hi, it's Nathan.'

He hadn't needed to say his name. She had recognized her brother-in-law's voice. She would have recognized it even in the clamour of a battlefield.

What do you want, you son of a bitch? she thought.

'What do you want, you son of a bitch?' she said aloud.

There was a moment's silence.

'You'll never forgive me, will you?'

'Nathan, forgiveness is for people who repent. Forgiveness is for people who try to repair the harm they've done.'

The man at the other end waited a moment, in order to let those words vanish into the distance that separated them.

'Have you seen Greta lately?'

'And you?' Vivien rounded on him, feeling the desire to hit him rise in her, that desire she felt every time she found herself in his presence or even just heard his voice. At that moment, if he had been sitting beside her, she would have smashed his nose with a dig from her elbow.

'How long is it since you last saw your wife? How long is it since you last saw your daughter? How much longer do you think you can hide?'

'Vivien, I'm not hiding. I—'

'Spare me your crap, you son of a bitch!'

She had shouted those words. And she had been wrong to do so. The contempt she felt for the man should not be manifested with a roar. It should be expressed with the hiss of the snake.

And a snake was what she became.

'Nathan, you're a coward. You always have been and you always will be. And when things got too tough for you, you did the one thing you know how to do: you ran away.'

'I've always provided for their needs. Sometimes, there are choices—'

'You didn't have choices,' she interrupted him sharply. 'You had responsibilities. And you should have assumed them. That lousy cheque you send every month isn't enough to compensate for your absence. Or even to soothe your conscience. So don't call me now to find out how your wife is. Don't call me to find out how your daughter is. If you want to feel better, get off your fucking ass and go see for yourself.'

She pressed the button so angrily to end the call that for a moment she was afraid she had broken it. For a few moments she looked straight ahead of her, driving and listening to the furious beating of her heart. A few ragged tears of anger ran down her cheeks. She wiped them with the back of her hand and tried to calm down.

To forget the place she had been that morning and the place she was going now, she took shelter in the one safe place she had: her work.

She tried to leave every other thought behind her and ordered her mind to concentrate on the new case. She recalled that arm emerging from the gap in the wall, the desolation of that shrivelled head resting on a shoulder that was only a residue of skin and bone.

Even though experience had taught her that everything was possible, that same experience made her fear that it was going to be very difficult to establish the dead man's identity. Construction sites were much favoured by the underworld as places to hide the victims of mob hits. When it was done by professionals, bodies were often buried naked or with all the labels torn off their clothes in case they were found. Sometimes the fingerprints were erased with acid. Examining the body today, she had noticed that this hadn't been done and that the labels were in their places, even though fairly deteriorated. That meant that this probably wasn't the work of a professional, but had been done by someone without the cool head or the experience to eliminate all traces.

But who could have hidden the body in a block of concrete? It wasn't an easy thing to do, unless you had expert help. Or maybe the culprit was an expert himself. Someone who worked for a construction company. Whatever the motive, the crime could have been the isolated act of an ordinary man.

The only lead they had was those photographs, especially that strange black cat with three—

'Shit!'

She had been so absorbed in her thoughts, she hadn't noticed that the junction with the Hutchinson River Parkway was blocked by a line of cars. She braked abruptly, swerving left in order not to bump the car in front. The driver of a big pick-up behind her sounded his horn loudly. In her rear-view mirror Vivien saw him leaning forward and showing her his middle finger.

She usually hated resorting to certain things when she wasn't on duty, but this evening she decided she was in a hurry. Her own distraction, more than the man's gesture, had made her nervous. She took the flashing light from behind the seat, opened the window, lit it and placed it on the roof.

With a smile, she saw the man abruptly lower his hand and back down. The cars in front of her, in so far as they could, pulled over to make it easier for her to get through. She made her way toward Zerega Avenue, and a couple of blocks after turning onto Logan she reached the church of Saint Benedict.

She parked the Volvo in a free space on the other side of the street and sat for a moment looking at the light brick facade, the short flight of steps that led to the three entrance doors surmounted by pointed arches, the columns and the friezes with which they were decorated.

It was a recent building. Vivien would never have thought that a place like that could one day become so familiar to her.

She got out of the car and crossed the street.

The semi-darkness that makes it hard to tell the colour of cats was already in the air, but there was still enough light to recognize a person. She was about to head for the priory when she saw Father Angelo Cremonesi, one of the priests attached to the parish, come out through the central door with a man and a woman. Confessions were usually heard on Saturdays from four to five, but nobody stuck rigidly to the rules, which in practice were quite flexible.

Vivien climbed the few steps and joined him. The priest stood waiting for her and the couple with him moved away.

'Good evening, Miss Light.'

'Good evening, father.'

Vivien shook his hand. He was a man in his sixties with white hair, a vigorous appearance and gentle eyes. The first time she had met him he had reminded her of Spencer Tracy in an old movie.

'Have you come for your niece?'

'Yes. I spoke with Father McKean, and we both think it's time to see if she can spend a couple of days at home. I'll bring her back here on Monday morning.'

Uttering the name of Michael McKean reminded her of him. He had an expressive face and eyes that gave the impression he could look through people and walls. Maybe it was because of this ability of his to see beyond things that he was always there when he was needed.

Father Cremonesi, who was docile but somewhat fussy, insisted on explaining the situation. 'Father McKean isn't here today, and he asked me to apologize. The kids are still at the pier. A kind person whose name I can't remember offered them a trip in a sailboat. John just called me. He knows about your agreement with Michael and told me to tell you that they were just getting their things together and that they'll be here soon.'

'That's all right.'

111

'Would you like to wait in the priory?'

'No thanks, father. I'll wait for them in the church.'

'I'll see you later, then, Miss Light.'

Father Cremonesi walked away. Maybe he had taken her intention to wait in the church for devotion. All she wanted for the moment was to be alone.

She pushed open the door and walked through the lobby with its light wood panelling, past the statues of Saint Teresa and Saint Gerard that stood in a niche in the wall. Another door, a less heavy one, led into the interior of the church itself.

It was cool here, quite dark, and silent. The altar at the far end of the one nave held out a promise of welcome and refuge.

Whenever she entered a church, Vivien found it hard to feel the presence of God in it. Young she might be, but in the time she had spent on the streets she had already met too many devils, and had felt just a weak human being shaken by the confrontation. Here, in this place, with these images, this longing for the sacred built to satisfy the needs of man, in the light of the candles lit in faith and hope, she couldn't share even a small part of that faith and that hope.

Life is rented accommodation. Sometimes God is an uncomfortable character to have around the house.

She sat down on a pew at the back. She realized one thing. In what for all believers was a place of peace and salvation, she had a gun hanging from her belt. And in spite of everything she felt defenceless.

She closed her eyes, replacing the dim light with darkness. While she waited for her niece Sundance to arrive, the memories arrived, too.

The day when she was sitting at her desk, just opposite the Plaza, in a chaos of papers and telephone calls and her colleagues joking and chattering. Then something happened that she would never forget. Detective Peter Curtin unexpectedly appeared in the doorway. He had been working at the 13th Precinct until quite recently. Then, in a shootout during a police operation, he had been quite seriously wounded. He had recovered physically, but emotionally he had realized he wasn't the same person any more. Under pressure from his wife, he had put in for a transfer. Right now he was with vice.

He came straight to her desk.

'Hi, Peter. What are you doing here?'

'I need to talk to you, Vivien.'

There was a hint of embarrassment in his voice, which made the smile on her face fade quickly.

'Sure, go ahead.'

'Not here. How about going for a walk?'

Surprised, Vivien left her desk, and soon they were outside. Curtin set off in the direction of Third Avenue and Vivien fell into step beside him. There was tension in the air and he attempted to lighten it. For whose sake she wasn't sure.

'How are things? Bellew still keeping you all on a tight leash?'

Vivien came to a halt. 'Stop beating about the bush, Peter. What's going on?'

He looked at her from another place. And it was a place that Vivien didn't like at all.

'You know what this city's like. Escort services, crap like that. Asian Paradise, Ebony Companions, Transex Dates. Eighty per cent of the places that advertise massage, health treatments, that kind of thing, are covers for prostitution. It happens everywhere. But this is Manhattan. This is the centre of the world, where there's more of everything . . .'

113

Peter came to a halt, and finally made up his mind to look her in the eyes.

'We had a tip-off. A luxury apartment on the Upper East Side. Used by men who like very young girls. Boys, too, sometimes. All minors, anyway. We went in, rounded up the people we found. And . . .'

He made a pause that for Vivien was a premonition. In a thin voice, she uttered a supplication as long as a single word. 'And?'

And the premonition became reality.

'One of them was your niece.'

The whole world started whirling like a carousel out of control. Vivien would have preferred to die than feel what she was feeling just then.

'I was the one who went into the room where . . .'

Peter didn't have the strength to add anything else. But his silence let Vivien's imagination run wild and that was worse.

'Luckily I knew her and managed by a miracle to keep her out of things.' Peter put his hands on her arms. 'If the story gets out, then social services get involved. With a family situation like yours it's possible she'd be put in an institution. She needs help.'

Vivien looked him in the eyes. 'You're not telling me everything, Peter.'

A moment's pause. Followed by something he'd have preferred not to say and she'd have preferred not to hear.

'Your niece is doing drugs. We found cocaine in her pocket.'

'How much?'

'Not enough to suggest she's dealing. But she must be doing quite a bit every day if she reached a point where . . .'

Where she prostituted herself to get money, Vivien completed the sentence mentally.

'Where is she now?'

Peter gestured with his head towards a point somewhere along the street. 'In my car. A female colleague is keeping an eye on her.'

Vivien shook his hand, to convey her gratitude and feel his warmth in return. 'Thanks, Peter. You're a friend. I owe you one. Hell, I owe you a lot.'

They walked to the car, Vivien going that short distance like a sleepwalker, with an urgency in her and at the same time a fear of seeing her niece and . . .

. . . the same anxiety with which she was waiting for her now.

A sound of footsteps behind her made her open her eyes again, bringing her back to a present that was only a little better than the past.

She rose and turned towards the entrance. Her niece was there, holding a gym bag. She was as pretty as her mother, and, like her mother, she had been broken in some way. But for her there was hope. There had to be.

John Kortighan had stayed back, in the doorway. Protective and vigilant, as always. But so discreet that he did not want to intrude on this private moment. He simply gave her a nod that was both a greeting and a confirmation. Vivien returned the greeting. John was the right-hand man of Father McKean, the priest who had founded Joy, the community that was taking care of Sundance and other kids who'd been through similar experiences.

Vivien lightly touched her niece's cheek with her hand. She couldn't help feeling guilty whenever they met. Guilty over all the things she hadn't done. Guilty over being so busy dealing with people who meant nothing to her that she hadn't realized that the person who most needed her was the one

115

closest to her, who, in her way, had asked for help and nobody had listened.

'Nice to see you again, Sunny. You're looking very pretty today.'

The girl smiled, with a wicked but not provocative gleam in her eye. '*You're* pretty, Vunny. I'm beautiful, you ought to know that.'

It was game they'd played since she was a little girl, when they'd given each other these nicknames as a kind of code. In those days, Vivien would brush her hair and tell her she'd be a great beauty one day. Maybe a model, maybe an actress. And together they would imagine all the things she could be.

All except what she'd actually turned out to be . . .

'What do you say, shall we go?'

'Sure. I'm ready.'

She picked up the bag, which contained a change of clothes for the days they would be spending together.

'Did you bring your rock gear?'

'You bet.'

Vivien had managed to get two tickets for the U2 concert at Madison Square Garden the next day. Sundance was a fan of the band. The concert had been one of the main reasons why she had been granted these two days away from Joy.

'Let's go, then.'

They walked back to where John was standing. He was a well-built man of medium height, simply dressed in sweat-shirt and jeans. He had a frank, open face and a positive air. He looked like a man who thought more about the future than the past.

'Bye, Sundance. See you on Monday.'

Vivien held out her hand, and he shook it. He had a firm grip.

'Thanks, John.'

'Thank you. You both enjoy yourselves now. Go on – I'm staying here for a while longer.'

They went out, leaving him in the quiet of the church.

The evening had chased away all trace of natural light, clothing itself artfully in artificial lights. They got in the car and set off for Manhattan. Vivien drove calmly, listening to what her niece was saying, letting her talk about whatever she wanted to talk about.

Neither of them mentioned the girl's mother, as if there was a tacit agreement between them that all dark thoughts were banned from now on. They weren't trying to betray or ignore their memories. They both knew, without having to say it, that what they were trying to rebuild wasn't only for the two of them.

As they drove on, Vivien had the feeling that with every turn of the wheel, every beat of their hearts, they were leaving behind the roles of aunt and niece and becoming more like friends. She felt something inside herself relaxing, as if the image of Greta that tormented her days was fading, along with the image of Sundance naked in the arms of a man older than her father that tormented her nights.

They had left Roosevelt Island behind them and were heading downtown along the East River when it happened. About half a mile ahead of them, on the right, a light suddenly appeared, wiping out all the others. For a moment it was like a distillation of all the lights in the world.

Then the road seemed to tremble under the wheels of the car and through the open windows they heard the hungry roar of an explosion.

CHAPTER 12

Russell Wade had just arrived home when a bright light suddenly and unexpectedly appeared over on the Lower East Side. The big ceiling-to-floor living-room windows framed that light, a light so vivid it seemed like part of a game. But it didn't go away, and continued to override all the other lights. Through the filter of the unbreakable window panes came the muted sound of a rumble that wasn't thunder but a destructive human imitation of it. It was followed by a cacophony of alarm systems set off by the blast, hysterical but futile, like little dogs uselessly barking behind an iron fence.

The vibration made him instinctively take a step back. He knew what had happened. He had realized immediately. He had already seen and felt that kind of thing in another place. He knew that glare meant incredulity and surprise, pain and dust, screams, injuries, curses and prayers.

It meant death.

And, in an equally sudden glare, a flash of images and memories.

'Robert, please . . .'
His brother was anxiously checking the cameras and the lenses and making sure he had enough rolls of film in the

pockets of his jacket. He wouldn't look him in the face. Maybe he felt ashamed. Or maybe he was already seeing in his mind's eye the photographs he was going to take.

'Nothing's going to happen, Russell. You just have to stay and be quiet.'

'And where will you go?'

Robert had smelled his fear. He was used to that smell. The whole city was imbued with it. You could breathe it in the air. Like an ugly premonition that comes true, like a nightmare that doesn't fade when you wake up, like the screams of the dying that don't end once they're dead.

He looked at him with eyes that might have been seeing him for the first time since they had arrived in Pristina. A scared boy who shouldn't be there.

'I have to go outside. I have to be there.'

Russell realized that this was the only way it could be. And at the same time he realized that he could never be like his brother, not even if he lived a hundred lifetimes. He went back into the cellar, through the trapdoor under the old carpet, and Robert went out the door. Into the sun and the dust and the war.

That was the last time he'd seen him alive.

As if reacting to these thoughts he ran into the bedroom, where one of his cameras was lying on the desk. He grabbed it and went back to the window. He switched off all the lights to avoid reflections and took a number of shots of that distant hypnotic glare with its sickly halo. He knew these photographs would never be used, but he did it to punish himself. To remember who he was, what he had done, what he hadn't done.

Years had gone by since his brother had gone out through that sunstruck doorway and for a few moments the distant bursts of machine-gun fire had grown louder.

119

Nothing had changed.

Since that day, there hadn't been a single morning when he hadn't woken with that image in front of his eyes and that sound in his ears. Since that day, every pointless photograph of his had been merely a new image of his old fear. As he continued clicking the shutter, he started shaking. It was animal rage, silent and instinctual, as if his soul was shuddering inside him and making his body vibrate.

The clicking of the lens became neurotic

click

click

click

click

click

like a homicidal maniac firing into his victim

Robert

all the bullets he has, unable to stop pulling the trigger, continuing as a kind of nervous habit, until all he hears in return is the empty dry snap of the firing pin.

That's enough, dammit!

Punctually, like a set answer to a set question, the shrill urgent sound of sirens came from outside.

Lights without anger.

Lights flashing, good lights, healthy lights, rapid lights. Police cars, fire engines, ambulances.

The city had been hit; the city was wounded; the city was asking for help. And everyone had come running, from all over, with all the speed that compassion and civic feeling gave them.

Russell stopped shooting and, in the light from outside, reached for the TV remote control. He switched it on, and found it automatically tuned to Channel One. The weather

120

report should have been on about now. The broadcast was interrupted two seconds after the screen lit up. The weatherman and his maps of sun and rain were replaced without warning by Faber Andrews, one of the channel's anchormen. His voice was deep and his face grave – appropriate to the situation.

'News just in that a building on the Lower East Side of New York City has been rocked by a powerful explosion. We have no idea yet how many casualties there are, but first reports suggest the number could be high. That's all we can tell you for now. At the moment we don't know the causes of this terrible disaster. We should be able to get a better idea soon. What everyone is hoping is that this wasn't a criminal act. The memory of other tragic events in the recent past is still fresh in our minds. Right now, the whole city, the whole of America, maybe the whole world is watching and waiting. Our reporters are already on their way to the scene, and we should soon be in a position to bring you more up-to-date news. That's all for now.'

Russell switched to CNN. Here, too, they were announcing what had happened. The faces and words were different, the substance exactly the same. He turned down the sound, letting the images carry the report. He sat there on the couch in front of the TV set, with nothing but the luminous fuzz of the screen to keep him company. The lights of the city beyond the windows seemed to come from the cold and distance of outer space. And in the bottom left-hand corner of the frame was that murderous sunlight devouring all the other stars. When his family had given him the apartment, he had been happy to be on the 29th floor with a fantastic view over the whole of downtown: the Brooklyn and Manhattan Bridges on the left, the Flatiron on the right and the New York Life Insurance Building just in front of him.

Now that view was only another cause of distress.

It had all happened so quickly since he had been released after his night in the cell. And yet, if he thought about it again, the images in his head moved in slow motion. Every instant was clear, every detail, every colour, every sensation. Like being condemned to relive those moments ad infinitum.

As if it was again, and for ever, Pristina.

The journey home from the police station had begun in silence. And that was how he thought it should have stayed. The lawyer, Corneill Thornton, an old friend of the family, had understood that, and up to a point had complied.

Then the truce had ended and the attack had begun. 'Your mother is very worried about you.'

Without looking at him, Russell replied with a shrug, 'My mother's always worried about something.'

He saw in his mind's eye the faultless figure and smooth face of Margaret Taylor Wade, a member of the Boston upper classes. Margaret was one of the city's most prominent citizens. Margaret moved with grace and elegance through that world, sweet faced, a woman who did not deserve what life had meted out to her: one son killed reporting on the war in former Yugoslavia and the other living a life that was, if possible, an even greater source of grief.

Maybe she had never got over either of those things. But she had continued her life of distinction and remembrance because it was inseparable from her. As for his father, Russell hadn't spoken to him since the day after that damned business with the Pulitzer.

From the first, Russell had suspected something about their attitude to him: it was possible that both of them thought the wrong brother had died.

The lawyer continued, and Russell knew perfectly well where it was all leading.

'I told her you were hurt. She thinks it would be opportune for you to be seen by a doctor.'

Russell felt like smiling.

Opportune . . .

'My mother's perfect. Not only does she always say the right thing at the right time, she always knows how to choose the most elegant word.'

Thornton leaned back in the leather seat. His shoulders relaxed, as if realizing he was dealing with a hopeless situation. 'Russell, I've known you since you were a little boy. Don't you think—'

'Counsellor, you're not here to condemn or absolve. There are judges for that. Or to preach to me. There are priests for that. You just have to get me out of trouble when you're asked to.' Russell turned to look at him, with a half- smile on his lips. 'It seems to me that's what you're paid for. Very well paid, with an hourly fee that's the equivalent of what a factory worker earns in a week.'

'Get you out of trouble, did you say? That's what I keep doing. Just lately, it seems to me I've had to do it more often than could reasonably be expected.'

The lawyer paused, as if to decide whether to say what he had to say or not.

'Russell, everyone has the constitutional right to destroy himself as he sees fit. The only thing limiting him is his imagination. And you have an extremely creative imagination when it comes to such things.' He looked Russell straight in the eyes, no longer a counsel for the defence but a gleeful executioner. 'From now on, I'll be happy to give up my fee. I'll tell your mother to look elsewhere when necessary. And

I'll sit there with a cigar and a glass of good whisky and watch the spectacle of your ruin.'

Nothing else was said because there was nothing else to say. The limousine dropped him outside his building on 29th Street, between Park and Madison. He got out without saying goodbye and without waiting for the lawyer to say goodbye to him. Not that he would have: his attitude was one of barely concealed human contempt combined with professional indifference. Russell grabbed his keys in passing from the doorman and went up to his apartment. He had just opened the door when the telephone started ringing. Russell was sure he knew who it was. He lifted the receiver and said, 'Hello?' expecting to hear a particular voice. And that voice had come.

'Hi, photographer. Things didn't work out too well for you yesterday, I hear. The game, the cops.'

Russell had an image in his mind. A big black man with his dark glasses and a double chin that his goatee didn't do much to conceal, sunk deep in the back seat of his Mercedes, his beringed hand holding a cellphone.

'LaMarr, I'm not in the mood right now to listen to your bullshit. What do you want?'

'You know what I want, boy. Money.'

'Right now I don't have any.'

'Then you'd better get some as soon as possible.'

'What do you plan to do? Shoot me?'

From the other end came a loud, contemptuous laugh. The threat in that laugh was particularly humiliating.

'That's very tempting. But I'm not so dumb I'll put you in a box with the fifty thousand dollars you owe me in your pocket. I'll just send over a couple of my boys to teach you some of the facts of life. Then I'll give you time to get over it. And then I'll send them over again and hope this time you'll have my money ready for them. Which by the way will be sixty thousand by then, maybe more, who knows.'

'You're a piece of shit, LaMarr.'

'Yes. And I can't wait to show you how much of a shit I am. Bye now, asshole. Try going on the Wheel of Fortune – maybe you'll have better luck.'

Jaws clenched, Russell put down the receiver, silencing the echo of LaMarr's laughter. LaMarr Monroe was one of the biggest sons of bitches ever to prowl the streets of New York. Unfortunately, Russell knew he wasn't talking for the sake of talking. He was a guy who kept his promises, and who'd do anything rather than lose face.

He went in the bedroom and undressed, throwing his clothes on the floor. The torn jacket ended up in the garbage. Next he went in the bathroom and forced himself to take a shower and a shave, avoiding the temptation to put the foam on the mirror instead of on his face. In order not to see his face. In order not to see his expression. After that, he found himself alone in the apartment. And by alone he meant having nothing to drink, not a single line of cocaine and not a cent in his pocket.

The apartment where he lived was unofficially his but in fact it was owned by one of his family's companies. Even the furniture had been chosen – tastefully – by a designer paid by his mother from among the vast choice available at budget prices from Ikea and similar stores. The reason was simple. Everyone knew that Russell would have sold anything of value he had in his possession and the money would have gone on gambling.

That had happened often enough in the past.

Cars, watches, paintings, carpets.

Everything.

With destructive rage and maniacal precision.

Russell sat down on one of the couches. He could have phoned Miriam or one of the other models he'd been seeing lately, but having them around meant that after a while he'd have to put a little white powder on the table. And he'd also have to have the money to take them out.

Or rather, a name.

Ziggy.

He'd met that colourless little man a few years earlier. He'd been one of his brother's informants, someone who some-times gave him tips about interesting things happening in the city, the kind of things he defined as 'over the edge', which were good to know about because they might turn out to be stories. Since Robert's death they'd kept in touch, though for very different reasons. One of these was that, in his brother's memory, Ziggy supplied him with what he needed and gave him credit. He even helped him out with a few small loans when, as was the case now, he was in a tight corner. Russell didn't know why Ziggy was so fond of him and trusted him like that. But it was a given, and when necessary he took advantage of it.

Unfortunately Ziggy didn't use a cellphone, and getting in touch with him usually took a while. After a bit of nervous pacing around the living room and bedroom, he came to a decision. He went down to the garage and took out the car, which he drove rarely and reluctantly. Maybe because it was a cheap Nissan that wasn't even registered in his name. He checked there was enough gas in the tank to get there and back. He knew where Ziggy lived, and he set off for Brooklyn. The journey was a kind of blur. He saw the city speed past without seeing it, paying it back for the fact that it didn't see him.

His lip hurt and his eyes smarted, in spite of his sunglasses.

He crossed the bridge, ignoring the skylines of Manhattan

and Brooklyn Heights, and plunged into neighbourhoods where ordinary people lived ordinary lives. Places that had no illusions any more, places where nothing ever worked out. Places roughly drawn in the faded colours of reality, where he often came because it was here that he found the secret gambling joints he liked to visit – it was here that anyone could find what they needed.

You just needed to have few scruples and a lot of money.

He reached Ziggy's place almost without realizing it. He parked just past the building, and after taking a few steps found himself pushing open the entrance door and descending the stairs that led to the basement. There were no doormen here, and the entryphone was a formality nobody bothered with any more. At the foot of the stairs he turned left. The walls were industrial brick, hurriedly painted in a colour that must once have been beige, and was now covered in stains. There was a smell of boiled cabbage and damp in the air. He turned the corner, and saw a line of faded brown doors in front of him. Someone was coming out of the one he was heading for, on the right-hand side towards the end of the corridor. A man in a green military jacket with a blue hood pulled down over his head, who moved quickly and resolutely to the end of the corridor and disappeared around the opposite corner.

Russell didn't pay much attention to him, thinking only that he was one of the people Ziggy came into contact with every day in his line of business. When he reached Ziggy's door, he found it ajar. He pushed the handle and his eyes took in the room and then everything happened as if he was seeing things frame by frame on a Moviola.

An image of Ziggy on his knees on the floor with his shirt all stained with blood, clutching at a chair and trying to pull himself to his feet

an image of himself approaching him and Ziggy's bony hand reaching out and clutching his arm

Ziggy supporting himself on the edge of the table and reaching out his hand towards the printer

himself not understanding

Ziggy pressing a button with his finger and leaving a red mark on it

himself listening without hearing as the printed sheet rustled onto the tray

Ziggy with a photograph in his hand

himself terrified

and finally Ziggy convulsing and drawing his last breath and blood spurting from his open mouth. He fell to the floor with a dull thud and Russell found himself standing in the middle of the room, holding a black and white photograph and a printed sheet of paper, both stained red.

And in his eyes the image of his brother lying in the dust covered in blood.

Moving like a puppet, hardly aware of what he was doing, he stuffed the sheet of paper and the photograph into his pocket. Then, with the logic and instinct of an animal, he fled, leaving reason behind him, in that place that smelled of boiled cabbage and damp. He reached his car without seeing anybody. He set off, forcing himself not to drive too quickly in order not to attract attention. He drove as if in a trance until his breathing and heartbeat returned to normal. At that point he stopped the car in a side street and started thinking. He told himself that, in running away, he had clearly made an instinctive choice, but at the same time he was certain it was the wrong choice. He should have called the police. But that would have meant having to explain why he was there and how he happened to know Ziggy. And God alone knew what kind of trouble Ziggy had got himself into. In addition, it was quite possible that the man in the green jacket was the person who had knifed the poor bastard. The thought that he might, for whatever reason, decide to come back was pretty scary. Russell had no desire to join Ziggy lying dead on the floor.

No. Better to pretend that nothing had happened. Nobody had seen him, he hadn't left any traces, and the neighbourhood was full of people who minded their own business and certainly weren't crazy about talking to the police.

As he was thinking and trying to decide what line to follow, he realized that the right sleeve of his jacket was stained with blood. He emptied his pockets onto the passenger seat, checked that nobody was about, then got out of the car and threw the garment in a dumpster. With a touch of self-deprecation that surprised him, given the situation, he told himself that, at the rate of two jackets thrown away per day, he would soon have serious problems with his wardrobe.

He got back in the car and returned home. From the garage, he took the elevator direct to his floor. That would save the doorman the effort of remembering that he had gone out wearing a jacket and come back in his shirtsleeves.

He had just put his things on the table when the explosion happened.

He got up from the couch and went and switched the light back on, his eyes turned to the glare in the east but his mind on the fact that he couldn't get away from what had happened in the afternoon. Now that he was thinking clearly, something occurred to him. Why had Ziggy used his last remaining strength, and the last moments of his life, to copy that sheet of paper and put it in his hands together with the photograph? What was so important about those things?

He went to the table, picked up the photograph, and stared at it for a few moments. He had no idea who that brown-haired young man with the black cat was, no idea what the photograph had meant to Ziggy. The sheet of paper, on the other hand, was a photocopy of a handwritten letter. The handwriting was clearly a man's. He started to read, trying to decipher the rough, imprecise writing.

And as he read the words and grasped their meaning, he kept telling himself that it couldn't be true. He had to read the paper three times to convince himself. Then, barely able to breathe, he put the letter and the photograph down on the table, with only Ziggy's bloodstains to confirm that in fact it was all real, that it wasn't a dream.

He looked back at the fire still burning in the distance.

His head was all mixed up. A thousand thoughts crossed his mind and he couldn't get a fix on any of them. The anchorman on Channel One hadn't mentioned the exact address of the building that had blown up. They were sure to report it on a subsequent news broadcast.

He absolutely had to know.

He went back to the couch and turned up the volume on the TV. He didn't know if what he wanted most was a denial or a confirmation.

He sat there, wondering if the void into which he could feel himself falling was death. Wondering if his brother had felt the same every time he tackled a new story or got ready to take one of his photographs. He hid his face in his hands and in the darkness of his closed eyelids turned to the one person who had really mattered to him. As a last resort, he tried to imagine what Robert Wade would have done if he had found himself in this situation.

CHAPTER 13

Father Michael McKean was sitting in an armchair in front of
an old TV set in his room at Joy, the community he had
founded in Pelham Bay. It was a top-floor room, an attic with
a partly sloping ceiling, white walls and a pine floor. In the
air there still lingered the smell of the preservative with which
the wood had been treated a week earlier. The cheap furniture
that comprised the spartan decor had been collected wherever
they could find it. All the books in the bookcase and on the
desk and the night table had arrived here by the same route.
Many were gifts from the parishioners, some made
specifically to him. But Father McKean had always chosen
the most worn and damaged things for himself. Partly that
was his character, but mostly it was because, if it was possible
to improve the everyday life of the community, he preferred
the kids to be the ones to benefit. The walls were bare, apart
from the crucifix over the bed and one splash of colour: a
poster of the Van Gogh painting in which the artist had
depicted, the poverty of his bedroom in the Yellow House in
Arles. Although they were quite dissimilar, you had the
impression, on entering, that those two rooms complemented
each other, that there was some kind of communication
between them, and that the poster on the white wall was an
opening into a distant place and a different time.

131

Beyond the curtainless window you could glimpse the sea reflecting the blue, windswept late April sky. When he was a child, his mother would tell him on bright days like this that the sun turned the air the colour of the eyes of angels and that the wind didn't let them cry.

But today there were bitter lines at the corners of his mouth and the expression on his face was grim. Those words of his mother, so full of imagination and colour, had stayed in his memory for ever. But the news on CNN today had other words and other images, scenes that from time immemorial had been associated exclusively with war.

And, like all epidemics, sooner or later war reached into every corner.

There, in close-up, was the face of Mark Lassiter, a reporter with a sharp, alert face, who looked as if he could hardly believe what he was seeing and saying, whose eyes and hair and shirt collar bore the marks of a sleepless night. Behind him lay the rubble of a shattered building, from which pathetic spirals of grey smoke still rose, the dying residue of the flames that for hours had illumined the darkness. The firefighters had fought all night to bring them under control and even now, on one side of the building, long jets of water indicated that the job wasn't completely over.

'What you can see behind me is the building that was partly destroyed by a powerful explosion last night. The experts are still at work trying to establish the cause. So far nobody has claimed responsibility, so we still don't know if we're dealing with a terrorist attack or a tragic accident. The only thing we know for sure is that the toll of the dead and missing is quite high. The rescuers are working around the clock to get the bodies of the dead out from under the rubble, although they haven't given up hope of finding survivors. Here are the images taken from our helicopter, which show better than any words could the extent of this tragedy that's shaken the city and the whole country and reminded us of other images and other victims that'll never be forgotten.'

A series of aerial shots now followed, with Lassiter heard as a voice-over. Seen from above, the scene was even more harrowing. The building, a twenty-two-storey redbrick construction, had been cut in half straight down the middle. The right side had collapsed but, instead of the building imploding, it had slid to the side, leaving the other half still standing like a finger pointing to the sky. The fracture was so sharp that on the standing side you could still see the rooms without their outer walls, and in them the remains of furniture and other relics of everyday life.

On the top floor, a white sheet had got caught on a trellis and was flapping in the wind caused by the displacement of air from the blades of the helicopter, like a flag of surrender and mourning. Fortunately, the part of the building that had come away had fallen on a wooded area, a small park with a children's playground, a basketball field and two tennis courts, missing other buildings. If it had hit them, the death toll would certainly have been greater. The explosion, occurring over toward the East River, had spared the buildings on the other side even though all the panes of glass within a significant radius had been knocked out by the blast. Around the shattered building and in among its debris was the highly coloured frenzy of rescue vehicles and men, bustling about full of energy and hope in a race against time.

The TV cut away from these images of desolation and death and back to a close-up of the reporter.

'Mayor Wilson Gollemberg declared a state of

emergency and rushed to the scene of the disaster. He took an active part in the rescue operations all through the night. We have his first statement, recorded last night soon after he arrived on the scene.'

They cut again, with that slight loss of quality that a recording made in those conditions involved. The mayor, a tall man with an open face who gave the impression of throbbing with anguish and at the same time conveying self-confidence and strength, was illumined by the motionless white lights of the TV cameras fighting against the background of unchecked flames behind him. At that moment of confusion and panic, his comments were few and to the point.

'It's impossible right now to draw any conclusion from this tragedy. The only thing I can promise as a mayor to all my fellow New Yorkers and as an American to all Americans is this. If any person or persons are responsible for this atrocity, I want them to know that there will be no escape for them. Their cowardice and savagery will receive the punishment they deserve.'

Back again to Mark Lassiter, reporting live from a place that for many people would never be the same again.

'For the moment, that's all from the Lower East Side of New York. A press conference is due to be held shortly. We'll let you know if there are further developments. I'm Mark Lassiter, returning you to the studio.'

Just as the anchorman reappeared on the screen, the cellphone on the small table next to the armchair rang. The priest turned down the volume on the TV and answered. From the other end came the voice of Paul Smith, the parish priest of Saint Benedict, slightly blurred with emotion.

'Michael, are you watching television?'

'Yes.'

'Terrible, isn't it?'

'Yes, it is.'

'All those people dead. All that despair. I can't come to terms with it. What goes through the mind of a person who could do something like that?'

Father McKean suddenly found himself overwhelmed by a strange, desolate tiredness, the kind that strikes the humanity of a man when he is forced to confront the total absence of humanity in other men.

'There's something we have to realize, Paul,' he said. 'Hate isn't an emotion any more. It's becoming a virus. When it infects the soul, the mind is lost. And people's defences against it are increasingly weak.'

At the other end there was a moment's silence, as if the elderly priest was thinking over the words he had just heard. Then he came to what was probably the true reason for his call.

'Given what's happened, do you think it's right to celebrate solemn mass? Don't you think something more modest would be better in the circumstances?'

McKean thought about it for a moment and shook his head, as if the parish priest at the other end could see him.

'I don't think so, Paul. I think that solemn mass, especially today, is both a statement of opposition and a specific response to this atrocity. Whatever its source. We won't stop praying to God in the way we consider most dignified. And in the same way, we'll pay tribute to the innocent victims of this tragedy.'

He paused briefly before continuing.

'The one thing I think we could do is change the reading. The planned reading for today was a passage from St John's Gospel. I'd replace it with the Sermon on the Mount. It's part of everyone's experience, even non-believers. I think it's very significant on a day like this, when mercy mustn't be overwhelmed by an instinctive desire for revenge. Revenge is the imperfect justice of this world. The justice we must speak of isn't worldly and is therefore uncontaminated by error.'

At the other end there was a moment's silence.

'Luke or Matthew?'

'Matthew. The passage from Luke includes an element of retribution that isn't in line with what our feelings should be. And for the hymns I'd suggest *The whole world is waiting for love* and *Let the valley be raised*. But I think we should consult Mr Bennett the choirmaster about that.'

Another pause, before Father Smith replied with relief in his voice, as if all his doubts had faded away. 'Yes, I think you're right. There's just one thing I'd ask you. And I'm sure everyone would agree with me.'

'Go on.'

'I'd like it to be you giving the sermon.'

Instinctively, Father McKean's heart went out to Father Smith. Paul was a highly sensitive man, and easily moved. His voice often broke when he had to deal with delicate subjects.

'All right, Paul.'

'See you later, then.'

'I'll leave in a few minutes.'

He put the cellphone down on the little table, got up and went to the window. He stood there with his hands in his pockets, looking at the familiar view without seeing it. The same shapes and colours as always, sea and wind and trees, which today seemed like alien spectators, images without meaning, incomprehensible. The news he had just watched on TV continued to superimpose itself on what he had in front of his eyes. He remembered the terrible period around September 11, the day that had changed the world for ever.

He thought again of how many crimes had been committed in the name of God, when God had nothing to do with them. Whichever God was being evoked. Instinctively Michael McKean felt like asking one question. Some time earlier, John Paul II had apologized to the world for the behaviour of the Catholic Church of some four hundred years earlier, at the time of the Inquisition. What was being done now that the then Pope would have to apologize for in four hundred years' time? What would *all* men in the world who professed a faith need to ask forgiveness for?

Faith was a gift, like love and friendship and trust. It was not born out of reason. Reason could only, in some cases, help to keep it alive. It was like a railroad track running parallel to reason, in a direction it was not given to men to know. But if faith made people lose their reason, then love, friendship, trust and goodness were also lost.

And so was hope.

In the time that Joy had been in existence, he had had kids around him who had never known hope, or who had lost it in the course of their brief, unhappy journeys through life. What they had had, instead of hope, had been a terrible certainty. That life was made up of dead ends, making do, dark shadows, unrealized wishes, blows, affection denied, beautiful things reserved for others. That in going against life and against themselves, they had nothing to lose, because there was nothing in their lives.

And in doing so, many had become lost.

There was a knock at the door. Father McKean walked away from the window and went to open it. In the doorway he saw the figure of John Kortighan, Joy's lay director.

Positive thinking personified. And God knew how much positive thinking was needed every day in a place like this.

John dealt with all the practical aspects of a structure that was, from a technical point of view, fairly easy to run but at the same time, for different reasons, quite complex. He was the organizer, administrator and financial director. When he had agreed to take on the running of Joy for a fairly modest – and not always very punctual – salary, Father McKean had at first been incredulous and then euphoric, as if he had been given a wonderful, unexpected gift. He hadn't been wrong in his judgement and had never had any reason to regret his choice.

'The boys are ready, Michael.'

'Good. Let's go.'

He took his jacket from the rack, left the room and shut the door. He never bothered to lock it. There were no bolts or locks at Joy. What he always tried to convey to his kids was that they weren't in a prison but in a place where everyone's actions and movements involved freedom of choice. Each of them was autonomous and could leave the community at any moment, if he or she saw fit. Many of them had ended up in Joy for the very reason that in the places they had lived earlier they had felt imprisoned.

Father McKean was well aware that the battle against drugs was long and hard. He knew that each one of these kids was struggling with a physical need that could turn into a genuine disease. At the same time each of them had to deal with all those things, inside and around him, that had driven him into the worst kind of darkness. With the certainty that the physical torture could cease and all the rest could be hidden or forgotten with a simple gesture: taking a pill, sniffing white powder, sticking a needle in your veins.

Unfortunately, some didn't make it. Some mornings they woke up and found themselves confronted with an empty bed. Every defeat of that kind was difficult to take. At such moments, the other kids would huddle around him. That display of affection and trust gave meaning to everything, and gave him the strength to continue, with all his bitterness absorbed as experience.

As they walked downstairs, John couldn't help commenting on what had happened the previous evening in Manhattan.

'Did you watch the news?'

'Not all of it, but quite a lot.'

'I had work to do this morning. Have there been any new developments?'

'No. Or at least no developments the media know about.'

'Who do you think it was? Islamic terrorists?'

'I really don't know. I haven't got any clear ideas yet. I don't think anyone has. The other time, the claim of responsibility was immediate.'

There was no need to specify. Both of them knew what *the other time* referred to.

'I have a cousin in the police, actually in a precinct on the Lower East Side. I spoke to him this morning. He was on the scene. He couldn't be specific but he told me it was really nasty.'

John stopped for a moment on the last landing, as if what he was about to say needed clarification.

'I mean, much nastier than it seems.'

They resumed walking and reached the bottom of the stairs in silence, both wondering what on earth could possibly make an atrocity like that even worse. They crossed the kitchen. Three of the kids, who were on work duty, and Mrs Carraro, the cook, were preparing Sunday lunch.

139

Father McKean walked to one of the stoves. Mrs Carraro had her back to him, and did not realize he was there. He lifted the lid of a saucepan. A whirl of steam rose toward the extractor fan, carrying with it the aroma of sauce.

'Good day to you, Mrs Carraro. What are you poisoning us with today?'

Janet Carraro, a middle-aged woman of ample dimensions – by her own definition, two pounds away from being fat – gave a start. She wiped her hands on her apron, took the lid from Father McKean's hands and put it back on the saucepan.

'Father McKean, for your information, this is a sauce that could be considered a sin of the throat.'

'So we don't have to fear only for our bodies, we have to fear for our souls, too?'

The kids who were cleaning and slicing vegetables on a cutting board on the other side of the room smiled. This kind of skirmish was common between the two of them, a little bit of play-acting born of mutual affection and offered for everyone's amusement. Mrs Carraro picked up the wooden spoon, dipped it in the sauce, and held it out to the priest with a defiant gesture.

'Here, try it for yourself, ye man of little faith. And remember St Thomas.'

McKean lifted the spoon to his lips, blowing on it to cool it down. His initially dubious expression changed to one of ecstasy. He immediately recognized the robust taste of Mrs Carraro's amatriciana sauce.

'I beg your pardon, Mrs Carraro. This is the best ragù I've ever tasted.'

'It's amatriciana.'

'Then you'll have to do it again, or it'll keep tasting like ragù.'

The cook pretended to be indignant. 'If you weren't who you are, just for that I'd put a huge dose of chilli in your plate when the time comes. And who's to say I won't anyway?'

But the tone of her voice and her smiling face belied her words. She gestured towards the door with her spoon.

'Now go and leave people to work, if you want to eat when you get back. Ragù or amatriciana or whatever.'

Father McKean rejoined John Kortighan, who was standing by the door to the forecourt, smiling at the little show he had just witnessed. As he held the door open for the priest, he gave his considered opinion.

'Very entertaining. You and Mrs Carraro should do it for a living.'

'Shakespeare already did it. Ragù or not ragù, that is the question, don't you remember?'

His colleague's sonorous laughter followed him into the open until it faded in the cool air. Once out in the forecourt, they walked towards the right-hand side of the building, where a rundown bus was waiting with the kids on board.

Father McKean stopped and raised his eyes for a moment towards the clear sky. In spite of the brief exchange of jokes, he had been overcome with a sudden feeling of unease. When he got on the bus and greeted the kids, the tenderness he felt for them and the pleasure of being together briefly dispelled the feeling that had just come over him like a bad omen. But as the old bus trundled down the unpaved drive towards the entrance to the property, leaving the house to dissolve in a cloud of dust behind it, that sense of impending threat once again took possession of his thoughts. He remembered the images he had seen on television, and had the impression that the wind that stopped angels and men from weeping had suddenly stopped blowing.

CHAPTER 14

Blessed are the poor in spirit, for theirs is the kingdom of heaven.

Blessed are they who mourn, for they shall be comforted.

Blessed are the meek, for they shall inherit the earth.

Blessed are they who hunger and thirst for righteousness, for they shall be satisfied.

Blessed are the merciful, for they shall obtain mercy.

Blessed are the pure of heart, for they shall see God.

Blessed are the peacemakers, for they shall be called children of God.

Blessed are they who are persecuted for the sake of righteousness, for theirs is the kingdom of heaven.

Blessed are you when people insult you, persecute you and falsely say all kinds of evil against you because of me.

Rejoice and be glad, because great is your reward in heaven.

Father McKean was standing at the lectern to the left of the altar, raised slightly above the floor of the church. When his deep voice reached the end of the reading, he remained silent for a moment, his eyes fixed on the page, and let his voice travel around the building. It wasn't a long journey, but it certainly wasn't an easy journey either, not today. Finally he raised his head and looked around the church, which was full.

Then he began speaking.

'The words you've just heard are from one of Jesus' most famous sermons. It's become famous not only because of the beauty of the language, or its power of evocation, but because of its importance in the centuries to come. In this short passage we find the essence of the doctrine he preached for the last three years of his life. In making himself a man, he brought to earth a new pact between men and the Father. With his message he gave us hope but did not ask us to surrender. It doesn't mean that we have to passively accept all the unjust, painful, tragic things that happen in a world made by God but ruled by men. But it does remind us that our strength and our sustenance in our everyday struggles lie in faith. And it asks us to have faith. It doesn't impose faith on us, but like a friend it simply asks us to have faith.'

He paused and again lowered his eyes to the lectern in front of him. When he raised his head again he allowed everyone present, without embarrassment, to see the tears running down his cheeks.

'You all know what happened in our city last night. The terrible images we all have before our eyes are not new, any more than the distress, the pain, the pity we feel when confronted with trials like these we have been called to overcome are new.'

He paused for a moment, giving everyone a moment to remember and understand.

'Which we are *all* called to overcome, every last one of us, because the pain that strikes one of us strikes the whole human race. Being made of flesh and blood, with our weaknesses and our frailties, when a tragic and unexpected event happens, an incomprehensible event that implicates our very existence and challenges our tolerance, the first instinct is to wonder why God has abandoned us. To wonder why, if we are His children, He allows such things to happen. Jesus did that, too, when on the cross he felt his human part demand the tribute of pain that the will of the father had required of him. But note this: at that moment, Jesus did not have faith . . .'

He paused. There was a new silence in the church, this Sunday.

'At that moment Jesus *was* faith.'

The priest had emphasized that sentence in a very particular way.

'If that happened to a man who came into the world with the desire to bring us redemption, it is understandable that it can happen also to us, who are the beneficiaries of that desire and that sacrifice, a sacrifice for which we give thanks every time we approach an altar.'

Another pause, and when he spoke again it was in the tone of a confidant rather than a preacher.

'You see, a friend is accepted for what he is. Sometimes we must do so even when we don't understand, because in some cases trust must go beyond understanding. So if we act in this way for a friend, who is and remains a human being, all the more reason we must do it for God, who is our father and at the same time our best friend. When we don't understand, we must offer in return that faith that is asked of us even when we are poor and afflicted, even when we are hungry and thirsty, even when we are persecuted, insulted, wrongly accused. Because Jesus taught us that it comes from our own goodness, from the purity of our hearts, from our mercy, from our desire for peace. And, remembering Jesus' words on the Mount, we will have that faith. Because what he promised is that if what we live in is an imperfect world, if what we grow old in is an imperfect time, what we will have one day in return will be a wonderful place, which is all ours. And it won't be constrained by time, because it will be for ever.'

With admirable synchronicity, as soon as he ended his sermon the evocative sound of the organ spread through the church, and the choir launched into a hymn that spoke of the world and its need for love. Every time Father McKean listened to the voices joined in the perfect fusion of harmony, he could not help feeling goose bumps in his arms. He considered music one of the greatest gifts given to men, one of the few that managed to involve the spirit in such a way that it affected the body. He moved away from the lectern and went back to his place next to the altar boys. He stood there, following the ritual of the mass and at the same time continuing to observe the faithful who had crowded into the church.

His kids, apart from those who were on work duty at Joy, were sitting in the front rows. As with everything else, he had left them a free choice over prayers and their presence at services. Joy was a place for human conversions rather than religious ones. The fact that the community was led by a Catholic priest was irrelevant to the choices the kids made. But he was conscious of the fact that almost all of them came to church because he was there and because they understood that he liked to know they were participating in a moment of togetherness.

And that was enough for him, at least for now.

The church of Saint Benedict was in the middle of a residential neighbourhood in the Bronx called Country Club, largely populated by people of Italian and Hispanic origin. At the entrance to the church, fixed to the wall around the statue of the Blessed Virgin, were brass plaques placed there in memory of the dead of the parish. Most of the surnames were Italian or Spanish. In fact, in the course of Sunday, to please the two ethnic groups, mass was celebrated in both languages.

When the time came for Holy Communion, Father McKean approached the altar and received the host directly from the hands of Father Paul Smith, who did not hesitate to give him a look of gratitude for his sermon. As the music swelled, and the worshippers turned to each other to exchange the sign of peace, and the smell of incense spread through the air, the voice of Father Smith led the mass to its conclusion.

Later, as was their custom, the priests stood at the entrance of the church to bid farewell to the faithful, exchanging impressions, listening to their stories, discussing the latest parish initiatives. During the winter months this farewell took place in the lobby, but on that fine late April day the doors had been flung wide open, and they stood spread out on the steps.

Father McKean was complimented on his sermon. Ellen Carraro, their cook's elder sister, came to him with watery eyes to express her emotion and remind him of her arthritis. Roger Brodie, a retired carpenter who sometimes gave his services free to the parish, promised he'd swing by Joy the next day to repair the roof. Gradually, the groups broke up and they all went back to their cars and their houses. Many had come on foot, as they lived very close to the church.

Father Smith and Father McKean found themselves alone again.

'You were very moving today, Michael. You're a great man. For what you say and how you say it. For what you do and how you do it.'

'Thank you, Paul.'

Father Smith turned his head and cast a glance at John Kortighan and the kids waiting at the bottom of the steps to return to Joy. When he turned his head back to him, McKean saw embarrassment in his eyes.

'I must ask a sacrifice of you, if it's not too much of a burden.'

'Go ahead.'

'Angelo isn't well. I know Sunday is an important day for you and your kids but do you think you could possibly replace him at the twelve-thirty mass?'

'No problem.'

The kids would feel his absence, but with the day being so unusual he knew he wasn't in the right mood to share their company at lunch. That sense of oppression had not left him, and he thought it best not to spoil the mood at table.

He descended the steps and joined the waiting kids.

'I'm really sorry, but I'm afraid you'll have to have lunch without me. I have something to do here in the parish. I'll join you later. Tell Mrs Carraro to keep me something hot, if you don't wolf it all down.'

He saw the disappointment on some of their faces. Jerry Romero, the oldest of the group, who had been at Joy the longest and was looked up to by many of his companions, made himself the spokesman for the general discontent.

'Seems to me if you want to be forgiven, you have to let us have a Fastflyx session.'

Fastflyx was a mail order DVD rental service that the community received free, thanks to John's diplomatic skills. In a place like Joy, where there was so much effort and so much abstinence, even watching a movie together was something of a small luxury.

McKean wagged a finger at the young man. 'That's

blackmail, Jerry. And I say that to you and your accomplices. However, given the common will, I feel forced to give in. In addition I think a surprise arrived only yesterday. In fact, a double surprise.'

He made a gesture to stop the kids asking questions.

'We'll talk about it later. Now go, the others are waiting for you.'

Arguing among themselves, the kids moved towards the Batmobile, the nickname they had given the bus. Father McKean watched them as they walked away. They were a colourful mass of clothes and a tangle of problems too great for their ages. Some were difficult to relate to. But they were his family and for part of their lives Joy would be their family.

John lingered a moment before joining them. 'Shall I come back to pick you up?'

'Don't worry, I'll get a ride from someone.'

'Okay. See you later, then.'

He stayed on the street while the vehicle disappeared around the corner. Then he climbed the steps and went back into the church, which was now deserted apart from a couple of women sitting in one of the rows near the altar, continuing on a personal level that contact with God that had been collective during the mass.

On the right, just past the entrance, was the confessional. It was made of clear shiny wood, with the two doors covered in burgundy velvet drapes. A red light indicated whether or not the priest was inside. The side reserved for the confessor was a narrow space containing a wicker chair beneath a screened wall lamp that cast a dim light from above on the blue wallpaper. The penitent's side was much more Spartan, with a prie-dieu and a grille allowing a privacy that many needed at such an intimate moment.

148

Here Father McKean sometimes took refuge, without switching on the light or indicating in any way that he was inside. He would stay there for a while thinking about the financial necessities of his work, collecting his thoughts when they threatened to fly away from him like migrating birds, concentrating on the case of a particularly difficult young person. Usually arriving at the conclusion that they were all difficult and all deserved the same attention, that with the money he had at his disposal they were performing genuine miracles and would continue to perform them.

Today, like many other days, he moved aside the drapes, entered and sat down, without turning on the little light above his head. The chair was old but comfortable and the semi-darkness an ally. He stretched his legs and rested his head against the wall. Those distressing television images took their toll on everyone, even those who had not been touched directly by the tragedy. Simply because everyone was human. There were days like today when he weighed his life in the balance and found that the greatest difficulty was to understand. In spite of what he had said in his sermon. Not only to understand men but also the will of the God he served. From time to time, he wondered what his life would have been like if he had not answered the call of God. If he'd had a wife, children, a job, a normal life. He was thirty-eight years old and many years earlier, when he had come to make that choice, he had been told what he was renouncing. But it was a warning – it wasn't based on experience. Now he some-times felt an emptiness to which he could not give a name. At the same time, he was certain that a similar emptiness was part of the experience of every human being. He had his revenge on that emptiness every day by living in contact with his kids and helping them to escape it. Ultimately, he told

149

himself, the most difficult thing was not to understand but, once you had understood, to keep going, in spite of the difficulty, to keep travelling along the road. Right now, that was the closest thing to faith he could offer himself and others.

And God.

'Here I am, Father McKean.'

The voice entered suddenly and without warning. It arrived from the semi-darkness and from a world without peace that he had forgotten for a few moments. Supporting himself on the armrest, he leaned towards the grille. On the other side, in the dim light, a barely glimpsed figure, a shoulder covered in a green fabric.

'Good day to you. What can I do for you?'

'Nothing. I think you're waiting for me.'

These words made him feel uneasy. The voice was hollow but calm, the voice of someone who wasn't afraid of the abyss he was staring into.

'Do we know each other?'

'Very well. Or not at all, if you prefer.'

The unease became a slight sense of dread. The priest found refuge in the only words he could offer him.

'You've entered a confessional. I assume you wish to make confession?'

'Yes.'

The monosyllable was resolute but nonchalant.

'Then tell me your sins.'

'I don't have any. I'm not looking for absolution because I don't need it. And anyway I know you wouldn't give it to me.'

On his side, the priest was stunned by this declaration of futility. From the tone of voice he sensed that it wasn't mere

150

presumption but came from something much bigger and more devastating. At any other time, Father Michael McKean might have reacted differently. Now he still had his eyes and ears full of images and sounds of death and the sense of defeat that takes hold after an almost sleepless night.

'If that's what you think, then what can I do for you?'

'Nothing. I just wanted to leave you a message.'

'What kind of message?'

A moment's silence. But it wasn't hesitation. He was simply giving him time to clear his mind of any other thoughts.

'It was me.'

'What do you mean?'

'I mean I blew up the building on the Lower East Side.'

That took Father McKean's breath away.

The images piled up in his mind. Dust, ambulances, the screams of the wounded, the blood, corpses taken away in sheets, the moans of the survivors, the anguish of those who had lost everything. The statements on television. A whole city, a whole country again transfixed with the fear that was, as someone had said, the only true horseman of the apocalypse. And the indistinct shadow on the other side of that thin barrier claimed to be responsible for all that.

Reason dictated that he take his time and think clearly. There were sick people in the world who liked to assume the guilt for murders and disasters they couldn't possibly be responsible for.

'I know what you're thinking.'

'What?'

'That I'm a fantasist, that there's nothing to prove what I'm saying is true.'

Michael McKean, a man of reason and a priest by belief,

was nothing at that moment but an animal with all its senses on the alert. And every shred of his ancestral instinct screamed at him that the man on the other side of the confessional was telling the truth.

He needed to breathe for a few moments, before continuing. The other man understood that and respected his silence. When he found his voice again, he appealed to a piety he already knew he wouldn't find.

'What do all those deaths, all that pain, mean to you?'

'Justice. And justice should never create pain. So much of it has been dispensed in the past that it has become an object of worship. Why should this time be different?'

'What do you mean by justice?'

'The Red Sea opening and closing. Sodom. Gomorrah. I have many other examples, if you want them.'

The voice was silent for a moment. On his side of the confessional, which at that moment felt like the coldest place in the world, Father McKean would have liked to shout out that these were just stories, that they shouldn't be taken literally, that . . .

He held back and missed the opportunity to retaliate. The other man took this as an invitation to continue.

'Men have had two gospels, one for their souls and one for their lives. One religious and one secular. Both have taught men more or less the same things. Brotherhood, justice, equality. There have been people who have spread them through the world and through time.'

The voice appeared to come from a place much further than the tiny distance separating them. Now it had become a mere breath, sour with disappointment. The kind of disappointment that gives rise not to tears but to anger.

'But almost nobody has had the strength to live according

to these teachings.'

'All men are imperfect,' Father McKean replied. 'That's part of nature. How can you not feel compassion? Haven't you repented what you did?'

'No. Because I will do it again. And you will be the first to know.'

Father McKean hid his face in his hands. What was happening to him was too much for one man. If this person's words corresponded to the truth, then this was a test beyond his strength. Or the strength of anyone who wore a priest's cassock. The voice pressed on. Not fierce now, but soft and persuasive. Full of understanding.

'In your words during the mass, there was pain. There was compassion. But there was no faith.'

He tried in vain to rebel, not against those words, but against his fear. 'How can you say that?'

'I'll help you regain it, Michael McKean,' the man continued, as if he hadn't heard the question. 'I can do that.'

There was another pause. Then the three words that set eternity in motion.

'I am God.'

CHAPTER 15

In many ways, Joy was the kingdom of almost.

Everything almost worked, was almost shiny, almost new. The roof was almost fine and the paint on the outside walls almost didn't need retouching. The few permanent employees received their salary almost regularly, the outside helpers almost always forewent theirs. Everything was second-hand, and in that display of the old and worn anything new stood out like the light of a beacon in the distance. But it was also a place where every day, with great difficulty, a new piece of the life raft was built.

As he drove the Batmobile along the unpaved drive towards the house, John Kortighan knew that in the bus with him he had a group of kids to whom life had been a terrible counsellor. Little by little it had devoured their trust, and they had been alone for so long they took solitude for the norm. Each one, with that originality typical of adverse fate, had found his or her own destructive way to go astray, and the indifference of the world had covered their traces.

Now in this place, together, they could try to find themselves, realizing that, logically and not by chance, they had a right to an alternative. And he felt fortunate and grateful to have been chosen to be part of that enterprise.

However hard and desperate it was.

John drove in through the gate and a minute or so later the van crossed the forecourt and pulled up under a canopy. The kids got out and headed for the back door of the kitchen, arguing and joking among themselves. For all of them Sunday was a special day, a day without ghosts.

Jerry Romero expressed everyone's opinion. 'Boy, we're hungry.'

Hendymion Lee, a young man of oriental descent, shrugged his shoulders in reply. 'So what's new? You're always hungry. I'm sure if you were the Pope, they'd have to give communion with slices of salami instead of the host.'

Jerry went up to Hendymion and grabbed his head in an arm lock. 'If it was up to you, gook, they'd do it with chopsticks.'

They both laughed.

Shalimar Bennett, a black girl with funny spiked hair and the body of a gazelle, joined in the joke. 'Jerry become Pope? He couldn't even become a priest. He can't stand wine. At his first mass he'd get so smashed they'd throw him out.'

John smiled. He lingered in the middle of the forecourt, watching them disappear inside the house. He was not fooled by that relaxed atmosphere. He knew how delicate the balance was, how in each of them memory and temptation were one and the same, until they could be transformed into just a memory. But what he witnessed every day was beautiful – the attempt at rebirth, the construction of a possible future.

Alone, standing in the middle of the forecourt, the sun directly overhead, John Kortighan lifted his eyes to the blue sky and looked at the house.

Joy had been built on the edge of that part of Pelham Bay Park that adjoined the Bronx, on a six-acre property facing the

155

stretch of sea that wove its way northward like a finger poking into the land. The main building was a two-storey construction in the shape of a square C, built according to the architectural dictates that characterized houses in New England, using mainly wood and dark brick. The free side was open towards the channel and the green coast beyond it, which, by contrast, descended southward like a hand holding back the sea.

There was the entrance, facing the garden, which you reached via a porch in the shape of a half-octagon, lit by large glass doors. On the ground floor were the kitchen and pantry, the dining room, a small infirmary, a library, and the games and TV room. On one of the short sides, two bedrooms with a shared bathroom for those members of staff who, like him, lived permanently at Joy. On the upper floor, the kids' bedrooms, and in the attic Father McKean's room.

The long side faced the forecourt, where a second building had been built to house a laboratory for those who opted for more manual activities instead of studying. In back of the laboratory was the vegetable garden, which stretched as far as the western edge of the property, where there was an orchard. Originally the vegetable garden and orchard had been developed as an experiment, with the idea of supplying a distraction for the kids at Joy, allowing them to experience something physical, and at the same time rewarding. In a short time, to everyone's surprise, the production of fruit and vegetables had grown until the community was almost self-sufficient. In fact, when the harvest was particularly good, a group of the kids went down to the market in Union Square to sell their products.

Mrs Carraro appeared in the kitchen doorway, wiping her hands on her apron. 'What's this about eating without Father Michael?'

'He's been delayed. He has to say the 12.30 mass.'

'Well, no one will die if we wait a bit. We can't have Sunday lunch without that man.'

'All right, colonel.' John pointed to the inside of the kitchen, from which came the high-pitched echo of the kids' conversation. 'But you tell the alligators.'

'They won't say a word. I'd like to see them try.'

'I'm sure you're right.'

John watched as she disappeared from the doorway, her face set for battle. Even though Mrs Carraro was greatly outnumbered by the kids, he had no doubt who would prevail. John left the kids to work it out with their cook. She was an apparently gentle and submissive woman but on several occasions had demonstrated how determined she could be. He knew that when she made a decision it was difficult to get her to change her mind, especially if the decision favoured Father McKean.

He turned left and walked slowly along the side of the house, breathing in the air, which had a slight salty taste.

Thinking.

The sun was already hot and the vegetation was starting to explode with that silent green clamour that always surprised the heart and the eyes and knocked down the cold gray walls of winter. He reached the front of the house and set off along the garden path. He walked until all he had in front of him was the shiny tabletop of the sea and the green of the park on the other side of the channel. He stopped with his hands in his pockets and his face lifted to the breeze.

He turned again to look at the house.

Bricks and wood.

Glass and concrete.

Technique and manual work.

All human things.

What was inside those walls, whether of brick or wood, went beyond that. It meant something. And, for the first time in his life, he felt part of that something, regardless of the point of departure and arrival and the unavoidable accidents along the way.

John Kortighan wasn't a believer. He had never managed to summon up any faith either in man or in God. And consequently not even in himself. But Michael McKean had somehow managed to open a breach in the wall that people had apparently built to keep him out, the wall that he had strengthened on his side in retaliation. God was still a distant, nebulous concept, hidden behind the obvious humanity of His representative. But in a way, even though John had never said this to him, Father McKean wasn't just saving the kids' lives, he was also saving his.

On the upper floor, behind the windows that reflected the sky, he glimpsed figures moving. Kids moving around in their rooms. Each had his experience, his fragment of life. Put all together by chance, like pieces of glass in a kaleidoscope, they made a vivid fragile image. Like all unstable things, it wasn't easy to decipher but was surprisingly colourful.

He walked back the way he had come, entered the house by the main door and started upstairs. As he climbed, step after step, he let his thoughts wander.

The story of Joy was both very simple and very complicated. And as was often the case, its foundation derived from a tragic event, as if some plans needed to be born out of pain in order to find the strength to become reality.

John wasn't living in the neighbourhood at that time, but he had heard about it from Michael, whose concise account had been corroborated by a couple of longer conversations with the parish priest of Saint Benedict.

It was ...

a Friday and they were holding a funeral.

A boy of seventeen, Robin Wheaters, had been found dead of an overdose in a corner of the park on the other side of the bridge, at the junction of Shore Road and City Island Road. A couple who were jogging had spotted a body lying on the ground, half hidden in the bushes. They had approached and found that he was unconscious but still breathing. The ambulance had rushed him to hospital, but to no avail. Robin had died soon afterwards in the arms of his mother, who had been taken there in a police car, after she had contacted the police to inform them that for some unknown reason her son had been out all night. Nobody in the family had ever had the slightest suspicion that he had been involved with drugs. The cause of death made his appalling end all the more horrifying. The post mortem and the absence of marks on his skin had revealed that in all probability it had been his first time. Fate had decided that there wouldn't be a second time.

His mother was the widowed sister of Barry Lovito, a lawyer of Italian extraction who practised in Manhattan but had chosen to continue living in Country Club. He was a rich man, unmarried and a workaholic, who had fought hard all his life to reach his position at the top of the heap. And had been so successful that the heap was now almost entirely his.

When his brother-in-law had died, his typically Italian sense of family had led him to take his sister and nephew into his house. The woman wasn't in good health, suffering from all kinds of psychosomatic symptoms, and the loss of her husband certainly hadn't improved her physical or mental condition. As for Robin, he was a sensitive, melancholy, suggestible boy. Left very much to his own devices, he had fallen into bad company, as often happens when solitude is forced on a person.

In church they were both there, the uncle and the mother. Counsellor Lovito was wearing an impeccably cut dark suit that marked him out in the middle of everyone as a wealthy person. His jaws were clenched and he kept his eyes fixed in front of him, out of grief and maybe also a sense of guilt. For him, the boy had been the son he had never had and, after a life spent chasing after success, was starting to miss. When his brother-in-law had died, he had deluded himself into thinking that he might be able to take his place, not realizing that the first duty of a parent is to be there.

The woman's face was gaunt with grief. It was clear from her hollow red eyes that she had no more tears in her, and from her expression that she was not only burying her son but also any desire to carry on living. She followed the coffin out of the church, leaning on her brother for support, her thin body in a black pant suit that suddenly seemed to have become a couple of sizes too big.

Father McKean was at the back of the church, surrounded by a group of teenagers, many of whom had been friends of Robin. He had followed the service with that sense of

As Barry Lovito came out of the church, he turned his head and saw him in the middle of all those kids. His glance had lingered longer than might have been expected on the figure of Father Michael McKean. Then he had turned away and, still supporting his sister, had continued his sad progress to the car.

Three days later, Father McKean saw him again, accompanied by the parish priest. After the ritual introductions, Paul left them alone. It was obvious the lawyer had come to talk to him, although he had no idea why. McKean had been at Saint Benedict for just under a year and had exchanged only greetings with him up until that moment. As if reading his mind, the lawyer hastened to satisfy his curiosity.

'I know you're wondering why I'm here. And especially what I've come to say. I'll only take a moment.'

He started walking slowly towards the priests' house.

'I've just acquired a property, up near the park. It's a big house, with a decent plot of land. Six acres, more or less. The kind of place that can house up to thirty people. With a view of the sea and the coast.'

Father McKean must have looked bewildered, because a half-smile appeared on Lovito's face. He made a reassuring gesture with his hand.

'Don't worry. I'm not trying to sell it to you.'

Lovito reflected for a moment, uncertain whether to continue with this preamble. Then he decided it wasn't necessary.

'I'd like that house to become the base for a community where kids with the same problems as my nephew can find help and comfort. It isn't easy, but I'd like at least to try. I know it won't bring Robin back, but maybe it'll give me a few hours of sleep without nightmares.'

Lovito turned his head away. They both knew perfectly well that both things were impossible.

'Anyway that's my problem.'

The lawyer paused, took off his dark glasses, and turned to face Father McKean full on, with the resolute air of a man who is not afraid to say or do anything.

Or to admit his own guilt.

'Father McKean, I'm a practical man and, whatever my motive, the result is the only thing that counts, the only thing that lasts. It's my wish that this community shouldn't be just a dream but become reality. And I want you to take charge of it.'

'Me? Why me?'

'I've been checking you out. And what I've learned has confirmed what I'd already guessed as soon as I saw you in the middle of those kids. Apart from all your other qualifications, I know you have a great influence on the young, and a great ability to communicate with them.'

The priest looked at him as if he was looking into the future. The lawyer, a man who had learned to know men, understood. And, being a lawyer, he hastened to forestall any possible objection.

'I'll provide most of the money. I can also get you a non-returnable loan from the state.'

He paused to let that sink in.

'You may be interested to know that I've already talked to people at the archdiocese. There wouldn't be any kind of objection. You can call the archbishop if you don't believe me.'

After a long conversation with Cardinal Logan he accepted, and the adventure began. The house was refurbished and a fund set up to guarantee Joy a monthly sum that could meet most of the expenses. Thanks to the influence of Counsellor Lovito word had got out and the first kids had arrived. And Father Michael McKean had been there waiting for them.

Robin's mother had been snuffed out like a fire abandoned on the shore a few months after the inauguration, eaten up by her own grief. The lawyer had gone the following year, cut down by a heart attack while working fourteen hours a day to. As often happens, he had left behind a lot of money and a lot of greed. Some distant relatives had emerged from the mists of indifference to contest his will, which had left the whole of his estate to Joy. The motives behind the action were many and varied, but they all had the same intention: to allow the plaintiffs to get their hands on the money. And while the verdict was still awaited, any further emolument to the community had been frozen. Right now, Joy's survival hung in the balance. But, bitter as the struggle was, it was worth fighting.

And they would fight it together, he and Michael.

Almost without realizing it, he found himself outside the priest's room on the top floor. He checked that nobody was coming up the stairs. Slightly anxious, knowing he was breaking a taboo, John opened the door and went in. He had done this before, feeling only a strange excitement, and no guilt at this violation of another person's privacy. He closed the door behind him and took a few faltering steps inside the room. His eyes were a camera, recording every detail. He let his fingers play over a bible lying on the desk, picked up a sweater thrown over a chair, and finally went and opened the closet. All Michael's meagre wardrobe was there in front of his eyes, on hangers. He stood there looking at the clothes and breathing in the smell of the man who, from the first, had fascinated and attracted him. Attracted him so much, there were times he had to walk away, for fear of what his face might reveal. He closed the closet and approached the bed. He ran his fingers over the blanket and then lay down on his stomach and put his head on the part of the pillow where Michael McKean's head had been. He took a deep breath. When he was alone and thought about Michael, there were times when he wanted to be with him. And there were other times, like now, when he wanted to be him. He was convinced that, if he stayed here, sooner or later he would succeed . . .

The cellphone started ringing from somewhere in his

pockets. He got up quickly from the bed with his heart in his mouth, as if that sound was the signal that the world had discovered him. He groped for the phone and answered.

'John, it's Michael. I'm on my way. Paul's saying mass instead of me.'

He was still agitated, as if the man at the other end could see him, could see where he was. But in spite of the fact that the voice on the phone came to him filtered through his own embarrassment, it wasn't the one John usually associated with Michael's face. It sounded broken or distressed, or both.

'What is it, Mike? Are you all right? Did something happen?'

'Don't worry. I'll be there soon. Nothing happened.'

'Okay. See you later.'

John hung up, and stood there looking at the phone as if it could help him decipher the words he had just heard. He knew Michael McKean well enough to know when something had affected him so strongly that he was no longer the person everyone was used to.

And this was one of those times.

When he had asked him if something had happened, he had replied that nothing had. But, in spite of his reassurances, his voice had the tone of a person to whom everything has happened. He left the room and closed the door behind him. As he walked back downstairs, he felt like a lonely, useless man.

CHAPTER 16

The fork went in and took two strands of spaghetti from the boiling saucepan.

Taking care not to scald herself, Vivien lifted them to her mouth. They were half cooked. She drained the pasta and placed it in the sauce that was waiting in the frying pan. She sautéed it for a few minutes on a high flame until the excess water had evaporated and everything was the right consistency, just as her grandmother had taught her when she was little. Her grandmother had been the only person in the family who'd never resigned herself to the fact that their surname had changed over the course of time from Luce to Light. She placed the frying pan on the worktop and with the tongs started to separate the spaghetti onto the two plates.

She didn't think it was necessary to sit down at table and had laid two places with bamboo mats on the counter.

'It's ready!' she called to her niece.

A few moments later Sundance appeared in the living room of Vivien's small apartment. She had just taken a shower and her long hair was still damp. The light coming from the window struck her full on. She had put on a T-shirt and a pair of jeans, and yet she looked like a queen. There were a few traces of her father, but mostly she was the image of her mother.

Beautiful, thin, fragile.

Hard to understand and easily hurt.

Vivien felt a pang in her heart. There were moments when the pain she carried inside her, congealed like a blood clot, suddenly broke free and overwhelmed her. It was pain at what had been, it was regret for all she could have been and fate hadn't wanted her to be.

In spite of this, she smiled at her niece.

She mustn't allow a sense of all the things they'd lost to spoil those that could still be recovered. Or to jeopardize those new, lasting things that could be built in what remained to her of the future. Time didn't always heal every wound. For Vivien it was enough that it didn't cause any more. The rest, as far as it was in her power to do so, she would provide. Not to silence the sense of guilt she carried inside her. Only to stop Sundance giving voice to hers.

The girl sat down on the stool and bent her head over the plate to breathe in the smell of the pasta. Her hair fell over the table like the branches of a willow tree.

'What is it?'

'Nothing special. Just spaghetti with tomato and basil.'

'Mmmh. It's good.'

'Are you taking that on trust?'

Sundance looked up at her with her clear blue eyes as if nothing had happened. 'Your spaghetti's always good.'

Vivien smiled and made an exaggeratedly self-satisfied gesture. 'That's quite a compliment! I think I'll put it in my personal ad.'

She sat down next to Sundance. They started eating in silence, each conscious of the other's presence.

After what had happened, Vivien had never talked directly to her niece about the things she had been involved in. There had been a psychologist for that, and a long, difficult and tortuous process that was far from over. Sometimes Vivien wondered if it ever would be. But she was the only stable point in Sundance's life now, since her sister Greta had fallen victim to early onset Alzheimer's and was moving closer to oblivion day by day. Sundance's father, Nathan, who'd been a shit all his life, though he'd been skilful at hiding it, had revealed his true colours and run away, trying to forget something that would never abandon him. If nothing else, he had left behind enough money to provide for his wife and daughter. Vivien had often thought, knowing him well, that this was the most they could expect from him. And that in any case anything else that came from him would be more of a hindrance than a help.

They finished the pasta almost simultaneously.

'Are you still hungry? I can make you a hamburger, if you like.'

'No. I'm fine. Thanks, Vunny.'

Sundance stood up and went to the TV set. She saw her take the remote control from the armrest of the couch and aim it at the set. The images and voices of Eyewitness Channel entered the room.

And a spectacle of desolation and death appeared on the screen.

Vivien took the plates from the counter and went and put them in the sink. The images the channel was broadcasting were a dramatic corollary of what they had seen for themselves at close quarters.

The previous evening, when the explosion had blocked the traffic in the city and made the world catch its breath, Vivien had immediately switched on the car radio, sure that in a few moments they would find out what had happened. Both had sat there in silence, listening to the presenter's words and at the same time seeing the glare of the flames in front of them, so vivid and violent it was as if they were burning souls as well as things. The fire had continued to blaze somewhere to the side of the car as they passed Alphabet City at 10th Street. Vivien was certain that the traffic in that area would be stopped very soon, which was why she had chosen to make a long detour to get to her home near Battery Park. She had crossed the Williamsburg Bridge and driven the length of the Brooklyn–Queens Expressway, emerging downtown through the tunnel. In all that time she'd hardly said a word, continuing to hop from station to station in order to get updates.

Once they got home they had rushed to switch on the TV. And the images of urban nightmare that had appeared confirmed what they had witnessed. They had followed the broadcasts until late at night, commenting on what they were seeing. They had listened to the words of the mayor and the brief statement from the White House, until tiredness had won out over despair.

They had fallen asleep side by side in Vivien's bed, the thunder of the explosion still in their ears, feeling that vibration of the ground that had followed the blast as if, in memory, it would never end.

Vivien opened the faucet and let the water run over the plates dirty with sauce. She added a few drops of detergent, and watched the foam bubble up. Behind her, she could hear the voices of the reporters, who were adding nothing to what they already knew, apart from an update on the death toll, which continued to grow.

The ringing of the telephone was a sign of life among all these tales of death. Vivien wiped her hands and picked up the cordless. She heard Captain Alan Bellew's voice, as strong and incisive as always, but with a slight hint of underlying tiredness.

'Hi, Vivien. Bellew here.'

He had never before called her at home, certainly never on her day off. She immediately knew what was coming next.

'What is it?'

There wasn't any need to specify the subject. Both of them knew only too well.

'It's a mess. I've just come out of a long meeting at One Police Plaza with the commissioner and all the precinct chiefs. I'm recalling all my men. I need to see you all tonight to bring you up to date with the situation.'

'Is it that bad?'

'Yes. What the press knows is nothing yet. Though I have to say we don't know much more than they do right now. There's a distinct possibility the city may be under attack. But I'll explain all that in person. Nine o'clock at the precinct.'

'OK. I'll be there.'

The captain lowered his voice. He was a friend now, not just a superior officer dealing with an emergency.

'I'm sorry, Vivien. I know how hard you've been working lately and I know all the things you've got on your plate. I know you were supposed to be going to the U2 concert with your niece. But all public gatherings have been suspended until further notice anyway.'

'I know. They just said that on TV.'

The captain paused. Out of sympathy, not embarrassment.

'How is Sundance?'

Bellew had two daughters not much older than her niece. Vivien thought he was probably seeing their faces as he asked that question.

'Fine.'

She said it softly, the way you cling to an illusion rather than a certainty. The captain understood and left it at that.

'See you tonight, then.'

'Bye, Alan. Thanks.'

Vivien hung up and put the phone down next to the sink. For a moment she looked at the two plates as if they were immersed in the depths of the ocean instead of a few inches of water.

When she turned, Sundance was standing on the other side of the counter. She was an adult at that moment, with old eyes in a girl's body. Everything around her was telling her that whatever we possess can be taken away without warning. More than ever, Vivien felt that she wanted to teach her, to show her that many beautiful things can happen just as unexpectedly.

How, she didn't yet know. But she would learn. And she would save both of them.

Her niece smiled at her, as if she had read her thoughts. 'We have to go back to Joy, don't we?'

Vivien nodded. 'I'm sorry.'

'I'll go pack my bag.'

She walked away down the corridor, towards the bedroom. Vivien went to the little safe, rather unimaginatively concealed behind a painting. She punched in the combination, opened it, and took out her pistol and shield.

Sundance was at the end of the corridor, waiting for her with her bag in her hand. There was no trace of disappointment on her face. Vivien would have preferred that, rather than this premature resignation.

They had planned to go running together along the Hudson in the afternoon, before enjoying an evening of fun, lost amid the concert crowd and carried on a wave of euphoria, the kind only music can give you.

Instead of which . . .

They went down onto the street and walked to the car. It was a gorgeous day, but right now the sun, the slight breeze and the intense blue of the sky seemed somehow mocking, as if nature was showing off rather than offering a gift to human beings.

Vivien pressed the remote control and opened the car doors. Sundance threw her bag on the back seat and then came and sat down next to her. As Vivien was starting the engine, the girl's thin voice caught her off guard.

'Have you been to see Mother lately?'

Vivien wasn't sure what to say in reply. They hadn't broached the subject in months. She turned to her niece, who was looking out the window as if ashamed of her question or afraid of the answer.

'Yes. I went yesterday.'

'How is she?'

Where is she? would have been a more accurate question.

That was the thought that came to her instinctively, but she didn't say it out loud. She tried to keep her voice as normal as possible as she told the truth, which was what she had decided to do.

'She isn't well.'

'Do you think I could see her?'

For a moment Vivien found it hard to breathe, as if the air inside the car had suddenly become rarefied. 'I don't know if that's such a good idea. I don't think she'd recognize you.'

Sundance looked at her, her face streaked with tears. 'I'd recognize her. That'd be enough.'

Vivien was suddenly overwhelmed with tenderness. It was the first time she had seen her niece cry since that terrible

171

business. She didn't know if the girl ever succumbed to the illusory solace of tears when she was alone. With her aunt and all the other people she came in contact with she was always self-possessed, as if she had built a wall between herself and her own humanity to keep pain out.

All at once she saw the girl Sundance used to be, relived all the wonderful times they had spent together. She leaned forward in her seat and embraced her, trying to wipe out the terrible things both of them needed to forget. Sundance took refuge in that embrace, and they were motionless for a long time, leaving all the space they had inside for that wave of emotion.

Vivien heard her niece's voice, broken by sobs, coming from somewhere beneath her hair. 'Oh, Vunny, I'm sorry for what I did. I'm so sorry. It wasn't me, it wasn't me, it wasn't me . . .'

She kept repeating these words until Vivien hugged her harder and placed a hand on her head. She knew that this was an important moment in their lives and she prayed to whatever being was responsible for human existence to help her find the right words.

'Shhhhhh. That's all over now. It's all over.'

She said that phrase twice, to convince her and to convince herself.

Vivien held her like that until Sundance's sobs subsided. When they moved apart, Vivien leaned towards the glove compartment, opened it, and took out a box of Kleenex.

She handed it to Sundance. 'Here. If we carry on like this, this car will soon be an aquarium.'

She said that to lighten the tension and seal this new-found bond between them. Sundance gave a little smile. She took one of the tissues and wiped her eyes.

172

Vivien did the same.

The girl's resolute voice surprised her as she wiped her eyes. 'There was a man.'

Vivien waited. The worst thing to do now would be to express impatience, to insist on the girl coming clean. But Sundance didn't need any prompting. Now that the wall had come down, it seemed that all the dark things hidden on the other side needed urgently to find daylight.

'It was someone I met, who gave me things. Someone who organized—'

Her voice cracked. Vivien understood it was still difficult for her to utter certain words and use certain expressions.

'Do you remember his name?'

'I don't know his real name. Everybody called him Ziggy Stardust. I think it was a nickname.'

'Do you know where he lives? Do you have his telephone number?'

'No. I only saw him once. And he was always the one who called me.'

Vivien took a deep breath to calm the beating of her heart. She knew what she would have to fight against in the next few days. Her anger and her instincts. The desire to track down that bastard and empty a full round of bullets in his head.

She looked at her niece. For the first time the look she got in return was direct and unclouded. Now she knew she could talk to her in a new way, a way she would understand.

'There's something happening in this city. Something very ugly that may cost the lives of many people. That's why the whole of the New York Police Department is on a state of alert, and that's why I have to be at the precinct tonight. To try to prevent what just happened from happening again.'

She gave her time to absorb what she had said. And to prepare her for what she was about to say.

'But I promise you one thing. I won't rest until I've made sure that man won't do anyone any harm ever again.'

Sundance simply nodded. For the moment, that was all that was needed between them. Vivien started the engine and set off towards Joy, which would be her niece's home for a little while longer. She was anxious to tell Father McKean about the progress they'd made, but as she joined the traffic, she couldn't help thinking about the new mission. Whoever this elusive Ziggy Stardust was, his life was about to become a living hell.

CHAPTER 17

Vivien opened the glass-fronted door and walked into the precinct house.

She left outside a bright sunny morning that showed not the slightest inclination to follow her in. This was usually a familiar place to her. A frontier outpost bang in the middle of civilization, which still gave her a sense of home she didn't find anywhere else.

Today was different. Today there was something abnormal in the air and inside her, a sense of anxiety and electric tension she couldn't define. She had read somewhere that, in times of peace, the warrior fights himself. She wondered what kind of war she would have to fight in the days to come. And how much space each of them would still have for his or her own inner conflict.

In a precinct house, peace wasn't a state of waiting. It was a dream.

She waved to the officers on duty behind the desk and went through the door leading to the upper floor. She started climbing the stairs, leaving behind her the roll-call room where, the night before, leaning on the desk, Captain Alan Bellew had updated all the off-duty officers on the situation.

He'd begun, 'As I guess you've all realized by now, this is a really nasty business. It's now been established that the building on 10th Street was blown up deliberately. The experts have found traces of explosive. The worst you could think of. TNT combined with napalm. That's one detail the media don't yet have, though you can bet they soon will. Whoever did this was aiming to cause the maximum damage, combining the incendiary effect of napalm and the explosive power of TNT. The building was mined with surgical precision. How the perpetrators managed to set the charges so carefully without attracting attention is still a mystery. You don't need me to tell you that everyone's working on this: FBI, NSA, CIA, you name it. And us, of course.'

Bellew had paused.

'This morning there was a meeting at the commissioner's office with the mayor and a couple of bigwigs from Washington. The Defcon level is on maximum readiness. That means all military bases and airfields are on a war footing. I'm telling you this so you can see how seriously everyone's taking this.'

Vincent Narrow, a tall, well-built detective sitting in the front row, had raised a hand. The captain gestured to him to speak.

'Has anyone claimed responsibility?'

They were all wondering the same thing. In spite of all the time that had passed, the ghosts of 9/11 were far from being exorcized.

Bellew had shaken his head. 'Nobody at all. For the moment we don't know any more about that than the TV channels. Al-Qaeda has put out a communiqué on the Internet disclaiming responsibility. The computer experts are checking if it's genuine. There's always a possibility some other group of fanatics is behind this, but these guys are usually very eager to take the credit.'

176

Another question came from the back of the room. 'Do we have any leads?'

'Not even the ghost of a lead. Apart from the unusual combination of explosives.'

Finally Vivien asked the question they were all afraid to hear the answer to. 'How many dead?'

The captain sighed. 'For the moment, more than ninety. The reason the number wasn't higher is that this was Saturday night, and a lot of people were out or away for the weekend. But it's bound to rise. Some were horribly burned. There won't be many wounded.'

The captain had left them all a moment to absorb the figure. And to join it in their minds to the images that TV channels were broadcasting all over the world.

'This isn't a massacre on the scale of 9/11, but when you take the expertise of the bombers into account, it may only be the beginning of something bigger. So what I ask all of you is this: keep your eyes and ears wide open. Pursue the investigations you've already been assigned, but in the meantime don't rule out anything, even the smallest detail. Spread the word among your informers. We have authorization to promise anything we like, from money to cutting deals on charges, to anyone who provides useful information.'

He took some photographs from his desk and showed them to his men.

'These were taken around the scene of the attack. They'll be displayed on the noticeboard upstairs. Maniacs often get a kick from going back to the scene of their crimes. They may not be any use, but who knows? Anyhow, take a look at them. You never know where a lead might come from. That's all for now.'

177

The meeting broke up and everyone left the room, commenting on the events. Some went back home, others hit the city to enjoy what was left of their Sunday. They all looked a lot more worried than when they'd come in.

Vivien, who had come directly from the Bronx to the precinct house, recovered her car from the parking lot and reluctantly joined the slow-moving traffic home. The next day, the city would wake up and resume its usual frenzied race towards some unknown goal. But for the moment there was calm and time to think. And that was what Vivien needed. As soon as she got home, she took a shower and went straight to bed, where she tried in vain to read a book. For what remained of the night she slept little and badly. The captain's words, combined with what she and Sundance had witnessed, preyed on her mind. In addition, she had been disoriented by Father McKean's behaviour when they had met at Joy. She had spoken with him of the progress she had made in her relationship with her niece, and how open Sundance had been. His response hadn't been what she had expected. He had greeted this news with a lukewarm smile and words that seemed more polite than enthusiastic. He hadn't seemed the person she'd come to know, the person she'd admired ever since she first met him. Several times, he'd turned the conversation around to the bombing, asking about the means used, the number of victims, how the investigation was going. Vivien had come away with a sense that something was eating Father McKean and she didn't know what it was.

Now, Vivien walked into the detectives' squadroom. Only a couple of her colleagues were at their desks. The Plaza was empty.

She gave a wave that took in everybody and nobody. The camaraderie which usually pervaded the room had disappeared. Everyone was silent, absorbed in their own thoughts.

She sat down at her desk, switched on the computer, and linked to the police database. She entered her user ID and password and, as soon as she had access, typed in the name Ziggy Stardust. After a few moments a photograph appeared, along with his record. She was surprised to find herself looking at a nondescript, bland face. He looked like the kind of person you meet and immediately forget. A complete nonentity.

'Here you are, you son of a bitch.'

She quickly read through all the things Zbigniew Malone alias Ziggy Stardust had been involved with. He was a type that Vivien knew well. A small-time crook, the kind who spends all his life on the edges of crime without ever really getting his feet wet. Someone who didn't enjoy a scrap of respect even among his own kind. He had been arrested several times for various offences. Bag snatching, drug dealing, pimping, crap like that. He had also done a little time, but less than Vivien would have expected, given his résumé.

She looked for his address, and saw that it was in Brooklyn. She knew a detective who worked out of the 67th Precinct, a bright, easy-going guy she'd once worked a case with. She picked up the phone and asked to speak with Detective Star. After a few moments, she heard his voice, slightly guttural, just as she remembered it.

'Star speaking.'

'Hi, Robert. It's Vivien Light, from the 13th.'

'Vivien, light of the human race. To what do I owe the honour?'

'I'm flattered by your description, though I'm not sure the human race agrees.'

She heard Star's laughter. 'I see you haven't changed. What do you need?'

'Information.'

'Shoot.'

'What do you know about a guy who goes by the name Ziggy Stardust?'

'I know a whole lot of things about him, but the first one that comes to mind is that he's dead.'

'Dead?'

'That's right. Murdered. Stabbed to death, to be precise. They found him yesterday in his apartment, lying on the floor in a pool of blood. According to the post mortem, the death occurred on Saturday. He was small fry, but someone decided he didn't deserve to live. We sometimes used him as an informer.'

Vivien added informer to the list of Ziggy Stardust's activities she already had in her possession. That would explain why he'd got off so lightly in his dealings with the law. Usually, in return for some reliable tip-offs, they turned a blind eye to illegal enterprises of lesser importance.

'Do you have the killer?'

She'd have liked to add that, if they did, she'd have gladly gone to the jail and given that person a medal, but she held back.

'No, and with all the crap that scumbag was into, I don't think it'll be easy. And let's be honest about this, no one's weeping tears over him. We're handling the case, but with all that's going down right now, finding whoever whacked this guy isn't exactly top priority.'

'I can believe that. Keep me informed. I may even tell you why, if I have to.'

'OK.'

Vivien hung up and sat there for a moment mulling over the information she had just received. Then she decided to print the file she had on the screen. She intended to show the photograph to Sundance, to confirm that he really was the man she had told him about. She couldn't summon up any shame over the small, mean sense of euphoria she felt inside her. Ziggy Stardust's ugly end showed that revenge and justice sometimes went hand in hand. What she had promised her niece had come to pass earlier than she had foreseen. Vivien's one regret was that she couldn't take any credit for it.

At that moment Brett Tyler, one of her colleagues, came out of the bathroom next to the Plaza. He was a dark, well-built guy, more stubborn than brilliant. And he could be rough with those who didn't deserve any other treatment. Vivien had seen him in action and she had to admit that, when he wanted, he could be extremely effective.

Tyler approached her desk. 'Hi, Vivien. Everything okay?'

'So-so. You?'

He spread his arms in a resigned gesture. 'Russell Wade is coming in to give me the lowdown on that gambling joint. I can hardly wait. It's going to be a truly thrilling morning.'

Vivien saw again the rumpled figure of Wade leaving the precinct house accompanied by his lawyer, and remembered Captain Bellew's comment on his chaotic, self-destructive lifestyle.

'Was it you who smashed his lip?'

'Yes. And strictly between the two of us, I quite enjoyed it. I just don't like the guy.'

Vivien didn't have time to reply, because just then the guy in question appeared at the door, accompanied by a uniformed officer. Vivien saw that he had got back on his feet compared with the first time she had seen him, even though his lip still bore the mark of Brett Tyler's tender loving care.

181

'Speak of the devil,' Tyler said softly.

The uniformed officer went back the way he had come, and Wade came towards them. Tyler made no attempt at cordiality, apart from a nod that was so formal as to appear vaguely sarcastic.

'Good morning, Mr Wade.'

'Any reason why it should be?'

'As a matter of fact, no. For either of us.'

The man turned his head for a moment to look at Vivien. He said nothing to her, and turned away again. As he did so, his glance fell briefly on the photograph lying on her desk. He immediately turned his attention back to Tyler.

'So, shall we get this whole thing over and done with?' The tone of the question was vaguely provocative.

Tyler accepted the challenge. 'Haven't you brought your lawyer?'

'Why, are you planning to hit me again?'

Vivien could have sworn she saw an amused gleam in Russell Wade's eyes. Maybe Tyler had seen it, too, because he darkened suddenly. Moving aside, he indicated a point to his right.

'This way, please.'

As they walked towards Tyler's desk, Vivien continued smiling for a few moments at the verbal skirmish between the two men. Then she opened the folder lying on her desk, which contained the file on the corpse found in the wall on 23rd. The medical examiner's report was there, along with a copy of the photographs she had found in the document holder on the ground next to the body. In spite of the captain's desire to handle all crimes committed in his patch, it was reasonably certain that the case would be transferred to the Cold Case Squad, which was why she went through the report quickly and without a great deal of interest. It confirmed, with a bit more technical jargon, the cause of death the ME had suggested at the scene. The date of death went back some fifteen years, although there was a small margin of error due to the conditions of the place in which the body had been preserved. Results of tests on the clothes hadn't come through yet, while tests on the teeth were still in progress. The body presented no unusual marks, except for a consolidated fracture of the humerus and the right tibia and a tattoo on one shoulder, still visible after all this time. Attached to the file was a photograph of this tattoo. It was a Jolly Roger, at the pirate flag. There was nothing exceptional about the design, but beneath it were the words

THE ONLY FLAG

written in characters appropriate to the image. Ironic, really, Vivien thought. Carrying the only flag hadn't saved the man from a nasty end. But the tattoo could be a useful lead in the identification of the body, if it turned out to be the symbol of some particular group or association.

That was all the documentation.

So far, this case was shaping up to be a fairly boring one. They'd have to contact the Department of Buildings for information on the two demolished buildings.

Take statements from the former owners and tenants.

Check missing persons reports from around that date.

She put down the file and picked up the two photographs. For a long time she stared at the young man in uniform in front of a tank, a protagonist in a war that had brought more shame than glory. Then she went on to the image of the same young man holding up that strange three-legged cat. She wondered about that. Was it a freak of nature or had someone mutilated the animal? She'd probably never know. She put everything back inside the folder, and sat back in her chair. She would have to write a report, but she didn't feel like it right now.

She stood up, crossed the room and went out on the landing where the coffee machine was. When the hot liquid had almost filled the paper cup, Russell Wade appeared by her side. He didn't look like someone who wanted a coffee.

Vivien took out the cup and turned to him. 'Finished with your tormentor?'

'With him, yes. Now I need to talk to you.'

'Me? About what?'

'The man whose photograph you have on your desk.'

Vivien's senses were immediately alert. There were times like that, when her experience – but above all her skill – told her something important was about to happen. And she had seldom been wrong.

'What about him?'

'I knew him.'

Vivien noticed the past tense. 'Did you know he was murdered?'

'Yes, I did.'

'If you have any information, I can put you in touch with the people handling the case.'

Wade looked puzzled. 'I saw the photograph on your desk. I thought you were handling it.'

'No. Brooklyn caught the case. It's pure chance that photograph was on my desk.'

Wade decided to get more specific. 'Actually, it's not Ziggy's death that's the important thing. At least not entirely. There's something else much more important. But right now

184

I'd like to talk in private with you and the head of this precinct.'

'Captain Bellew is very busy at the moment. Believe me, I'm not just saying that.'

He paused, looking her in the eyes. Vivien remembered that moment when he had passed her in the car, the day he had been released. That sense of sadness and solitude he had conveyed to her. She had no reason to feel any respect for the man, but once again she found it hard to remain insensitive when faced with the depth in those eyes.

'If I told you I have information that could lead to the arrest of the person who blew up the building on the Lower East Side,' Russell Wade said calmly, 'do you think Captain Bellew might find a minute to hear me out?'

CHAPTER 18

He was sitting on a plastic chair in a small waiting room on the second floor of the 13th Precinct. A nondescript room, with faded walls that bore witness to stories that had also faded with time. But his time was now, and his story belonged to the present.

He got up and went to the window that looked out on the street. He put his hands in his pockets and, for better or worse, felt part of the world.

After the discovery he had made in Ziggy's apartment, after reading the paper he had passed on to him before dying, and realizing with dismay what it was about, Saturday and Sunday had been spent in long and tormented reflection, interspersed with watching the TV news, reading the newspapers and seeing images of the bloodstained man who had died in his arms.

At last, he had come to a decision.

He didn't know if it was the right one, but at least it was his.

In this uncertain situation, one thing was now clear to him. That something in his life had ended and something else was about to start. And he would do everything he could to make it something good, something important. By a strange twist of fate, at the very moment he had found himself alone, burdened with a huge responsibility, the knot he had carried inside him for years had loosened. As if the ship had needed a real storm to demonstrate that it was seaworthy.

At first, overwhelmed by doubt, he had wondered what Robert Wade would have done if he had been in his shoes. Then he had realized it was the wrong question to ask. What mattered was what *he* ought to do. And he had finally turned his back on the mirror in which, however hard he had looked for his own face, he had continued for years to see the image of his brother.

For the whole of Sunday night, he had lain on the bed, looking up at the ceiling, which was like a clear roof in the semi-darkness.

All you had to do was search. The most difficult thing to understand was not who, or how. It was where. And that was always somewhere closer than you thought. In the morning, when the signs and the street lamps had gone out and the sun had come up again, he had got out of bed and taken a shower that had completely wiped out any lingering trace of tiredness due to his sleepless night.

He had found himself in the bathroom, naked in front of the mirror. There, on the shiny surface, was his body and his face. He knew now who he was – he knew that, if there was something he had to prove, then he had to prove it to himself and no one else.

But above all, he wasn't afraid any more.

The door opened behind him. In the doorway appeared the young woman who had introduced herself as Detective Vivien Light. When some time ago

when was that?

he had been released and had gone out onto the street with the lawyer, Thornton, and got into the car, he had seen her

187

there on the steps, motionless, as if unsure whether or not to descend. The car had passed her and their eyes had met. A fleeting moment, a brief glance in which there had been no judgement and no condemnation. Only a curious sense of understanding that Russell hadn't forgotten. At that time he hadn't known she was a police officer but, when he had found her sitting at a desk with Ziggy's photograph next to her, he had realized she might be the right person to talk to.

He would know very soon if he had been right.

The detective stepped aside and indicated the corridor. 'Come with me.'

Russell followed her until they reached the door with a frosted-glass pane and the words

Captain Alan Bellew

painted in cursive lettering by a steady hand. It reminded Russell of images from black and white crime movies of the Forties. The detective opened the door without knocking and they found themselves in an office with furnishings that were anything but austere.

Filing cabinets against the wall to the left, a closet on the right, a small table with two armchairs and a coffee machine on its wooden surface. Walls of an indefinable colour. A couple of questionable paintings and a few plants in a vase fixed to the wall with a wrought-iron ring.

A man was sitting behind a desk facing the door. Russell couldn't see him very well because he was silhouetted against the light from the window, made only slightly less bright by the Venetian blinds.

The man pointed to a chair in front of the desk. 'I'm Captain Bellew. Take a seat, Mr Wade.'

Russell sat down and the young woman detective came and stood a couple of feet from him. She was observing him curiously, whereas the captain, if he was curious about him at all, didn't show it.

Russell decided he was a man who knew his job. He was a cop, not a politician, someone who had earned his rank by results, not through public relations.

Bellew sat back in his chair. 'Detective Light tells me you claim to have some important information for us.'

'It's not just a claim. I do have it.'

'We'll see. For the moment, let's take it from the beginning. Tell me about your relationship with this Ziggy Stardust.'

'First I'd like to talk about my relationship with you.'

'I'm sorry?'

'I know that in cases like these, you have considerable discretionary powers over concessions to anyone who provides useful evidence. You can offer money, you can even offer immunity from prosecution, if necessary.'

The captain's face darkened. 'Do you want money?'

Russell Wade shook his head, a half-smile on his lips. 'Up until two days ago, an offer like that would have tempted me. It might even have persuaded me . . .'

He lowered his head, leaving the sentence unfinished, as if suddenly pursuing a thought, or a memory. Then he looked up again.

'Today's different. There's only one thing I want.'

'And are we allowed to know what that is?'

'I want exclusive rights to this story. In return for what I'm going to give you, I want the chance to follow this investigation at close quarters.'

The captain thought about this for a moment. When he

spoke, he spoke clearly and emphatically, as if determined to make himself understood. 'Mr Wade, I'd have to say you don't come with the best references.'

Russell made a vague gesture with his hand. 'Captain Bellew,' he said, adapting his tone to the captain's, 'my story is common knowledge. Everyone knows I won a Pulitzer I didn't deserve and that it was quite rightly taken away from me. I don't deny that – in fact I know it better than anyone. I'm not going to excuse what I did in the past. At best, I might be able to explain it. But this doesn't seem to me the right time to do that. I beg you to believe that I have some very important things to say even though, as you said, I don't have the best of credentials.'

'Why do you want this?'

Russell was aware that the answer he gave was a crucial one.

'I could give you a whole list of reasons. But what I really want is to stop being a coward.'

Silence fell in the room.

The captain looked him in the eyes for a long time. Russell held his gaze without any difficulty.

'We could hold you as a suspect in the homicide of Ziggy Stardust.'

'Of course you could, but I don't think you will.'

To make these words seem less presumptuous, he decided to be a little more specific.

'Captain, I'm not a vulture. If I'd wanted a scoop I'd have gone to the *New York Times*, however difficult that might have been for me. But, believe me, that would have thrown the whole city into total panic. And I haven't the slightest intention of playing with the lives of thousands of people. Because that's what's at stake here . . .'

He paused briefly, looking from one to the other.

'The lives of thousands of people.'

He had repeated that last phrase to make sure the idea was as clear to them as it was to him. Then he reinforced it with a statement that was as difficult to say as it was to accept.

'If what I'm thinking is correct, Saturday's explosion is only the first in a long series.'

He got to his feet and took a few steps around the room.

'For a whole series of reasons, one of which is pure chance, I've chosen Detective Light and you to tell this to. But it's not my intention to keep any information to myself that could save the lives of so many people. I could go to the FBI, but I think it's best if everything starts here, in this room.'

He came back to the desk, put his hands on the desktop and leaned slightly towards the captain.

It was his turn now to look the other man in the eyes.

'All I want is your word that you'll let me follow the investigation at close quarters.'

Russell knew there was a long-standing rivalry between the various investigating bodies. And he knew the biggest was between the NYPD and the FBI. Captain Bellew seemed like a good cop and a good man. But he was still a human being. The idea that his precinct could solve this case and get the credit for it had to weigh heavily with him.

The captain pointed to the chair. 'Sit down.'

Russell did as he was told. Captain Bellew waited until he was seated before speaking.

'All right. You have my word of honour that, if what you have to say is of interest to us, I'll let you follow the investigation. But if I find you've made us waste our time, I'll personally kick you down the stairs.'

A pause. They looked at each other to seal their pact – and accept its possible consequences.

'Now talk.'

The captain motioned to Vivien, who had been silent so far, listening to the conversation from her position next to the desk. Russell realized that from now on she would be leading the way.

Which was what she did.

'What's your connection with Ziggy Stardust?'

'For reasons of my own, I was at his place on Saturday afternoon.'

'What kind of reasons?'

Russell Wade shrugged. 'You know me. And I think you know Ziggy and what he did. For now, can I just say the reason doesn't matter?'

'Go on.'

'Ziggy lived in a basement apartment. When I got to his place and turned the corner at the bottom of the stairs, I saw a man in a military jacket start up the stairs at the other end of the corridor. He seemed to be in a hurry. I thought he was a customer of Ziggy's who couldn't wait to get out of there.'

'Would you be able to recognize him?'

Russell was favourably impressed by the young woman's transformation. She had gone from being a mere spectator to being the person who asked the questions, and it was clear she knew her business.

'I don't think so. I didn't see his face. He was of average build, I'd say. He could have been anyone.'

'What did you do then?'

'Ziggy's door was open, and I went in. He was still alive, but there was blood all over him. On his pants, on the front of his shirt. It was even coming out of his mouth. He was trying to stand up and get to the printer.'

The captain interrupted at this point. 'The printer?'

Russell nodded. 'That's what he did. I also wondered why. He grabbed hold of me and pressed a button on the printer. There was this orange light flashing, like when there's no paper and the machine goes on stand by.'

'And then?'

'With his last strength he took the sheet of paper that had just been printed and put it in my hand. Then he slid to the floor and died.'

Russell paused a moment. Neither of the two police officers said or did anything to make him continue.

'When that happened, I panicked. I stuffed the paper in my jacket pocket and ran out. I know I should have called the police, but I was scared. I thought the killer might come back. When I got home, I saw the explosion on the Lower East Side from the windows of my apartment and everything else went out of my mind. Once I'd calmed down a bit, I remembered the paper in my pocket and took a look at it. It was a photocopy, clearly part of a longer letter, because it begins and ends in mid-sentence. It's handwritten, and quite difficult to read with all the bloodstains on it.'

Once more, Russell paused. When he spoke again, his tone was that of a man who couldn't, in spite of everything, quite believe what had happened.

'I had to read it twice before I realized what it meant. And when I did realize, I felt as if the whole world had come crashing down on my head.'

'What on earth was in it?'

Russell Wade put his hand in the inside pocket of his jacket, took out a sheet of paper folded in four, and held it out to Vivien. 'Here it is. This is a photocopy of the original. Read it for yourself.'

Vivien took it, opened it and started reading. By the time she got to the end, her face was white and her lips drawn. Without a word, she passed the paper to the captain.

and that's why I left. So now you know who I am and where I'm from, just as you know who you are. As you see, my story didn't take long to tell, because after a while not much happened to me. But it was difficult to tell, because it was difficult to live through. During my life, I couldn't pass anything on to anyone. I preferred to keep my resentment and hate to myself. Now that the cancer has done its work and I'm on the other side, I can pass something on to you, the way every father should do to his son and I should have done a long time ago but couldn't. I never had much money. All I had, minus the funeral expenses, is here in the envelope, in thousand-dollar bills. I'm sure you'll make good use of it. All my life, before and after the war, I worked in the construction industry. When I was young and working for a man who was like a father to me, I learned to use explosives for demolition. The army taught me the rest. All the time I was working in New York, I hid bombs in many of the places I helped to build. TNT and napalm. I learned about napalm the hard way. I'd have liked to be the one to blow them up, but seeing as how you're reading these words it means life, and my lack of courage, decided otherwise. In this letter I've put the addresses of the buildings that have been mined and instructions on how to blow them up in my place. If you do that, you'll be avenging me. Otherwise I'll just be one of the many victims of the war who never had the consolation of justice. I recommend you learn the addresses and the

technical details by heart and then destroy this letter.
The first building is on the Lower East Side, on 10th
Street at the corner of Avenue D. The second

That was where the letter ended. The captain, too, was white by the time he had finished reading. He put the sheet of paper down, put his elbows on the desk, and hid his face in his hands. His voice was muffled as he made one last attempt to convince himself that what he had just read wasn't true.

'Mr Wade, you could have written this yourself. How do I know this isn't another of your hoaxes?'

'The TNT and the napalm. I checked. Nobody mentioned it, either on TV or in the newspapers. I assume they don't yet know about it. If you can confirm that was the cause of the explosion, I think that's sufficient proof.'

Russell had said this to Vivien, who was pale and didn't seem able to speak. All three of them were thinking the same thing. If what was written in the letter was true, it meant they were at war. And the man who had started this war had, on his own, the power of a small army.

'And there's another thing. I don't know how useful it might be.'

Again Russell Wade put his hand in the inside pocket of his jacket. This time he took out a bloodstained photograph. He held it out to the detective.

'Along with the paper, Ziggy gave me this.'

Vivien took the photograph and stared at it for a moment or two. A kind of electric shock seemed to go through her.

'Wait a moment. I'll be right back.'

She disappeared into the corridor, barely leaving Russell and Captain Bellew time to wonder what she was up to. There was only one flight of stairs between the captain's office and her desk, so it didn't take her long to pick up the yellow folder and get back. She closed the door and approached the desk.

'A couple of days ago, during demolition work at a site on 23rd Street, a body was found inside a cavity wall. According to the ME, it had been there for about fifteen years. We didn't find any significant clues, apart from one thing.'

Assuming that the captain already knew most of this, Russell realized that Detective Vivien Light's presentation was for his benefit. That meant she was respecting their pact.

'On the ground next to the body,' she continued, 'we found a document holder containing two photographs. Here they are.'

She gave the captain the black and white enlargements that were in the folder. Bellew examined them for a few moments. When Vivien was certain he had digested them, she passed him the photograph Russell had shown her.

'And this is what Ziggy gave Mr Wade.'

As soon as he saw it, the captain couldn't stop himself crying out, 'Holy fucking shit!'

He continued looking from one photograph to the other for what seemed like for ever. Then he leaned across the desk and held them out to Russell. In one, there was a young man in uniform standing in front of a tank: an image that looked as if it dated from the Vietnam war. In the other, the same young man, in civilian clothes, was holding a big black cat up to the camera, a cat that seemed to have one leg missing.

Now Russell knew why Detective Light had behaved the way she had, and why the captain was so surprised. The young man and the cat in the photograph found next to a body that had been dead for fifteen years were the same as those in the photograph Ziggy Stardust had put in his hands before dying.

CHAPTER 19

I am God . . .

Ever since Father Michael McKean had opened his eyes, those three words had been echoing in his head as if they were on some kind of endless tape loop. Up until last night there had still been, somewhere inside him, a small hope that it was all the ramblings of a madman, ramblings that hurt no one but the madman himself. But reason and instinct, which were usually in conflict, told him it was all true.

And in the sunlight everything seemed clearer and more final.

He remembered the end of that strange conversation in the confessional, when the man, after making that terrible declaration, had changed his tone and become soft spoken, conspiratorial, uttering words of menace in a voice that artfully combined guilt and innocence.

'Now I'm going to stand up and leave. And you won't follow me, or try to stop me. If you did, the consequences would be very unpleasant. For you and the people who are dear to you. You can trust me on that, just as you can trust everything I've said.'

'Wait. Don't go. At least tell me why—'

The voice interrupted him, once again firm and precise. 'I thought I'd made myself clear. I have nothing to explain.

Only announcements to make. And you'll get them before anyone else.'

The man continued with his ravings as if they were the most natural thing in the world.

'This time I reunited darkness and light. Next time, I will bring together earth and water.'

'What does that mean?'

'You'll understand, in time.'

The voice was full of a calm, inexorable menace. Terrified that he would disappear at any moment, Father McKean asked him a last desperate question.

'Why have you come to me? Why me?'

'Because you need me more than anyone else. I know that.'

There followed a silence that, coming from a man who claimed to be the master of eternity, seemed infinite. Then he uttered his final words. His farewell to a world that was doomed.

'Ego sum Alpha et Omega.'

The man stood up and left, almost noiselessly, a rustle of green beyond the grille, a glimpse of a face in the semi-darkness. Father McKean sat there alone, breathing with difficulty but devoid of fear, because what he was feeling was so big and so nameless it left no room for anything else.

He left the confessional white faced, and when Paul came to find him he was startled by his pained look.

'What's the matter, Michael, aren't you feeling well?'

He didn't see any point in lying. In any case, after what had happened he really didn't have the strength to celebrate the noon mass. Mass was a moment of joy and togetherness, and the thoughts he had inside him could only contaminate it.

'No. To tell the truth, I don't feel well at all.'

'Okay. Go home. I'll take the service.'

'Thanks, Paul.'

Paul had had some visitors from outside the parish, and he found him a ride back to Joy. A man Father McKean didn't know introduced himself as Willy Del Carmine and pointed to a large car. He could barely remember the colour. For the whole of the brief journey he was silent, looking out the window, emerging from his thoughts only to give directions to the driver. He didn't even recognize the road he had travelled along a thousand times.

When he was in the forecourt, hearing the noise of the car as it drove away, he realized he had not even thanked or said goodbye to the man who had been so kind as to give him a ride.

John had been in the garden when he saw the car pull up, and now he joined Father McKean. He was a man of uncommon sensitivity and a keen ability to read people's moods.

Father McKean knew he would realize something was wrong. He had already sensed it in the tone of his voice when he had phoned from Saint Benedict to say he was on his way back. As if to confirm the opinion he had of him, John approached him now as if afraid he was being intrusive.

'Everything all right?'

'Everything's fine, John. Thank you.'

His colleague did not insist, confirming another of his qualities, discretion. They knew each other too well by now. He knew John was confident that, when the time was right, his friend Michael McKean would open up to him. He wasn't to know how different things were this time.

The problem was insoluble.

And it was the source of an anguish he had never felt before. In the past he had talked with other priests who had been told about crimes in the confessional. Now he understood their turmoil, their sense, as human beings, that they were in conflict with their roles as ministers of the church they had chosen to serve.

The seal of the confessional was inviolable. That was why it was forbidden to betray anyone who unburdened himself there.

Such a violation was not permitted even where the confessor's life or other people's lives had been threatened. The priest who violated the secrecy of the confessional would be automatically subject to the excommunication known as *latae sententiae*, which could be lifted only by the Pope. And that was something the Holy Father had rarely done over the course of the centuries.

If the sin confessed was a criminal act, the confessor could suggest or demand of the penitent, as an indispensable condition for absolution, that he hand himself in to the authorities. That was all he could do, though: he certainly couldn't inform the police himself, not even indirectly.

There were cases where part of the confession could be revealed to others, but always with the permission of the person involved and always without revealing his identity. This was valid for some sins that could not be forgiven without the authorization of the Bishop or the Pope. All this, however, supposed one crucial thing. The request for absolution was dependent on repentance, or the desire to free the soul from an unbearable weight. In this particular case, Father McKean was dealing with neither.

A man had declared war on society.

Destroying buildings, claiming victims, sowing grief and despair. With all the determination of the God who, in his madness, he claimed to be, the God who had destroyed cities and wiped out armies in the days when the law was still based on an eye for an eye and a tooth for a tooth.

After that tentative conversation in the forecourt with John, he headed for the kitchen to avoid having to explain himself further. As far as he could, he put on his best mask and went in the house to have lunch with the kids, who were pleased to have him with them for their little Sunday feast.

Not everyone was fooled. Mrs Carraro for one. And in the hubbub of laughter and comments and jokes around the table, a couple of the kids realized something was up. Katy Grande, a seventeen-year-old girl with a funny freckled nose, and Hugo Sael, a boy who was particularly sensitive to the world around him, looked at him every now and again with a questioning air, as if wondering where the Father McKean they knew was hiding.

In the afternoon, while most of them were in the garden enjoying the sunshine, Vivien and Sundance joined them. If Sundance was unhappy at the turn of events that had forced the authorities to postpone the concert, she didn't show it. She was quite calm, and seemed happy to be back at Joy.

She and her young aunt appeared much more united than the day before when Vivien had come to fetch her. All the embarrassment there had been between them seemed to have vanished. It looked as if their uneasy relationship had taken a completely new direction.

This impression was confirmed when Vivien, in words that were close to euphoric, told Father McKean what had happened with her niece, and about their new-found, hard-won intimacy and togetherness.

Now, in the light of a new day, he realized how unresponsive he had been to that enthusiasm. He hadn't been able to stop himself asking the detective about the tragedy on 10th

Street and its consequences and implications, trying almost obsessively to find out if the police had a lead, an angle, any idea about who might have committed that atrocity. He had barely been able to suppress the temptation to take her aside and tell her what had happened, what he knew.

Now he realized that he'd had all the answers he was going to get, given that this was still an ongoing situation and that whatever information Vivien might have, as a police officer, was strictly confidential.

They both had their secrets. And both were duty bound to keep them. They had both taken vows to that effect, one secular, the other religious.

Ego sum Alpha et Omega . . .

Father McKean looked out the window at that green and blue spring landscape that usually filled him with a sense of peace. Now he found it almost hostile, as if winter had returned, not because of anything external, but because of the eyes with which he was now looking at it. After he had got up from his bed like a sleepwalker, he had taken a shower, dressed and said his prayers with a new fervour. Then he had walked up and down the room, barely able to recognize the objects around him. Poor, familiar things, everyday objects that, even though they represented the everyday difficulties of his life, seemed all at once to belong to a happy time that was now lost for ever.

There was a knock at the door.

'Yes?'

'Michael, it's John.'

'Come in.'

Father McKean had been expecting him. They usually met on Monday mornings to discuss the week's activities and objectives. Whatever the difficulties, it was a gratifying time, which confirmed them in their commitment to achieve the aims the small community of Joy had set itself. But today John entered with the air of someone who would have liked to be in another place and time.

'Sorry to bother you, but there's something I absolutely have to discuss with you.'

'No bother. What's going on?'

Given their familiarity and mutual respect, John decided to start with a little preamble. 'Mike,' he said, 'I don't know what's happened to you, but I'm sure you'll tell me in due course. And I'm sorry to be troubling you now.'

Yet again, Father McKean was made aware of John Kortighan's great tact and how lucky he was to have a man of his calibre on the staff.

'It's nothing, John. Nothing important. It'll pass, trust me. But tell me what's on your mind.'

'We have a problem.'

At Joy there were always problems. With the kids, with the money, with members of staff, with the temptations of the outside world. But judging by John's face, this was a particularly tricky one.

'I had a word with Rosaria this morning.'

Rosaria Carnevale was a parishioner at Saint Benedict, of Italian extraction, who lived in Country Club but ran a branch of the M&T Bank in Manhattan, which handled the community's financial interests and administered Barry Lovito's estate.

'What does she say?'

What John said next was something he had hoped never to have to say. 'She says that while this case has been going on, she's bent over backwards to keep sending us the monthly allowance, as laid down in our charter. But now, after a petition by Mr Lovito's presumptive heirs, she's received

203

another court order. All payments are suspended until the dispute has been resolved.'

This meant that until the judge had pronounced, apart from the contribution by the state of New York, the community would lose its main source of income. From now on, Joy would have to rely for its general needs on its own resources and on spontaneous offers from people of goodwill.

Father McKean again looked out the window, silent and pensive. When he spoke, John Kortighan heard the unease in his voice.

'How much do we have in reserve?'

'Little or nothing. If we were a company, we'd be bankrupt.'

The priest turned with a small, colourless smile on his lips. 'Don't worry, John. We'll manage. As we always have done. We'll manage this time, too.'

But although his words might be full of confidence, there was little trace of it in his tone of voice. It was as if he had said these words more to delude himself than to convince the person he was talking to.

John felt the cold wind of reality gradually take possession of the air in the room.

'All right,' he said. 'I'll leave you now. We'll talk about the other things later. They're minor in comparison with what I've just said.'

'Yes, John, you can go. I'll be with you soon.'

'Okay, then. I'll wait for you downstairs.'

Father McKean watched as his right-hand man left the room and gently closed the door behind him. He didn't like the fact that John felt so bad about the situation, but what really hurt him was the feeling that he, Michel McKean, had disappointed him.

204

I am God . . .

He wasn't God. He had no wish to be. He was only a man conscious of his earthly limits. Up until now he had been content to serve God as best he could, accepting everything that was offered him and everything that was asked of him.

But now . . .

He picked up the cellphone from the desk and after a brief search in the address book dialled the number of the archdiocese of New York. He waited impatiently as the phone at the other end rang a few times. When at last a voice answered, he identified himself to the switchboard operator.

'I'm Father Michael McKean from the parish of Saint Benedict in the Bronx. I'm also the director of Joy, a community that takes in teenagers with drug problems. I'd like to talk to the archbishop's office.'

Usually his introductions were much more concise, but he had preferred to emphasize his status to make sure his call was put through immediately.

'One moment, Father McKean.'

The switchboard operator put him on hold. A few moments later another voice came on. A young, polite voice.

'Hello, Father. I'm Samuel Bellamy, one of Cardinal Logan's colleagues. How can I help you?'

'I need to speak to His Eminence as soon as possible. In person. It's a matter of life and death.'

He must have conveyed his own distress very effectively, because there was genuine regret in the tone of the answer, as well as a hint of anxiety.

'Unfortunately, the cardinal left this morning for a short stay in Rome. He'll be meeting with the Holy Father, and won't be back before Sunday.'

All at once, Michael McKean felt lost. A week. He'd hoped

to be able to share his burden with the archbishop, to get some advice or instruction. A dispensation was far too much of a miracle to even think about, but the consolation of a superior's opinion was vital to him right now.

'Can I do anything, Father?'

'Unfortunately not. The one thing I can ask is that you make sure I get an appointment with His Eminence as soon as possible.'

'As far as it's in my power to do so, I guarantee I will. And I'll contact you personally at your parish to let you know.'

'I'm very grateful.'

Father McKean hung up and sat down on the edge of the bed, feeling the mattress yield under the weight of his body. For the first time since he had decided to take his vows, he felt alone. And as someone who had always taught love and forgiveness, for the first time he felt like asking God, the only true one, why He had abandoned him.

CHAPTER 20

Vivien left the precinct house and walked towards her car. The temperature had dipped. The sun, which had seemed unassailable in the morning, was now battling it out with a west wind that had appeared without warning. Clouds and shadows struggled for possession of the sky and the earth. That seemed to be the preordained fate of this city.

She found Russell Wade exactly where they had arranged to meet.

Vivien still didn't have a clear idea of the man. Every time she had him pinned down, some new, unexpected aspect of him surfaced to muddy the picture she was building in her mind.

And that bothered her.

As she approached him, she went over the whole crazy story in her mind.

When, at the end of the meeting in the captain's office, the three of them had realized that there was nothing more to say, Vivien had turned to Wade and said, 'Could you wait for me a moment outside, please?'

The unfortunate winner of an undeserved Pulitzer Prize had stood up and walked to the door.

'No problem. Goodbye, captain, and thank you.'

There was a formal politeness in Bellew's reply belied by the tone in which the words were said.

'Don't mention it. If this thing leads to what we're hoping for, there'll be many people who'll want to say thank you to you.'

Including the editor of some newspaper . . .

Vivien thought.

The man went out, gently closing the door behind him, and leaving her alone with her chief. Her first impulse was to ask him if he'd gone crazy, promising what he'd just promised to a guy like Russell Wade.

'What do you think, Alan? This story of the bombs, I mean.'

'I think it sounds crazy. I think it sounds impossible. But since 9/11 I've realized that the limits of what's crazy and what's possible have gotten a whole lot wider.'

Tacitly agreeing with him, Vivien tackled another subject. The one that worried her the most. The weak link in the chain.

'And what do you think of Wade?'

The captain shrugged. Which could mean everything or nothing.

'For the moment he's given us the only lead we have. And we're lucky to have one, whatever the source. In normal circumstances I'd have kicked that daddy's boy out of here. But these aren't normal circumstances. Nearly a hundred people have died, and there are other people out there who don't know the risk they're running right now of meeting the same fate. As I said during the meeting, we have a duty to explore every avenue. Besides, that business of the photograph is strange. It turns what looked like a routine case is something of vital importance. And it seems genuine. Only reality could be fantastic enough to create a coincidence like that.'

Vivien had often thought the same thing. A thought her experience seemed to endorse a little more every day.

'Do we keep this information to ourselves?'

Bellew scratched his ear, as he often did when he was thinking. 'For now, yes. I don't want to run the risk of spreading panic or having every local politician and every police department in the country laughing behind my back. It's always possible the whole thing could burst like a soap bubble, though I don't think it will.'

'Do you trust Wade on that? It's as clear as daylight that he's looking for a scoop.'

'He already has one. And that's why he won't talk. Because it's not in his interest. We won't either, for the same reason.'

Vivien asked for a confirmation of what she already knew. 'Does that mean I have to take him with me from now on?'

The captain spread his arms as if acknowledging the inevitable. 'I gave him my word. And I usually keep it.'

As if everything had been said on that matter, it was the captain who changed the subject this time.

'I'm phoning the 67th immediately to have them send you the file on the investigation into this Ziggy. If you think it's worth it, you can also search his apartment. How about the guy in the wall, who seems to be a major player in this all of a sudden? Do you have any ideas?'

'Yes. I have a lead. Not a big one, but it's a start anyway.'

'Good. Let's get down to work. And whatever you need, you only have to let me know. For the moment, I should be able to give you what you want without having to spill the beans to anyone else.'

Vivien didn't find that hard to believe. She knew that Captain Alan Bellew boasted an old friendship with the

Police Commissioner, and unlike Elisabeth Brokens wife of Charles Brokens, he wasn't just boasting.

'Okay. I'm going.'

Vivien turned to leave the office. When she was at the door, about to leave, Bellew called her back.

'Vivien, one last thing.'

With a sly smile, he had looked her in the eyes.

'As far as Russell Wade is concerned, remember this, if you need to. I gave him my word of honour.'

A pause for emphasis.

'*You* didn't.'

Vivien left the room with the same smile on her lips. She found Russell Wade standing with his hands in his pockets in the little room where he had waited some time earlier.

'Here I am.'

'Tell me what to do, detective.'

'If we have to spend a little time together, you can call me Vivien.'

'Okay, Vivien. What happens now?'

'Give me your cellphone.'

Russell took his phone from his pocket. Vivien was surprised it wasn't an iPhone. In New York, every VIP had one. Maybe Wade didn't consider himself a VIP or maybe he'd used his as a chip in a poker game.

Vivien took the phone and dialled her own number. When she heard it ring, down below on her desk, she hung up and gave the phone back to its owner.

'There. My number's in the memory. Just outside this building, on your left, is a silver grey Volvo. That's my car. Go to it and wait for me.' She loaded the following sentence with sarcasm. 'I have things to do and I don't know how long I'll take. I'm sorry, you'll just have to be patient.'

Russell looked at her. A film of sadness passed over his eyes, the same sadness Vivien had caught in them a few days earlier.

'I've been waiting more than ten years. I can wait a little while longer.'

He turned his back on her and left. Standing at the top of the stairs for a few moments, feeling slightly perplexed by him, Vivien watched him descend and disappear on the floor below. Then she descended the stairs in her turn and went back to her desk. Along with her excitement at the importance of the task that had fallen into her hands, the impact of the words she had read in that letter had not gone away. Crazy words carried on the wind like poisonous seeds, which had somehow found the right soil in which to grow. Vivien wondered what kind of suffering the man who had left that message had endured and what kind of sickness afflicted the man who had received it, if he had decided to accept his inheritance and carry out his father's posthumous revenge.

The limits of what's crazy have grown wider . . .

Maybe in a case like this, it would have been more correct to say that the limits had been completely abolished.

She sat down at her desk and connected to the police database. She typed in the words 'the only flag' and waited for the results. Almost immediately, a photograph of a man's bare back appeared on the screen, bearing a tattoo exactly like the one found on the dead body. It was the emblem of a group of bikers based in Coney Island who called themselves the Skullbusters. There were other photographs: members of the group who had been in trouble with the law. Next to the name of each one, their offences were listed, large and small. The photographs seemed quite old and Vivien wondered if any of them was the person who had rested for years in the

211

foundations of a building on 23rd Street. It would be the greatest of ironies. But she wouldn't have been too surprised. As the captain had pointed out earlier, their work relied a lot on coincidence. The fact that photographs of the same young man and the same cat had been found in two places so distant in time and space was tangible proof of that.

As she was noting down the address of the bikers' meeting place, the file on the Ziggy Stardust case arrived by email from the 67th precinct. Bellew had wasted no time. Vivien now had all the available material on her computer: the ME's initial findings, the report drawn up by the detective in charge of the case, and the photographs taken at the scene of the crime. She zoomed all the way in on one photograph taken from the angle that interested her. There, clearly visible, was a red mark on one of the buttons of the printer, a red mark, as if someone had pressed the button with a bloodstained finger. Something else to support Russell Wade's story.

The other photographs showed the body of a slightly built man lying on the floor covered in blood. Vivien looked at them for a long time without feeling the slightest pity: the bastard had got what he deserved. For what he had done to her niece and God knew how many other kids. Not for the first time, she was forced to realize how much personal involvement changed your perspective on things.

Vivien took the remote control from her pocket and opened the car doors automatically. By the time Vivien got in, Russell Wade was busy putting on his seatbelt. As she observed him, she caught herself thinking that he was a handsome man. She immediately called herself a fool. None of this was putting her in a good mood.

He looked at her expectantly. 'Where are we going?'

'Coney Island.'

'To do what?'

'See people.'

'What people?'

'Wait and see.'

As the car slipped into the flow of traffic, Russell sat back in his seat and stared at the street in front of him. 'Are you in some kind of state of grace today,' he asked, 'or are you always this talkative?'

'Only with important guests.'

Russell Wade turned to her. 'You don't like me, do you?'

The words sounded more like a statement of fact than a genuine question. Vivien was pleased with such a direct approach. For the sake of their present and future relations, she expressed her opinion without beating about the bush.

'In normal circumstances, I wouldn't give a damn about you. People can do whatever they like with their own lives. Even throw them away, as long as they don't harm anybody. There are a lot of people around who need help because they've got into trouble through no fault of their own. Anyone who's adult and conscious and goes looking for trouble, as far as I'm concerned, can look after themselves. That isn't apathy, it's common sense.'

Russell Wade nodded eloquently. 'OK. At least we know where we stand.'

Vivien swerved and pulled up at the kerb, provoking a reaction from the motorists behind her. She let go of the wheel and turned to Russell.

'Let's get one thing straight,' she said. 'You may have charmed the captain with that story about your redemption, but I'm not such a pushover.'

Russell sat looking at her in silence. His dark, apparently

213

defenceless eyes made her think she was being made fun of. When she next spoke, it was with a harshness that was uncharacteristic of her.

'People don't change, Wade. We are what we are, and we all have our own place. However much we stray, we always come back to it in the end. And I don't think you're any exception.'

'What makes you think that?'

'You came to the precinct with a photocopy in your pocket of the sheet of paper Ziggy gave you. That means you still have the original, the one that's stained with his blood. And in case we didn't believe you and threw you out, you'd have used it to show to the FBI or the NSA or whoever.'

Vivien continued the onslaught.

'If for any reason we'd asked you to empty your pockets we'd have found only the photocopy of a page you could have passed off as something you'd dreamed up. Passing off one thing for another seems like a speciality of yours.'

Her words did not seem to have fazed Russell. This was a sign either that he had amazing self-control or that he was used to it. In spite of her anger, Vivien leaned more towards the second of these hypotheses.

She grabbed the wheel, pulled away from the kerb, and resumed her journey to Coney Island. Russell's next question took her by surprise. Maybe he, too, was trying to form an opinion of his travelling companion.

'Detectives usually have partners. How come you don't have one?'

'Right now, I have you. And your being here reminds me why I usually work alone.'

After that curt reply, silence fell in the car. During the

214

conversation, Vivien had driven the car downtown and was now crossing the Brooklyn Bridge. When they had left Manhattan behind them, Vivien tuned the radio to Kiss 98.7, a black music station. She drove the Volvo along the Brooklyn–Queens Expressway and then onto Gowanus.

Russell was looking out the window on his side. When a particularly rhythmical song came on, he started, perhaps without realizing it, to beat time with his foot. Vivien realized that this whole thing had fallen on her shoulders at a particularly difficult time. Sundance's situation and Father McKean's curious behaviour had affected her ability to think clearly and calmly. Or at least made her too harsh in her judgement.

As she parked the car on Surf Avenue in Coney Island she felt a slight pang of guilt.

'Russell, I'm sorry for what I said earlier. Whatever your motives, you're helping us a lot and we're grateful to you for that. The other stuff, it's not for me to judge. It's no excuse, but I have a few personal problems right now, and I guess I'm not acting normally.'

Russell smiled, apparently impressed by her sudden openness. 'It's OK. I should understand better than anyone the way personal problems can influence our choices.'

They got out of the car and walked to the address that Vivien had pulled out of the file on the Skullbusters. It turned out to be a large Harley Davidson dealership, with a workshop for repairing and personalizing motorbikes. The place looked clean, efficient and businesslike, a long way from Vivien's experience of bikers' hangouts in the Bronx or Queens.

They went in. To their left was a long line of bikes, different models but all Harleys. To the right, a display of gear and accessories, from helmets to coveralls to mufflers.

Facing them was a counter, from behind which a tall, sturdy man in a pair of jeans and a black sleeveless T-shirt emerged and came towards them. He had a black bandana, sideburns and a drooping moustache. As he approached, she realized the moustache was dyed, the bandana was probably there to cover a bald patch, and beneath his tan he must be well over seventy. On his right shoulder he had a tattoo of a Jolly Roger with the same words they'd found on the body walled up fifteen years earlier.

'Hello. My name's Vivien Light.'

The man smiled, amused. 'Like in the movie?'

'No, like in the police,' she replied curtly and took out her shield. The fact that her name was similar to Vivien Leigh had bugged her all her life.

The man didn't skip a beat.

A thick skin or an easy conscience, Vivien thought.

'I'm Justin Chowsky, the owner. Is there something wrong?'

'I believe this used to be the headquarters of a group of bikers called the Skullbusters.'

'It still is.' Chowsky smiled at Vivien's look of surprise. 'Things have changed a bit since the old days. We used to be a pretty wild bunch of guys. Some of us even had problems with the law. Me too, to be honest. Nothing big, you can check. A few joints, a few fights, a few benders too many.'

For a moment, he stared at one of the windows as if scenes from his youth were projected on it.

'We were hotheads but we weren't delinquents. The really heavy guys left of their own accord.'

He made a circular gesture with his hand, taking in both the space around them and his visible sense of pride.

'Then one day, I decided to open this place. Before too

long, we were one of the biggest centres for sales and personalization in the state. And the Skullbusters became a quiet group of nostalgic old men who still go around on bikes like they were kids.'

Vivien looked at Russell, who so far had kept back and hadn't introduced himself. She liked that. He knew his place.

She turned her attention back to the man in front of her. 'Mr Chowsky, I need some information.'

She took the man's silence as consent.

'About fifteen years ago, did a member of your group suddenly disappear without a trace?'

The reply came without a moment's hesitation, and Vivien felt her heart swell with hope.

'Mitch Sparrow.'

'Mitch Sparrow?' Vivien repeated the name, as if afraid it would immediately vanish from their memories.

'That's the one. Now let me see, it happened . . .'

Chowsky removed his bandana. Vivien had been wrong: he still had a full head of hair in spite of his age, although it was clearly dyed. He passed his hand through it, as if that would help him to remember.

'It happened exactly eighteen years ago.'

Vivien noted that the date fitted the margin of error in the ME's report. 'Are you sure?' she asked.

'One hundred per cent. My youngest son was born a few days later.'

From the inside pocket of her jacket, Vivien took one of the two photographs she had brought with her, the one with the cat, and held it out to Chowsky.

'Is this Mitch Sparrow?'

He did not even need to take it from her. 'No. Mitch had fair hair and this guy's dark. And anyway he was allergic to

217

cats.'

'Have you ever seen this person before?'

'Never saw him in my life.'

For a moment, Vivien considered the implications of that statement. Then she did what her job required and continued with her questions. 'What kind of a man was Mitch?'

Chowsky smiled. 'When he first joined us, he was a fanatical biker. Took better care of his bike than his mother. He was a good-looking guy, too, but he treated women like Kleenex. You know, used them, then threw them away.'

Chowsky seemed to be the kind of person who loves the sound of his own voice. Vivien pressed him. 'And then?'

Chowsky shrugged, as if to say: That's life. 'One day he met a girl who wasn't like the others, and he fell for her. He spent less time with his bike and more time in bed. The girl ended up pregnant. So Mitch found a job and got married. We all went to the wedding. We were drunk for two whole days.'

Vivien didn't have time for an old biker's memories of drinking sprees. She tried to stick to the point. 'Tell me about his disappearance. What happened?'

'There's not much to tell. One fine day he vanished. Just like that. His wife told the police. They even came and asked me questions. From the 70th Precinct, I think. But they never got anywhere. You know what the French say. *Cherchez la femme.*'

He seemed very pleased with himself for saying something in a foreign language.

'Are you still in touch with his wife?'

'No. For a while, when she still lived around here, she and my wife used to see each other from time to time. But a couple of years after Mitch disappeared, she found someone

218

else and moved away.' Chowsky anticipated the next question. 'I don't know where.'

'Do you remember her name?'

'Carmen. Montaldo, Montero, something like that. She was Hispanic. A tall woman, quite a looker. If Mitch did run off with another woman, then that was one of the dumbest things he ever did in his life.'

Vivien couldn't tell Chowsky that this was one dumb thing Mitch probably hadn't done. Though maybe he had done something even dumber, to end up inside a concrete wall.

She didn't think she would get any more information from Chowsky for the moment. She had a name, she had a time period, she had a missing persons report filed by a woman called Carmen, Montaldo or Montero or something like that. Now she had to find that report and trace the woman.

'Thank you, Mr Chowsky – you've been a great help.'

'Don't mention it, Miss Light.'

They left the man to his bikes and headed for the door. Just as they were about to leave, Russell stopped. He looked at her for a moment, unsure of his next step. Then he turned to Chowsky, who was now back behind the counter.

'One last thing,' he said, 'if you don't mind.'

'Go ahead.'

'What kind of work did Mitch Sparrow do?'

'He worked in the construction industry. He was really good. He'd have become a site supervisor, if he hadn't vanished like that.'

CHAPTER 21

As soon as they were some distance from the shop, Vivien took out her BlackBerry and dialled the captain's direct number. After a couple of rings, he replied.

'Bellew.'

'Alan, it's Vivien. I have something.'

'Good.'

'I need you to run a really quick check.'

The captain could hear the thrill of the chase in Vivien's voice, and it infected him. 'Quicker than that, if I can. Go on.'

They were both experienced police officers. They both knew that a case like this was, more than anything, a race against time. And the man they were after had time on his side.

'Write this down.'

Vivien gave the captain a couple of seconds to find pen and paper.

'Shoot.'

'In all probability, the name of the guy in the wall is Mitch Sparrow. A witness has confirmed that he belonged to a group of bikers called the Skullbusters. They were based in Coney Island, on Surf Avenue. There should be a missing persons report filed with the 70th Precinct eighteen years ago by a woman named Carmen Montaldo or Montero. A couple of years later she found a new partner and moved to an

220

unknown address. I need to trace her.'

'OK. Give me half an hour and I'll get back to you.'

'One last thing. This Mitch Sparrow was a construction worker.'

That made the captain understandably excited. 'Holy shit.'

'Precisely. We'll need to take a look at the union registers. Can you get someone on that?'

For a whole lot of reasons, most construction companies only used people supplied by the union. If Sparrow had been a construction worker, he had to have been a union member.

'Consider it done.'

Vivien hung up.

Russell had been walking in silence beside her, listening to her end of the conversation. 'I must apologize,' he said.

'What for?'

'For earlier, I mean. The way I butted in. It was instinctive.'

Vivien had in fact been taken by surprise by the question Wade had asked Chowsky, and had regretted the fact that she hadn't thought of it first. But she was honest enough always to give credit where credit was due.

'It was a good question, a really good question.'

Russell went on to explain his motivation, as if surprised by his own intuition. 'It occurred to me that the reason this Sparrow guy ended up in a block of concrete must have been because he found out something he wasn't supposed to know, or saw something he wasn't supposed to see.' He paused for reflection. 'So I thought again about the letter I gave you.'

A shadow passed over his face, and Vivien was sure he was reliving the circumstances in which he had obtained that letter. She, too, remembered the words clearly, and could see the rough masculine handwriting.

All my life, before and after the war, I worked in the

construction industry.

She finished Russell's line of thought for him. 'And you concluded there's a strong likelihood the man who killed Sparrow and the man who wrote the letter are one and the same.'

'Precisely.'

By now they had reached the parking lot. On the other side of it, beyond a small row of trees, they could see the big tents of the amusement park and the skeletal outlines of the rollercoaster and the Parachute Tower. There weren't many cars parked here, and it occurred to Vivien that Monday probably wasn't the busiest day of the week for an amusement park, even on a beautiful if strange day like today.

She looked at her watch. 'With all that's going down I forgot about food, but now I'm starting to feel hungry. We have to wait for the captain to call back. How about a burger?'

Russell gave a vague, doubtful smile. 'I'm not eating. But I can keep you company, if you like.'

'Are you on a diet?'

The smile turned into an expression of unconditional surrender. 'The truth is, I don't have a cent on me. And my cards have been pretty much worthless for a while now. In the city there are places that'd give me credit, but here I'm in Comanche territory. Not sure how I'm going to survive.'

In spite of all she knew about Russell Wade's erratic lifestyle, Vivien couldn't help feeling sorry for him, a feeling that immediately relegated him to a place where he couldn't cause trouble.

'You've had it bad lately, I guess?'

'Everyone's feeling the pinch right now. You're a police officer, you must know about that forger they arrested in New Jersey.'

'What forger?'

222

'He's been making twenty-five-dollar bills, because these days he can't make his costs back with just twenty-dollar bills.'

In spite of herself, Vivien burst out laughing. A couple of young black men dressed in strict hip-hop style who were crossing the parking lot turned to stare at them.

She looked Russell Wade in the eyes as if seeing him for the first time. Behind the look of amusement, she saw him as someone who was used to being on the margins, and she wondered if, after a certain point in his life, it hadn't been something he'd chosen for himself rather than having it imposed on him by the world.

'How about if it's on me?'

Russell made a desolate gesture with his head. 'I'm in no position to refuse. I admit I'm so hungry, you just need to give me a jar of mayonnaise and I could eat the tyres of this car.'

'Come on, then. We still need those tyres. And standing you for lunch will cost me less than replacing them.'

They crossed the parking lot to the seashore. There was nobody on the beach, apart from a few people walking their dogs and a few indomitable joggers. The reflection of the sun and clouds on the water made for a magical interplay of air, light and shade. Vivien stopped to look at it, her face to the wind, the same wind that moved the waves and flecked them with foam. There were occasional moments in her life like this. Moments when, faced with the indifferent splendour of the world, she would have liked to sit down, close her eyes and forget everything.

And hope that everyone would forget her.

They continued along the boardwalk until they came to a stand selling hot dogs, souvlaki and hamburgers. The smell of the grilled meat, carried on the wind, had preceded and guided them. Next to it was a canopy with a wooden table and chairs under it, allowing customers to eat in the shade when the weather was hot and look out at the sea.

'What would you like?'

'Maybe a cheeseburger.'

'One or two?'

Russell gave her a sheepish look. 'Two would be great.'

Again, Vivien found herself smiling. There was no reason to, but this man seemed to have the ability at times to bring out her lighter side, in a way that could triumph over any mood.

'Okay, little orphan boy. Sit down and wait for me.'

She went up to the counter and gave the order, while Russell sat down in the shade of the canopy. Vivien soon joined him, holding a tray with the food containers and two bottles of mineral water. She pushed the cheeseburgers towards Russell and ostentatiously placed one of the bottles in front of him.

'I got this to drink. I assume you would have preferred a beer. But seeing as how you're with me, we can both consider ourselves on duty, so no alcohol.'

Russell smiled. 'A period on the wagon won't do me any harm. I think I may have overdone it a bit lately . . .' He left the sentence hanging, with all that it implied. Suddenly his expression and tone of voice changed. 'I'm sorry about all this.'

'What?'

'Forcing you to pay.'

Vivien replied with a nonchalant gesture. 'You'll be able to pay me back with dinner. My choice. If this thing works out the way we hope, you'll have a great story to tell. And great stories usually bring fame and money.'

'I'm not doing this for the money.'

He had uttered these words in a low voice, almost casually. Vivien was sure he hadn't spoken them only for her. In his mind, he was talking to someone else. Or maybe lots of people.

For a while they ate in silence, lost in their own thoughts.

'Would you like to know the truth about *The Second Passion*?'

Russell's words had come suddenly, out of nowhere. Vivien raised her head to look at him. His face was turned towards the sea, his dark hair blowing in the wind. From the tone of his voice, she realized that this was an important moment for him. It was the end of a long journey, like coming home and at last seeing a face in the mirror you're happy to call your own.

Russell did not wait for her to reply. He launched straight into his story, following the thread of a memory.

'My brother Robert was ten years older than me. He was a very special person, the kind of person who makes everything he comes in contact with his own.'

Vivien decided that the best thing to do at a moment like this was to listen.

'He was my idol. He was everyone's idol: the school, girls, his family. He didn't try to be, it was just the way he was. I don't think I've often heard in anyone the kind of pride my father had in his voice whenever he talked about Robert.'

He paused, and in that pause was the fate of the world and the meaning of his life.

'Even when I was around.'

Indirectly, words and images started to crowd into Vivien's mind. As Russell continued with his story, voices and faces from her own life slotted right in beside his.

. . . and of course Greta has been made head cheerleader. Not because she's my daughter, but really I don't see who

225

else, apart from her, could have . . .

'I tried to copy everything he did, but he was inimitable. And he was crazy. He loved taking risks, putting himself to the test. He was very competitive. Looking back now, I think I know why. It's because he was competing against himself.'

. . . Nathan Green? Greta, you mean that Nathan Green is coming to pick you up tonight? I can't believe it. Of all the boys at school, he's the most . . .

'Robert was unstoppable. He always seemed to be looking for something. And I think he found it when he became interested in photography. At first, it seemed to be just another of the thousand things he'd tried out, but it wasn't long before he showed that he had a real talent. He had this innate ability to get to the heart of things and people with his camera. Looking at his photographs, you had the feeling he saw beyond the surface, that his eyes went further than most people's.'

. . . you're beautiful, Greta. And I don't think there's ever been a more beautiful bride around here. In the whole world, I think. I'm so proud of you, my dear . . .

'The rest is well known. His love of extreme situations led gradually to his becoming one of the best-known war reporters. Wherever there was a conflict, he was there. Anyone who questioned why the heir to one of the richest families in Boston was risking his life going around the world with a Nikon in his hand just had to look at the results. His photographs were published by newspapers all over America and around the world.'

. . . Police academy, you say? Are you sure? Apart from the fact that it's a dangerous job, I don't think . . .

With an effort, Vivien wiped the images from her mind, before Greta's beautiful face appeared out of the past to

226

remind her of the pain of the present.

'And you?'

She had interrupted Russell's story with that simple question, although she couldn't explain to him that she was asking it of both of them.

'Me?'

Russell said this as if only now remembering that he, too, had a place in the story he was telling. A place of his own, which he had sought for a long time to no avail. A shy smile appeared on his face, and Vivien realized that he was smiling at his own past naivety.

'To copy him, I also started messing around with cameras. When I told my father I'd bought a few cameras, he looked like someone who sees his own money being thrown out the window. Robert, on the other hand, was really supportive. He helped and encouraged me in every way he could. And he taught me everything I know.'

Vivien noticed that, even though he had said he was hungry, he hadn't finished even one of his two cheeseburgers. She knew from personal experience how easily powerful memories could take away your appetite.

As Russell continued, Vivien had the impression that this was the first time he had talked about these things to anyone. She wondered why he had chosen her.

'I wanted to be like him. I wanted to show my father and mother and all their friends that I amounted to something, too. So when he left for Kosovo, I asked him to take me with him.'

So far, he had been looking away, but now he turned to her, with a new familiarity.

'Do you remember the war in the Balkans?'

Vivien didn't know that much about it. For a moment she

felt embarrassed by her own ignorance. 'More or less.'

'At the end of the Nineties, Kosovo was an autonomous province of former Yugoslavia, with an Albanian Muslim majority, ruled with a rod of iron by a Serb minority that suppressed the separatists who wanted to join Albania.'

Vivien was fascinated by Russell's voice, his ability to tell a story in such a way that he made the person listening part of it. It struck her that this might be his true talent. She was certain that, when this was all over, he would be able to tell a great story.

His great story.

'It all started a long time ago. Hundreds of years ago, in fact. To the north of Pristina, the capital, there's a place called Kosovo Polje. The name means 'the plain of blackbirds'. At the end of the third century, there was a battle there between a Christian army composed of a Serbian and Bosnian coalition led by a man named Lazar Hrebeljanovic and an army of the Ottoman Empire. The Christians were wiped out. The Serbs in particular suffered enormous losses. After that defeat, a monument was built on the site that I think is unique in the world. It has a curse inscribed on it, wishing any Serb who doesn't take up arms against the enemies of the Serbian people the loss of everything they possess, now and for ever. I've been there. Standing in front of that monument I realized one thing.'

He paused briefly, as if searching for the right words to sum up his idea.

'Wars end. Hate lasts for ever.'

Vivien wondered if he was again thinking of the words of the letter and all they implied.

All my life, before and after the war, I worked in the construction industry . . .

'Robert told me that in 1987 Slobodan Milošević swore

that no one would ever again lift a hand to a Serb. That declaration of intent turned him overnight into the leading light of the Serbian nationalist movement, and he became president. In 1989, exactly six hundred years after the battle of Kosovo Polje, he stood in front of that monument and made a warlike speech to more than five hundred thousand Serbs. That day, all the Albanians stayed home.'

Russell made a gesture, as if to hold time in his hand.

'We arrived at the beginning of 1999 when the repression, and the fighting between the government and the Kosovo Liberation Army, had persuaded the international community to intervene. I saw things I'll never forget. Things that Robert was so used to, he was quite impervious.'

Vivien wondered if Russell would ever be free of the ghost of Robert Wade.

'One night, just before the NATO bombardment began, all the journalists and photographers were expelled. The reasons weren't openly stated, but it was widely believed that they planned to carry out ethnic cleansing on a grand scale. The prefect of Pristina had summed it up by saying that he wished those who left a safe journey, but couldn't guarantee anything to those who stayed. Some didn't make that journey. And we were among them.'

Vivien ventured a question. 'Are you sure Robert was really a brave man?'

'I used to think so. Now I'm not so sure.'

Russell continued with his story, and there was both relief and strain in his voice.

'Robert had a friend, Tahir Bajraktari, if I remember correctly, a schoolteacher who lived on the outskirts of Pristina with his wife Lindita. Robert gave him money and before leaving the city he hid us in his house, in a cellar that you reached through a trapdoor under a carpet, at the back of the building. We could hear the sounds of fighting outside. The Kosovo Liberation Army would attack, strike, and then vanish into thin air.'

Vivien had the impression that if she had looked deep in his eyes she would have seen the images he was reliving.

'I was terrified. Robert did everything he could to calm me. He stayed with me for a while, but the call of what was happening outside was too strong to resist. A couple of days later, with machine-gun fire still echoing on the streets, he left our hiding place with his pockets full of rolls of film. That was the last time I saw him alive.'

Russell picked up the bottle of water and drank deeply from it.

'When he didn't come back I went out to look for him. Even now I don't know how I summoned up the courage. I walked through the deserted streets. Pristina was a ghost town. The people had run away, leaving some of the houses with their doors open and the lights on. I reached the centre, and after a while found him. Robert was lying on the sidewalk, in a little tree-lined square, surrounded by other bodies. He had been hit in the chest by machine-gun fire, still clutching his camera in his hand. I grabbed the camera and ran back quickly to hide. I wept for Robert and I wept for myself, until I didn't even have the strength to do that. Then the NATO bombardment began. I don't know how long I hid there, listening to the bombs fall, without washing, rationing the food I had, until I realized that the voices coming from outside were speaking English. That was when I realized I was safe and came out.'

He drank again, greedily, as if the memory of his tears had dried every trace of liquid from his body.

'When I managed to develop the photographs in Robert's

camera and took a look at them, I was struck by one shot in particular. I immediately realized that it was an exceptional photograph, the kind a photographer spends his whole life chasing after.'

Vivien remembered the image well. Everyone knew it. It had become one of the most famous photographs in the world.

It showed a man being hit by a bullet in the heart. He was wearing dark pants, but his chest and feet were bare. The impact of the bullets had made the blood spray out from him and at the same time had raised him off the ground. By some weird chance – the kind that could make a war reporter's fortune – he had been caught by the camera with his arms outspread and one foot in front of the other, the body hanging in a position that recalled the figure of Christ on the cross. Even the man's gaunt face, long hair and small beard fitted the traditional Christian iconography. The title of the photograph, *The Second Passion*, had come almost as a matter of course.

'I got swept up in something I can't explain. Envy, anger at Robert's ability to capture the moment, ambition. Greed, maybe. I showed the photograph to the *New York Times* and told them I'd taken it. The rest you know. I won a Pulitzer Prize with that photograph. Unfortunately, the brother of the dead man had seen Robert taking it and told the newspapers. That's how everyone found out the photograph wasn't mine.'

He paused, before coming to a conclusion that had cost him ten years of his life.

'And if I have to be honest, I'm not at all sure I was sorry.'

Vivien had instinctively placed a hand on Russell's arm. When she realized, she pulled it away, hoping he hadn't noticed.

'What did you do after that?'

'I survived by accepting any work I could find. Fashion articles, technical photographs, even weddings. Mostly I drew on my family's money a few too many times.'

Vivien was searching for the right words to lift the burden of that confession from his shoulders, but just then her cellphone rang. She saw the name on the display: *Bellew*.

She took the call. 'Hello, Alan.'

'A real stroke of luck. I called the head of the 70th and asked him to run a check. When I asked him if he could put every man available on it, he thought I was crazy.'

'I can imagine. Did they find anything?'

'The woman's name is Carmen Montesa. When she moved, she wisely went to the police and told them she was moving. We checked out the address. It's in Queens, and we also have an active phone number registered to her.'

'Alan, you're quite a man.'

'The first woman who told me that was the midwife who brought me into the world. Join the line. Keep up the good work, and stay in touch.'

Vivien stood up and Russell did the same. He had realized that the break was over and it was time to move.

'Anything new?'

'Let's hope so. For now we have the woman. Let's take it from there.'

She wiped her mouth, threw the paper napkin on the table and headed for the car. Russell cast a melancholy glance at the food he had barely touched. Then he followed Vivien, leaving behind him a story that, however hard he tried, he suspected would never end.

CHAPTER 22

Carmen Montesa loved numbers.

She had always loved them, since she was a little girl. At elementary school she was the best in her class. Working with numbers gave her a feeling of order, of peace. She liked putting them in little squares on the paper, each little graphic sign representing a quantity, placed side by side or in a column, all in her childish but precise handwriting. And, unlike many of her school friends, she found it a very creative subject. In her little girl's mind, she had even assigned colours to numbers. Four was yellow and five was blue. Three was green and nine was brown. Zero was a clear, immaculate white.

Even now, sitting in her old leather armchair, she had a Sudoku magazine lying on her lap. Unfortunately not much had remained of those girlish fantasies. Numbers had become black marks on white paper in a periodical, nothing more. Over time, the colours had disappeared and she had discovered that, applied to the lives of people, zero wasn't a nice shade.

She would have liked a different life. She would have liked to study, go to college, choose a subject connected with numbers that she could then make her career. Circumstances had decided otherwise.

In a movie she had seen once, one of the characters had said that life is very difficult in New York if you're Mexican and poor. When she had heard that, she had agreed inside. Compared with most girls in her situation, she'd had one advantage: her beauty. And that had helped her a lot. She hadn't had to compromise herself, although over the years she'd had to tolerate a few too many straying hands, a few too many bodies rubbing up against hers. There was just the one occasion when, to make sure of a place at nursing school, she had given the director a blow job. When she had seen her fellow students and noticed how many of them were pretty, she'd realized she hadn't been the only one to take that particular entrance test.

Then Mitch had come on the scene.

She moved aside the magazine when she realized that a tear had fallen onto the Sudoku diagram. The number she had just written, the five, was now surrounded by a bluish halo, making it too round and too similar to zero.

It isn't possible – after all these years I'm still crying . . .

Calling herself a fool, she put the magazine down on the low table beside her. But she let the tears come, and with them the memories. They were all she had left of a happy time, maybe the one true bright spot in her existence. From the moment she'd met him, Mitch had changed her life in every way.

There was before, and there was after.

With him she had found true love, discovered what love could be and do. He had given her the greatest gift in the world: he had made her feel loved and desired and a woman and a mother. All the things he had taken back from her when, from one day to the next, he had vanished into thin air, leaving her alone with a small son to raise. Carmen's mother had always hated him. When it was clear that her son-in-law wouldn't be coming back, she hadn't made any overt comment, but the words *I told you so* were written all over her face. Carmen had tolerated her veiled allusions because she needed her mother to look after the child when she was at work, but she had never agreed to go back to her parents' home. She would spend her evenings in her – their – apartment with Nick, who was the spitting image of his father, reading stories and watching cartoons and leafing through biker magazines.

Then, one day, she had met Elias. He was a Chicano like her, an OK guy, who worked as a cook in a restaurant in the East Village. They had gone out together for a while, just as friends. Elias knew her situation – he was a gentle, respectful man, and it was obvious from a mile away that he was in love with her. But he had never asked her for anything, had never even tried to touch her.

She felt comfortable with him and they talked a lot. Nick liked him. She didn't love him, but when he had suggested they live together, after much hesitation she had agreed. They had obtained a mortgage and bought a little house in a working-class area of Queens that Elias had insisted on putting in her name.

Carmen smiled through her tears at the memory of that tender, innocent man.

Poor Elias. They had made love for the first time in their house. He was gentle and shy and inexperienced, and she'd had to take him by the hand like a child and show him, step by step, how to please her. A month later she had discovered she was pregnant, and exactly nine months after their first night together Allison was born.

So then she had a family. A son, a daughter and a partner who loved her, all sitting together at the same table. She wasn't with the man she secretly wished was still there, and this wasn't the wildly happy life she'd known with Mitch. A quiet life was what it was, the kind that, when you had it and were content with it, made you realize you were starting to

235

get old.

Unfortunately, it didn't seem to be her destiny to keep hold of a man.

Elias had gone, too, carried away by an acute form of leukaemia that had consumed him in a short time. She still remembered the grim expression on the face of Dr Myra Collins, an internist at the hospital where she was working then, who had taken her aside and explained what the results of the first tests meant. To Carmen's ears, those clear, courteous words had already sounded like words of condolence.

And once again, she had been left alone. She had decided that was how she was going to live her life from now on. Alone with her children, just the three of them. Nick was a gentle, lovable boy and Allison a girl with a very strong character. Then one day Nick had confessed to her that he was gay. Carmen had already guessed that, but had been waiting for him to bring up the subject. As far as she was concerned, it changed nothing. Nick was and would always be her son. She considered herself a fairly intelligent woman and too much of a loving mother to allow a sexual preference to jeopardize the respect she had for him as a person. He had spent one whole afternoon talking about the humiliations he had suffered and the torments he had gone through before coming to terms with what he was, in a community where machismo was a way of life for most young men. Then he had told her that he and his companion would be going to live in the West Village.

Carmen stood up, went to the kitchen, took a sheet of paper from the roll on the worktop, and wiped her eyes. Now that she came to think of it, the full line spoken by the boy in that movie was that it isn't easy to live in New York if you're poor, Mexican, and gay.

She opened the refrigerator and poured herself a glass of apple juice.

Enough crying, she told herself.

She had shed sufficient tears in her life. Although Nick's life hadn't been easy at first, he was an assistant in a boutique in SoHo now, he was in love and he was happy. She, too, had a good job, she didn't have too many money worries and for years she'd had a discreet relationship – no strings attached – with her boss, Dr Bronson. It could have been thought an acceptable life. True, Allison had turned from a lively child into a difficult teenager. Every now and again, without warning, she would stay out all night. Carmen knew she was with her boyfriend when he had his parents' house to himself. Still, she would have preferred to be told when that happened. She was sure that, once they'd got past the inevitable generational conflicts, their relationship would get better with time. Over the years, Carmen had learned to understand people but, like everyone, she'd never really learned to understand herself or those she was emotionally involved with. Sometimes, she suspected that all her certainties about Allison were just self-delusion.

She was about to go back to her armchair and her Sudoku when the doorbell rang. She wondered who it could be. Her few friends rarely visited her without phoning first. And anyway, at this hour of the day they were all at work. She left the kitchen and walked down the corridor to the front door.

Framed in the glass-fronted door, visible through the blind, were the silhouettes of two people.

When she opened the door she found herself facing a determined-looking young woman, the kind who are always too busy to remember they're also beautiful, and a tall man of about thirty-five, with dark hair, intense black eyes and two days' growth of beard that gave him an engagingly bohemian look. If she were still young, Carmen thought, she'd have found the girl attractive enough to be considered a rival and the man sexy enough to be considered a quarry. But these were the foolish illusions of memory, a game she played with herself every time she met new people, whether young or old, but would never follow through on. At her age, she had no desire to play the game, because life had taught her how it was going to end in most cases. All things considered, it boiled down to numbers, yet again.

'Mrs Carmen Montesa?'

'Yes.'

The young woman held up her shield. 'My name's Vivien Light. I'm a detective with the 13th Precinct in Manhattan.' She gave her time to check her photograph, then indicated the man beside her. 'This is Russell Wade, my partner.'

Carmen felt a pang of anxiety. Her heart started beating faster, as always happened to her when she felt emotional. 'What's the matter? Is it Allison? Has something happened to my daughter?'

'No, don't worry. I just need to have a word with you.'

The relief was like balm to the soul. She was too excitable, she knew. She couldn't help it – it was her nature. At work she was admirably cool and efficient, but when she went back to being a woman and mother she became vulnerable again.

'All right,' she said, relaxed now.

The young woman smiled and pointed inside the house. 'I'm afraid this is going to take a while. Can we come in?'

Carmen stood aside, an apologetic expression on her face. 'I'm sorry. I was so relieved, I forgot my manners. Of course you can come in.'

She held the door open. As the man passed her, it struck Carmen that he smelled nice. The woman, on the other hand, smelled of vanilla and leather. As she closed the door, she wondered what they would have thought of her if they could have heard what had passed through her mind.

She went past them and led them into the living room. She heard the young woman's voice behind her.

'I hope we're not bothering you.'

Carmen was surprised that a police officer would apologize. Usually they were quite rude. Especially when they were gringos like these two and you were Hispanic. That was when she knew they hadn't come to her house bearing good news.

They were all in the living room now. Carmen turned to look at the young woman so that she could see the words she was about to say weren't simply said out of politeness.

'No bother. Today's my day off. I was enjoying a lazy afternoon.'

'What kind of work do you do?'

As she was about to reply, she wondered why a half-smile had appeared fleetingly on the man's face when he heard the young woman ask that question.

'I'm a nurse. For a long time I worked at the Bellevue, in Manhattan. Now I'm the OR assistant to a plastic surgeon named Dr Bronson.' She pointed to the couch behind the two visitors. 'Please, make yourselves at home. Would you like anything? Coffee?'

She sat down in the armchair only after the other two had settled on the couch.

'No thanks, we're fine,' the young woman said with a smile.

Carmen had the impression she was dealing with a person

who, when she wanted, knew how to put other people at their ease. Maybe because she was usually that way herself. The man, on the other hand, seemed a bit more fidgety. He didn't look like a police officer. He didn't have that no-nonsense air they usually carried around with them as an emblem of their power.

She saw Vivien looking around, letting her gaze wander over the walls, the wallpaper, the kitchen counter glimpsed through the door to the right, the little dining room at the other end of the corridor. It was a quick but keen visual tour.

'It's very nice here.'

Carmen smiled. 'You're very kind and very diplomatic. It's the house of a woman who lives on her salary. Really nice houses are different. But I'm fine here.'

She stopped and waited, looking intently at the young woman. Vivien realized that the pleasantries were over and she had to get to the reason for her visit.

'Eighteen years ago you reported your husband, Mitch Sparrow, missing.'

It wasn't a question – it was a statement. Carmen was caught off guard. Especially as she'd only just been thinking about Mitch. In addition to which she would never have imagined that the story was still of any interest to anyone else but her.

'Yes, that's right.'

'Can you tell us what happened?'

'There isn't much to tell. One day he left home and never came back. I waited until it was dark, and then late at night I called the police.'

'And what did they find out?'

'He'd been at work, as always. He'd left the site where he was working at the usual hour, but never came home. My

240

husband was a construction worker.'

Carmen had the impression that the two of them already knew that last detail.

'What kind of man was your husband?'

'A very special person. When I met him all he thought about was his bike. And girls. But when we met it was love at first sight.'

'No problems, no quarrels, nothing that might have made you think of—'

Carmen interrupted her. 'Another woman, you mean?'

She had understood where the young detective was going with her question. Looking at her, she also had the impression she already knew the answer, that she had only asked the question because it was part of her job.

But Carmen thought it was important to tell her how things had really been between her and her husband. Especially after what she had been thinking before these two people arrived and dredged up the story.

'Believe me, Mitch and I and were in love, and he was crazy about his son. I'm a woman and I know when a man is distracted by other thoughts. Desire is the first thing that goes. Mitch thought about no one but me, day and night, especially night. And I felt the same about him.'

As another woman, Carmen knew Vivien would understand what she was talking about. Indeed, the detective seemed satisfied with what she'd said and changed the subject.

'Can you confirm that your husband had a tattoo on his right shoulder?'

'Yes. It was a pirate flag. You know, with the skull and crossbones. There were words underneath it, but I can't for the moment remember what they were.'

'*The only flag*, maybe?'

'That's it. It was the symbol of those weird biker friends of his. We used to live in Coney Island and Mitch—'

'Yes, we know about the Skullbusters,' Vivien interrupted her, gently but firmly.

Carmen remembered that she had reported her husband missing to the 70th Precinct. She wondered what could have happened for the police to come here from a precinct in Manhattan.

'Did your husband have any broken bones?' the detective continued, in the same professional tone, forceful but at the same time reassuring.

'Yes. He fell off his bike once. Broke his humerus and tibia, I seem to remember. That was how we met. He was admitted to the hospital where I worked. When he was discharged, he made me write my phone number on the plaster. We spoke often on the phone and when he came back to take off the armour, as he called it, he asked me out.'

'One last thing. Where was your husband working when he disappeared?'

Carmen made an effort to call up long-buried memories. 'His company was renovating a building in Manhattan, around Third Avenue, I think.'

Vivien was silent for a moment, as if searching for the right words. There are words people say, it occurred to Carmen, which are like mathematical equations. However you change the order of the words, the result remains the same. What Vivien said next confirmed that fleeting thought.

'Mrs Sparrow, I'm afraid I have some bad news for you. We've found a body hidden in a cavity wall of a building on the corner of 23rd Street and Third Avenue. In the light of what you've just told us, we have reason to believe that it's your husband.'

Carmen felt something come and go simultaneously, like a long-awaited wave that only makes the boat sway before sinking back into the open sea. In spite of what she'd said earlier, after so much time spent speculating, now that there was certainty tears started to run down her cheeks. She bowed her head and hid her face in her hands. When she looked up again, straight at Vivien, Carmen had the feeling they would be her last tears.

'I'm sorry.'

She got up and went into the kitchen. When she came back she had a pack of paper handkerchiefs in her hand. As she sat down, she asked the question that had suddenly occurred to her.

'Do you have any idea who . . .'

Vivien shook her head. 'I'm afraid not. That's why we're here, to see if we can get a clearer idea. Even identification is very difficult after all this time. We'll only know for sure after the DNA tests.'

'I have his pony tail.'

'I'm sorry?'

Carmen got up from the armchair. 'I won't be a minute.'

She walked across the room and out into the corridor, where there was a door beneath the stairs. She knew where what she was looking for was kept. She remembered everything to do with her only husband.

Her only man.

And there it was, when she opened the door, a trunk full of things low in price but big in value. She snapped open the lock and lifted the lid. What she was looking for was on top of everything else, wrapped in a light cloth. She took out the package,

243

removed the cloth, and looked at the object for a moment. There was a bitter taste in her mouth, the taste of the tenderness this strange relic aroused in her. She also took out an old photograph, from around the period when Mitch had disappeared.

Then she went back to the living room and showed her two visitors what she had brought with her. It was a dark wooden frame inside which, lying on a green cloth under glass, was a braid of fair hair.

Carmen smiled at the memory.

'When Mitch started work,' she said, speaking with the same clarity with which she was reliving the episode, 'he cut his hair, which he used to wear in a pony tail. Before he did that, I gathered it into a braid and had it framed as a souvenir. You can take this. If you can find any of the bulbs, you can get DNA from hair.' Then she handed Vivien the photograph. 'And this is a photograph of my husband. One of the last.'

Carmen saw a hint of self-satisfaction on Vivien's face. She had noticed that, all this time, the man had remained silent, looking at her intensely with those dark eyes that seemed to dig deep inside her. She had told herself that, of the two, the woman was the one who called the shots.

Vivien took the photograph and placed it beside her on the couch. 'A couple more things, if you don't mind.'

She took an object from the inside pocket of her jacket. She held it out and Carmen saw that it was a document holder.

'Did this belong to your husband?'

Carmen took it in her hands and examined it carefully. 'No, I really don't think so. It isn't his style. He only had things with the Harley brand name on them.'

'Have you ever seen this person?'

Carmen looked at the photograph Vivien handed her, a

244

photograph of a dark-haired young man and a big black cat posing for the camera.

'No, never.'

As Vivien put the objects back in her pocket, Carmen had the impression that what she had just said had disappointed the detective but not surprised her.

'As far as you know, did anything strange, anything out of the ordinary ever happen in your husband's work? Anything he may have told you about, maybe not thinking it was that important.' She gave Carmen time to think, then said to encourage her, 'For obvious reasons I can't tell you anything, but I want you to know that it's extremely important.'

There was a hint of sadness in her tone, which conveyed a sense of anxiety to Carmen.

She thought it over for a while, then made a resigned gesture with her hands. 'No. Mitch may have been wild in the past, but we led a quiet life. Every now and again he saw his old friends, the Skullbusters I mean, but apart from a couple of nights when he came back home with a few too many beers under his belt, he was a hard worker, always did what he was told. At home he didn't talk much about his work. He played with Nick all the time.'

Vivien was about to reply when they were interrupted by the noise of a key in the lock and the front door opening. They stopped talking and listened to footsteps in the corridor that seemed more eloquent than words. Carmen's daughter appeared in the doorway of the living room.

She had short hair made spiky with gel, heavily made-up eyes, purple lipstick and black half-gloves on her hands. Her jeans seemed a couple of sizes too big for her and she had on a short T-shirt that left her pierced navel exposed.

She didn't seem surprised to find her mother in the company of two strangers. She looked smugly at the strangers, then at her mother.

'You didn't have to call the cops. You know I always come back.'

'They aren't—'

'They have cop written all over their faces,' the girl said, more bored than upset, and looking away as she put her key in her bag. 'You think I was born yesterday?' Then she looked at her mother again. 'Anyway, the bad girl's come home again, so your two bloodhounds can go back where they came from. And tell them if they don't have a search warrant, they can't take anything from this house, not even a tablecloth.'

Carmen saw a shadow descend over Vivien's eyes. As if she already knew this situation, as if she had already lived through it before.

'We aren't here for you,' Vivien said to Allison, forcing herself to be patient. 'We're here because we had some news for your mother.'

But Allison had already turned her back on them, as if the conversation didn't interest her. She disappeared round the corner, leaving only the sound of her voice.

'Who the hell cares?' she said, as she climbed the stairs to her room. Before too long, cutting through their silence and embarrassment, the noise of a door being slammed came from upstairs.

Carmen didn't know what to say. It was Vivien who spoke first. The scene she had just witnessed seemed to inspire a new familiarity in her.

'Carmen, can I go up and say a few words to your daughter?'

Carmen was startled for a moment. 'Yes, I suppose so.'

'I'm afraid they may be rather rough words,' Vivien added.

246

'I see. Well, I don't think they'll do her any harm.'

Vivien stood up.

Carmen gave her a small, knowing smile. 'First room on the right, at the top of the stairs.'

Vivien disappeared behind a corner, knowing that what she was about to say was something it was right to say to that person at that moment.

The man who had introduced himself as Russell assumed an expression of slightly forced irony. Up until now he had remained silent but when he spoke, his voice was exactly as Carmen had expected it to be.

'Vivien is a very determined woman.'

'So I see.'

'And also very direct, when she wants to be.'

With a touch of self-satisfaction, Carmen agreed. 'I'm sure she is.'

They sat there in silence until Vivien returned. She had not been gone for long. Calmly, she sat down again on the couch.

'It's done. She'll have slightly red cheeks for the next few hours, but she ought to have understood the way things are.'

She took out her business card and placed it on top of the Sudoku magazine. Carmen saw her pick up the felt-tip that was next to it and write something on the back. Then she leaned towards her and held out the card.

'This is my number. On the back is my cell number. If you remember anything connected with your husband, or have any more problems with your daughter, call me.'

Vivien took the frame and stood up, and Russell immediately did the same, a sign that their visit was over. Carmen walked them to the door. As they were about to leave, she placed a hand on Vivien's arm.

'Vivien.'

'Yes?'

'Thank you. It's something I should have done myself a long time ago, but thanks all the same.'

Vivien smiled and shrugged, downplaying what had happened. But at the same time there was a tiny gleam in her eyes. 'Don't mention it. Goodbye, Carmen.'

Carmen waited until they were at the foot of the steps and then closed the door. She walked back to the living room, thinking over the whole story.

Mitch, damn you, for however long it lasted I hope I made you realize how much I loved you . . .

She knew that the difficult part would come that night, when she had turned out the lights and found herself alone with her ghosts. For the moment she decided to switch on the TV and ask the world to keep her company.

When the screen lit up, there was a news item about Saturday's explosion on 10th Street in Manhattan. The images of destruction reminded her of something. She leaped to her feet, ran to the door and opened it. Russell and Vivien were still outside on the sidewalk opposite, standing by a car, as if they had stopped to discuss the outcome of the visit.

She waved at them to attract their attention, and called out, 'Vivien!'

The detective and her partner turned their heads in her direction.

'What is it, Carmen?'

'I just remembered something. It was a long time ago, and my memory—'

An excitable Vivien interrupted her with a touch of impatience in her voice. 'Go on.'

Carmen was embarrassed. For the first time in her life she

was playing a role in a police investigation, and she was afraid of looking foolish or saying something they would think was stupid.

'I don't know if this is important at all, but I just remembered that a long time ago the company Mitch worked for, Newborn Brothers, renovated a house on North Shore, Long Island. The house of an ex-soldier, I seem to remember. A major or a colonel, something like that.'

Vivien pressed her. 'And?'

Carmen paused again, then at last came out with what she had to say. 'About a year after the end of the work, the house blew up.'

Even though it was dusk and the light was dimming, Carmen saw, as clear as if it was day, the young detective's face turn pale.

CHAPTER 23

Through the car window Russell and Vivien saw Carmen Montesa slowly close the house door, a lonely desolate figure trying in vain to keep outside the door something that would surely get in through the window. At night and with teeth bared. A moment later Vivien had already picked up the car phone and was punching in the captain's number. Sitting beside her, Russell counted three rings before the answer came.

'Bellew.'

Vivien came straight to the point. 'Alan, we have something.'

The question that followed took Vivien by surprise. 'Is Wade there with you?'

Vivien instinctively turned to look at Russell. 'Sure.'

'Can you put me on speakerphone?'

'Sure.'

'Good. Both of you need to hear what I have to say.'

Vivien was bewildered. She found this procedure highly unusual. Though of course this whole business was unusual. Even crazy. Then she told herself that, in line with the promise he had made, the captain must have decided to include Russell in their conversations. Or maybe he had something to say that particularly concerned him. Vivien pressed a button.

'You're on.'

The captain's voice came through the car speakers, loud and clear. 'Tell me what you have first.'

Vivien updated the captain on their progress. 'I'm almost sure the guy in the wall is this Mitch Sparrow I told you about. I may even have something that can be used as the basis for a DNA test. But we have to move quickly.'

'Let me have what you've got, and consider it done. Anything else?'

Russell was fascinated by the laconic but clear way the two police officers communicated. They spoke the same language, which they'd learned by experience.

'Years ago,' Vivien continued, excited, 'Sparrow worked for a small construction company called Newborn Brothers. His wife just told me. They did renovation work on a house at North Shore, Long Island. And listen to this: apparently the house belonged to an ex-soldier and one year after the end of the work it blew up. According to the experts it wasn't an accident, but a bomb. What do you think?'

'I think you found yourself a good lead.'

Vivien continued, certain that her chief was taking notes at the other end. 'We have to check out Newborn Brothers and the company that did the building on the Lower East Side, and look through the personnel records, if they still exist. See if there was anyone who worked on both buildings. And find out the names of the heads of the company.'

'I'll get the men on it straight away.'

The captain changed tone. Now it was his turn to update them.

'I've been moving in the meantime. I had a talk with Commissioner Willard. A private talk, if you know what I mean.'

'Perfectly.'

'When I showed him the letter, he almost jumped out of his chair. But, as I expected, he distanced himself and started to stall. He said he thought it was a pretty slim lead, though of course we can't rule out anything. He wants to have the letter examined by a criminologist or a psychologist, but someone outside the police or the FBI. Someone who'll keep it hush-hush, obviously. He's looking at a list of names. He agreed that for the moment we should proceed with caution, keeping it strictly between ourselves, as agreed. It's a tricky situation for everyone. People have died. Others may be in danger. As far as we're concerned, we may end up praised to the skies, or we may be out on our ears. I'm talking about us, Vivien.'

Russell had the impression that Vivien had expected these words. Her only reaction was to say, 'Received.'

'Wade, can you hear me?'

Russell instinctively moved his head into the area he supposed the microphone to be. 'Yes, captain.'

'I didn't tell the commissioner about our arrangement. If anything gets out before this thing is over, your life will be worse than your worst nightmares. Do I make myself clear?'

'Very clear, captain.'

This meant that from now on their lives were inextricably linked, for better or worse. When Vivien next spoke, it was in a calm, detached voice. Russell admired her self-control, something he himself was quite lacking in.

'Good. We've established that. Any other news?'

The captain's tone retuned to being the professional tone of a police officer examining the elements of an investigation. The emotional break was over. They were getting back to work.

'The good news is that, if we need it, we have the whole of the NYPD at our disposal. And the power to drag anyone from their beds at any time of the night, starting with the commissioner.'

There was a noise of papers being leafed through.

'I have here in front of me the results of the first tests. The experts think they've identified the kind of primer used. It's a simple but very ingenious device, which emits a series of radio impulses at different frequencies and in a specific sequence. Given all the radio waves in this city, this stops the mines from exploding at a chance signal.'

Russell had a question that had been nagging at him since this crazy story had started. He again intervened in the conversation.

'The building that blew up was built some years ago. How come the bombs were still working after all this time?'

That question was one that the captain must also have asked himself, because he let out a sigh before answering. In spite of his experience, it was a small mark of his incredulity at the genius of madness.

'No batteries. The son of a bitch connected the primer to the building's current. It may be that in the course of years some deteriorated and are no longer active, but God knows how many places the man put that shit."

There was a strange sound, and for a moment Russell was afraid that they had been cut off. Then Bellew's voice again spread through the car.

'You're doing great work, guys. I wanted to tell you that. Great work.'

Vivien took over again and ended the conversation. 'I'll wait to hear from you, then. Call me as soon as you have anything.'

'As fast as I can.'

Vivien hung up and for a few moments only the muted

noise of the traffic competed with their thoughts in the silence of the car. Russell looked out at the street and the lights shining through the dark. On this day without memory, time had preceded them and the darkness had caught them almost by surprise.

It was Russell who spoke first, with words that reciprocated the trust Bellew had placed in him. 'Do you want the original?'

Distracted by her thoughts, Vivien didn't immediately grasp what he was saying. 'What original?'

'You were right when you accused me of coming to you with a photocopy of the paper I got from Ziggy. The real one I put in an envelope and sent to my home address. It's a system he taught me. I think it's in my mailbox right now.'

'Where do you live?'

Russell was pleased that Vivien had made no other comment. 'Twenty-ninth Street, between Park and Madison.'

Vivien drove in silence along Queens Boulevard and across the Queensboro Bridge. They emerged onto Manhattan at 60th Street, turned left onto Park Avenue and drove south, at the mercy of the traffic.

'Here we are.'

Vivien's voice reached his ears like a memory and Russell realised that he had dozed off. The car was now parked on 29th at the corner of Park, just across from his building.

Vivien saw him rubbing his eyes. 'Are you tired?'

'Afraid so.'

'You'll have time to sleep when this is all over.'

Without saying that what he was hoping for was not sleep, Russell took advantage of the green light and crossed to the other side of the street. When he got to the entrance to his building, he pushed open the glass door into the lobby. The building, like all those of a certain standing in New York, had the services of a doorman twenty-four hours a day. He approached the doorman behind his desk and was surprised, at this hour, to find Zef, the building manager, with him. Zef was a friendly man of Albanian origin, who had worked hard to get to his current position. Russell had always been on good terms with him. He was convinced that Zef, for all the dubious activities he'd been a witness to, was secretly his only fan.

'Good evening, Mr Wade.'

Russell not only led a wild life, but was also a tad absent-minded. That was why, after losing several bunches, he always left his keys with the doorman. Usually whichever of them was on duty would hand them over as soon as he arrived, without even needing to be asked. The fact that this didn't happen now told him that something unusual was going on. His suspicions aroused, Russell turned to his friend.

'Hi, Zef. Have you lost the keys this time?'

'I'm afraid there's a problem, Mr Wade.'

The man's words, not to mention his expression, made him even more suspicious. The thought that now crossed his mind wasn't so much a conjecture as a certainty, but he asked the question anyway. 'What problem?'

The man's embarrassment was obvious on his face, in spite of which he had the decency to look him in the eyes. 'A representative of Philmore Inc. came here today. With him was a lawyer bearing a letter from the executive director addressed to me. And one for you.'

'And what was in them?'

'The one addressed to you I didn't open, obviously. I put it with the rest of your mail.'

'And the other?'

'The one addressed to me says that the company apartment

255

in this building is no longer at your disposal. With immediate effect. So I can't give you the keys.'

'What about my things?'

Zef shrugged his shoulders in a gesture that meant: Don't shoot me, I'm only the piano player. Russell felt like laughing.

'The person in question went up to the apartment and put all your personal effects into suitcases. They're over there, in the storage closet.'

He seemed really upset by what had happened, and, given their relations in the past, Russell had no reason to doubt that he was genuine. In the meantime, the doorman had fetched the mail and placed it on the marble desktop. Russell recognized the logo of Philmore Inc. on an unstamped yellow envelope. He took it and opened it. When he unfolded the sheet of paper, he immediately recognized his father's handwriting.

Russell,

Any rope, however resistant, finally snaps if you pull on it too hard. Mine snapped some time ago. It was only your mother's gentle soul that grabbed the ends and kept them joined, providing you – without my knowledge – with money and the apartment you've been living in until today. After your last stunt, I fear that even her strength is exhausted. She has found herself faced with a choice: whether to maintain relations with a man she married some decades ago and who in the course of time has given her a thousand proofs of his love, or with a son who is beyond redemption, a son who has never, even at the best of times, been anything but a severe embarrassment to this family.

The choice, although painful, was freely made.

To use language you can understand: From now on, kid, you're on your own.

Jenson Wade

P.S. If you had the good taste to change the name you bear, it would be a gesture greatly appreciated by us.

As Russell put it, when he finished reading, 'So my bastard of a father has kicked me out.'

Zef assumed a fitting expression, which even included an embarrassed half-smile. 'Well, I would have phrased it differently, but that's more or less the idea.'

For a moment, Russell was lost in thought. In spite of everything, he didn't feel like blaming his father for his decision. On the contrary, he was surprised it had been so long in coming. He wouldn't have given himself all that time.

'It's all right, Zef, it doesn't matter.'

He took the envelopes from the desk and put them in the inside pocket of his jacket.

'Can I leave the bags here for now?'

'As you wish, Mr Wade.'

'Good. I'll pick them up later. And I'll swing by every now and again to see if there's any mail.'

'You know I'm always pleased to see you.'

'OK, then. Goodbye my friend.'

Russell turned and headed for the door.

Zef's voice held him back. 'One last thing, Mr Wade.'

Russell turned and saw Zef leave his post and cross the lobby. He placed himself between Russell and the doorman and said in a low, conspiratorial voice, 'I assume your situation is a little precarious right now.'

Russell had always been amused by the man's decorous language. This time was no exception.

257

'I think that pretty much sums it up.'

'Well, Mr Wade, if you'll allow me . . .'

Zef held out his hand as if in farewell, and when Russell shook it he felt the thickness of a few banknotes in the palm of his hand.

'Zef, look, I can't—'

'It's only five hundred dollars, Mr Wade,' Zef interrupted him, with a knowing look. 'It'll help you to keep going. Don't repay me until you're back on your feet.'

Russell withdrew his hand and put the money in his jacket pocket. He accepted it for what it meant. To him and to the person who had offered it to him so generously and so discreetly. At this major turning point in his life, the only tangible help he had received came from a near-stranger. He put a hand on Zef's shoulder.

'You're a good man, my friend. I promise you'll get it back. With interest.'

'I'm sure I will, Mr Wade.'

Russell looked Zef in the eyes, seeing in them a sincerity and trust that he, for one, was very far from possessing. He turned his back on Zef and walked out onto the street. Here, he stopped for a moment to think again about what had just happened. He put his hand in his pocket to make sure it was all true, that people like that still existed.

At that moment, out of the corner of his eye, he saw a movement behind him. A hand reached out of the semi-darkness and grabbed his arm. He turned his head to the right and found himself confronted with a tall, solidly built black man, dressed all in black. On the other side of the street, a large dark car switched on its lights and pulled away from the kerb. It stopped in front of them and, at the same time, as if the two things had been synchronized, the back door opened.

258

Instinctively Russell looked around, trying to figure out what was happening. His guardian angel thought he was looking to escape, and saw fit to underline the reality of the situation.

'Get in the car. Don't do anything stupid. It'll be better for you, believe me.'

Through the open door, Russell saw the thick legs of a man sitting in the back seat. With a sigh he got in the car and sat down, while the big guy who had so politely invited him to get in took his place in the front.

Russell greeted the man who was sitting next to him in the tone of an Egyptian greeting a plague. 'Hello, LaMarr.'

The usual sardonic smile played over the fat man's lips. His well-cut suit couldn't compensate for his graceless figure, nor did his dark glasses provide any kind of protection against his coarse-grained features.

'Hello, photographer. You don't seem yourself. Anything bothering you?'

As the car pulled away from the kerb, Russell turned to look through the rear window. If Vivien had seen what had happened, she hadn't had time to intervene. She might be following them. But he hadn't seen any other car move out from the kerb on the other side of Park Avenue.

He turned to LaMarr again. 'What's bothering me is that you're still using the wrong deodorant. Sitting next to you would make anybody's eyes water.'

'Good joke. Give the man a great big hand.'

LaMarr was still smiling. He signalled to the man in the front, who leaned over and punched Russell in the face. For a moment, the noise of flesh on flesh was the only sound inside the car.

Russell felt a thousand hot little needles puncture his cheek. A yellow bulb danced in front of his eyes.

Nonchalantly, LaMarr put a hand on his shoulder. 'As you can see, my boys have kind of a strange way of showing their appreciation of humour. Got any more jokes like that?'

Russell sank resignedly into his seat. In the meantime, the car had turned onto Madison and was now heading uptown. At the wheel was a guy with a bald head and the same build, Russell estimated, as the man who had just given him such tender loving care.

'What do you want, LaMarr?'

'I told you. Money. I'm not usually involved in collecting, but with you I want to make an exception. It's not every day I get to rub shoulders with a celebrity, which is what you are. Not to mention the fact that you're really pissing me off.'

With a nod of the head, he indicated the man who had just hit Russell.

'It'd be a pleasure for me to sit in the front row and see you go a few rounds with Jimbo.'

'There's no point. Right now I don't have your fifty thousand dollars.'

LaMarr shook his large head. His double chin wobbled slightly, shiny with sweat in the light from outside. 'Wrong. You don't seem any better at math than poker. It's sixty thousand, remember?'

Russell was about to reply but held back. He preferred to avoid another encounter with Jimbo's hand. His first experience of that hadn't been one that left him feeling nostalgic.

'Where are we going?'

'You'll see. Somewhere quiet, where we can have a man-to-man talk.'

Silence fell in the car. LaMarr didn't seem inclined to give any further explanation. Russell didn't need any. He knew perfectly well what was going to happen when they got to their destination, wherever that destination was.

In a short time, carried on the stream of lights and auto-mobiles, the car reached an area of Harlem that Russell knew well. There were a couple of places here that he visited when he wanted to hear great jazz, and another couple of places, much less well publicized, that he visited when he had a bit of money in his pocket and felt like shooting craps.

The car stopped in a dimly lit street, in front of a closed shutter. Jimbo got out, opened the padlock and pulled the handle up. Lit by the car's headlights, the metal wall rose to reveal a large, bare space, an L-shaped warehouse with a line of concrete pillars in the middle.

The car glided in through the entrance and the shutter came down again behind them. The car turned left round the corner and stopped at a slanting angle. A few moments later, a couple of bare dirt-encrusted bulbs hanging from the ceiling came on, spreading a dim light.

Jimbo opened the door on Russell's side. 'Get out.'

He took Russell's arm in his iron grip and made him walk around to the other side. Russell had the pleasure of seeing LaMarr struggling to get out through the door. He avoided making any comment that would simply have earned him more of Jimbo's brand of applause.

To their left was a desk with a chair. In front of it, another chair, a wooden one with a straw bottom. Despite the precariousness of the situation, Russell found the setting quite traditional. Clearly, LaMarr was a nostalgic.

Jimbo pushed him towards the desk and pointed at the top of it. 'Empty your pockets. All of them. Don't force me to do it myself.'

With a sigh, Russell put everything he had in his pockets

on the desk. A wallet with the documents and letters, the five hundred dollars Zef had just given him, and a pack of cinnamon-flavoured chewing-gum.

The fat man walked to the chair behind the desk. He smoothed the collar of his jacket, took off his hat, sat down, and placed his fat forearms on the table. The rings on his fingers glittered as he moved. It struck Russell that he looked like a version of Jabba the Hutt.

'All right, Mr Russell Wade. Let's see what we have here.'

He pulled Russell's things towards him. He opened the wallet, and threw it straight back down again as soon as he saw it was empty. Ignoring the envelopes, he picked up the banknotes and counted them.

'Just look at that. Five hundred dollars.'

He leaned back in his chair, as if trying to recall something he remembered perfectly well.

'So now you owe me sixty-five thousand.'

Russell didn't think it wise to point out that only a little while earlier LaMarr had been demanding sixty thousand. In the meantime, his guardian angel had made him sit down on the chair in front of the desk and had taken up a standing position next to him. Seen from below, he looked even bigger and more threatening. The driver had got out of the car as soon as they had arrived and vanished through a door behind them, into what was probably a bathroom.

LaMarr ran his thick fingers through his short curly hair. 'Now how do we go about paying the rest?' He pretended to think.

It was clear to Russell that LaMarr was playing with him like a cat with a mouse, and savouring yet another demonstration of his own power.

'I'm going to be generous. Seeing as how I've just

collected, I'll let you off another five hundred.'

He nodded toward Jimbo. The punch in the stomach arrived with impressive speed and a force that knocked the air out of Russell's lungs, maybe out of the entire atmosphere. He felt acid rising in his throat, and bent forward, retching. A thread of saliva dropped from his mouth onto the dusty floor. LaMarr looked at him with a self-satisfied expression, the way you look at a child who's done his homework properly.

'So now there's sixty-four thousand left.'

'Right now, I'd say that should be enough.'

These words of Vivien's, firm and confident, came from somewhere behind Russell. Three heads turned simultaneously in that direction, only to see a young woman emerge from the shadows into the pool of light cast by the bulbs. As if some spell had been broken, Russell started breathing again.

The fat man turned incredulously to Jimbo. 'Who's this fucking whore?'

Vivien raised her hand and aimed her gun at LaMarr's head. 'This whore is armed, and if the two of you don't go stand against the wall with your legs wide apart, she might decide to show you how offended she is by your insinuations.'

The rest happened before Russell had time to warn Vivien. The door to the bathroom burst open and the man who'd been in there ran out and flung his arms around her chest, immobilizing her. Vivien's reaction was instant.

Instead of trying to wriggle free, Vivien pressed her body against his, raised her legs and brought the heels of her heavy boots down on the tips of her attacker's shoes. Russell distinctly heard the sound of his toes cracking. A strangulated cry, and the arms surrounding Vivien loosened their grip as if by magic. The man collapsed to the floor and lay on his side, cursing, his legs pulled up to his chest.

Vivien aimed the gun at him and looked defiantly at the other two men. 'OK. Now who else wants to try?' She gestured to Jimbo. 'Are you armed?'

'Yes.'

'OK. Take out your gun with two fingers, lay it on the ground, and kick it towards me. Nice and slowly. I'm a little edgy right now.'

Keeping her eyes on Jimbo, Vivien bent over the man on the floor, frisked him with her left hand and took a big revolver from his jacket. She straightened up. A moment later, the other man's automatic came sliding across the floor to her feet. She slipped the revolver into her belt and bent down to collect the new trophy from the floor. Then she turned and Russell saw her use the barrel of the gun to indicate the man lying on the floor to Jimbo.

'Good. Now move slowly and lie down next to him.'

When she was sure she had the two men under control, she approached the chair where Russell was sitting.

'Are you armed?' she asked LaMarr.

'No.'

'I hope for your sake I don't find out you're lying.'

'I'm not armed.'

Given that he was looking down the barrel of a gun, he might be telling the truth.

'Can you stand?' Vivien asked Russell.

His legs didn't seem to want to obey him, and his stomach was tight with cramps. But somehow he managed to get to his feet and walk to Vivien. She handed him a big dark pistol and nodded at the two men on the ground.

'Keep an eye on these two. If they move, shoot.'

'I'd be glad to.'

Russell had never used a firearm in his life but the punch

264

he'd had from Jimbo was a good incentive to start. And from that distance it was impossible to miss.

Vivien relaxed and turned to LaMarr, who had followed the scene with a certain apprehension from behind the desk.

'What's your name?'

The man hesitated, licking his dry lips before replying. 'LaMarr.'

'OK. This fucking whore is called Vivien Light and she's a detective with the 13th Precinct. And she's just been an eyewitness to a kidnapping. Which, as you know, is a federal offence. Now how much do you think it's worth for me not to call the FBI and drop your name to them?'

LaMarr had realized where she was going with this. 'I don't know. How about sixty-four thousand dollars?'

Vivien leaned over and took from his fat, sweaty hand the dollars he was still clutching. 'Let's say sixty-four thousand five hundred and the deal's done. And that's the end of it. Do I make myself clear?' She straightened up and put the money in the pocket of her jeans. 'I'll take your silence for consent. Let's go, Russell. There's nothing more to do here.'

Russell took the envelopes and the wallet from the desk and put them in his pocket. He took the pack of chewing-gum, looked at it for a moment and then put it down with exaggerated grace in front of LaMarr. 'I'll leave you this. In case you want to sweeten your breath.' He smiled seraphically. 'Use it wisely. It's worth sixty-four thousand dollars.'

There was anger in the fat man's eyes, and there was death. He joined Vivien, and they retreated in silence, shoulder to shoulder, keeping their eyes on the little group. They reached the shutter and Russell saw that Jimbo, when they had arrived, had not lowered it completely. That was how Vivien had managed to get in without making any noise.

265

This time she bent down and raised it.

Within a minute they were sitting in her car. Russell noticed that her hands were trembling with the drop in adrenaline. He wasn't feeling much better. He consoled himself with the observation that not even someone trained in this kind of thing ever really got in the habit.

Russell tried to relax and find his voice again. 'Thanks,' he said.

The reply was a curt one. 'Thanks my ass.'

He turned abruptly and saw that Vivien was smiling. She put her hand in her pocket, took out the five hundred dollars and gave it to him.

'Part of this will go to pay the laundry. And I hope for your finances I haven't ruined my jacket, rolling on the floor like that.'

Russell accepted this clear invitation to relieve the tension. 'As soon as I can, I'll buy you a whole shop full of jackets.'

'Added to the dinner.'

Russell looked at her profile as she drove. She was young, strong and beautiful. A dangerous woman, seen from the wrong end of a gun barrel.

'There's something I have to say to you.'

'What?'

Russell tightened his seat belt to stop the buzzer from sounding. 'When I saw you coming around that corner . . .'

'Yes?'

Russell closed his eyes and sank back in his seat. 'It was like an apparition, like the Virgin Mary appearing to the faithful. From now on I'll worship at your shrine.'

In the semi-darkness of his closed eyelids, he heard the sound of Vivien's cool laughter. Then Russell felt things fading away and he, too, smiled.

CHAPTER 24

The key turned in the lock, opened the door and disappeared again into Vivien's pocket. She entered and switched on the light.

'Come in, sit down.'

Russell entered, carrying a bag in each hand, and looked around. 'It's nice here.'

Vivien looked at him with a touch of self-satisfaction. 'Do you want me to say what Carmen Montesa said when you made the same comment about her apartment?'

'No, I mean it.'

He had expected to find an untidy apartment. Vivien struck him as a tough cookie, not at all the type you'd expect to be houseproud: not patient or meticulous enough. Instead of which the small apartment was a model of good taste in its furnishings, and full of an unusual attention to detail. There was something here he had never experienced before. Not the insane chaos of his own apartment, nor the antiseptic splendour of his parents' house, but real love on the part of the occupant for the things she had around her.

He put the bags down, while continuing to examine the apartment. 'Do you have a cleaning woman?'

Vivien was at the refrigerator, getting a bottle of mineral

water. 'I assume you're kidding,' she replied, with her back to him.

'What do you mean?'

'There aren't many people in the NYPD who could afford a cleaning woman. Cleaners in New York are as expensive as plastic surgeons, and their work needs going over, too, though usually a whole lot earlier.'

As she poured herself a glass of water, Vivien indicated the two-seater couch facing the television. 'Sit down. Would you like a beer?'

'A beer would be good.'

He walked to the counter and took the bottle that Vivien had opened and pushed towards him. It wasn't until he felt the cold liquid going down his throat that he realized how thirsty he was. He would carry the after-effects of Jimbo's punch with him for several days. He walked towards the comfortable-looking couch, and as he did so noticed a picture frame of unusual design on top of a cabinet. In it there was a photograph of a woman with a girl of about fifteen. It was obvious at first glance that they were mother and daughter, so alike did they look. They were both very beautiful.

'Who are they?'

'My sister and my niece,' Vivien replied, in a tone that suggested she had said all she had to say on the matter.

It seemed clear to Russell that there was some unhappy episode connected with these two people and that she didn't want to talk about it. Rather than ask any more questions, he sat down on the couch and moved his hand over the bright leather upholstery.

'Comfortable. And pretty, too.'

'My ex-boyfriend was an architect. He gave me a hand choosing the furniture and decorating the apartment.'

'And where is he now?'

Vivien gave a self-deprecating half smile. 'He's a good architect – let's say he went on to other projects.'

'How about you?'

Vivien spread her arms. 'My personal ad goes something like this: *Young woman, interesting job, single, not looking for anybody*.'

Once again, Russell didn't ask any more questions. All the same, he couldn't help feeling pleased to hear that Vivien didn't have anyone in her life right now.

She finished her glass of water and put it in the sink. 'I think I'll take a shower. Make yourself comfortable, watch television, finish your beer. You can have the bathroom after me, if you want to take a shower.'

Russell could feel the dust of centuries on him. The idea of warm water running over his body, washing away all trace of that day, made him quiver with pleasure. 'OK. I'll wait here.'

Vivien disappeared into the bedroom and came out a couple of minutes later wearing a bathrobe. She slipped into the bathroom and almost immediately Russell heard the water running. He couldn't help imagining Vivien's strong, agile body naked under the shower. The beer suddenly didn't seem cold enough to reduce the heat he could feel rising inside him.

He got up and went to the window with its view of part of the Hudson. The evening was clear but there were no stars.

On the way back from Harlem, he and Vivien had exchanged their impressions of the events they had just been involved in. When she had seen him disappear inside the big sedan, Vivien had immediately realized that something was wrong. And when the car had headed out she had started to follow it, discreetly, always keeping two other cars between them but managing not to lose sight of it. When she saw the car turn onto a dead-end street, she pulled up to the kerb and quickly got out, in time to see the sedan disappear through the entrance to the warehouse. She went closer and saw that the shutter hadn't been pulled all the way down. There was enough of a gap between the shutter and the ground to let her enter without attracting attention. Following the direction of the voices, she cautiously peered around the corner. She saw LaMarr sitting at his desk and the gorilla standing next to Russell. From her vantage point on Park, she had lost visual contact a couple of times because of the passing cars, and had assumed the gorilla was also the driver, which was why she hadn't suspected that there might be a third man.

Then Russell told her what had happened in the lobby when he'd arrived home. He didn't mind her smiling over his disinherited state. In fact, he smiled, too. And then he told her about Zef's kindness in lending him five hundred dollars.

'What will you do now?'

'Find a hotel.'

'Is the money I gave you back all you have?'

'Right now I'm afraid it is.'

'If you want somewhere decent, that money's only going to last you a couple of days, and that's being optimistic. I don't want to be in the same car as a guy who sleeps in the kind of place you can afford.'

Deep down, Russell could only agree with her disconcertingly clear summary of his situation. He was forced to come clean. 'I don't have any choice.'

Vivien made a vague gesture. 'There's a sofa bed in the living room of my apartment. I don't think we're going to get much sleep in the next few days. If you really want to follow this story, it's best you stay with me. I don't want to be forced to look all over town to find you. If you can live with it, it's yours.'

Russell did not hesitate. 'It'll be like staying at the Plaza.'

Vivien burst out laughing, and Russell wasn't sure why. She hastened to explain. 'Do you know what we call the cell at the precinct house where they put you when they arrested you?'

'Don't tell me. Let me guess. The Plaza, right?'

Vivien nodded.

Russell accepted the joke. 'Seems I can't help being indebted to you right now. Mind you, being in debt to other people is something I've always been good at.'

Now, thinking back on it, Russell found the memory of that conversation quite comforting.

It was as if a kind of bond had been formed between them in the car. A reaction of the heart, a brief refuge from the knowledge that they were pursuing a killer who had already killed a hundred people and was getting ready to do it again.

He left the window and opened one of the bags he had brought with him. In it were his laptop and his cameras, the only things he considered sacred. Before coming to Vivien's apartment, they had swung by the precinct house to leave the captain the frame containing Mitch Sparrow's hair, and then gone on to 29th Street, where Russell had packed his bag from the things abandoned in the storage closet of what was no longer his home.

He took out the laptop checked his mail. There wasn't much, and all of it predictable. Time Warner Cable explaining why they were cutting off his service, an agency explaining why he would soon be getting a letter from its lawyer and Ivan Genasi, a very good photographer friend of his – and the only person he didn't owe money to – asking what had become of him. The other messages were all about missed payments or loans that hadn't been repaid. Russell felt ill at ease. He had the feeling, as he read these emails, that he was violating the privacy of someone he didn't know, so distant did he feel right now from the man who had inspired these messages.

He closed down his email and opened a new Word document. He thought about it for a moment, then decided to call the file *Vivien*. He started by noting down some of the thoughts that had occurred to him since this whole thing had started. In the absence of a notebook, he had been making mental notes every time something significant had emerged. Before too long, the words started to flow uninterruptedly, as if there was a direct connection between his thoughts and his fingers on the keyboard. He didn't know, and didn't really care, whether it was the story taking him over or him taking over the story. All that mattered was that sense of total possession he had while writing. By the time Vivien's voice surprised him, he had already written two pages.

'Your turn, if you want it.'

He turned and saw her. She had put on a light sweatsuit and flip-flops. She looked the picture of freshness and innocence. Russell had seen her react to an attack by a man three times her size and render him harmless. He had seen her hold other men at bay with a gun. He had seen her treat a slimeball like LaMarr as the dirt he was.

He had thought of her as a dangerous woman. And it was only now, when she looked completely defenceless, that he realized how dangerous. He turned and glanced at the picture frame on the cabinet, the photograph of the smiling woman and girl. Vivien's natural place was with them, he thought. She was as beautiful as they were.

He turned his eyes away from the photograph and stared at her in such a way that she asked, 'Hey, what's going on?'

'One day, when this is all over, you must allow me to photograph you.'

'Me? You're kidding, right?' Vivien pointed to the photograph in the picture frame. 'My sister's the model of the family. I'm the police officer, the one who's almost a man, remember? I wouldn't even know what to do in front of a camera.'

What you're doing now would be more than enough, Russell thought.

He realized that, much as she might protest, she had been pleased by his request. And what he saw on her face was not only surprise but an unexpected shyness, which it was possible she hid at other times by holding a badge in front of her.

'I mean it. Promise me.'

'Don't talk crap. And get out of my kitchen. I left clean towels for you in the bathroom.'

Russell saved what he had written and went to get clean clothes from his bag. He slipped into the bathroom, where he found a pile of towels placed on a cabinet next to the washbasin.

It was only a detail, a trifle. But it made him feel at home all the same.

He stepped into the shower and let the water and foam wash away all the fatigue. After the business with Ziggy and then the explosion, he had felt truly alone for the first time in his life, totally inadequate to the burden that had been placed on him.

When he came out of the bathroom, Vivien was sitting in front of the laptop. She had opened the document named for her and was reading what Russell had written.

'What are you doing?'

Vivien continued reading, without even turning her head, as if it was quite natural for her to open someone else's computer. 'What I should be doing as a police officer. Investigating.'

Russell protested, without a great deal of conviction. 'This is a flagrant violation of privacy and press freedom.'

'If you don't want me to stick my nose in, then don't give my name to a file.'

When she finished reading, she stood up and, without making any comment, walked to the kitchen counter. Russell noticed there was a saucepan on the boil, and a frying pan of red sauce next to it. Vivien increased the volume of the extractor fan, then pointed to the water, which was starting to boil.

'Penne all'arrabbiata. Or spaghetti, whichever you prefer.'

Russell looked surprised.

'I'm Italian,' she said. 'I know how to make it. You can trust me.'

'Of course I trust you. I just wonder how you managed to rustle together a sauce in such a short time.'

Vivien threw the pasta in the saucepan and put the lid over it, to keep the steam in. 'Is this your first visit to earth? Aren't there freezers and microwaves on your planet?'

'On my planet we never eat at home.'

Russell approached Vivien, who was on the other side of the counter. He sat down on a stool and looked curiously at the frying pan.

'Actually, I've always been fascinated by people who can cook. I once tried boiling some eggs and managed to burn them.'

Vivien was still concentrating on the pasta and the sauce, undistracted by Russell's little joke. 'I keep asking myself who you really are,' she said.

Russell shrugged. 'An ordinary guy. I don't have any particular qualities. I've had to make do with particular defects.'

'You do have one quality. I read what you wrote. It's beautiful. Convincing. It reaches out to the reader.'

This time it was Russell's turn to be pleased with the compliment and not let it show. 'Really? It's the first time I've done it.'

'Really. And if you want to know what I think, then I'd add one thing.'

'What?'

'If you hadn't spent your life trying to be Robert Wade, you might have discovered that his brother could be just as interesting.'

Russell felt something stir inside him, something he couldn't give a name.

All he knew was that there was one thing he wanted to do. And he did it.

He walked around to the other side of the counter, took Vivien's face in his hands and gently kissed her on the lips. For a moment she returned the kiss but then immediately put a hand on his chest and pushed him back.

Russell noticed that her breath was coming faster.

'Hey, calm down,' she said. 'This wasn't what I intended when I invited you here.'

She turned, as if to erase what had just happened. For a few moments she occupied herself with the pasta, leaving Russell a view of her back and the smell of her hair. Then she murmured a few words, under her breath.

'Or maybe it was. I don't even know myself. The one thing I know is that I don't want complications.'

'Neither do I. But if they're the price to pay to have you, I accept them gladly.'

After a moment, Vivien turned off the hob and put her arms around his neck. 'Then to hell with the pasta.'

She raised her head and this time the kiss wasn't accompanied by hands pushing him away. Her body against his was exactly the way Russell had imagined it would be. Strong and soft, immature and ripe. As he moved his hand under her sweater and found her skin, he asked himself why here, why now, why her, why not before. Vivien continued kissing him as, with eyes closed, she drew him to the bedroom. The semi-darkness welcomed them, convincing them that this was the right place for them.

As he lost himself inside her, as he forgot names and people, Russell wasn't sure if Vivien was the light before the dawn or a glow after sundown.

He knew only that she was like her name. Light, period.

Afterwards, they lay clinging together as if the skin of one was the natural clothing of the other. Russell felt himself slipping into the warmth of sleep and immediately shook himself, for fear of losing her. He realized that he must have fallen asleep for a few minutes. He reached out his hand and found the bed empty.

Vivien had gone to the window. He saw her against the light that filtered through the curtains, accepting the glow that came from outside in return for the prospect that her body offered him.

He got up and went to her. He embraced her from behind, feeling her lean body against his. She moved closer in to him, naturally, as if this was meant to be.

Russell put his lips on her neck and breathed in the scent of her skin, the skin of a woman after making love. 'Where are you?'

'Here. There. Everywhere.' With a vague gesture, Vivien

indicated the river beyond the window and the whole world.

'And am I with you?'

'I think you always have been.'

She added nothing, because there was nothing to add.

Beyond the window, the river flowed calmly. They were still standing there, looking out, exchanging the consolation of presence and fragments of regret, when all at once a blinding light appeared on the horizon and filled the spaces between the buildings opposite, imprinting them in the frame of the window like a photographic negative.

A few moments later, they heard the obscene, arrogant roar of an explosion.

CHAPTER 25

'We're in deep shit.'

Captain Alan Bellew threw down the *New York Times*, adding it to the other dailies that already lay strewn over the desk. After the previous night's explosion, all the newspapers had produced special editions. They were full of theories, conjectures, suggestions. All of them were asking what the police were doing to ensure the safety of the citizens. The television channels could talk about nothing else, pushing all other world events into the background. All eyes were on New York. Correspondents were arriving from all over the world, as if America was in a state of war.

The latest explosion had occurred after nightfall on the banks of the Hudson, in Hell's Kitchen in a warehouse on Twelfth Avenue, near the corner with 46th Street, right next to the Sea-Air-Space Museum, where the aircraft carrier *Intrepid* was on display. The building had disintegrated. Fragments had hit the moored ship and damaged the planes and helicopters displayed on the bridge, like a tragic echo of the wars they had fought. The window panes in the neighbouring buildings had been shattered by the blast. An elderly man had died of a heart attack. The street had partly slid into the Hudson. For a long time, burning fragments had floated on the water. It had been a desolate scene. Only the late hour had prevented another major massacre. The death toll amounted to no more than twenty, plus an unspecified number of wounded, none of them seriously. A group of night birds, whose only fault was to be in the wrong place at the wrong time, had been blown apart and their remains strewn over the asphalt. No trace had been found of the warehouse's night watchman. Some passing cars had been struck by the explosion and flung away as tangles of crumpled metal. Others had not braked in time and had ended up in the river together with the detritus of the street. The passengers had all died. The firefighters had fought for a long time to bring the blaze under control and the crime scene team had started their investigations as soon as the place had become accessible.

They were expecting the results at any moment.

After a sleepless night, Russell and Vivien were in the captain's office, sharing his feelings of frustration, his inability to defeat the man who was defying them in this way.

One invisible man.

Bellew finally stopped pacing about the room and sat down, although that didn't make him any less restless.

'There's been a lot of phoning going on. The president, the governor, the mayor. Anyone with any authority in this country has grabbed the phone and called someone else. Who then called the commissioner. Who of course called me straight afterwards.'

Russell and Vivien waited in silence for him to finish.

'Willard feels as if he's sinking, and he's dragging me down with him. He feels guilty for being too cautious.'

'What did you say to him?'

Bellew made a gesture that seemed to say that the answer was obvious and at the same time far from obvious. 'I told him two things. One, that we don't know for certain that we're pursuing the right lead. Two, that the more people who know about this the more likely it is that the news will get out. If it reached the ears of Al-Qaeda, we'd have a real disaster on our hands. We'd have a ruthless competitor searching for that list. Think what a field day they'd have if they found it. The city already mined, just waiting to be blown up. If it was common knowledge, New York would be a desert in the space of three hours. You can just imagine it. Clogged highways, fighting, people dispersed all over the fucking map.'

Vivien could well imagine the picture the captain had conjured up. 'What are the FBI and NSA saying?' she asked.

The captain rested his elbows on the table. 'Not much. You know how close to their chests those people like to keep things. Apparently they're still pursuing the terrorism angle. Which means there's not too much pressure coming from over there. Not for the moment, anyway. That's one good thing, I guess.'

Russell had been lost in thought throughout the conversation between Vivien and Bellew. Now he intervened.

'The only thing linking us to the person who set the bombs is Mitch Sparrow. As far as I'm concerned, there's no doubt he was the guy in the wall. Nor is there any doubt that the document holder with the photographs isn't his, which makes it likely that it was accidentally left behind by whoever stuck the poor guy in the concrete. So the two photographs, the one with the cat and the one taken in Vietnam, have to show his killer. What I think happened is that Sparrow discovered what he was doing, and the man killed him to stop him talking.'

The captain thought this over. 'So they were co-workers.'

'Whether continuously or occasionally, I don't know. One thing's for sure. That they were working in the same place when Sparrow disappeared.'

280

Russell took another moment to think, as if putting his ideas in order. Vivien was fascinated by his degree of concentration.

'The person we're looking for is clearly the son of the man who planted the bombs. The father was a Vietnam veteran, who came back with huge psychological wounds. Many soldiers were transformed by the war. Some never lost the taste for killing, even when they got back to civilian life. My brother saw this many times.'

Vivien heard the ghost of Robert Wade in Russell's voice, but without any sense of anxiety. She looked at him and saw a face she knew looking out at the world with different eyes. She felt her heart swell for a moment before thoughts of the immediate problems facing them gained the upper hand.

Russell had not noticed a thing. Clearly and rationally, he continued, 'Unfortunately, if whoever wrote the letter and planted the bombs had mental problems, his son seems to have inherited them tenfold. I get the impression from that letter that he never knew his father, and only found out about him after his death. I wonder why.'

Russell paused, leaving that crucial question hanging.

As if granting them a pause for thought, the telephone on the desk started ringing. The captain reached out his hand and lifted the receiver to his ear.

'Bellew.'

He listened in silence to whatever the person at the other end was telling him. Vivien and Russell saw his jaw gradually clench. When he hung up, it was clear from the expression on his face that he would have liked to smash the telephone.

'It was the head of the explosives team that's been examining the debris on the Hudson.'

He paused, then said what they were all expecting to hear.

'It's him again. Same explosive, same kind of primer.'

Russell stood up, as if he needed to move after that confirmation.

'Something just occurred to me. I'm no expert, but for this man to have decided to carry out what his father had planned, he has to be a sociopath or something like that, with all that that implies.'

He turned to look at Vivien and Bellew.

'I've read that people like that usually develop compulsive patterns of behaviour. The first blast took place on Saturday evening. The second between Monday and Tuesday. Nearly two days later. If that madman has fixed that in his mind as the interval between one explosion and the other, we should have two more days to catch him before he decides to act again. I don't even want to think . . .'

He left the sentence hanging. Then he concluded it, expressing in his tone all the gravity of the situation.

'I don't even want to think about what would happen if another explosion took place. Maybe in a building where thousands of men and women work.'

He had saved the worst hypothesis until last.

'Not to mention that he might even decide to blow up all the buildings on the same day.'

Vivien saw the captain looking at Russell as if, in spite of everything, he was still wondering who this guy was and what he was doing in his office. A civilian discussing with them facts that according to the rules should have been confined to the police. The situation that had been created was absurd but had its own warped logic. The three of them were linked by a secret that must not be divulged at any cost, that it was in nobody's interest to divulge.

Bellew stood up and leaned with his clenched fists on the desk. 'We urgently need a name to put with those photographs. We can't publish them with the words *Who knows this man?* If he saw that, the son might realize we're on to him, panic and start to blow up the buildings one after the other.'

Vivien realized that they were referring to these two unknown people as the father and the son. Absurdly, memories of her childhood welled up to underline the tragic irony of the situation.

In the name of the Father and of the Son and of the Holy Spirit . . .

The image of herself, still a child, in a church with the scent of incense around her was erased by other images: buildings in flames and bodies being put in ambulances.

There was a knock at the door. Detective Tyler entered the office holding a file. His stubbled chin and generally dishevelled appearance indicated a sleepless night. When he saw Russell, a grimace of disapproval crossed his face for a moment.

Ignoring Russell and Vivien, he said, 'Captain, I have the results you wanted.'

His tone was that of someone who had done hard, boring work and knew that it wouldn't be recognized. The captain reached out his hand, took the file and looked through it quickly.

He spoke without raising his eyes from the paper. 'OK, Tyler. You can go.'

The detective went out, leaving a trace of stale cigarettes and surliness in the room. Bellew waited for him to move away from the door, before informing Vivien and Russell of what he had just read.

'I put a couple of three-man teams on it. Telling them as little as I could. This is what he have.'

He turned his attention back to the papers in his hands.

'The house that blew up on Long Island belonged to an ex-

283

soldier, a Major Mistnick. Apparently he served in Vietnam. That may not mean anything, but it's curious all the same. The firm that built it was indeed a small company in Brooklyn, Newborn Brothers. The company responsible for the building on the Lower East Side on the other hand is called Pike's Peak Buildings. And here we've had a real stroke of luck. Some time ago, the management hired an IT company to put all its data on computer. That means we can look at everything, even from years ago.'

'That's good news,' Vivien said.

'There's more.' There was no joy in the captain's voice. 'We need to look at the company that fixed up Twelfth Avenue and built the warehouse in Hell's Kitchen, the one that blew up last night. It was a municipal contract, so the company must have used union labour, which means the data should still be available. We'll proceed in the same way with the company that renovated the building on 23rd Street, where the body was found. If we can get hold of the names of the people who worked on those four sites, we can compare them and see if any coincide.'

Bellew passed his hand through his hair, maybe thinking that he was too old for his professional expertise to be put to the test like this.

'It's not much of a lead but it's all we've got. I'll ask the commissioner for backup, and put as many men to work on this as I can. I'll tell them it's a Code RFL.'

Russell frowned. 'Code RFL?'

Vivien intervened with an explanation. 'It's a code that doesn't exist but every police officer in New York knows. RFL stands for *Run for Life*. In police jargon it means those cases where speed is of the essence.'

She looked back at her chief.

'I want you to talk to Newborn Brothers. If it was a small company, with not many workers, the direct contact may be more productive. Someone may remember something. While you're on your way down, I'll ask the switchboard to get the number. You can pick it up from the desk officers.'

Vivien stood up, glad to do so. As they left the office they heard Bellew's voice: he was already on the phone, getting them what he had promised.

They walked downstairs. Russell was in front of her, and Vivien could smell his eau de cologne. She remembered his lips in the hollow of her elbow and his hand in her hair. Then she remembered the blinding flash and the thunderous sound that had abruptly pulled them out of the time and space they had carved out for themselves.

After the blast they had dressed quickly, saying nothing. They had gone into the living room and switched on the TV. After a few minutes' wait, Channel One had interrupted its broadcasts with news of the attack. They had continued hopping from one channel to another as the news was updated minute to minute. The magic there had been between them had vanished, lost in the flames now leaping on the TV screen.

Bellew had sent them a text. A few words only: *7.30 tomorrow in my office*.

There wasn't much more to say. Both she and the captain knew there was nothing they could do right now, except wait a few hours. The night had ended and the light through the windows had surprised her and Russell sitting on the couch, concerned and incredulous, close without touching, as if what they were seeing could come out of the screen and contaminate them.

As she descended the stairs, responsibility gripped her

285

chest. The lives of so many people depended on her, on what she would do in the next few hours. It made her a little dizzy, and she was happy to reach the bottom of the stairs.

As soon as he saw her come through the door, a uniformed officer held a sheet of paper out to her.

'Here it is, detective. It's a cell number, if that's OK. The man's name is Chuck Newborn and he's working on a big site in Madison Square Park.'

Vivien was grateful to code RFL, which was making everything move at a speed she wasn't accustomed to.

They left the precinct house and walked to Vivien's car. Silently they climbed in, both lost in their thoughts. After switching on the engine but before heading out, Vivien gave voice to hers.

'Russell, about last night . . .'

'Go on.'

'I just wanted to say that I . . .'

'I know. That you don't want complications.'

That wasn't what Vivien had meant to say. But Russell's words and detached tone brought her up short, on the threshold of a place she could enter only if she was invited in.

'That's fine by me,' he went on.

She turned to look at him but saw only the back of his head. Russell was looking intently out the window on his side. By the time he turned back to look at her, he was back in the present.

'Traffic's pretty heavy.'

Vivien put off any response to what he had said earlier in favour of more urgent priorities. 'Now you'll see how useful is to be a police officer.'

She took the flashing lamp and put it on the roof. The Volvo pulled away from the kerb and set off at speed.

They reached Madison Square Park after going west along

286

23rd street at a speed that had left Russell stunned.

'You'll have to lend me that gadget sometime.'

He had gone back to being the way Vivien had known him at the beginning. Ironic and detached, friendly and at the same time distant. She had to admit, with a touch of resentment towards herself, that the previous night had been a mistake, never to be repeated.

'When this is all over, I'll buy you a police car.'

They immediately saw the place they were looking for. To their left, facing the park, was a building under construction, not so high as to be called a true skyscraper, but with enough storeys to be imposing. There was all the activity of an anthill, in the swinging of cranes and the bustle of men with their coloured hard hats on the scaffolding.

Russell looked around. 'It's a recurring number. Everything seems to be happening on this street.'

'What do you mean?'

He gestured to a point behind her. 'We're on 23rd street. Sparrow's body was found on this street, only further east.'

Vivien would have liked to reply that in her work that kind of synchronicity was much more common than in the plots of movies. Most investigations stood or fell by the whims of fate and the thoughtlessness of human beings.

They parked the Volvo in front of the site. A worker wearing a yellow hard hat turned to them and protested, 'Hey, you can't park here.'

Vivien approached and flashed her shield. 'I'm looking for Mr Newborn. Chuck Newborn.'

The worker pointed to a sheet-metal hut on the left-hand side of the building, near a large embossed terrace on the third floor. 'You'll find him in his office.'

Vivien led Russell towards the temporary white-painted

287

construction. The door was open. They climbed the steps and found themselves in a room that was bare except for a desk and a chair. Two men were bent over the desk, studying a plan.

One of the two looked up. 'Can I do something for you?'

Vivien approached the desk. 'Mr Chuck Newborn?'

'Yes, that's me.'

He was a tall, bulky man in his early thirties, with sparse hair and clear eyes and the hands of someone who never shirks away from heavy work. He was wearing a worker's reflecting jacket over a denim jacket.

Vivien flashed her shield again. 'I'm Detective Light, 13th Precinct. This is Russell Wade. Can we talk to you for a moment?'

The man looked both puzzled and slightly alarmed. 'Sure.'

Vivien decided to underline the nature of the interview. 'Alone.'

Chuck Newborn turned to his companion, a thin, indolent-looking man. 'Tom, go check that concrete.'

Aware of being superfluous, the man called Tom picked up his hard hat and left without a word. Vivien was sure he considered her and Russell only a glitch in his day's work. Newborn folded the plan and stood waiting on the other side of the desk.

Vivien came straight to the point. 'Have you been working for Newborn Brothers for a long time?'

'Since I was a boy. My father and my uncle started the business, and I started working here when I was eighteen. My cousin arrived straight after college. He's in charge of administration. Now the old guys have retired and the two of us run the business.'

'Were you around when Major Mistnick's house on Long

Island was built?'

In Chuck Newborn's mind alarm bells must have gone off. He didn't have to search long and hard in his memory to know what the detective was talking about. 'Yes. A weird business. A year later—'

'—the house blew up.'

The man raised his hands. 'There was an investigation. The police questioned us. We were cleared of any wrongdoing.'

'I know, Mr Newborn. I'm not accusing you of anything. I'd just like to ask you a few questions concerning that period.'

She gave Newborn a few moments to calm down before continuing with her questioning. 'Do you remember if a man named Mitch Sparrow worked on that site?'

'The name sounds familiar, but I can't put a face to it.'

Vivien showed him the photograph she had been given by Carmen Montesa. Even before the man spoke, the expression on his face made it clear that his memory had been jogged.

'Oh, him. Of course. He was a good guy. Crazy about bikes, but a good worker.'

'You're sure about that?'

He shrugged. 'In those days, Newborn Brothers wasn't how it is now. We dealt mostly with renovations and small buildings. We didn't have so many workers. They were great days, and I remember them well.'

The man made no mention of his former worker's disappearance. Vivien suspected he didn't know about it. She preferred not to add a new element to the interview for the moment.

'As far as you were aware, did Sparrow have any particular friends, anyone he spent a lot of time with?'

'No. He was a quiet guy. He'd finish work and go straight

home to his wife and son. They were all he ever talked about.'

'Did anything strange happen on the site? As far as you can remember, any particular episodes, any people that attracted your attention?'

'No, not that I recall.' Then he gave a half-smile. 'Apart from the Phantom of the Site.'

'I'm sorry?'

'There was this one guy with scars all over his face and hands. A real monster. Everyone thought they were burns.'

At these words, others words appeared in the minds of Russell and Vivien.

Newborn lowered his head and looked at his hands, embarrassed perhaps by what he was about to say. 'You know how cruel you can be when you're young. My cousin and I used to call him the Phantom of the Site, like the Phantom of the Opera.'

'Do you remember his name?'

'I'm afraid not.'

'Do you have copies of the pay slips?'

'This was almost twenty years ago. We aren't required to keep records all that time.'

Vivien assumed the most reassuring tone she could muster. 'Mr Newborn, I'm not with the IRS. I'm here for an extremely important reason. Any detail can be crucial, even the most insignificant.'

Chuck Newborn decided to come clean. 'In those days, to keep costs down, we used to hire workers off the books. It wouldn't be possible now – the company's too big for that kind of thing. But in those days we were forced to do it to survive. These guys I'm talking about were paid in cash, no questions asked, no paperwork.'

'Do you remember any other details about this man?'

'My father talked about him one evening at dinner. He'd just showed up and offered his services, for a price my father and uncle liked a lot. Plus, he was really good. As they were standing there talking the guy calculated, just by looking, how much iron and concrete was needed for the foundations.'

'And did he ever work for you again?'

'No. Immediately after we finished the Mistnick house he left.'

Vivien was worried she was going too fast. She granted Newborn, who had been getting increasingly nervous as the conversation proceeded, a moment's pause.

'And what can you tell me about the accident?' she next asked.

'One night the house just exploded, killing the major and all his family. Or to be more precise, it imploded. Just crumpled in on itself. There was hardly any damage to the surrounding houses.'

Vivien looked at Russell. Both of them had thought the same thing. The man had shown the same fiendish skill in calculating the quantity of explosives to plant and how to set them off as he had earlier shown in calculating the amount of iron and concrete for the foundations.

'Did you mention him to the police at the time?'

Guilt fell like a shadow over Chuck Newborn's face. 'I'm afraid not.'

The reason was obvious from what he'd said earlier. Mentioning the man would have been the equivalent of handing himself in to the IRS, with the inevitable consequences. Vivien felt anger come over her like a gust of hot air.

'Didn't it occur to you there was something suspicious about the man's behaviour, given the circumstances?'

Newborn bowed his head, unable to find a plausible excuse

for what he was being accused of.

Vivien sighed. As she had done with Carmen Montesa, she took a business card from her bag, wrote her cellphone number on the back and held it out to the man.

'We're through for now. Here are my numbers. If you remember anything, let me know, any time.'

The man took the card and looked at it for a moment, as if afraid it was an arrest warrant. 'I will, don't worry.'

'Goodbye, Mr Newborn.'

He said something in reply, but in such a low voice they barely heard him. Vivien and Russell walked to the door and went out. Neither of them could prove it, but deep down they were both sure that the man with the burned face who had been called the Phantom of the Site as a joke was the person they were looking for. They walked down the steps and headed for the car, leaving Chuck Newborn alone with the feeling that he'd done something terribly wrong, even though he didn't know what it was. It would have been easy enough to tell him, if they had been able to. It might not have been so easy for him to accept.

If Newborn Brothers hadn't been so determined to cut costs, the man would have been arrested, and years later hundreds of human lives might have been saved.

CHAPTER 26

Russell and Vivien were back on the street.

The sky had turned blue again and the city had absorbed the latest outrage. Madison Square Park looked the way it usually did on a fine spring day. Senior citizens in search of sun, and dogs in search of trees. Mothers with children still too young to go to school and adolescents too lazy to want to. In the middle, a mime dressed up as the Statue of Liberty waited motionlessly for someone to throw coins in the can on the ground in front of him, at which point he would respond with a couple of movements. As she looked at the familiar scene, Vivien had the feeling that one of these people would suddenly turn to her and reveal a face ravaged with scars.

She stopped Russell, who was already walking towards the car. 'Are you hungry?'

'Not really.'

'We ought to eat something. We have time now, while we're waiting for results, but there probably won't be time later. I know from experience that a rumbling stomach isn't good for concentration.'

At the corner of the park, on the other side of the street, was a grey-painted stand serving hot dogs and hamburgers. In its very simplicity it had a certain elegance and did not jar with the natural setting. Vivien indicated a line of people.

'The guides say it's the best in New York. At lunchtime the line stretches all the way to Union Square.'

'OK. A hamburger would be fine.'

They crossed the street and joined the line. As they waited, Vivien expressed in words what they had surely both been asking themselves.

'What do you think about what Newborn said? The man with the scars, I mean.'

Russell took a moment before coming out with his conclusion. 'I think he's our man.'

'So do I.'

Those words sealed their fate. From that moment on, this was the lead to follow, with all the means they had at their disposal. If it turned out to be the wrong one, then, rightly or wrongly, they would have the deaths of many people on their consciences.

In the name of the Father . . .

Almost without realizing it, Vivien found herself at the window where the orders had to be placed. She ordered two cheeseburgers and two bottles of water and paid for them. In return she received a small electronic receiver that would inform her when the food was ready to be collected.

They moved away from the stand to a nearby bench. As they sat down, Russell had a slightly downcast expression. 'I promise you this is the last time.'

'The last time for what?'

'The last time you pay for me.'

Vivien looked at him. He was genuinely sorry. She knew how humiliated he felt, and that was a remarkable thing in itself. The last trace seemed to have gone of the man that Russell Wade had been until a few days earlier.

It had happened abruptly, like an evil spell taken away at

the utterance of a magic word. Unfortunately, the other person who seemed to have vanished without a trace was the man she had spent the night with.

She told herself it was stupid to regret something that had never really existed. She lowered her eyes to the object she had in her hands, which was the size of an old TV remote control.

'It must be something like this he uses.'

'Who does, and to do what?'

'The man who set off those bombs. It must be a gadget like this that he used to send the impulses that set off the explosions.'

As she was looking at that innocuous device of plastic and Plexiglas, which in another situation might become a lethal weapon, the receiver buzzed, almost making them jump.

Russell stood up and took the receiver from her hands. 'I'll go. Let me do that at least.'

Vivien watched as he presented himself at the window, handed over the receiver and got a tray with the food in return. He came back and placed the tray on the bench between them.

They unwrapped the hamburgers and started eating in silence. The food was the same, but the atmosphere was very different than when they had eaten together in Coney Island, facing the sea. When Russell had confided in her and she had been sure she understood him.

Now it occurred to her that she had only understood what she wanted to understand.

It depends on which wolf you feed more . . .

The ringing of her cellphone jolted her out of these thoughts. She looked at the number on the display without recognizing it.

She took the call. 'Detective Light.'

She heard a familiar voice. 'Hello, Miss Light. This is Dr Savine, one of the doctors treating your sister.'

The voice and the words brought images flooding into Vivien's mind. The Mariposa Clinic in Cresskill, Greta gazing into the distance with sightless eyes, white coats that meant both safety and anguish.

'What is it, doctor?'

'Unfortunately it isn't good news.'

Vivien waited in silence for him to continue, instinctively clenching her fist.

'Your sister's condition has suddenly worsened. We don't know exactly what to expect and so I don't know exactly what to tell you. But it isn't looking good. I'm being honest with you. You told me that was what you wanted, right from the start.'

Vivien bowed her head, and let the tears run down her cheeks. 'Of course, doctor, and I'm grateful. Unfortunately I can't be there right now.'

'I quite understand. I'll keep you informed, Miss Light. I'm very sorry.'

'I know. Thanks again.'

She hung up, and rose abruptly from the bench, turning her back on Russell and wiping her eyes with the back of her hand. Her first impulse was to drop everyone and everything, take the car to see her sister. But she couldn't. For the first time in her life she cursed her work, the duty that confined her like a cage, the significance of her shield. She cursed the man who, in his madness, was keeping her away from the person she most loved and making that person seem ever more distant.

'Let's go.'

296

Russell understood that she had received some upsetting news. Anyone would have understood that. Obeying her curt voice, he got up from the bench, threw the tray in the garbage and followed her in silence to the car.

Vivien was grateful to him for that.

They went back to the precinct house the same way they had come, using the flashing light and the siren to get through the traffic.

They reached their destination without exchanging a word. The whole time, Vivien had driven as if the fate of the world depended on the speed with which they returned to base. She had barely seen the cars they passed – she had seen only her sister's face.

As she loosened her belt, Vivian wondered if her sister was still alive right now. She raised her face and looked at Russell. She realized that for the whole of the journey she had forgotten he was even there.

'I'm sorry. Today's not a very good day for me.'

'No problem. Tell me if I can help in any way.'

Of course you can help me. You could take me in your arms and let me be an ordinary girl crying on someone's shoulders and . . .

She erased the thought. 'Thanks. It's over now.'

They got out of the car, entered the precinct house and went straight upstairs to the captain's office. By now, the presence of Russell was taken as an established fact, even though it might not have been accepted by everyone. Without supplying too many details, the captain had told his men that he was someone who had information about a particular investigation and was collaborating with Vivien on it. Vivien knew her colleagues weren't stupid and that sooner or later one or other of them would suspect something. But for the moment, whatever surliness they encountered, they just had to pretend everything was all right until the case was solved.

When he saw them come in, the captain looked up from the papers he was signing. 'Well?'

'We may have a lead.'

Bellew immediately closed the file he had in front of him. Russell and Vivien sat down in front of his desk. Briefly, Vivien told him about Mr Newborn and the Phantom of the Site, a man with a disfigured face who'd been suspiciously eager to work on Major Mistnick's house. She told him how perfectly the house had imploded and how carefully the charges must have been positioned to obtain such a result.

The captain leaned back in his chair. 'Thinking about the letter, and how precise these recent explosions were, then yes, it could be the right person.'

'That's what we think, too.'

'Now we just have to check if he worked on other sites, and find out his name. How we do that, and how long it'll take, I don't know. One useful thing we could do in the meantime is find out more about this major. We need to contact the army. Bowman and Salinas have just called me from Pike's Peak. They have the material we're looking for. I think they'll be here soon. Nothing yet from the other men I sent out.'

The telephone on the desk starting ringing. Vivien saw from the light on the front of the apparatus that the call came from the lobby. The captain reached out his hand and lifted the receiver to his ear. 'What is it?'

He listened for a moment, then allowed himself an angry outburst. 'Christ almighty, I told them to come to me as soon as they got back. Now they're suddenly concerned with

298

etiquette and don't ask for me? Send them up, and fast.'

The telephone returned to its natural home with a little more force than necessary. The light went off.

'Fucking assholes!'

Vivien was surprised by this flare-up. Bellew was usually a restrained person, who tended to stay deadpan under pressure. Everyone in the precinct had had at least once to bear the brunt of his calm, cold voice, which made the dressing down they were receiving all the more effective. An outburst such as this wasn't like him. Then she told herself that in these circumstances, with the burden of all those deaths and the prospect of other deaths to come, it would become increasingly difficult to say what was like him or anyone else.

Preceded by footsteps on the stairs, the outlines of two officers appeared on the frosted glass of the door. In a loud voice, and not without a touch of sarcasm, Bellew said, 'Come in!' before either of them had had time to knock.

Officers Bowman and Salinas entered, looking grim faced, each carrying a large, heavy cardboard box. The desk sergeant had clearly conveyed the captain's words to them.

Bellew pointed to the floor next to the desk. 'Put them down over here.'

As soon as the boxes were on the ground and Vivien was able to look inside, she felt a distinct sense of discouragement. They were full of printouts. If the employee lists from the other companies were as voluminous as these, it would take a very long time to look through them. She glanced up at Russell and realized that he was thinking the same thing.

The captain, still bent over and looking inside the boxes, expressed everybody's thoughts. 'This is like the fucking Encyclopaedia Britannica.'

Officer Bowman tried to rehabilitate himself and his colleague in his chief's eyes by placing a thin square of black plastic on the desk. 'We also had a CD made with all the data.'

'Great work, boys. You can go.'

Freed by the captain's words, the two officers headed for the door. Vivien could sense how curious they were about all this research they'd been asked to do without knowing the reason why. In fact, there was a general curiosity in the air. She was sure that by now everyone had figured out that it was connected with the two explosions that had taken place in the space of three days.

Russell was the first to express his anxieties. 'If we want to be quick, we're going to need a lot of men for this.'

If the captain had been overwhelmed with the same discouragement for a moment, he had already got over it. His voice was positive and determined as he came out with the only possible reply.

'I know. But we can't afford to fail. I can't do anything for now, until the other data gets here. But we'll have to get it done, even if it means putting every police officer in New York on the job.'

Vivien went to one of the boxes, and took out a file. She sat down again and placed it on her lap. There was a long list of names, in alphabetical order, on the white and blue lines of the pages. To get rid of the sense of stagnation that everyone was feeling she started running through the names.

The endless series of letters became almost hypnotic as her eye slid down the page.

A
Achieson, Hank
Ameliano, Rodrigo

Anderson, William
Andretti, Paul

and then all the rest down to the next page

B
Barth, Elmore
Bassett, James
Bellenore, Elvis
Bennett, Roger

and then more names and another page

C
Castro, Nicholas
Cheever, Andreas
Corbett, Nelson
Cortese, Jeremy
Crow . . .

Vivien stopped abruptly. The name had jumped out at her, reminding her of a face smiling with contentment after she had treated poor Elisabeth Brokens like dirt. She leaped to her feet, dropping the papers on the floor.

Russell and Bellew looked on in surprise as she rushed to the door, crying out just two words.

'Wait here.'

She descended the stairs as fast as she could without breaking her neck. There was a rush of adrenaline inside her. After so many *if*s and *maybe*s, so many *I can't remember*s, at last a small stroke of luck. By the time she reached the lobby, she was praying that this didn't turn out to be another illusion.

On the steps she stopped and looked around her for a moment.

A car with two officers was reversing out of the parking lot next to the entrance. Vivien waved to them and ran down the short flight of steps. She reached the car, and saw the reflection of the sky disappear from the side window as the officer lowered it.

'I need a ride to 23rd and Third.'

'Get in.'

She opened the back door and sat down in a seat usually reserved for arrested people. But she was in too much of a hurry to register that.

'Use the siren.'

Without asking for explanations, the driver switched on the flashing light and pulled out quickly, with a slight screech of tyres. She was so impatient to arrive that the journey seemed very long, even though it was only three blocks. When she saw the orange plastic barriers around the site, she relived the discovery of the body of Mitch Sparrow, which at first had seemed to be yet another case to be filed away in the records, but which had in fact given a whole new direction to this crazy business, and might even help to bring it to a conclusion. The madness of chance, as well as of human beings, was turning out to be the one thing connecting all the threads of this case.

The car had not yet come to a compete halt when Vivien opened the door and jumped out.

'Thanks, boys. I owe you one.'

She didn't hear the reply, didn't hear the car drive off. She had already approached a worker who had just come out of the gap in the perimeter fence and took him aback with the urgency of her request.

'Where can I find Mr Cortese?'

The man indicated a point beyond the fence. 'He's right behind me.'

After a moment, the figure of Jeremy Cortese appeared. He was wearing the same jacket as on the day they had first met. When he saw her coming towards him, he recognized her immediately. Difficult to forget someone who reminds you of the discovery of a corpse!

'Hello, Miss Light.'

'Mr Cortese, I need to ask you a few questions.'

Surprised, but realizing there was no way out, he said, 'Go ahead.'

Vivien drew Cortese aside. The place where they were standing, between the fence and the barriers, was used by the workers and she didn't want them to be disturbed, or for them to disturb her. She took up a position facing Cortese and spoke as clearly as possible, as if she and the man were speaking two different languages.

'I need you to dig deep into your memory. I know it's been a long time, but your answer's important. Very important.'

He nodded to confirm that he had understood, and waited in silence for the question.

'I know you worked for the company that constructed the building on the Lower East Side, the one that was blown up last Saturday.'

A hint of fear and alarm appeared in his eyes, as if she had just told him that the police were investigating him personally. His shoulders drooped a little and when he spoke, there was a distinct unease in his voice. 'Before we go on, I'd like to ask you a question. Do I need a lawyer?'

Vivien tried to put him at his ease. 'No, Mr Cortese,' she said, as reassuringly as possible, 'you don't need a lawyer. I

303

know perfectly well you had nothing to do with that. There are just a few things I need to know about.'

'Go on.'

'Among the men who worked with you on that building, do you remember if there was one with a heavily scarred face?'

The answer came without hesitation. 'Yes.'

Vivien's heart skipped a beat. 'Are you sure?'

Now that his fears had been calmed, Cortese seemed reassured by the turn taken by the interview, and was eager to reply. 'He wasn't in my team but I do remember seeing the guy a few times. With a face like that, you couldn't exactly miss him.'

Vivien's heart was standing still in her chest. 'Do you remember his name?'

'No. I never even spoke to him.'

The disappointment Vivien felt at this lasted only a brief moment before it was wiped out by a new thought that suddenly occurred to her.

'God bless you, Mr Cortese. God bless you a thousand times. You have no idea how helpful you've been. You can go back to work now, and don't worry.'

The briefest of handshakes, and Vivien had already turned her back on him, leaving him standing there on the sidewalk, surprised and relieved. She took out her cellphone and dialled the captain's number.

She didn't even give him time to say his name. 'Alan, it's Vivien.'

'What's going on? Where the hell are you?'

'You can call off the men. We won't need to search through those names any more.'

She waited a moment, to give Bellew time to prepare for what she was about to ask him.

'You need to send officers to the oncology departments of every hospital in New York to check if they had any patient with a strongly disfigured face who died in the last year and a half.'

Now that the cancer has done its work and I'm on the other side . . .

Bellew, like the others, knew that letter by heart by now. Vivien's excitement immediately became his.

'Great work, Vivien. I'll put the men on it right away. We're waiting for you here.'

Vivien folded the cellphone and put it back in her pocket. As she walked briskly back to the precinct, surrounded by the crowd, she would have given anything to be just a normal person. Instead of which, every person she passed aroused the anxious question of whether this was one she would lose or one she would save. For them, too, there was still hope. Maybe the man who had left a trail of bombs behind him, like a trail of stones in a tragic fairy tale, had, at the time of death, also left behind him a name and an address.

CHAPTER 27

Father McKean reluctantly made his way through the crowd thronging the Boathouse Café. His face bore clear traces of his sleepless night, spent in front of the television absorbing the images on the screen with all the avidity of a thirsty man and at the same time dismissing them from his mind as too horrible to contemplate.

I am God . . .

Those words continued to echo in his head, like a ghastly soundtrack to the visions his memory continued to play back to him. The destroyed cars, the damaged buildings, the fires, the wounded and bloodstained people. An arm, torn from a body by the violence of the blast, lying on the sidewalk, pitilessly framed by the TV cameras.

He took a deep breath.

He had prayed for a long time, asking for comfort and enlightenment where he usually found it. Faith had always been his consolation, his point of departure and point of arrival, whatever the nature of the journey. It was because of faith that his adventure with the community had begun, and thanks to the results he had achieved with many kids he had allowed himself to dream. Other Joys, other houses spread all over the state, in which young people attracted by drugs would be able to stop feeling like moths drawn to a flame. After a certain point, the kids themselves had been his strength.

But this morning he had wandered among them trying to hide his pain, smiling when he was asked to smile and replying when he was asked to reply. But as soon as he was alone it all crashed down on top of him, like objects falling out after being crammed into a closet.

For the first time in his life as a priest, he didn't know what to do.

He had found himself in that situation before, when he still lived in the world, before realizing that what he wanted to do in his life was to serve God and his fellow man, and he had resolved his doubts and anxieties then by entering the peace of the seminary. This time it was different. He had called Cardinal Logan without a great deal of hope. If he had been in New York, he would have met with him more for moral support than to obtain an authorization he knew would never come. Not in the time or the circumstances that would be needed. He knew perfectly well the iron rules that governed that aspect of the relationship with the faithful. It was one of the fixed points of their creed, guaranteeing as it did that anyone could approach the sacrament of confession with a free heart and without fear and receive absolution in return for repentance. In his capacity as a minister, the Church condemned him to silence – and simultaneously condemned hundreds more people to death, if those attacks continued.

'So you're the famous Father McKean, the founder of Joy.'

He turned in the direction of the voice and found himself facing a tall woman in her forties, with dark, impeccably groomed hair. She was too heavily made-up, too elegant, probably too rich. She was holding two glasses full of what must have been champagne.

307

The woman did not wait for his answer. Anyway, it hadn't been a question, but a statement of fact.

'They told me what a charismatic and fascinating man you are. And they were right. '

She held out one of the two glasses. Taken aback by these words, Father McKean took it instinctively. He had had the impression that, if he hadn't, the woman would have let go and it would have fallen on the ground.

'My name's Sandhal Bones and I'm one of the organizers of the exhibition.'

The woman shook the hand he held out and kept it in hers a moment longer than necessary. Father McKean added embarrassment to all the emotions already churning inside him. He looked away from her and saw little bubbles rising vivaciously to the surface of the flute.

'So you're one of our benefactors.'

Mrs Bones tried, without too much success, to downplay her role. 'Benefactor is pitching it a little high. Let's say I like to give a hand where it's needed.'

Father McKean, although with no desire to drink, lifted the glass to his lips and took a small sip. 'It's thanks to people like you that Joy continues to thrive.'

'It's thanks to people like you that it exists at all,' she replied, taking him by the arm.

He smelled a delicate and doubtless highly expensive perfume, and heard the swish of her dress.

'And now let's go and see the work of your protégés. I've heard great things about them.'

Making her way nonchalantly through the crowd, Mrs Bones moved to the other side of the balcony overlooking the little lake.

The Boathouse Café was an elegant venue in the middle

308

of Central Park, joined to the rest of the city by East Drive. A single-storey building, its facade consisted of wide windows that allowed the customers a view of the water and the greenery as they dined. When the weather was fine, tables were put out on the terrace that ran all the way alongside it, and visitors could eat in the open air.

It was here that an exhibition of paintings, sculptures and crafts involving kids in the care of institutions similar to Joy had been organized by a committee whose name Father McKean could never remember. It was a way of allowing them to communicate with people, both personally and through their artworks. When the idea had been suggested, Father McKean had approached Jubilee Manson and Shalimar Bennett. The two of them were still in the middle of a difficult journey, but eventually he had become convinced, as had John, that this experience could only do them good.

Shalimar was a white girl from a normal middle-class family. They had managed to get her off heroin, as well as the self-harming that had covered her arms with scars. Father McKean wouldn't have admitted it to anyone, not even the Inquisition, but she was his favourite. She had a face that inspired tenderness and a wish to protect her. And light seemed to radiate from her eyes whenever anyone complimented her on her work, which was halfway between sculpture and jewellery. Original and colourful bracelets, necklaces, earrings were all made from materials that were not so much random as rudimentary.

Jubilee, a seventeen-year-old black boy, came from a very different kind of family, one where there were no rules and where in order to survive you had to fight. His mother was a prostitute and his father had been stabbed to death in a fight.

309

His brother Jonas claimed to be a rapper, under the stage name Iron7. In reality, he was the head of a gang mainly involved in drugs and prostitution. When his mother had found crack in Jubilee's room, she had realized that her younger son was about to follow in his brother's footsteps. In one of her rare lucid moments, by some lucky intuition, she had taken him to see Father McKean at Joy. The same afternoon she had killed herself.

Once past his initial difficulties, Jubilee had adapted well to the life of the community and soon after his arrival had shown marked artistic gifts, which had been encouraged and cultivated. Now some of his most interesting works – although quite immature and needing allowances to be made – formed part of this exhibition in Central Park.

Father McKean and Mrs Bones reached the area where three of Jubilee's paintings were displayed on easels. The influence of pop-art, and particularly Basquiat, was obvious but the bright colours, and the originality with which they were juxtaposed, showed great promise for the future.

The young painter was standing next to his works. Mrs Bones stopped in front of the pictures, in order to cast an eye over them.

'And this is our young artist.'

She examined the works with great attention, not devoid of a certain bewilderment. 'Well, I'm no critic and this certainly isn't Norman Rockwell. But I have to say they are . . . they are . . .'

'Explosive?'

Having suggested this definition Father McKean winked at Jubilee, who was trying hard not to laugh.

Mrs Bones turned to the priest as if she had seen the light. 'Of course. That's exactly what they are. Explosive.'

'That's what we all think.'

Having gratified both the artist's ego and Mrs Bones' obsession with patronage, Father McKean started to find her presence annoying. A short distance away, he saw John Kortighan talking to a group of people and threw him a glance that contained a desperate plea for help.

John immediately grasped the situation. He freed himself from the people he had been talking with and came towards them.

Father McKean made as if to get away. 'Mrs Bones . . .'

In return, she gave him a look in which there was a little too much fluttering of the eyelashes. 'You can call me Sandhal, if you prefer.'

Just then, John reached them and released him from his ordeal.

'Mrs Bones, this is John Kortighan, who works with me. He's the principal architect of the smooth running . . .'

As he introduced him, Father McKean turned his head to look at him. John was standing with his back to the water, and the priest's eyes were drawn past him, past the crowded balcony, all the way to the cycle track that ran alongside the little lake on the left.

Standing there with his hands in the pockets of his jeans was a man in a green military jacket. Father McKean felt as though the breath had been knocked out of him. A wave of heat rose to his face. He somehow managed to finish the introduction.

'. . . of our little community.'

John held out his hand, diplomatic as always. 'Pleased to meet you, Mrs Bones. I know you're one of the principal architects of this event.'

The woman's little laugh came to him as if in a trance. 'As

311

I was saying to Father McKean, I've always been ready to do something for my fellow human beings.'

The words seemed to come from a great distance, as if muffled by space and fog. He couldn't take his eyes off that man standing alone, looking in his direction, while bicycles passed close by him. He told himself jackets like that were very common and that an event like this was bound to attract the attention of outsiders. It was perfectly normal for a person to stop and look to see what was going on.

It was a reasonable attempt to reassure himself, but he knew that wasn't the case. He knew this was no ordinary person but the man who had whispered those sacrilegious words to him inside the confessional along with his murderous intentions.

I am God . . .

The faces and the noise and the people around him had vanished. Only that disquieting figure drew his attention, his thoughts, his eyes. His longing for mercy. Somehow he was certain that the man had seen him and that, of all the people there, he, Father McKean, was the one he was staring at.

'Excuse me a moment.'

He didn't even hear what John and Mrs Bones said in reply.

He had moved away from them and was making his way through the crowd, straight to the other end of the balcony. Losing and finding again the sombre eyes of that stranger who had taken up residence inside him like a harbinger of doom. He wanted to reach him and try to talk to him, try to make him see reason, even though he knew it was a desperate enterprise. On his side, the man continued to watch him as he walked, waiting, as if he had come to the Boathouse Café with the same intention.

312

Father McKean suddenly found two black men barring his way.

One was just a little shorter than him and was wearing a hooded down jacket that was much too big for him and much too heavy for the season, a black cap with the peak at the side, jeans, and a pair of heavy sneakers. On his chest, a glittering gold chain.

The man who loomed behind him was huge. It didn't seem possible that a man that size could actually move. He was dressed all in black, and his head was covered in a kind of bandana that looked like one of those hairnets men used to wear at night to straighten their hair.

The thinner of the two men put his hand on Father McKean's chest and stopped him. 'Where are you going, priest man?'

Annoyed by this hitch, Father McKean instinctively turned to look to his right. The man in the green jacket was still there, observing the scene without expression. Reluctantly, he turned his attention back to the person in front of him.

'What do you want, Jonas? I didn't think you'd been invited.'

'Iron7 doesn't need an invitation if these assholes can get in. Right, Dude?'

The big man merely nodded impassively.

'Well,' Father McKean said, 'now that you've demonstrated how strong you are, I think you can leave.'

Jonas Manson smiled, revealing a small diamond encrusted in one of his incisors. 'Hey, hold on a minute, priest. What's the hurry? I'm the brother of one of the artists. Can't I admire his work like everyone else?'

He looked around and, beyond Father McKean, glimpsed Jubilee still standing next to his paintings and commenting on them to other people.

'There he is. There's my boy.'

The man who called himself Iron7 pushed Father McKean aside and headed towards his brother, followed by the impressive hulk of Dude. People instinctively stepped aside for them. Father McKean walked behind them, trying to keep the situation under control.

Jonas reached the paintings and, without even greeting his brother, assumed a dramatic studio pose in front of them. On seeing him coming, Jubilee had fallen silent, taken a step backwards and started shaking.

'Hey, great stuff. Really great stuff. What do you think, Dude?'

Again the fat man, without speaking, confirmed his chief's words with a movement of his head. John, who had grasped the tricky nature of the situation, approached, trying to put his body between Jonas and his brother.

'You can't stay here.'

'Oh yes? Who says so? You, runt?' The rapper turned to the giant and smiled. 'Dude, get this asshole out of the way.'

The man reached out his huge hand, grabbed John by his shirt collar, pulled him towards him as if he were weightless and then pushed him back again so that he hit the balustrade. Father McKean intervened to stop John trying to react. If a fight broke out, others might get involved.

'Let it be, John. I'll deal with this.'

Jonas let out a vulgar laugh. 'Oh, great. You'll deal with this.'

In the meantime a void had formed around them. All the people who had been standing nearby, while not quite sure exactly what was happening, had decided that it was better to move away from these two gaudy characters with their rude behaviour and unappetizing faces.

314

'You and I have to talk business, priest.'

'We don't have any business with each other, Jonas.'

'Get off your high horse. I know things aren't going too well in that place of yours. I'd like to give you a hand. I thought twenty grand might come in useful.'

Father McKean wondered how this delinquent had found out about Joy's financial difficulties. Certainly not from his brother, who was terrified of him and avoided him like the plague. It was clear that right now, given how empty the community's coffers were, twenty thousand dollars would be like manna from heaven. But they couldn't take it from a man like that, with the kind of things he was involved in.

'You can keep your money. We'll manage.'

Jonas put his index finger on the priest's chest and started to prod him as if trying to perforate his sternum. 'Are you refusing my money? Do you think it's dirty?'

He paused, as if reflecting on the implications of what he had just heard. He again looked at Father McKean.

'So my money is no good . . .'

Then he pointed to the people around him and his anger exploded.

'But these assholes' money is all right, is that it? These men in their jackets and ties who look so respectable and buy the whores and the other shit that I sell. And all these women who act like little plaster saints but go around grabbing as much black dick as they can get hold of.'

A rustle and a moan behind him. Without turning, Father McKean realized that one of the women present had fainted. The rapper continued spreading his venom.

'I only wanted to do some good. Help my brother and that fucking place where you live.'

Jonas Manson put his hand in his pocket and when he took it out he was clutching a knife. Father McKean heard it open with a dry snap and saw the blade glitter in the light. The noise around them increased, becoming the shuffle of feet on the wooden terrace. A couple of women screamed hysterically.

With the knife in his hand, Jonas turned towards Jubilee, who was watching him in terror.

'Did you hear that, little brother? Did you hear how high and mighty this priest thinks he is?'

Jubilee took another step back, while Jonas approached the paintings. Father McKean moved to try to intercept him, but Dude moved with an agility that was impressive for someone of his size. He put his arms around the priest's chest to immobilize him, and squeezed, knocking the air out of his lungs and sending a sharp pain shooting through his muscles.

'Hold still, priest,' Jonas said, 'this is a family affair.' He turned to Jubilee, who seemed to be about to faint. 'And you don't even say a word. You just let this piece of shit insult your brother.'

He made a quick movement, there was a tearing sound, and a long diagonal cut appeared on the painting in front of him. He was about to do the same thing to the next painting when from somewhere on their right came a voice.

'All right, guys, you've had your fun. Now put the knife down and lie on the ground.'

Father McKean turned his head and saw a uniformed officer, standing on the lawn holding a gun aimed at Jonas. The rapper looked at him nonchalantly, as if having a gun pointed at him was a normal occurrence.

The officer made an impatient gesture with his weapon. 'Did you hear what I said? Lie down on the ground with your hands behind your head. And you, gorilla, drop that man.'

Father McKean felt the pressure lessen, and air started returning to his lungs. Dude let go of him and joined his boss. Slowly, as if it was their own thoughtful concession rather than something imposed by a third party, they lay down on the floor and put their hands over their heads.

While the officer kept his eye on them and radioed for backup, Father McKean, free at last, turned towards the lake. He peered anxiously around the shore and the cycle track, searching for someone he couldn't find.

His nightmare, the man in the green jacket, had vanished.

CHAPTER 28

Vivien listened anxiously to the variations in the noise of the engine as the helicopter descended.

She didn't like flying. She didn't like being at the mercy of a vehicle she couldn't control, in which every patch of turbulence made her jump and every change in the turning of the blades got her nervous. She looked out the window at the ground coming closer. Hanging in a black mass of darkness that seemed to have invaded the earth, the lights of the world lay beneath them. The triumphal light of a great city and the more isolated lights of the smaller towns surrounding it like satellites. The helicopter tilted and made an agile turn to the right. Below, directly in line with the front of the vehicle, signal lights marked the runway of a small airport.

The voice of the pilot over her headphones took her by surprise. Not a word had been spoken since the start of the flight.

'We'll be landing shortly.'

Vivien was glad to hear it. She hoped that by the time she started on the return journey she'd have a result that would allow her to face that interlude of emptiness and darkness in a different mood.

Darkness had overtaken them halfway through the journey, and Vivien had understood why it had been necessary to use a helicopter equipped with blind flight, even though she couldn't figure out how the pilot could possibly make anything of that mass of screens he had in front of him.

Beside her, leaning towards the window on his side, his head tilted slightly back, Russell had taken off his headphones and was sleeping, even snoring a little. Vivien sat looking at him for a few moments in the reflected light from the control panel and remembered his head resting on the pillow, his regular breathing in the semi-darkness, on the night she had got out of bed and gone to the window.

The night when the world had exploded, in every meaning of the word.

As if that image had been thrust forcefully into his sleep, Russell opened his eyes. 'I must have dozed off.'

'Unless you snore while you're awake, I'd say you're right.'

He yawned and turned to look out the window. 'Where are we?'

'Almost there. We're descending.'

'Good.'

Vivien went back to studying the terrain beneath them which, after that brief absence, was preparing to receive them again, although many miles away from the place they had started. She felt the urgency of the situation sucking her down like a vortex, and the responsibility weigh on her more than the pressure of the air above her.

After her conversation with Jeremy Cortese, it had taken most of the rest of the day to get a result. Bellew had contacted Commissioner Willard, who had immediately arranged the backup needed for that kind of research. An unspecified number of officers had dispersed to the hospitals, large and small, of Manhattan, the Bronx, Queens and Brooklyn.

Code RFL.

They had extended the search to hospitals in New Jersey, calling on the support of the local police. Bellew, Vivien and Russell had waited in the second-floor office.

Vivien divided her time between longing for the captain's telephone to ring and fear that her own cellphone would ring, bringing bad news from the clinic where Greta was being treated. Russell sat down in an armchair, and had put his legs up on the little table in front of him and stared into space, demonstrating a power of abstraction she wouldn't have thought him capable of. The captain continued reading reports, but Vivien was prepared to bet that he had not absorbed a single word on those pages. The silence became like a spider's web none of them wanted to escape. Words would only have led to other conjectures and other hopes, whereas what they needed now was something concrete, a message from reality.

By the time the phone on the desk rang, the light beyond the windows was stamping the approach of dusk on the walls. The captain lifted the receiver to his ear.

'Bellew.'

The captain's impassive expression didn't give anything away to Russell and Vivien.

'Wait.'

He had taken a pen and paper and Vivien saw him quickly write something.

'Terrific work, boys. Congratulations.'

The receiver was not yet back in its place when the captain raised his head and held out what he had just written. Vivien took it gingerly, like an object that had just been pulled out of a fire.

'We have a name. From Samaritan Faith Hospital in

Brooklyn. A couple of nurses remember the guy well. They say he really was a monster, disfigured all over his body. He died just over six months ago.'

Vivien lowered her eyes to the piece of paper. On it were the words

Wendell Johnson – Hornell NY 7 June 1948.
140 Broadway Brooklyn

in the captain's rapid, sloping handwriting.

Vivien found it incredible that a shadow they had been chasing in vain had suddenly become a human being with a name and address and date of birth. But what was equally incredible was the number of victims linked to that name and how many others would eventually have to be added to the list.

As she read, Bellew was already going into action. He was already talking to the switchboard.

'Get me the police in Hornell, New York State.'

As he waited to be put through, he put the call on speakerphone, so that they could all listen. A professional voice came out of the small speaker.

'Hornell police headquarters. How can I help you?'

'This is Captain Alan Bellew of the 13th Precinct in Manhattan. Who am I speaking to?'

'Officer Drew, sir.'

'I need to speak with your chief. As soon as possible.'

'One moment, sir.'

Bellew was put on hold. A jingle played briefly, followed after a few moments by a deep voice sounding much more mature than the previous one.

'Captain Caldwell.'

'I'm Captain Alan Bellew of the NYPD.'

At the other end there was a brief silence.

'Good evening, captain. What can I do for you?'

'I need information on a man named Wendell Johnson. All I know is that he was born in Hornell on 7 June 1948. Do have anything on him in your files?'

'Just a moment.'

Only the noise of fingers moving rapidly over a keyboard. Then Captain Caldwell's voice returned.

'Here he is. Wendell Bruce Johnson. The only prior I have is an arrest for driving while intoxicated, in May 1968. There's nothing else on him.'

'Are you sure?'

'Give me another moment, please.'

Again the noise of fingers on keys and then again the voice. Vivien imagined a corpulent man trying to come to terms with a technology he didn't quite understand, a man whose main objective in life was to hand out as many fines as possible to justify his salary to the city council.

'There was someone taken in with him, for resisting arrest. A man named Lester Johnson.'

'His father or his brother?'

'From the date of birth, it has to be the brother. There's only a year between them.'

'Do you know if this Lester is still living in Hornell?'

'Unfortunately, I'm not from around here. In fact I've only just started in the job. I don't yet know many people. If you give me another few seconds I'll check.'

'That would be very helpful.'

Vivien saw on Bellew's face the temptation to explain that all those seconds added up to days and months. And they were having difficulty finding hours in a situation like this.

In spite of everything, Captain Caldwell replied calmly and politely, 'There's no Wendell Johnson in the phone book. But there is a Lester Johnson, at 88 Fulton Street.'

'Good. I'm sending you a couple of people in a helicopter. Can you provide a place where they can land?'

'There's Hornell Municipal Airport.'

'Perfect. They'll be arriving as soon as possible. After that, I'm going to need your help.'

'Whatever you need.'

'If you could go to meet them personally that would be great. In addition it's vital that this conversation remain confidential. Very confidential – have I made myself clear?'

'Loud and clear.'

'I'll speak to you soon then.'

The captain hung up and looked at Vivien and Russell.

'As I think you heard, you need to take a little trip. In the meantime I'll send a team to search this Johnson guy's address in Brooklyn. It's a formality, because I don't think we'll find anything, but in a case like this you never know.'

Within fifteen minutes Bellew had requested and obtained the use of a helicopter equipped for night flights. Vivien and Russell were driven at high speed to a soccer field on 15th Street, on the banks of the East River. The helicopter arrived soon afterwards, a graceless, overgrown insect that moved agilely in the sky. No sooner did they get on than the earth spun away from them and the city became a sequence of houses and towers down below until it had disappeared behind them. The plunge into darkness happened in slow motion, with only an ever thinner blade of light on the horizon to recall that the sun still existed.

*

The pilot brought the helicopter down smoothly next to a long, narrow building lit by a string of lampposts. On an open space to their left, a number of small tourist aeroplanes were parked. Cessnas, Pipers, Socatas and other models that Vivien didn't know. As she opened the door, a police car that had been waiting next to the building came towards them.

The car stopped and a uniformed officer climbed out. He was tall, in his forties, with salt and pepper hair and a moustache. He came towards them with the phlegmatic, shambling gait of a basketball player. As she shook his hand and looked into his eyes, Vivien realized that the judgement she had formed when she had heard his voice on the telephone had been a hasty one. He inspired confidence, the sense that he wasn't a man who abused the position he occupied.

'Captain Caldwell.' His handshake was firm and resolute.

'Detective Vivien Light. This is Russell Wade.'

The two men nodded to each other. The urgency that was driving them seemed to have also infected Hornell's chief of police. He immediately pointed to the car.

'Shall we go?'

They got in, and the vehicle pulled out while they were still putting on their seat belts. They drove out of the airport, leaving the lights of the runway behind them, and took Route 36 heading south.

'Fulton Street isn't far. It's in the north part of Hornell. We'll be there in a few minutes.'

There wasn't much traffic at that hour but Captain Caldwell nevertheless put on the flashing light.

Vivien insisted on one thing. 'I'll need you to switch it off when we get closer. I'd prefer to arrive unannounced.'

'Sure.'

If he, too, was dying of curiosity, he didn't let it show. He drove in silence, his face illuminated by the dim light of the dashboard. Vivien felt the presence of Russell in the back seat, silent, apparently absent. But judging by what she had read on his computer, that dreamy air of his concealed the ability to capture aspects and moods in a very involving way. After participating in something, he was able to make the reader feel as if he had actually been there with him. It was a completely different way of treating a subject, different from anything she had seen before in a newspaper article.

What they needed now was the truth. The press, once they'd had enough of reporting the attacks and their aftermath, and speculating on the possible perpetrators, would soon launch a virulent campaign against the police and the other investigating bodies, accusing them of not doing enough to guarantee the safety of the public. Criminal acts like those that were devastating the city would soon have political reper-cussions, offering a valid pretext to anyone who wanted to attack Willard or the mayor or whoever. Anyone with the slightest involvement in the investigation, her included, would be caught up in the storm, which, although starting at the top, would inevitably affect those at the bottom, too.

The cellphone in her pocket started ringing. On the display she saw Bellew's number.

She replied, with the absurd hope that he would tell her it was all over.

'Hello, Alan.'

'Where are you?'

'We just landed and now we're on our way to the subject's house.'

By now names were gone, as were all traces of identity, replaced by cold, impersonal words that referred to a human being only as 'the subject' or 'a suspect'.

325

'Great. We discovered something strange at this end, and I'm not sure what to make of it.'

'What is it?'

'We checked out Wendell Johnson's apartment. Obviously, no one was there. But get this: the guy knew he was terminally ill, but just before he was admitted to hospital he paid a year's rent.'

'That is strange.'

'That's what I thought.'

Captain Caldwell switched off the light on the roof. Vivien realized that they were nearing their destination.

'Alan, we're there. I'll call you as soon as I know anything.'

'OK.'

The car turned left onto a short street called Fulton Street, drove past a row of identical houses and stopped at the end, outside number 88. It was a small house that, from what they could see of it, could have done with a coat of paint and some repairs to the roof. There were lights on in the windows. Vivien was grateful she wouldn't have to drag anyone from their bed. She knew that when that happened, it usually took a while before people were in a fit state to talk.

'Here we are.'

They got out of the car in silence and walked in Indian file down the short drive. Vivien let Captain Caldwell lead the way, so that he could feel he was still in charge.

Caldwell rang the bell next to the door. A few moments later, light filtered through the frosted glass. There was the sound of bare feet approaching quickly and lightly. The door opened and a blond, freckled boy of about five peered out. He was surprised to see a man in uniform towering over him, but did not seem afraid.

Caldwell bent slightly. 'Hello there, champ,' he said in a calm, friendly voice. 'What's your name?'

The boy reacted suspiciously to this attempt at communication. 'I'm Billy. What do you want?'

'I need to speak to Lester Johnson. Is he home?'

The boy ran away, allowing the door to swing open. 'Grandpa, the police want you.'

Straight ahead of them was a corridor ending in a staircase that led to the upper floor. To the right was a small lobby, and to the left a door, through which the boy disappeared. Before long, a man came out. He was an energetic-looking man in his sixties, wearing a blue shirt and a pair of faded jeans. He still had a thick head of hair and alert eyes that looked them rapidly up and down. It struck Vivien that this was the way prison inmates sometimes behaved.

She let Captain Caldwell take the initiative. It was his territory and Vivien owed that to him. She hoped that when the time came he would be shrewd enough to step aside.

'Mr Lester Johnson?'

'Yes, that's me. What do you want?'

That phrase seemed to be part of the family's linguistic heritage: the boy had used it, too.

'I'm Captain Caldwell. I—'

'Yes, I know who you are. Who are these people?'

Vivien decided that this was the moment to step forward. 'I'm Detective Vivien Light, from the NYPD. I need to speak with you.'

Lester Johnson gave her a quick, self-satisfied appraisal, which above all took in her physical appearance. 'OK. Come on in.'

He led them to the door through which he had emerged and the boy had disappeared. They found themselves in a large living room, with couches and armchairs. On one of these Billy was sitting watching cartoons on a flat screen TV. However rundown the exterior of the house might have looked, the interior was neat and tidy, with an excellent choice of fabrics and wallpaper, all in natural colours. Vivien saw a woman's hand in the matching shades.

'Billy, it's time for bed,' Lester Johnson said to his grandson in an authoritative tone.

'But grandpa . . .' the boy protested weakly.

'I said it's time for bed. Go to your room and don't make a fuss.'

His voice made it clear he would accept no compromise. The boy switched off the TV and walked sulkily past them, and without saying goodnight to anyone disappeared around the corner. A few moments later they heard the sound of his bare feet on the stairs grow weaker until it faded completely.

'My son and sister-in-law are out for the evening. And I'm a bit more lenient with the boy than his parents.'

After that brief insight into his family life, he indicated the couch and the armchairs. 'Take a seat.'

Vivien and Caldwell sat down on the couch and Lester Johnson on the armchair facing it. Russell chose the one that was further away.

Vivien decided to get straight to the point. 'Mr Johnson, are you related to a man named Wendell Johnson?'

'He was my brother.'

'Why do you say *was*?'

Lester Johnson gave a vague shrug. 'Because early in 1971 he left for Vietnam and that's the last we heard of him. He was never declared either dead or missing in action. Which must mean he got out alive, but never got in touch with us. Well, that's his business. He stopped being my brother a long time ago.'

Hearing a relationship between brothers dismissed like that, Vivien instinctively turned to look at Russell. His eyes had hardened for a moment, but immediately afterwards he resumed the stance he had decided to adopt, one of attentive silence.

'Before he left for Vietnam, did Wendell work in the construction industry?'

'No.'

That monosyllable rang in Vivien's ears like a bad omen. She sought refuge in illusion. 'Are you sure?'

'Miss, I'm old enough to be a little soft in the head. But not so soft that I can't remember what my brother did when he was still here. He wanted to be a musician. He played the guitar. He would never have done any job where he risked damaging his hands.'

From the inside pocket of her jacket, she took the photographs that had brought her to Hornell. She held them out to Lester Johnson. 'Is this Wendell?'

Lester did not take them from her, but leaned forward to look at them. After what seemed an eternity, he said, 'No. I've never seen this guy before in my life.' He leaned back in his chair.

Russell, who had been silent until now, surprised everyone by speaking at this point. 'Mr Johnson, if that isn't your brother, it might be someone he knew in the army. Usually, guys who went to Vietnam sent home photographs of themselves in uniform. Sometimes alone, but often with a group of friends. Did he happen to do the same?'

Lester Johnson looked at him sharply, as if the question had put paid to any hope he might have had that these intruders would leave his house soon. 'Wait a minute,' he said. 'I'll be right back.'

He got up from the couch and left the room. When he returned, he was holding a cardboard box. He handed it to Vivien and sat down again.

'These are all the pictures I still have of Wendell. There should be some from Vietnam among them.'

Vivien opened the box. It was full of photographs, some in colour, some in black and white. She looked through them quickly. The subject was always the same: a pleasant-looking, fair-haired boy, alone or with friends. At the wheel of a car, as a child on a pony, with his brother, with his parents, with long hair held in a band while he hugged a guitar. She had already gone through most of them when she found it. It was in black and white and showed two soldiers in front of a tank. One was the smiling boy she had seen many times in the previous photographs; the other was the young man who had been holding up a three-legged cat in the photographs they had in their possession.

Vivien turned it over and saw on the back in faded letters

The King and Little Boss

written in irregular handwriting that had one major characteristic: it was completely different from the handwriting in the letter that had started this whole madness.

She handed the photograph to Russell, so that he could see the result of his intuition. When she got it back, she passed it to Lester Johnson. 'What do these words on the back mean?'

The man took the photograph and looked first at the front and then at the back. 'The King was what Wendell called

330

himself as a joke. I assume Little Boss was the other boy's nickname.'

He handed the rectangle back to Vivien.

'I'm sorry if I told you I'd never seen him. I don't think I've looked at these photos for thirty years.'

He leaned back in the armchair again and Vivien was surprised to see tears welling in his eyes. Maybe his cynical attitude was only a kind of self-defence – maybe the fact that he'd never heard from his brother again had hurt him more than he wanted to admit. Her arrival must have reopened an old wound.

'And you really have no idea who that person with Wendell could be?'

The man shook his head, without saying anything. His silence was worth more than a thousand words. It meant that tonight he had lost his brother for a second time. It also meant that they had lost the one real lead they had.

'Can we keep this photograph? I promise you'll get it back.'

'All right.'

Vivien had stood up. The others realized that they had no reason to stay here any longer. All the energy seemed to have drained out of Lester Johnson. He walked them to the door in silence, maybe thinking to himself how little it takes to dredge up old memories and how much they hurt.

As Vivien was about to leave, he held her back. 'Can I ask you a question, Miss?'

'Go ahead.'

'Why are you looking for him?'

'I can't tell you that. But there's one thing I can say for certain.' She paused, as if to isolate what she was about to say. 'The reason your brother never got in touch with you isn't because he didn't want to. Your brother died in Vietnam, just like so many others.'

She saw the man take a deep breath. 'Thank you. Goodnight.'

'Thank *you*, Mr Johnson. Say goodnight to Billy for us. He's a great kid.'

When the door closed behind them, she was pleased that she had resolved his uncertainties. For them, on the other hand, she thought as they walked to the car, certainty was still a distant target. She had arrived in Hornell convinced she had reached the finishing post, instead of which she had come up against a new and very uncertain point of departure.

Wars end. Hate lasts for ever.

That phrase of Russell's came back to her as she opened the car door. Hate kept alive for years had led a man to plant bombs all over a city. Hate had led another man to detonate them. The illusion that she might return to New York in a different mood had faded. She knew that the return journey she would be thinking of the consequences of war and the power it had, after many years, to still claim victims.

CHAPTER 29

When the alarm went off, Vivien did not open her eyes immediately.

She lay in bed, enjoying the touch of the sheets on her body, lethargic after a night of intermittent sleep and no rest. Shifting a little, she realized that she was lying diagonally across the bed, a sign that the restlessness that had made her change position a hundred times in her half-waking state had continued even after she had fallen asleep. She reached out a hand to switch off the alarm. It was nine o'clock. She stretched and took a deep breath. The pillow next to her still bore traces of Russell's smell.

She allowed herself a glance into the half-lit, familiar landscape of her bedroom. The next stage of the investigation was out of her hands for now, and Bellew had allowed her a night off. She had smiled at those words. As if taking time off was possible, with the cellphone on the night table next to her that could ring at any moment, bringing news that would make her hide her head under the blankets and wish she could wake up a thousand years and a thousand miles away.

She got out of bed, put on a soft terrycloth bathrobe, picked up the phone and walked barefoot to the kitchen, where she started making coffee. This morning, contrary to habit, she was in no mood for breakfast. The very idea of food turned her stomach. And to think that the last time she'd eaten had been with Russell at the stand in Madison Square Park!

Russell . . .

As she put the filter in the machine, she felt a momentary anger. With all that she was going through, with a madman somewhere out there threatening to blow up half the city, with Greta lying on a bed in a clinic in a desperate condition, it didn't seem either possible or fair that there could still be room in her brain to think of that man.

Last night, after they got back from Hornell, he had come to the apartment with her, taken his things and left. He hadn't asked to stay, and she knew that if she'd suggested it, he would have refused.

Standing in the doorway on his way out, he had turned to look at her with a mixture of sadness and determination in his dark eyes. 'I'll call you tomorrow morning.'

'OK.'

She had stood there for a few moments looking at the closed door.

She poured coffee into a cup. However many sugars she added, she knew it would always be too bitter.

She told herself that what had happened was the kind of thing that happened many times in life. Too many times, maybe. It had been a night full of the only kind of love that time did not cover with frost, the kind that blazed into life at night only to fade with the sun the following morning. That was how he had taken it and that was how she had to take it, too.

But if that's the price I have to pay to have you, I gladly accept . . .

'Go fuck yourself, Russell Wade,' she said out loud, and continued standing there, leaning on the counter, drinking coffee she didn't really want. She forced herself to think of something else.

At Hornell Municipal Airport, just before the helicopter lifted off to take them back to New York, she had called the captain to update him on the bad news. After she had told him what had happened, a brief silence at the other end had told her that Bellew was trying to hold back a curse.

'So we're back to square one.'

Vivien had not admitted defeat. 'There's still one lead we can pursue.'

'Go on.' There was a slight hint of mistrust in the captain's voice.

'We have to go back to the period of the Vietnam war. We absolutely need to find out what happened to the real Wendell Johnson and this other kid nicknamed Little Boss. It's the only angle we have.'

'I'll call the commissioner. At this hour I don't think it's possible to do anything, but I'll start the ball rolling first thing tomorrow morning.'

'OK.'

The reply had been drowned by the blades as they started to churn up the air. She and Russell had got into the helicopter, and for the whole journey there had been no sound strong enough to break their silence.

The telephone next to her rang. As if her thoughts had called him up, Bellew's appeared on the display.

'Vivien here.'

'How are you feeling?'

'I'm still alive. Any news?'

'Yes. And it isn't good.'

She waited in silence for the cold shower to hit her.

'Willard contacted the army early this morning. The name

Wendell Johnson is classified. There's no way to access his files.'

Vivien felt anger clutch her stomach. 'They're crazy. In a case like this—'

'I know,' Bellew interrupted her. 'But you're forgetting two things. The first is that we can't tell them what we're working on. The second is that even if we could, it's too flimsy a lead to break through that wall. The commissioner has asked the mayor to intervene. Maybe Gollemberg can approach the president. But there are procedures to go through that take time, even for the most important man in America. And if Russell is right, time is the very thing we don't have.'

'It's crazy. All those people dead . . .'

She left the sentence unfinished, with a powerful implied reference to those who might still die.

'I agree. But there's nothing we can do for now.'

'Anything else?'

'One small thing you might be pleased to hear. The DNA test has proved that the man in the wall really is Mitch Sparrow. You were right.'

At any other moment, that would have been a great success. A victim identified and his killer already punished. Now it was only a source of pitiful pride and no consolation at all.

Vivien had tried to react against her sense of discouragement. There was one thing she could do, in the meantime. 'I want to take a look at . . . that man's apartment.'

She had been about to say Wendell Johnson's apartment but had realized that the name no longer applied. He wasn't Wendell Johnson any more – he was the Phantom of the Site.

'I told them not to touch anything, because I knew you'd want to do that. I'll send an officer to wait for you with the keys.'

'Great. I'll head out right now.'

'There's one strange thing. In the whole apartment there are almost no fingerprints. And the few there are certainly don't match the prints of Wendell Johnson that Captain Caldwell sent me.'

'Does that mean he wiped them?'

'Maybe. Or it could mean our man didn't have any prints. Probably wiped out when he got those burns.'

A phantom.

No name, no face, no prints.

A man who, even after death, didn't accept an identity. Vivien wondered what kind of things the creature had experienced, what sufferings he had endured, to become what he had become. She wondered how long he had cursed the society around him, the society that had taken his life away from him and given him nothing in return. Exactly how he had cursed it they already knew. Dozens of deaths had demonstrated that.

'OK. I'm heading out.'

'Keep in touch.'

Vivien hung up and put the phone in the pocket of her bathrobe. She rinsed the cup in the sink and put it in the rack to dry. She went in the bathroom and turned on the shower. After a moment or two, enjoying the warm water on her naked body, she couldn't help thinking that this case verged on the grotesque. Not because of how elusive the solution remained, but because of the way fate kept presenting absurd new escape routes, the way the truth kept finding unexpected hiding places for itself.

She got out of the shower, dried herself and put on clean clothes. As she put yesterday's clothes in the laundry basket, she seemed to smell the scent of disappointment, which in her imagination was like the smell of dead flowers.

When she was ready, she picked up the telephone and called Russell.

An impersonal voice told her that his telephone was off, or unobtainable.

Strange.

It seemed impossible that he could be so negligent, given his eagerness to follow the case, the opportunity it was providing him, and the insight he had demonstrated during the investigation. Maybe he was still asleep. People accustomed to an easy life developed the ability to sleep on command, and for an excessive length of time, just as they managed to stay awake longer than most.

Well, it's his loss . . .

She would search the apartment on her own. That was how she usually worked, and in her opinion it was still the best way.

When she reached her car, she found Russell standing next to it.

He had his back to her. She saw that he, too, had changed: his clothes had the smell clothes get when they have been in a bag for too long. He was looking at the river, where a barge was moving slowly upstream, drawn by a tugboat. It was like an image of victory against adverse fate, an image it was difficult to share right now.

Hearing footsteps behind him, Russell turned. 'Hi.'

'Hi. Have you been here long?'

'A while.'

Vivien pointed to the front door of her building. 'You could have come up.'

'I didn't want to bother you.'

What he really meant, Vivien thought, was that he hadn't wanted to be alone with her. But it made no difference.

'I called you and your telephone was off. I thought you'd thrown in the towel.'

'I couldn't do that. For a whole lot of reasons.'

Vivien decided not to ask what they were.

'Where are we going?' he asked as she started the engine.

'One-forty Broadway, Brooklyn. Where the Phantom of the Site lived.'

They turned onto West Street, heading south. Before too long they had left the entrance to the Brooklyn Battery Tunnel behind them and were heading for F.D. Roosevelt Drive. As they proceeded, Vivien updated Russell on what Bellew had told her: that Wendell Johnson's story was classified and that it wouldn't be easy to get around that fact in a short time. He listened in silence, with his usual intent expression, as if pursuing an idea he didn't see fit to express. In the meantime they had started across the Williamsburg Bridge and the water of the East River glittered beneath them, barely ruffled by a light wind. At the end of the bridge they turned right onto Broadway and soon found themselves in front of the building they were looking for.

It was an apartment block, with the same kind of down-at-heel look as the hundreds of anonymous hives that housed equally anonymous people in this city. It was in places like this that people lived for years without leaving any trace of their presence and sometimes died without anyone thinking to look for them for days.

Outside the front door, which had the number 140 on it, a patrol car was waiting. Vivien parked just opposite. Officer Salinas got out of the patrol car and came towards them.

He didn't deign to look at Russell. By now, that appeared to have become the official attitude of the 13th Precinct to him. Even the friendly attitude Salinas had always shown him seemed to have vanished.

'Hi, Vivien,' he said, handing her a bunch of keys. 'The captain told me to give you these.'

'Perfect.'

'It's Apartment 418B. Do you want me to go up with you?'

'No sweat. We can manage.'

The officer did not insist, pleased to get away from the place and the company. As they watched the patrol car drive off, she was surprised by Russell saying, 'Thank you.'

'For what?'

'That officer asked if he could go up with you. It was obvious he meant only you. When you replied you said "we", meaning me, too. I'm grateful to you.'

Vivien realized she had got so used to having him with her that she had answered like that unconsciously. But she was obliged to consider her own thoughtfulness. 'For better or worse,' she said, 'we're a team.'

Russell accepted the definition with a half-smile. 'I don't think it's making you too many friends in the precinct.'

'It'll pass.'

They waited for the elevator in a lobby that smelled of men and cats. The elevator's arrival was signalled by some incomprehensible squeaks and creaks. They went up to the fourth floor and immediately located the apartment, sealed by a couple of yellow ribbons.

Vivien removed them and turned the key in the lock.

No sooner had they opened the door than they were hit by that desolate feeling you get in places that have been uninhabited for a while. The door led straight into a room that

340

doubled as kitchen and living room. It was obvious at a glance that this was the apartment of a man who had lived alone. Alone and without any interest in the world. To the right, there was a kitchen corner and a refrigerator next to a table with one chair. Opposite the oven, next to the window, an armchair and an old TV set on a shabby little table. Over everything, a thin layer of dust bearing traces of the police search the previous day.

They entered the apartment as if entering a temple of evil, holding their breaths. For years a man had lived within these walls.

Now that they had reached a point where they had an inkling of his story, they knew the true extent of the resentment that, day after day, had nourished his madness.

He had chosen to kill people under the illusion that in doing so he was destroying his own memories.

They took a quick look around the bare room, which was devoid of any object that was not strictly utilitarian. No paintings, no ornaments, no concessions to personal taste, unless that very absence could be considered a kind of personal taste. Next to the refrigerator was the only trace of normal life and humanity in the room. A shelf filled with aromatic essences, a sign that the man who had lived here had cooked for himself.

They concluded their visit of the tiny apartment in the adjoining room. Against the wall to the right of the door was a closet, and opposite it was a single bed pushed almost up against the wall. To the right of the bed, dividing it from the wall, a night table and a grim-looking lamp. To the left was a rack with two parallel shelves. The upper shelf was the height of a normal table, the lower one some twenty inches from the floor. In this room was only the second chair in the

341

whole apartment, an old office armchair on wheels, which looked so shabby it might have been acquired from a junk-yard rather than bought. The walls were bare, apart from a large map of the city hanging on the wall above the rack.

There were some objects on the lower shelf. Mostly books. A few magazines. A pack of cards that made them think of endless games of solitaire. And a big grey cardboard folder containing sheets of paper.

Vivien went closer.

If this was where he prepared his devices, then any tools or other things that could be analysed would already have been taken away by the team that had searched the apartment the previous day. But the captain had assured them that everything had been left intact, which made it likely that they hadn't found anything.

She bent down and looked at some of the books. A Bible. A cookery book. A thriller by Jeffery Deaver. A tourist guide to New York.

She picked up the folder and placed it on the upper shelf. When she opened it, she found it full of drawings. Oddly, none of them were on normal paper. They had all been executed on stiff sheets of transparent plastic, as if the artist had wanted to express his originality, not only through his talent but also through the medium he had used.

She started looking at the drawings, one by one.

It soon became clear that the medium was the only original thing about them, because, even to an untrained eye, the drawings revealed no artistic talent at all. The composition was approximate, the line wavering, and the use of colour lacked both taste and technique. The person who had lived in this apartment seemed to have been obsessed with constellations. Each drawing was of a different constellation, but according to a map of the stars unknown to anyone but the artist.

Constellation of Beauty, Constellation of Karen, Constellation of the End, Constellation of Wrath . . .

A series of points joined by different-coloured lines. Sometimes stars, drawn in a childlike hand, sometimes circles, sometimes crosses, sometimes just tangled brush strokes. Russell, who had held back until now, came closer to see what Vivien was looking at.

He allowed himself a judgement she couldn't help but share. 'Horrible, aren't they?'

She was just about to agree when her cellphone started ringing. She put a hand in her pocket, planning to turn it off without even looking to see who was calling her. But then she took it out reluctantly and looked at it, afraid that she would see the number of the Mariposa clinic on the display.

Instead, it showed the name of Father McKean.

'Hello.'

She heard his voice, familiar but oddly different. It sounded tense, almost frightened, without any trace of the energy it usually conveyed. 'Vivien, it's Michael.'

'Hi. What is it?'

'I need to see you, Vivien. As soon as possible, and alone.'

'Michael, I'm tremendously busy right now, I can't—'

'It's a matter of life and death, Vivien,' he said as if he had rehearsed these words to himself many times. 'Not mine but that of many people.'

A moment's hesitation. A moment that, to judge by his next words, must have seemed endless to him. 'It's to do with those explosions, may God forgive me.'

'The explosions? What's your connection with the explosions?'

'Come quickly, I beg you.'

343

Father McKean hung up. Vivien stood there in the middle of the room, in the square of sunlight cast on the floor from the window. She realized that while she had been on the telephone, as often happened when she was engrossed, she had moved, so that she was now back in the living room.

Russell had followed her and had stopped in the doorway to the bedroom.

She looked at him. She wasn't sure what to say. Michael had asked to speak with her alone. Taking Russell with her might mean annoying Michael and perhaps inhibiting him from saying what he had to say. At the same time, it meant confessing that her niece was in a community for drug addicts, and that was something she couldn't deal with right now.

She made a quick choice, putting off until later the question of whether she had chosen rightly or wrongly. 'I have to go somewhere.'

'Does that mean you have to go alone?

Russell knew something was up: during her phone conversation, he had heard her let slip the word *explosions*.

'Yes. I have to see someone and I have to see him alone.'

'I thought we had an agreement.'

She turned her back on him, and immediately felt ashamed of doing that. 'The agreement doesn't apply to this.'

'The captain gave me his word I could follow the investigation.'

She felt anger rising inside her.

She turned abruptly, a hard expression on her face. 'The captain gave you his word,' she said curtly. 'I didn't.'

The following second lasted a century.

I can't believe I really said that . . .

Russell turned pale. Then he looked at her for a moment,

344

the way you look at someone who is leaving and will never return.

Finally, in silence, he walked to the door. Vivien did not have the strength to say or do anything. He opened the door and went out into the corridor. The last sign of life from him was the door gently closing.

Vivien felt more alone than she had ever felt in her life. Her impulse was to go out in the corridor and call him back, but she told herself she couldn't do that. Not now. Not before finding out what Father McKean had to tell her. Many people's lives were at stake. Hers and Russell's didn't matter. From now on she would need all her willpower and all her courage, too much to use part of it admitting she was in love with a man who didn't want her.

She waited a few moments, long enough to give him time to leave the building. As she waited, she remembered the words he had said to her as they were coming in. They were like an accusation now.

She had said they were a team.

He had trusted her and she had betrayed him.

CHAPTER 30

When Vivien opened the door she saw the deserted, dimly lit corridor. The semi-darkness, and the thought that the man had walked down it for years, that every day he had planted his feet on that carpet, which had become an indefinable colour, made the place feel malign and hostile.

A wrinkled old black woman with incredibly crooked legs emerged around the corner of the landing and walked towards her, supporting herself with a stick. In her free arm she carried a shopping bag. When she saw Vivien closing the door, she couldn't help making a comment.

'Ah, so they finally rented it to a human being.'

'I'm sorry?'

The old woman didn't bother to give any other explanation. She stopped outside the door opposite the one Vivien had just come out of and unceremoniously handed her the bag. Presumably, her age and condition had taught her to impose, instead of asking. Or maybe she thought her age and condition in themselves gave her the right to whatever she wanted.

'Hold this. But remember, I don't give tips.'

Vivien found herself with the bag in her hands. A smell of onions and bread rose from it. Still supporting herself with her stick, the woman searched in the pocket of her coat. She took out a key and put it in the lock. She answered a question no one had asked.

'The police came yesterday. I knew that man wasn't a decent person.'

'The police?'

'Yeah. They're great people, too. They rang but I didn't open.'

After such an open declaration of mistrust, Vivien decided not to identify herself as a police officer. She waited for the old lady to open the door. Immediately, a big black cat poked its head out. When it saw that its owner was with a stranger, it ran away. Instinctively, Vivien checked that it had all four legs.

'Who lived here before me?'

'A guy with his face all scarred. A real monster. Not just the way he looked, the way he acted, too. One day, an ambulance came and took him away. To an asylum, I hope.'

In her concise, pitiless judgement, the woman had hit the target. That would have been the right place for the man, whoever he was, to spend his days. The old woman walked into her apartment and indicated the table with a nod.

'Put it there.'

Vivien followed her in and saw that the apartment was a mirror image of the one she had just been inspecting. In the room there were two other cats, in addition to the black one. A white and ginger cat was sleeping on a chair and didn't take any notice of them. A second one, a grey striped cat, jumped on the table. Vivien put down the bag, and the cat immediately ran to sniff it.

The woman gave it a cuff on its backside. 'Get away, you. You can eat later.'

The cat jumped to the floor and went and hid itself under the chair where its companion was still sleeping.

347

Vivien looked around. The room was a triumph of the unmatched. Not one chair was similar to another. The glasses on the shelf over the sink were all different among themselves. The place was a chaos of colours and old things. The cat smell in the apartment was worse than the one in the lobby.

The old woman turned to Vivien and looked at her as if she had just seen her for the first time. 'What was I saying?'

'You were talking about the man who had the apartment opposite.'

'Oh, yes, that guy. He never came back. That other guy came to see it a couple of times. But he can't have liked it, because he didn't rent it. God knows what state it was in.'

Vivien's heart leaped. 'Which other guy? The landlord didn't tell me there'd been anyone else interested in the apartment.'

The old woman took off her coat and threw it on the back of a chair. 'It happened a while back. A tall guy, in a green jacket. A military kind, I think. He was as strange as the first one. He came a couple of times then never came back. I'm glad he didn't take the apartment.'

Vivien would have liked to stay and ask her more questions without making her suspicious: she had made it clear right from the start how she felt about the police. But that would take time, and the urgency in Father McKean's voice required an immediate response. She promised herself that as soon as she'd seen the priest she'd come back and delve deeper.

The woman approached the kitchen area. 'How about a coffee?'

Vivien looked at her watch, as if seriously considering the idea. 'I'm sorry. I'd love to, but I'm in a hurry.'

A slight disappointment was visible on the old woman's face. Vivien came to her rescue.

'What's your name?'

'Judith.'

'Well, Judith, I'm Vivien. I tell you what we'll do. I'll go to my appointment and when I get back I'll knock at your door and we'll have that coffee. Like good neighbours.'

'Not between three and four. I have to go see the doctor because my back is—'

Oh no. Not now, not the list of aches and pains.

Vivien interrupted the start of what might turn out to be a long litany of arthritis and stomach aches. 'Look, I really have to go now. I'll see you later.'

She got to the door and before leaving threw her new friend a smile.

'And keep that coffee warm. We'll have plenty to talk about.'

'OK. But remember, I don't give tips.'

Vivien found herself alone again in the corridor, wondering how reliable that addle-headed old lady was. But she had given her some small ideas for leads, however slender. As Bellew had said several times, in their situation they couldn't afford to rule out anything.

The elevator took her down to the lobby. Out on the street, an officer was standing by her car, issuing a ticket. She reached the car just as the officer was lifting the windshield wiper to leave the ticket.

'Excuse me, officer.'

'Is this your vehicle?'

'Yes.'

'You know this space is reserved for loading and unloading merchandise?'

Without a word, Vivien flashed her shield.

Grumbling, the officer removed the ticket from the

349

window. 'Next time make sure you show the sign. That way we don't waste time. Either of us.'

Time, in fact, was the one thing Vivien didn't have. Not even to counter a neighbourhood cop's reasonable comments. 'I'm sorry,' she said. 'It wasn't my intention.'

The officer walked away, mumbling a goodbye. Vivien got in her car and started the engine. She again used the flashing light. She headed north, took the Brooklyn–Queens Expressway and then followed the 278 until, after the bridge, it became the Bruckner.

During the journey, after a lot of thought, she tried calling Russell a couple of times. His telephone was still off. To counter her own bad mood, she told herself she had done the right thing. With the best will in the world, she had to admit that part of her had gone with Russell when he had left.

She forced herself to go over the whole story in her mind, examining each aspect to see if they had overlooked anything. Ziggy, the letter, Wendell Johnson, Little Boss, that bizarre three-legged cat. The bombs a madman had planted before his death.

And finally that crazy cat lady, Judith. Was she to be trusted or not? Russell had seen a man in a green jacket leaving Ziggy's apartment. A man wearing the same kind of jacket had been seen in the other apartment. The question was: Was it the same person? If it was, it couldn't be a tenant, because the captain had said that the apartment had remained empty for a year. The reason for his presence there wasn't clear. Unless, together with the letter, the father had also sent his son the keys to his apartment. If that was the case, then the person they were so desperately seeking really had been in that apartment.

She deliberately left Father McKean's tense, anxious voice out of the equation, even though it was still echoing in her ears.

It's to do with those explosions, may God forgive me . . .

She didn't know what to expect.

Time and speed seemed to be going in two different directions. One was too fast, the other too slow. She tried once again to call Russell. More to pass the time than out of real interest, she told herself.

Nothing.

The telephone was off, or unobtainable. She yielded to her human feelings and allowed herself the fantasy of being somewhere else, with him. She felt a warm stream of desire lapping at her groin. She told herself that this was wrong, but it was the only sign she had that she was still alive.

When she turned on to the unpaved road, and after a few bends the roofs of Joy appeared, a sudden dread seized hold of her. She wasn't at all sure she wanted to know what Father McKean had to tell her. She slowed down. The priest was waiting for her on the edge of the garden, a black stain against the green of the vegetation. She saw that he was wearing his cassock. As she got out of the car and walked towards him, Vivien had the impression that this choice was not a random one, but meant something specific. As if Father McKean needed to assert his own identity in some way and was doing it with the only means at his disposal.

When she got close to him, she realized that her suppositions were probably not far from the truth. His eyes were lifeless and evasive. Not even a hint of the vitality and benevolence that were usually an integral part of his character.

'I'm so glad you're here,' he said.

'Michael, what's so urgent? What's happened?'

Father McKean looked around. A couple of kids at the far end of the garden were repairing a perimeter grille. A third was standing next to them and handing them the tools.

'Not here. Follow me.'

He started walking to the house. They passed the main entrance and came to the door of the room next to the office, which functioned as a small infirmary. Father McKean opened it.

'Come in. No one will disturb us here.'

Vivien followed him. The room was completely white: the walls and the ceiling and on the right, against the wall, a metal bed covered in a snow-white sheet. Just beyond it, in the corner, was an old hospital screen, restored and upholstered in cotton that was still white. On the opposite side was a small medicine cabinet of the same colour. The priest's cassock stood out like an inkstain on snow.

Father McKean came and stood in front of her. He didn't seem able to look her in the eyes for more than two seconds at a time. 'Vivien,' he said, 'do you believe in God?'

Vivien wondered why he was asking her that. He couldn't possibly have summoned her with such urgency only to question her about her faith. If Father McKean had asked her that, she decided, there had to be a reason.

'In spite of the work I do, Michael, I'm a dreamer. That's the most I can allow myself.'

'That's the difference between us. A dreamer hopes that his dreams will come true.' He paused, and looked at her with eyes that for a moment looked as they had always done. 'A believer is certain they will.'

He turned and went to the cabinet. He placed a hand on the top and stood looking at the boxes of medicines inside.

He spoke without looking at her.

'What I'm about to tell you goes against that certainty. It goes against the teachings I've followed for years. Against everything I've learned. But there are times when the dogmas of the Church become unintelligible when confronted with human suffering. So much human suffering.'

He turned to look at her. His face was ashen.

'Vivien, the man who set off the bombs on the Lower East Side and the Hudson confessed to me.'

For Vivien, it was like diving into the icy waters of the Arctic. And she stayed under for a long time, until she was able to resurface and find her breath again.

'Are you sure?'

The question had come to her instinctively and carried with it many implications. In return she got a calm, measured reply, the reply of someone able to explain something that is difficult to believe.

'Vivien, I have a degree in psychology. I know the world is full of crazy people ready to confess to all the sins on earth in order to get their fifteen minutes of fame. I know how difficult it is in certain cases for the police to concentrate on searching for the guilty party and avoid wasting time on people who merely claim to be guilty. But this is different.'

'What makes you think that?'

The priest shrugged. 'Everything and nothing. Details, words. But since the second bomb I've been sure it's him.'

After her initial shock, Vivien had regained her self-control, revived by an unnatural rush of adrenaline. She realized the importance of what Father McKean had just told her. At the same time, she knew what kind of inner battle he had won and lost in order to be able to say it.

'Do you mind going from the beginning?'

Father McKean nodded, and waited. Now that it was out in the open he knew that Vivien would know what to ask and the right way to ask it.

'How many times have you seen him?'

'Once.'

'When was that?'

'Sunday morning, the day after the first bomb.'

'What did he say?'

'He confessed what he had done. And he told me what he intended to do in the future.'

'How? Do you remember his exact words?'

'As if I could forget. He said that the first time he had reunited light and dark. The next time he would reunite water and earth.'

He left her time to think. Then he arrived at the conclusion for her.

'And that's how it was. The first explosion happened at dusk, when the light and the dark are reunited. The second took place on the shores of the river. In that way the earth and water became one and the same. Do you know what that means?'

'It means he's working his way through Genesis, only destroying instead of creating.'

'Precisely.'

'Did he tell you why he's doing it?'

Father McKean sat down on a stool, as if his strength was starting to desert him. 'I asked him that question, using almost the same words.'

'And what did he reply?'

'He replied "I am God".'

That phrase, repeated in a low voice for the first time outside the confessional, gave both of them a sharp sense of the madness.

354

Father McKean recalled his studies of psychology. 'This man, whoever he is, is much more than just a serial killer or a mass murderer. He combines both pathologies. And what he presents of both pathologies is the rage and the total lack of discrimination.'

Vivien found herself thinking that, if they caught this man, there would be psychiatrists ready to pay money just to study him. And many people who would pay to be able to kill him with their bare hands.

'Can you describe him?' she asked.

'Brown hair, young, tall, I think. A soft voice, but calm, and cold as ice.'

'Anything else?'

'If it's any use, I had the impression he was wearing a green military-style jacket. But clothes don't mean much.'

On the contrary, they mean everything.

Vivien felt excitement roll over her like a wave, and her lungs swelled as if she had breathed pure helium.

So Judith, who didn't give tips, had been right. She blessed her, vowing to herself that she would have that coffee and listen to her complaints about every single ailment. She crouched in front of Father McKean, who was looking desolately at the floor, and placed her hands on his knees. At that moment it didn't seem like excessive familiarity, only a mark of solidarity.

'Michael, it would take too long to explain how I know, but it's him. You were right. It's him.'

This time the incredulous question came from the priest, uncertain if he should yield to his own relief. 'Are you sure?'

Vivien sprang to her feet. 'One hundred per cent.'

She paced a little up and down the room, thinking at a speed she did not believe herself capable of. Then she came to a halt, but that desperate search for a solution continued.

'Did he tell you he'd be back?'

'I fear he will.'

A thousand thoughts were crowding into her head, a thousand images turning around in rapid succession.

It was finally clear to her what she would do.

'Michael, if it became known that you had betrayed the secret of the confessional, what would the consequences be for you?'

Father McKean stood up, looking like a man who feels his own soul sinking. 'I'd be excommunicated. Permanently barred from the ministry.'

'It won't happen. Because nobody will know.'

Vivien explained how she intended to proceed. As she did so, she was thinking of the man who was with her in that white room and what was best for Joy and what was being done there every day for young people like Sundance.

'I can't put a bug in the confessional. I'd have to explain too many things. But there's something you could do.'

'What?'

'If the man comes back, call me on my cellphone. Leave it on between you, so that I can hear your conversation. That way I'll be the only one to hear him, and I'll be able to control the operation and make sure that he's arrested away from the church.'

Michael McKean, a priest who had lost every certainty, saw hope shining on the horizon. 'But when you've caught him, the man will tell it all.'

'And who'll believe him if you and I deny it all? I have another witness who saw a guy in a green jacket somewhere else. He can take all the credit for himself. You'd come out completely clean.'

Father McKean remained silent, examining the proposal

as if Vivien were standing there holding out an apple to him. 'I don't know, Vivien. I don't know anything any more.'

Vivien put her hands on his arms and squeezed them. 'Michael, I'm hardly the right person to preach to you. I don't go to church very much and I'm not a very fervent worshipper. But one thing I'm sure of. The Christ who died on the cross to save the whole world would surely be able to forgive you for saving the lives of many people.'

'All right. I'll do it.'

Vivien felt overcome with gratitude and liberation and had to force herself not to embrace Father McKean.

As for the priest, he had never felt so close to mankind as at that moment when he believed that his soul had strayed from God.

'How about going out in the garden?' Vivien suggested. 'I really want to see my niece right now.'

'The kids are just going to lunch. Will you stay with us?'

Vivien realized she was hungry. Optimism had set her stomach working again. 'I'd love to. Mrs Carraro's cooking always deserves to be celebrated.'

Without saying anything else, they left the room and closed the door behind them.

After a few moments the figure of John Kortighan emerged from behind the screen. He stood there for a few moments looking at the door, grim faced and with tears welling in his eyes. Then he sat down on the bed and, as if that movement had cost him an immense effort, hid his face in his hands.

CHAPTER 31

Seated in a comfortable red armchair, Russell waited.

He was used to waiting. He had been waiting for years, without even knowing what he was waiting for. Even now, when he was almost breathless with impatience, he sat quietly, casually observing his surroundings.

He was in the waiting room of an ultra-modern Philippe Starck-designed office that occupied one whole floor of an elegant skyscraper on 50th Street. Crystal, leather, gilt, a touch of moderate kitsch and deliberate craziness. In the air, a vague aroma of mint and cedar. Attractive secretaries and solid-looking executives. Everything put together in such a way as to welcome and astonish visitors.

It was the New York office of his father's company, Wade Enterprises. A company with its headquarters in Boston and various branch offices in the major cities of the United States and a number of world capitals. The company had its fingers in many pies, from construction to supplying technology to the army, and from finance to commodities, principally petroleum.

He looked down at the tobacco-coloured carpet with the company logo. It must have cost a fortune. Everything around him was a silent, discreet act of homage to Mammon and his worshippers. He knew them well, and he knew how loyal they could be.

Russell, on the other hand, had never cared much about money. Now less than ever. The only thing that mattered to him right now was that he didn't want to feel like a failure any more.

Never again.

That had always been his life. He had always been in the shadows. Of his father, his brother, the name he bore, the great headquarters building in Boston. And the protecting wing of his mother, who up to a certain point had managed to overcome the distress and embarrassment some of his actions had caused her. Now the time had come to get out from under those shadows. He hadn't asked himself what Robert would have done in this situation. He knew for himself. The only possible way to tell the world the story he had in his possession was to get to the end and then start from the beginning.

Alone.

When he had finally realized this, the memory of his brother had changed. He had always idealized him so much, he had refused to consider him as a person, with all his qualities and all his defects – indeed, for years he had stubbornly rejected the idea that he had any defects. Now he wasn't a legend any more, but a friend whose memory was with him, a point of reference, not an idol on an excessively high pedestal.

A bald, bespectacled man in an impeccable blue suit came in and walked up to the reception desk. Russell saw the woman who had greeted him get up from her desk and lead the man into the waiting room.

'Please, Mr Klee. If you don't mind waiting a few moments, Mr Roberts will see you straight away.'

The man nodded in gratitude and looked around for

somewhere to sit. When he saw Russell, he reacted with disgust to his crumpled clothes and went and sat down in the chair furthest from him. Russell knew that his presence struck a wrong note here, in this padded kingdom of harmony and good taste. He felt like smiling. It seemed that his greatest talent had always been to be a nuisance.

Vivien's words forced themselves back into his mind, the night he had kissed her in her apartment.

The one thing I know is that I don't want complications . . .

He had said the same, but at the same time he knew he was lying. He felt that Vivien was something new, a bridge he wanted to cross to discover what was on the other side. For the first time in his life, he hadn't run away. And he had been made to suffer what he had often made women suffer. With the bitter taste of irony in his mouth, combined with embarrassment, he had heard himself say words that he, too, had uttered many times before turning his back and leaving. He hadn't even given Vivien time to finish what she had to say. In order not to be hurt, he had preferred to hurt her. Afterwards, he had sat in the car, looking out the window, feeling alone and useless, debating with himself the only truth: that night clung to him like a made-to-measure suit. And in spite of everything, the complications had come.

When, in front of his very eyes, Vivien had suddenly turned into a person he didn't know, he had left the apartment on Broadway weighed down with disappointment and resentment. He had entered a bar to get something to drink, something strong that would go down and warm that cold knot he felt in his stomach. By the time the barman reached him, he had changed his mind. He had ordered a coffee and started thinking about his next move. He had no intention of giving up his search but was aware of the difficulties he would have in getting a result using only his own resources. Reluctantly, he had had to admit that he had no choice but to turn to his family.

He didn't have either battery or credit on his cellphone, but he had seen a pay phone at the other end of the bar. He had paid for his coffee and asked for a handful of quarters. Then he had walked to the phone booth to make one of the most difficult calls of his life.

The coins had fallen in the slot with a sound like hope, and he had dialled the number of his home in Boston, pressing the keys like a wireless operator launching a desperate SOS from a sinking ship.

Naturally, the impersonal voice of a servant had answered. 'Hello. Wade Mansion.'

'Hello. This is Russell Wade.'

'Hello, Mr Russell. This is Henry. What can I do for you?'

The butler's prim face had superimposed itself on the advertising cards in front of him. Medium height, punctilious, impeccable. The right person to run a household as complicated as the Wade family residence.

'I'd like to speak with my mother.'

An understandable moment of silence. The servants, as his mother persisted in calling them, had a very efficient grapevine, and he was sure everyone knew about his difficult relations with his parents.

'I'll see if Madam is at home.'

Russell had smiled at the butler's tact. What his cautious reply actually meant was, 'I'll see if Madam wants to speak to you.'

After what seemed an interminable length of time and another couple of quarters

tlink tlink

swallowed by the telephone, he heard his mother's kindly but suspicious voice.

'Hello, Russell.'

'Hello, Mother. It's nice to hear your voice.'

'Yours, too. What are you up to?'

'I need your help, Mother.'

Silence. An understandable silence.

'I know I've abused your support in the past. And given you nothing but trouble in return. But this time, I don't want money, and I don't need legal help. And I'm not in any trouble.'

A hint of curiosity in his mother's aristocratic voice. 'What do you need, then?'

'I need to talk to Father. If I call his office and give my name they'll tell me he isn't there, or he's in a meeting, or he's on the moon.'

Her curiosity had suddenly turned to apprehension. 'What do you want from your father?'

'I need his car. For something serious. The first serious thing in my life.'

'I don't know, Russell. That may not be such a good idea.'

He had understood his mother's hesitation. In a way, he felt sorry for her. She was caught between a rock and a hard place, her respectable husband on one side, her wayward son on the other. But he couldn't give up now, couldn't admit defeat, even if he had to beg.

'I realize I've never done anything to deserve it, but I need your trust.'

After a few moments Margaret Taylor Wade's aristocratic voice admitted surrender.

tlink

'Your father's at the New York office for a couple of days. I'll talk to him now and call you back.'

This was an unexpected stroke of luck. Russell had felt euphoria spread through his body more effectively than any alcoholic drink.

'My cellphone isn't working. Just tell him I'm going to his office and I'll wait there until he sees me. I won't leave until he does, even if I have to wait all day.'

He paused. Then he said something he hadn't said in years. 'Thank you, Mother.'

tlink

He hadn't had time to hear her reply, because the call had been cut off as the last coin had fallen.

He had gone out on the street and invested his last few dollars in a taxi ride to 50th Street. Now he had been here for two hours, being stared at by people like Mr Klee, waiting for his father to grant him an audience. He knew he wouldn't see him straight away, that he wouldn't miss the opportunity to humiliate him by making him wait. But he didn't feel humiliated at all, only impatient.

And he had waited.

A tall, elegant secretary had appeared in front of him. The carpet had muffled the sound of her heels in the corridor. She was beautiful, as the surroundings dictated, and he assumed that if she had been chosen for that job she was also highly efficient.

'Mr Russell, please come with me. Mr Wade is waiting for you.'

He realized that, as long as his father was alive, there would only ever be one 'Mr Wade'. But he could change that if he wanted, and he wanted it with all his might.

He got up from the armchair and followed the secretary

down a long corridor. As he watched the woman's bottom move gracefully under her skirt, he felt like smiling. Maybe a few days before he would have indulged in some vulgar comment, embarrassing the woman and consequently displeasing his father. Then he reminded himself that, until a few days earlier, he would never have dreamed of coming to this office to see Jenson Wade.

The secretary stopped in front of a dark wooden door. She knocked lightly and, without waiting for a response, opened the door and motioned to him to enter. Russell took a couple of steps and heard the swish of the door closing behind him.

Jenson Wade was sitting behind a desk placed diagonally between two corner windows that offered a breathtaking view of the city. The backlighting was compensated for by lamps artfully placed around the large room, which was one of his father's command posts. They hadn't met in person for a long time. He looked older but in excellent shape. Russell stood looking at him while he continued reading documents and ignoring him completely. Jenson was the image of his younger son. Or rather, it was Russell who bore a resemblance that had proved uncomfortable for both of them on several occasions in the past.

Jenson Wade raised his head and looked at him with steady, uncompromising eyes. 'What do you want?'

His father didn't like beating about the bush. Russell came straight to the point. 'I need help. And you're the only person I know who can give it to me.'

The reply was curt and predictable. 'You aren't getting a cent from me.'

Russell shook his head. Although he hadn't been invited, he calmly chose an armchair and sat down. 'I don't need a cent from you.'

His father looked straight at him, without a trace of affection in his eyes. He must be wondering what Russell had got up to this time. But he found himself unexpectedly confronted with something new. His son had never before had the strength to sustain his gaze.

'What do you want, then?'

'I'm pursuing a lead on a news story. A big one.'

'You?'

In that incredulous monosyllable, there were years of photographs in the scandal sheets, lawyers' bills, betrayed trust, money thrown away. Years spent mourning two sons: one because he was dead, the other because he was doing everything he could to be considered dead.

And had finally succeeded.

'Yes. I might add that many people will die if I don't obtain your help.'

'What kind of trouble have you got yourself into this time?'

'I'm not in any trouble. But a lot of other people are, even though they don't know it.'

Curiosity was starting to take hold. His voice softened a little. Maybe he had sensed that the person facing him had a decisiveness different from the Russell he was used to. But all those past disappointments obliged him to proceed with extreme caution.

'What's it all about?'

'I can't tell you. That's a point against me, I know. I'm afraid you'll just have to trust me.'

He saw his father lean back in his chair and smile as if at a witty joke. 'With you, the word trust seems a little out of proportion, to say the least. Why should I trust you?'

'Because I'll pay you.'

The smile became a sarcastic grimace. When it came to money, the powerful Mr Wade was on home ground. And Russell knew he had few equals there.

'With what money, may I ask?'

He returned the smile. 'I have something I'm sure you're going to like more than money.'

He put his hand in the inside pocket of his jacket and took out a sheet of letter paper folded in three. He opened it, got up from his armchair and placed it carefully on the desk in front of his father. Jenson Wade picked up his pair of glasses and read what was written on the paper.

I, the undersigned, undertake to work for Wade Enterprises for three years from the beginning of June this year for the sum of one dollar per month.
Russell Wade

Russell saw first surprise, then temptation, play over his father's face. The thought of having him in his power, being able to humiliate him just as he liked, must be an enticing prospect. The sight of Russell in coveralls, cleaning the floors and the toilets, would surely take many years off him.

'Let's say I agree. What would I have to do?'

'You have a whole lot of connections in Washington. Or rather you have a whole lot of people in your pocket, both in politics and in the army.'

He took his father's silence as a self-satisfied admission of his power.

'I'm following a lead, but I've come up against a brick wall and I don't see any way of getting through it. Maybe with your help I could.'

366

'Go on.'

Russell approached the desk. From his pocket he took the photograph of the young man and the cat. Before handing over the original to Vivien he had scanned it and printed a spare copy for himself. He had felt a little guilty at the time, but now he was glad he'd done it.

'It's something connected with the Vietnam war. From 1970 onwards. I have the name of a soldier called Wendell Johnson and this photograph of an unknown man who fought with him. I think both of them were involved in something unusual, something that's still classified. I need to know what it is. And I need to know as soon as possible.'

Jenson Wade thought about it for quite a while, pretending to look at the images. Russell did not know that it wouldn't be his words that convinced his father, but the tone in which he had said them. That impassioned tone that only the truth possesses.

He saw his father indicate the armchair in front of the desk. 'Sit down.'

When Russell was seated, Jenson Wade pressed a key on the telephone.

'Miss Atwood, get me General Hetch. Now.'

While waiting, he put the call on speakerphone. It occurred to Russell that there were two reasons for that. The less important was to allow him to hear the subsequent conversation. The other, the main reason, was that he was about to give Russell yet another demonstration of what his father's name meant.

After a while, a rough, slightly hoarse voice floated into the room. 'Hi, Jenson.'

'Hi, Geoffrey, how are you?'

'Just finished a game of golf.'

'Golf? I didn't know you played golf. One of these days we'll have to have a game.'

'That'd be good.'

'You can count on it.'

At this point, the courtesies were over. Russell knew his father spent huge sums every year to keep his phones safe from tapping, so he was sure this would be a call in which both men said what they meant.

'Good. What can I do for you?'

'I need a big favour, something only you can do for me.'

'Try me.'

'It's really very important. Do you have pen and paper handy?'

'Just a moment.'

General Hetch was heard asking someone near him for a sheet of paper and something to write with. A moment later, he came back on the phone and into the office. 'Go ahead.'

'Write down this name. Wendell Johnson. Vietnam War, 1970 or later.'

The silence indicated that the general was writing.

'Johnson, you said?'

'Yes.' Jenson Wade waited a moment before continuing. 'He and another soldier were involved in something that's still classified. I want to know what.'

Russell realized that his father, in telling the general what he wanted, had used almost the same words with which he had earlier formulated his request.

That little touch put him in a good mood.

From the other end of the phone came an energetic protest – 'Jenson, I can't just go rummaging around in—' which was strangled at birth by Jenson Wade's harsh voice.

'Yes, you can. If you think about it, you'll see you can.'

368

That phrase was full of innuendo, allusions to things only the two of them knew.

The general's tone changed abruptly. 'All right. I'll see what I can do. Give me twenty-four hours.'

'I'll give you one.'

'But, Jenson—'

'Call me as soon as you have anything. I'm in New York.'

Jenson hung up before the general had time to reply. He got up from his chair and threw a distracted glance out the window. 'Now we just have to wait. Have you eaten?'

Russell realized he was starving. 'No.'

'I'll tell my secretary to bring you something. I have some people to meet with in the conference room. I'll be back by the time Hetch calls.'

Without saying another word, he went out, leaving Russell alone to breathe the air in the office, which smelled of expensive cigars, wood, and secret passages. He went to the window and stood there for a few moments looking out at that endless horizon of roofs, with the East River in the middle like a street of water glittering in the sun.

After a while the door opened and the secretary entered with a tray. There was a plate covered with a silver lid, and next to it a half bottle of wine, a glass, bread and flatware. She put the tray down on a small glass table in front of the couch.

'Here you are, Mr Russell. I took the liberty of ordering your steak rare. Is that OK?'

'Perfect.'

Russell walked towards the woman, who was standing there, looking at him curiously. And somehow suggestively. With a smile on her lips, her head tilted to one side, and her long hair tumbling over her shoulders.

'You're very famous, Russell,' she said. 'And very handsome.'

'Do you think so?'

She took a step forward. In her hand she clutched a business card. With a smile, she slipped it into his jacket pocket. 'I'm Lorna. This is my number. Call me if you like.'

He watched her as she walked to the door. Before going out she turned one last time, invitation still in her eyes.

Russell was alone. He sat down and started eating his steak, without touching the wine. He went and got a bottle of water from the minibar hidden in a cabinet opposite the couch. He remembered a moment of sun, sea, wind and closeness.

With another woman.

But seeing as how you're with me, we can both consider ourselves on duty, so no alcohol . . .

Recalling Vivien's advice, he forced himself to finish the food. He didn't know when he'd next get the chance to eat.

He stood up and went back to the window. He spent a long time looking out, trying to overcome his impatience and to get Vivien's face out of his mind. He didn't succeed in either.

His father's entrance took him by surprise. Russell checked his watch and realized that almost an hour and a half had passed since his father had gone out.

'The general's called back. I asked for the call to be put through to here.' He walked quickly to the desk, sat down and activated the speakerphone. 'Jenson here. Found anything?'

'Yes.'

'So what are we dealing with?'

'Just your common or garden cover-up.'

'Meaning what?'

There was the sound of paper being crinkled.

'Here it is. Wendell Johnson, born in Hornell, 7 June 1948. He was living there when he was drafted. He was part of the 11th Mechanized Cavalry Regiment stationed at Xuan-Loc. Status 1Y.'

Russell made an impatient gesture, opening and closing his fist.

'Get to the point. What happened to him?'

'All I was shown were his personal details. For the rest I'm telling you what I remember, because I couldn't get direct access to the papers. I had to go about it in a roundabout way, which is why I can only report what was said to me.'

'All right, but for Christ's sake do it.'

The general's voice picked up Jenson's urgency. 'In 1971, Johnson's platoon took part in an operation in the north of Cu Chi District, an operation that intelligence had advised against but that went ahead anyway. They were all wiped out, apart from Johnson and one other soldier, who were taken prisoner and later used by the Vietcong as human shields against a bombing raid.'

Russell would have liked to ask questions directly to the general. He took a notebook and pen from the desk and wrote

Then?

and put the sheet in front of his father, who nodded to say he'd understood.

'And then?'

'The person who ordered the aerial incursion, Major Mistnick, knew from the reconnaissance that they were there but pretended he didn't. The planes went in and spread napalm over the whole area. The major had already given signs of being unbalanced on a number of occasions, which was why he was removed and the whole thing covered up to avoid

371

embarrassment. It was a time when public opinion was turning against the war, so I'm not surprised by what they did.'

Russell wrote another phrase: *The two soldiers?*

This time, too, Jenson Wade gave voice to Russell's thought. 'What happened to the two soldiers?'

'Johnson suffered severe burns and was taken care of by the troops who arrived there soon afterwards. They saved him by a miracle, and he spent some time in a military hospital for rehabilitation, I don't remember where.'

Another note.

The other man?

'And what about the other man?'

'He burned to death.'

His hand trembling, Russell wrote the thing that most interested him.

Name?

'Do you know what his name was?'

'Wait, they told me that, too. Here . . .'

A sound of papers being leafed through. Then, at last, a name.

'Matt Corey, born Corbett Place, 27 April 1948, lived in Chillicothe, Ohio.'

Russell quickly wrote down this information, threw his arms up in the air in a gesture of elation, then gave his father a thumbs-up sign.

'That's good, Geoffrey. Thanks for now. Don't forget that game of golf.'

'Any time you like.'

Jenson Wade pressed a key and eliminated the presence of General Hetch from the office, leaving his last words hanging in the air. An incredulous Russell was clutching in his hands the name he had pursued for so long.

'I have to go to Chillicothe.'

His father looked at him for a moment, evaluating this new person he found himself confronted with. Then he pointed up at the ceiling. 'This is an office building. We don't have a swimming pool on the roof, but we do have a landing strip. If you go up now, I can have you picked up by our helicopter in ten minutes.'

Russell was even more incredulous. This unhoped-for offer of help filled him with an energy and a clear-headedness he didn't think himself capable of. He looked at his watch. 'It must be about five hundred miles to Ohio as the crow flies. Can I make it before dark?'

A shrug that was worth a few billion dollars. 'No problem. The helicopter will take you to La Guardia, where we keep the company jets. One of them can land you at whichever's the closest airport to Chillicothe. While you're in the air, I'll ask my secretary to make sure there's a car waiting for you when you arrive.'

Russell was speechless, standing there in front of the desk looking at the man he had most feared in his life. He said the only thing that came into his head. 'I don't know how to thank you.'

'You have a way.' From the inside pocket of his jacket, Jenson Wade took the paper on which Russell had made his commitment. He leaned forward, placed it in the centre of the desk, then sat back in his leather armchair with a smug expression on his face. 'You're going to be working for me for the next three years, remember?'

CHAPTER 32

'Do you have a cigarette?'

Russell woke up, wondering who the fuck . . .

A haggard face, cheeks covered with a sparse beard, hung a few inches from his face. Two bleary little eyes were looking at him. A tattoo poked out of a dirty shirt collar near the left ear. The man's breath smelled of alcohol and rotting teeth.

'What?'

'Do you have a cigarette?'

Russell suddenly realized where he was. He sat up, feeling his joints creaking. Spending a night on a bunk in a cell wasn't the most comfortable position for the body. When he had been arrested the previous night, this skinny, down-at-heel guy hadn't been there. They must have brought him to the jail while he was sleeping. He was so tired he hadn't heard a thing.

Clearly more desperate than ever for a smoke, the man said in a hoarse voice, 'So, do you have that cigarette or not?'

Russell stood up. The man instinctively took a step back.

'You can't smoke here.'

'I'm already in jail, boy. What can they do, arrest me?'

His cell companion underlined his joke with a catarrh-filled laugh. Russell didn't have any cigarettes, and he wasn't in

374

any mood to continue this conversation.

'Leave me alone.'

Realizing he wasn't going to get anywhere the man walked away, muttering an incomprehensible oath, and lay down on the bunk against the wall opposite. He turned his back to Russell and lay there with his jacket rolled up under his head as a pillow.

A moment later he was snoring.

Russell approached the bars. Facing them was a wall, part of a corridor that disappeared to the left. To the right, he assumed there was another cell, but no noise came from it. Maybe the honest folks of Chillicothe didn't give the authorities much reason to use these cells. He went back to his bunk, lay down and looked up at a ceiling that seemed recently repainted, thinking about how he had come to spend yet another night in jail.

His father had been as good as his word.

Five minutes after he had come out onto the roof of the building, a helicopter had appeared out of the sky. The pilot must have been informed how urgent this all was, because he had not turned off the engines. A man had emerged from the passenger seat and walked towards him, stooped over to withstand the displacement of air by the helicopter blades. He had taken him by the arm, gesturing to him to walk the same way, and accompanied him to the machine.

No sooner had he closed the door and fastened his seat belt than they were in the air. The city passed below them at high speed, soon becoming the runway reserved for private flights at La Guardia Airport. The pilot brought the helicopter down next to a small Cessna CJ1+ bearing the insignia of Wade Enterprises.

The engines were already on. A stewardess was waiting for him at the foot of the staircase, a blond girl in a tobacco-coloured uniform and a light blouse, recalling the colours of the company logo. As Russell walked towards her, he heard the helicopter take off.

'Good evening, Mr Wade. I'm Sheila Lavender. I'll be your attendant during the flight.' She pointed to the inside of the plane. 'Please.'

Russell went up and found himself in an elegant sitting room with four comfortable seats. Two pilots were sitting in their places in the cabin.

Sheila indicated the seats. 'Please sit down, Mr Wade. Can I get you something to drink?'

Russell went and sat down on one of the seats, and felt the soft embrace of the leather envelop him. He had decided not to drink, but maybe he deserved one after all. It occurred to him that the rules governing what he could do 'on duty' were much less constricting than Vivien's.

'Is there a bottle of whisky from my father's reserve on this plane?'

The stewardess smiled. 'Yes, there is.'

'Good. Then I'll have a drop of that. With a little ice, if possible.'

'I'll be right back.'

The stewardess walked away and started bustling about in front of a drinks cabinet.

The pilot's voice came over the intercom. 'Mr Wade, I'm Captain Marcus Hattie. Good evening and welcome on board.'

Russell returned the greeting with a gesture in the direction of the cabin.

'We chose this plane for its size, which will allow us to land and take off from the runway at Ross County Airport.

376

Unfortunately we have a problem with heavy air traffic right now. We're being kept in a holding pattern and I'm afraid we're going to have to wait a few minutes before we get the go-ahead for take-off.'

Russell took this news on board. It was disappointing. Sheila's return with a glass appeased him a little. Looking out the window, he sipped the whisky as calmly as he could. After an interminable quarter of an hour, they at last moved onto the runway. A powerful thrust of the engines, a sense of emptiness, and they were in the sky, turning until the front of the plane was directed towards Chillicothe, Ohio.

Russell looked first at his watch, then at the sun on the horizon, trying to estimate the journey time. The answer came from the pilot, when he next spoke.

'We plan to reach our destination in just under two hours.'

During the journey he tried a couple of times to call Vivien on the plane's telephone, but her cellphone was always engaged. And with everything that had happened he wasn't even sure she would want to talk to him.

The captain gave you his word. I didn't . . .

At the memory of those words, the taste of the whisky suddenly turned bitter. The only thing that would improve that taste would be revenge, the revenge he would have when he revealed to her that he had found by himself what the two of them had pursued together in vain.

After another couple of drinks, the pilot's voice informed him that they had begun their descent towards their destination. Again, as on that earlier journey a few days before, darkness had overtaken them during the flight.

The landing was perfect and the plane was skilfully guided to the terminal. When finally the door was opened and he set

377

foot on the ground, he found himself in a place almost identical to the small airport at Hornell.

Next to the long, low terminal building a man was waiting beside a black Mercedes sedan that looked shiny and clean under the lights. His father had clearly spared no expense. Then Russell remembered that he would be paying for these luxuries with the sweat of his brow.

He walked to the car, and was greeted by a tall thin man who looked more as though he was in the habit of renting hearses than automobiles.

'Mr Russell Wade?'

'That's me.'

'I'm Richard Balling, from Ross Rental Services.'

Neither of the two held out his hand in a friendly gesture. Russell suspected that Mr Balling was a little contemptuous of someone who came out of a private jet and found a Mercedes waiting for him. Even though he himself had supplied it.

'This is the car that was reserved for you. Do you need a driver?'

'Does the car have GPS?'

The man gave him an outraged look. 'Of course.'

'Then I'll drive.'

'That's your choice.'

He waited for the man to fill in the documents with his details, signed them and got in the car.

'Could you give me the address of the sheriff's office, please?'

'Twenty-eight North Paint Street. In Chillicothe, of course. Could you give me a ride into town?'

Russell gave him a conspiratorial smile and started the engine. 'Of course not.'

He pulled out, wheels skidding on the gravel, heedless of Mr Balling's legitimate concern for his vehicle. As he drove, he programmed the GPS. There was the road, and there was his destination, some nine miles away, with a journey time of about twenty-one minutes. He allowed the soothing female voice of the GPS to guide him until it advised him to turn right onto Route 104. As he neared the town, he started to think about his next move. He didn't have a specific plan. He had a name. He had photographs. He would ask the sheriff for information, then decide what to do on the basis of that. He had reached this point by following his instinct and improvising. That seemed like the best way to continue. Without his realizing it, the long straight road had led him to press his foot down hard on the accelerator. Suddenly, a flashing light and a sharp sound behind him brought him up short.

He pulled up on the right and waited for the inevitable. He lowered the window just in time to see the officer touch his hat in greeting.

'Good evening, sir.'

'Good evening, officer.'

'Would you mind showing me your licence and car registration, please?'

Russell handed the rental certificate and licence through the window. The officer, who bore the insignia of Ross County, examined them, but did not give them back. He was a thickset man, with a broad nose and pockmarked skin.

'Where are you from, Mr Wade?'

'New York. I just landed at Ross County Airport.'

The grimace he received in return made him realize his mistake.

'Well, Mr Wade, I'm afraid there's a problem.'

'What kind of problem?'

'You were going along like a bat out of hell. And from your breath, I'm pretty sure I know why.'

'I'm not drunk, officer.'

'We'll soon see. All you have to do is breathe into a balloon, just like you did when you were a kid.'

He climbed out of the Mercedes and followed the officer to his car. He did as he was asked, but unfortunately the result wasn't the same as when he was a kid, thanks to Jenson Wade's personal whisky reserve.

The officer looked at him with a self-satisfied smirk. 'You'll have to come with me. Will you come quietly or do I have to put cuffs on you? Don't forget, resisting arrest is an aggravating factor.'

Russell knew that only too well. He had learned it the hard way. 'You don't need cuffs.'

With no thought for Mr Balling, he left the Mercedes in a lay-by and climbed in the patrol car. As he was getting out at 28 North Paint Street, he realized there was one bright spot in all this. He had been looking for the sheriff's office and now here he was.

Hearing footsteps in the corridor, he got up from the bunk and approached the bars. A moment or two later, a man in uniform stopped in front of the cell door.

'Russell Wade?'

'That's me.'

Unceremoniously, the officer made a sign with his nearly bald head. He looked like the good brother of the guy who was sleeping – and snoring – on the other bunk.

'Come on, your backup's here.'

After the snap of the lock and the clatter of the bars, he

found himself following the man along the corridor. They stopped in front of a wooden door. A sign on it indicated that Thomas Blein was the sheriff of Ross County. The officer knocked, and immediately opened. He motioned to him to enter and closed the door behind him.

In the office were two men and a vague smell of cigars. One was sitting behind a desk piled high with papers. It was obvious he was the Thomas Blein mentioned on the door. He was tall with thick white hair, and a calm but resolute face. His uniform both emphasized his slender build and conferred the right degree of authority.

The man sitting on the chair just in front of the desk was a lawyer. He didn't look like one, but the fact that he was there, plus the officer's words, made it seem likely. Confirmation came when the man, who had an easygoing air but sharp eyes, stood up and held out his hand.

'Hello, Mr Wade. I'm Jim Woodstone, your lawyer.'

The previous evening he had taken advantage of the one call allowed him to call the plane on the number the stewardess had given him. After explaining the situation he was in, he had asked that his father be contacted and brought up to date. Sheila Lavender hadn't sounded at all surprised.

Russell shook the lawyer's hand. 'Pleased to meet you.' Then he turned to the man behind the desk. 'Good morning, sheriff. I'm sorry if I caused you any inconvenience. That wasn't my intention.'

In the light of what they knew about him, this submissive attitude seemed to surprise both men, who for a moment found themselves on the same side of the barricades.

Blein simply nodded at him. 'Are you Russell Wade, the rich guy?'

'My father's the rich guy. I'm the wild guy who got disowned.'

The sheriff smiled at this brief but comprehensive self-description. 'You get yourself in the news a lot. Quite rightly, I think. Would you agree?'

'I think I would, yes.'

'What do you do in life?'

Russell smiled. 'When I don't spend my time getting arrested, I'm a journalist.'

'What paper do you work for?'

'I don't work for any at the moment. I'm freelance.'

'And what brought you to Chillicothe?'

Woodstone intervened, with professional shrewdness. After all, he had to justify the bill he'd be sending Wade Enterprises. 'Mr Wade, you don't have to answer if you don't want to.'

Russell made a gesture with his hand that meant that everything was fine and he would satisfy the sheriff's curiosity. It was easy – all he had to do was tell the truth. 'I'm doing an article about the Vietnam war.'

Blein raised an eyebrow, in a vaguely cinematic manner. 'Is anyone still interested in that?'

More than you might imagine . . .

'There are certain things still unresolved that I think the public has a right to know about.'

He noticed a heavy brown envelope on the sheriff's desk. It looked like the one in which they'd placed the contents of his pockets the previous evening, just before they photographed him, took his fingerprints, and threw him in the cell.

'Are those my meagre belongings?'

The sheriff took the envelope and opened it. He extracted

382

the contents and put them on the desk in front of him. When Russell looked closer, he saw that nothing was missing. Watch, wallet, the keys of the Mercedes . . .

The sheriff's eyes fell on the photograph of the young man with the cat. There was a puzzled look on his face as he moved forward in his chair and placed his elbows on the desk. 'May I?'

Russell said yes without quite knowing what he was saying yes to.

The sheriff picked up the photograph, looked at it for a moment, then put it back among Russell's personal effects. 'Mind telling me how you got hold of this photograph, Mr Wade?' he asked, then immediately turned and threw a significant glance at the lawyer. 'Of course you don't have to answer, if you don't want to.'

Russell stopped the lawyer before he could reply, and took the plunge. 'According to my information, that young man died in Vietnam. His name was Matt Corey.'

'That's right.'

The words echoed in his ears like the sound of a parachute opening. 'Did you know him?'

'We worked together when we were young. I used to earn myself a few dollars in my spare time, working as a bricklayer on construction sites. He was a couple of years older than me and was working for a company I was with for a whole summer.'

'Do you remember what it was called?'

'Sure, it was Ben Shepard's old firm. He was based over towards North Folk Village. Matt was like a son to Ben. He even lived in a room attached to the main building.' Blein pointed at one of the two photographs. 'With Waltz, that weird three-legged cat.'

Without holding out too much hope, Russell asked, 'Is this Ben Shepard still alive?'

The sheriff's reply was not only unexpected, but tinged with a barely concealed hint of envy. 'More alive than ever. The old dog's almost eighty-five, but he's straight as a rocket and bursting with health. And I'm sure he still screws like a rabbit.'

'Where can I find him?'

'He has a house at Slate Mills, not far from his old place. I'll write down the address.'

Blein took paper and a pen, scribbled a few words, and placed the paper on top of the photographs. Russell took that gesture as a good omen. Those images had been the start of everything. He hoped that what was written on the sheet of paper represented the beginning of the end.

Russell felt impatience fluttering in his stomach like a flight of butterflies. 'Can I go?'

Blein made a gesture with his hands that meant freedom. 'Of course. Your lawyer and the bail he put up say you can.'

'I'm very grateful, sheriff, and I mean that. In spite of the circumstances, it's been a pleasure.'

Woodstone got up from his chair, and he and Blein shook hands. They presumably saw a lot of each other, given their respective jobs in a small town like Chillicothe. In the meantime Russell had already reached the door and was opening it.

He was stopped by the sheriff's voice.

'Mr Wade?'

He turned in the doorway and saw the sheriff's clear eyes fixed on him. 'Yes?'

'Seeing as how you just interrogated me, can I ask you a question now?'

'Go ahead.'

'Why are you interested in Matt Corey?'

Russell lied shamelessly, trying his damnedest not to let it show. 'According to reliable sources, he performed an act of heroism that has never been recognized. I'm writing an article to draw attention to his sacrifice and that of other soldiers like him who've also been ignored.'

He didn't stop to wonder if his patriotic tone had deceived such a mature lawman. In his head he was already sitting in front of a former builder named Ben Shepard. Assuming the old dog, as Blein had called him, agreed to talk to him. Russell remembered perfectly well how difficult it had been to be received by that other old dog, his father.

He followed Woodstone outside, crossing the part of the office open to the public, where a young woman in uniform was behind the desk and another officer sat filling out forms. He found himself back in America. Chillicothe was the essence of it.

Russell saw his rented Mercedes parked on the other side of the street.

Following the direction of his gaze, the lawyer gestured towards the car. 'Mr Balling sent someone with a second set of keys to get the car. I gave instructions that they bring it here.'

'Good work. Thank you, Mr Woodstone. I'll tell the person who contacted you.'

'It was your father actually.'

Russell couldn't hide his surprise. 'My father, personally?'

'Yes. I thought it was a joke at first, but when I heard you'd been arrested . . .'

The lawyer broke off, realizing he had made a gaffe. He seemed to be saying that he'd been more convinced by the news that Russell Wade was in jail for speeding and for drunk driving than by a voice on the telephone claiming to be Jenson Wade in person.

Russell felt like smiling, and hid it by scratching his nose. 'How did my father sound?'

The lawyer shrugged, as if trying to erase his embarrassment. 'That's what fooled me. When I heard his voice on the telephone, I had the impression he was trying hard not to laugh.'

Russell allowed himself that smile after all.

Discovering after all this time that Jenson Wade had a sense of humour was weird, to say the least. He wondered how many other things he didn't know about his father. He immediately told himself, with a touch of bitterness, that there were at least as many things his father didn't know about him.

CHAPTER 33

Russell stopped the car in front of the house and switched off the engine.

He sat for a few moments in the middle of that rural landscape, beneath an unsmiling sky. He had gently but firmly refused Woodstone's offer to go with him, in spite of the fact that he claimed to have known Ben Shepard for decades. Whether that was true or not, his eyes had glittered with curiosity as he made the offer. Russell had understood why. This was a small town and being in possession of new information could make anyone the centre of attention.

The house he was looking at now was of stone and wood, had wide windows, and gave the impression of solidity. Its owner had clearly built it according to his own needs and his own aesthetic criteria, which were admirable. It was a two-storey house at the top of a hill. In front of the house was a lawn and a well-tended garden and in back was what looked, from the position in which he was parked, like a vegetable garden. About a hundred yards to his right there was an asphalted road that went around to the rear of the house, which was where the garage must be.

He got out of the car and approached the fence that surrounded the property. Next to the small gate was a green painted letterbox with the name Shepard on it in white letters. The gate was not locked and there were no signs warning of dogs. Russell opened it and walked along the path, which was marked out with slabs embedded in the grass. He was a few steps from the house when someone emerged from around the corner to his left. He was an elderly but still vigorous-looking man of above average height, with a lined and tanned face and surprisingly young blue eyes. His work clothes and the basket he had in his hand indicated that he had come from the vegetable garden.

When he noticed Russell, he came to a halt. 'What do you want?' he asked calmly but firmly.

'I'm looking for Ben Shepard.'

'In that case, you've found him.'

Russell was impressed by the old man's character. Instinctively, he decided that the one way to deal with him was to tell him the truth.

'My name's Russell Wade and I'm a journalist from New York.'

'Good. Now you've told me, you can take your car and go back where you came from.'

Ben Shepard walked unhurriedly past him and climbed the steps leading to the porch.

'This is very important, Mr Shepard.'

'I'm nearly eighty-five, young man,' Ben Shepard replied, without turning around. 'At my age, the only important thing is to open your eyes again the next morning.'

Russell realized that if he didn't say something, the encounter would finish before it had even started. 'I came here to talk to you about Little Boss.'

On hearing that name, which for years had probably been spoken nowhere but in his memory, the old man stopped on

388

the steps. 'What do you know about Little Boss?' he asked, coming back down.

'I know it was the nickname of a boy whose real name was Matt Corey.'

The reply was curt and determined. 'Matt Corey died many years ago in Vietnam.'

'No. Matt Corey died in New York just over six months ago.'

Ben Shepard's shoulders appeared to droop. He seemed affected by the news, but not surprised. He stood there for a few moments, head bowed. When he looked up again, Russell saw that his eyes were watery. He recalled the tears Wendell Johnson's brother Lester had tried to hold back.

The old man nodded towards the house. 'Come in.'

Russell followed Ben Shepard inside and found himself in a spacious living room that occupied the whole front part of the house. On the right, over towards the fireplace, there was a pool table with a rack for the cues. The left side of the room was given over to the TV area, with armchairs and couches. The whole room was furnished in a sober and surprisingly modern style, even though the furniture didn't look new. In the past, Russell thought, that room must have been cutting-edge of its kind. Everywhere, as a unifying element, there were pictures and objects representing a lifetime's memories.

Shepard walked to the living room area. 'Take a seat. Would you like a coffee?'

Russell collapsed into an armchair that promised comfort. 'Yes, I would. I just spent a night in jail. A coffee would be great.'

The old man made no comment on this, but appeared to appreciate his honesty. He turned towards the door on the other side of the living room, through which the kitchen could be glimpsed.

'Maria!'

A dark-haired, olive-skinned woman appeared in the doorway. She was young and quite pretty and Russell understood where the sheriff's sly comment about his host had come from.

'Could you make us some coffee, please?'

Without saying a word, the woman went back in the kitchen. The old man sat down in the other armchair, facing Russell. He crossed his legs and looked at him curiously. 'Who put you inside?'

'One of the sheriff's officers, out on Route 104.'

'Big guy with a pockmarked face, looks like a cowboy who's lost his cows?'

'Yes.'

The old man nodded, as if to say: a leopard never changes his spots. 'Lou Ingraham. He thinks the world ends at the county line. He doesn't like strangers and never misses an opportunity to harass them. He has quite a collection of scalps.'

At that moment Maria came in carrying a tray with a coffee pot, a jar of milk and two cups. She approached Shepard and placed everything on the little table next to his armchair.

'Thanks, Maria. You can take the day off. I'll see to everything here.'

The woman gave a smile that lit up the room. 'Thanks, Ben.'

Russell realized that his host's idle chatter had only been a way of gaining time until he was free of this possibly indiscreet presence. This cheered him and at the same time put him on his guard.

'How do you like your coffee?'

'Black, no sugar. I'm a cheap date, as you can see.'

As the old man poured the coffee from the thermal pot, Russell decided to take the initiative.

'Mr Shepard, I'll say my piece first. If what I say is correct, then if you allow me to, I'll ask you a few questions. But if it isn't correct, then I'll do what you told me to do. I'll get in my car and go back the way I came.'

'OK.'

Russell began his presentation of the facts. With a certain apprehension, given that he was not entirely sure things had actually happened that way.

'Matt Corey worked for you and lived on your premises. He had with him a cat that, by some freak of nature, or something someone had done to it, had only three legs. It was called Waltz.'

From his pocket, he took the photograph of the young man with the cat and placed it in Ben Shepard's lap. The old man lowered his head slightly and looked at it, but did not pick it up.

'In 1971, he left for Vietnam. 11th Mechanized Cavalry Regiment, to be precise. At Xuan-Loc he met a young man named Wendell Johnson. The two of them became friends. One day, they took part in an operation that ended up in a massacre, and they were the only survivors of their platoon. They were taken prisoner and were later used by the Vietcong as human shields against an air raid.'

Russell paused, wondering if he might be going too fast. He saw that Ben Shepard was looking at him with interest, perhaps paying more attention to his attitude than his words.

'In spite of the fact that they were there, the raid went ahead. Wendell Johnson and Matt Corey were hit with napalm. One burned to death, the other was rescued but had

391

severe burns all over his body. After a long period of rehabilitation in a military hospital, he was discharged, but in a damaged state, both physically and mentally.'

Russell paused again, and in the silence he realized they were both holding their breaths.

'I have reason to believe that, for some reason I can't explain, the two men's dogtags got mixed up. Matt Corey was declared dead and everyone thought the survivor was Wendell Johnson. And when he recovered, he accepted this change of identity. There were no photos or prints to contradict him. His face was completely deformed and it's quite likely he didn't have any prints left.'

Silence fell in the room. A silence evoking memories and provoking the appearance of ghosts. Ben Shepard allowed a tear held back for years to roll from his eyes and drip onto the photograph.

'Mr Shepard—'

The old man interrupted him, looking at him with eyes uncorrupted by age or men. 'Ben.'

In the light of this unexpected bond, Russell asked his next question in a calm voice.

'Ben, when did you last see Matt Corey?'

The old man took an eternity to answer. 'In the summer of 1972, just after he left the military hospital.'

After this admission, the old man decided at last to pour himself some coffee. He picked up the cup and took a long sip.

'He came to see me and told me the same story you just told me. Then he took the cat and left. I never saw him again.'

Russell decided that Ben Shepard wasn't a good liar, and that what he had just told him, even if not a lie, was only a half-truth. But at the same time he realized that if he got something wrong, the old man would clam up and he wouldn't get anything more out of him.

'Did you know Matt had a son?'

'No.'

The way Ben Shepard lifted the cup to his mouth again immediately after uttering that monosyllable struck Russell as a little too hurried. He realized that he had no alternative but to let the old man know how important any information he had was.

And there was only one way to do that.

'Ben, I know you're a man of honour, in the best sense of that word. And I want to give you credit for that. I'm going to tell you something I'd never dream of revealing if you weren't the man I think you are.'

Ben made a gesture with the cup to thank him and invite him to continue.

'It's a hard story to tell, because it's a hard story to believe.'

He said that for Ben's sake, but at the same time to confirm to himself the absurdity of the whole story. And the absolute necessity to bring it to an end as soon as possible.

'Have you been following the news of the attacks in New York?'

Ben nodded. 'Terrible business.'

Russell took a deep breath before continuing. He couldn't do it physically, but in his mind he had his fingers crossed. He looked Ben straight in the eyes. 'Matt Corey moved to New York after the last time you saw him, and spent the rest of his life working in the construction industry.'

Instinctively, the old man was pleased. 'He was very good. It was the thing he was born for. He understood more at his age than many people who'd studied.'

There was both affection and regret on Ben Shepard's face.

393

But Russell felt his own face drawn with anxiety. He took care that what he was about to say should seem an expression of compassion and not an insult.

'Matt was a very sick person, Ben. And after what had happened to him, the solitary life he led all those years made his mental state even worse. During his career, he planted bombs in many of the buildings he worked on. New York is full of them. Six months after he died, they started exploding.'

Abruptly, the old man's face turned pale.

Russell gave him time to absorb what he had said. Then, with all the conviction he could muster, he said, 'If we don't find Matt Corey's son, those explosions will continue.'

Ben Shepard put the cup down on the little table next to him, then stood up and went to the window. He stood there for a few moments. He might have been listening to the song of the birds or the beating of his heart or maybe the wind in the branches. Or else something that didn't come from outside but from inside. Maybe the last words he and Matt Corey had said to each other, many years earlier, were echoing in his mind.

Russell thought it best at this point to clarify his own role. 'I'm here because I'm working in collaboration with the New York Police Department. It's a privilege I was given because I had some information they thought would help them. If you talk about it to me, you have my word that I'll tell them only what's absolutely necessary to stop the attacks, without involving you.'

Ben said nothing, and still did not turn around. Russell decided to insist on the gravity of the situation.

'More than a hundred people have died, Ben. And others will die. I can't say how many, but next time the death toll could be even higher.'

The old man started speaking without turning around.

'When I met him, Matt was in a reformatory up north, near the state border. I'd won the contract to renovate the building. When we got there and started putting up the scaffolding, the other kids looked at us suspiciously. Some of them made fun of us. But Matt was interested – he liked the way things kept changing in front of his eyes. He asked me questions, wanted to know what we were doing and how we were doing it. In the end I was convinced, and I asked the warden if he could work with us. The warden wasn't too crazy about the idea at first, but he agreed in the end, though he warned me the boy was a difficult character. His family background was enough to make anyone shudder.'

Russell realized that Ben was reliving an important moment of his life. He didn't know why, but he had the feeling he was the first person to hear any of this.

'I became fond of the boy. He was quiet and touchy, but he was a quick learner. When he left reformatory, I took him to work for me permanently and gave him that room to live in. There was a gleam in his eyes when he went in there for the first time. It was the first place he'd ever lived in that was really his.'

The old man moved away from the window and came and sat down again facing Russell.

'Matt soon became the son I never had. And my right-hand man. It was the other workers who gave him the nickname Little Boss, because of how he ran things whenever I was away. If he'd stayed, I'd have left him the business, instead of selling it to the asshole who bought it. But one day he told me he'd volunteered for Vietnam.'

'He volunteered? I didn't know that.'

'This is the really lousy part of the story. The kind of story that makes you ashamed to be a man.'

Russell said nothing, but waited. Ben had decided to share with him a bitter pill he'd never, in all that time, managed to swallow alone.

'One day we were called in to work on an extension to the house of the county judge. Herbert Lewis Swanson, God curse him wherever he is. That was when Matt met Karen, the judge's daughter. I was there the first time they met. I knew right away that something had happened between them. And I also realized it'd lead to nothing but trouble.'

The old man smiled at the memory of that love.

'They started seeing each other in secret. It may have been the only happy time in Matt's life. Sometimes I like to kid myself that the time he spent with me was happy, too.'

'I'm sure it was.'

The old man shrugged, as if to say: what's the point in remembering the past? Look at me now.

'Anyway, it was no use. Chillicothe's a small town, and not an easy place to hide in. Sooner or later, everyone notices everything. The judge soon found out his only daughter was seeing a boy. Then he found out who the boy was. Karen's life was all mapped out. She was beautiful, rich, intelligent. A guy like Matt wasn't quite what her father had planned for her. And her father was a very, very powerful man at the time. He practically owned the town.'

Ben allowed himself a few more sips of his coffee. He seemed reluctant to turn that memory into words, as if doing so meant being hurt a second time.

'Around about that time there was a double murder, down by the river. A couple of hippies camping out in the open were found dead. Both stabbed. They never found the killer, and they never found the murder weapon. The sheriff at the time was a man named Duane Westlake and he had a deputy named Will Farland. Both of them were tied hand and foot to Swanson, who'd bought them with privileges and money. A few nights after the bodies had been discovered, these two burst into Matt's room with a search warrant signed by the judge himself. Among his things they found marijuana, and they also found a big hunting knife, which could have been the murder weapon. Matt told me later that he'd been forced to put his fingerprints on the handle of that knife.'

The old man's voice was full of anger.

'I'm sure Matt had never sold an ounce of that stuff to anyone. And he'd never owned a knife.'

Russell had no reason to do so, but he was inclined to believe him.

'They dragged him to jail. And there they told him what could happen to him. A charge of using and dealing narcotics, and the much more serious charge of homicide. They were the ones who put the grass in Matt's room. As for the knife, I can't quite bring myself to believe the two of them killed the hippies on purpose. But the sheriff had been the first person at the scene of the crime, and getting rid of the weapon would have been child's play for someone like him. In addition, seeing that Matt was living at my place, those two sons of bitches told him they could charge me with being an accessory. Then they offered him an alternative to being tried and sentenced. He could volunteer for Vietnam.'

Ben finished his coffee.

'And he agreed. The rest you know.'

'A story as old as the world.'

Ben Shepard looked at him with his blue eyes, in which the pain was now fully accepted. 'The world's still too young to make sure stories like that never happen again.'

'What happened to Karen?'

'She couldn't believe it when he made that decision. She was incredulous at first, then desperate. But one of the conditions of the agreement he made with the sheriff was that he couldn't tell anyone. Not her, not me.'

Without asking, his host poured some more coffee into Russell's empty cup.

'After a period of training at Fort Polk, in Louisiana, Matt was granted leave, like everyone before they left for Nam. He snuck back here, and spent a month practically shut up at my place. Karen would come and join him there. They spent all the time they could in that room and I hope every one of those minutes lasted years, although that's not usually how it is. A month and a half after he left, Karen came to see me and told me she was pregnant. She also wrote him about it. We never got a reply, because soon after that we heard that he'd died.'

'What became of her?'

'Karen was a strong woman. When her father found out she was pregnant, he tried every way he could to persuade her to have an abortion. But she held out, threatened to tell everyone who the father of the child was and that the judge wanted her to have an abortion. That wouldn't have looked good for his political career, so the bastard chose the lesser of two evils, the scandal of his daughter becoming an unmarried mother.'

'But then Matt came back.'

'Yes. In the state you know.'

There was a pause, during which Russell saw images of that encounter in Ben's eyes.

'When I saw him and recognized him, I felt a grief inside me that's taken years to pass. That boy must have suffered tremendously. He must have gone through things it isn't right for a human being to go through.'

Ben took a handkerchief from the pocket of his old

cardigan and wiped the corners of his mouth with it. Without realizing it, he had used almost the same words he had spoken to Matt the night he had found him hiding out on his premises.

'Because of what he'd become, he didn't want Karen to know he was still alive. He made me swear I wouldn't tell her.'

'And then?'

'He asked me if he could stay there for a few hours, because he had something to do. As soon as he'd finished, he'd come back to pick up the cat and leave. I saw him walking into town. That was the last I ever saw of him.'

Another pause. Russell knew Ben was about to tell him something important.

'The next day, the bodies of Duane Westlake and Will Farland were taken from the burned-out remains of the sheriff's house. And I hope they're still burning in hell.'

In Ben Shepard's eyes there was an open challenge to anyone who might not care to agree with what he had just said. By this point, Russell had lost the ability to judge. He only wanted to know.

Ben sat back in his armchair. 'About ten years later, Judge Swanson joined his cronies.'

'What became of the child?'

'While he was still small, Karen would bring him to see me from time to time. Then we kind of lost touch. I don't know who was more to blame, her or me.'

Russell realized that, in his honesty, he was assuming a share of the responsibility, although he did not really think he had any.

'And then what happened?'

'A while later, I went through a difficult time, financial problems, that kind of thing. To solve them, I rented the business out to someone and spent three years working on an oil rig as an explosives expert. When I came back, I found out Karen had sold everything and gone away. I never saw her again.'

Russell felt disappointment burn his throat. 'You don't know where she moved to?'

'No. If I did, I'd tell you.'

The old man allowed himself a few moments to take stock. 'I realize how important it is that you find the person you're looking for. I feel enough remorse already – why should I add more?'

Russell looked out the window. At least it was a lead, he told himself.

It wouldn't be difficult for the police to find Karen Swanson, which meant it shouldn't be too difficult to trace his son as well. What they didn't have was time. If he was right, the next explosion would happen at night. He turned back to Ben, who, realizing how disappointed he was, had been waiting to speak again.

'Russell, there's one more thing I can tell you, though it seems such a long shot, I really don't know if it amounts to anything.'

'In a case like this, anything could amount to something.'

The old man looked for a moment at his age-stained hands, and the palm that contained all the familiar lines of his life. 'For years,' he said, 'my cousin managed the Wonder Theatre, here in Chillicothe. It was nothing special, mostly local shows, concerts by small groups and half-known singers. With a few touring companies every now and again to bring us a bit of novelty and an illusion of culture.'

Russell waited, hoping that what he suspected turned out to be true.

'One day, some years after Karen and her son left, a variety

400

show came to town. Magicians, comedians, acrobats, that kind of thing. My cousin is willing to swear that one of the performers was Manuel Swanson. Now remember, quite a few years had passed – he was using a stage name – but that was what my cousin thought. And he'd have bet any money on it. He told me he actually asked the boy if they'd met before, and the boy said no, this was the first time he'd ever been to Chillicothe in his life.'

Russell stood up, nervously smoothing his pants. 'That's certainly something, but it's going to take a while to find him. I'm afraid we don't have all that time.'

'Would a photograph help?'

At those words, Russell turned abruptly. 'That'd be the best thing of all.'

'Wait.'

Ben Shepard got up from his armchair and went and picked up a cordless phone lying on a cabinet. He dialled a number and waited for the reply.

'Hi, Homer, Ben here.'

A few moments listening. A few anxieties at the other end.

'No, don't worry. I'll be going bowling tonight. I called you about something else.'

He waited for the person at the other end to calm down.

'Homer, you remember what you told me once about young Swanson and that variety show?'

Russell had no idea what the other man was saying, but waited for Ben's next words.

'Among all your stuff, did you keep theirs?'

The answer must have been a short one, because Ben immediately replied, 'Great, I'm sending someone to see you. His name's Russell Wade. Do whatever he asks you. If you don't trust him, trust me.'

There must have been protests, a demand for an explanation. Ben Shepard cut him short.

'Just do it. Bye, Homer.'

He hung up and turned to Russell.

'In all those years, my cousin kept copies of posters of all the artists who performed in his theatre. A kind of collection. I think he plans to write a book about it, one of these days. He has a poster with a photograph of the person you're looking for.'

He took a notepad and a ballpoint pen from next to the telephone and wrote down a name and an address. He handed the paper to Russell.

'This is his address. It's all I can do.'

Russell followed his instinct. He took the paper and immediately hugged Ben Shepard. The sincerity and emotion of the gesture wiped out any surprise the old man might have. Russell hoped it would also wipe out any regret he might feel when he was alone.

'Ben, I have to go. You don't know how grateful I am.'

'But I do. And I also know you're a good person. I hope you find what you're looking for.'

Ben Shepard's eyes were moist again, but his handshake was firm and quick. Russell was already crossing the garden, on his way to the car. A few moments later, as he entered the address Ben had given him in the GPS, he told himself that he couldn't handle the information he now had all by himself. He would need the resources of the police. He had to get back to New York as soon as possible, once he'd obtained the material he needed from Homer. As he started the car and headed back to town, he wasn't sure if the excitement he felt inside him came from the discovery he had just made or the thought that he would soon see Vivien again.

CHAPTER 34

From the window of the clinic, Vivien had seen the sun come up. For Greta, there wouldn't be any new day. There wouldn't be any more dawns or sunsets, until the day came for a resurrection she had always found it difficult to believe in. She put her forehead against the window pane and felt the damp coldness of the surface on her skin. She closed her eyes, and dreamed of waking up in a time and place where none of this had happened and she and her sister were children, happy as only children can be. Earlier, as she had held Greta's hand and heard the beep-beep-beep of the monitor getting slower and slower until it was just a straight green line that came from nothing and led towards nothing.

In the past she had always supposed this was a privilege reserved for the dying, allowing them to become aware of the duration of their own lives. In this case, it had seemed absurdly short. Maybe because she was the one left behind and everything seemed fragile and vain, with that sense of emptiness that would remain with her for a very long time.

She went back to the bed and placed her lips on Greta's forehead. The skin was smooth and soft and Vivien's tears slid down her sister's temple onto the pillow. She reached out a hand and pressed a button next to the bedhead. She heard a buzzing sound. The door opened and a nurse appeared.

A quick glance at the monitor, and the woman immediately grasped the situation. She took an internal telephone from her pocket and sent a signal. 'Doctor, can you come to Room 28, please?'

Before long Dr Savine entered the room, preceded by the sound of his rapid footsteps in the corridor. He was a balding man, of medium height and middle age, with a capable air and a patient, professional manner. He approached the bed, pulling his stethoscope from the pocket of his white coat. He moved the sheet down and put the stethoscope to Greta's frail chest. It took him a moment to register the truth, and another moment to turn to Vivien with an expression that seemed to encompass all the similar situations he had experienced in his medical career.

'I'm sorry, Miss Light.'

The voice and the words were not merely formal. Vivien knew that the doctors and staff of the Mariposa had taken Greta's case to heart. And their powerlessness to halt the progress of the disease had been accompanied day after day by a sense of defeat, which they had shared with her. She turned away from the bed, so as not to see the sheet being pulled up to cover Greta's face.

The grief and fatigue made her feel dizzy. She swayed and put a hand against the wall to stop herself falling. Dr Savine immediately went to her to support her. He led her to a small armchair and helped her to sit down. Vivien felt his expert fingers looking for her pulse.

'Miss Light, you're exhausted. Don't you think you should rest a little?'

'I'd like to, doctor. But I can't. Not now.'

'If I remember correctly, you're a police officer. Am I right?'

Vivien looked up at the doctor, her face full of effort and urgency. 'Yes. And I absolutely have to get back to New York. It's a matter of life and death.'

'There's nothing more you can do here. If you believe in prayer, it can reach its destination from wherever you send it. In case you don't already have one, the clinic can supply you with the names of some undertakers who are very capable and very discreet. They'll see to everything.' Savine turned to the nurse. 'Meg, prepare the papers for the death certificate. I'll come and sign them.'

As soon as they were alone, Vivian rose from the armchair. Her legs felt stiff and wooden.

'Doctor, I have a big day ahead of me. And I can't afford to fall asleep.' She paused to overcome her embarrassment. 'It's a strange thing for a police officer to ask you, but I need something to keep me awake.'

The doctor gave her a strange knowing smile. 'Is this a trap? Am I going to end up in handcuffs?'

Vivien shook her head. 'No. But you will be in my prayers.'

Savine thought it over for a moment. 'Wait here.'

He went out, leaving Vivien alone. Before long, he returned with a white plastic container. He shook it to indicate that there was one pill inside.

'Here. Take this pill if and when you need it. But make sure you don't drink alcohol.'

'There's no danger of that. Thank you, doctor.'

'Good luck, Miss Light. And once again, my condolences.'

Again, Vivien was alone. She tried to convince herself that her sister was no longer in that room, that what was lying on the bed under the sheet was only an envelope that for years had contained her beautiful soul, a borrowed envelope that would soon be surrendered to the earth. In spite of this, she couldn't help giving Greta a final kiss and a final look.

On the night table there was a half-full bottle of water. She opened the container the doctor had just given her and tipped the pill straight out onto her tongue. She swallowed it with a sip of water that, to her, tasted like tears. Then she moved away from the bed, took her jacket from the coat stand, and left the room.

She walked along the corridor, her eyes stinging. She got in the elevator and glided smoothly and noiselessly down to the lobby, where she found a couple of young women in uniforms behind the reception desk. Within a few moments she had made arrangements for Greta's body with an undertaker whose number had been supplied by one of the two women.

Then she looked around at this place where there was now nothing more for her to do, but above all where there was nothing more she could do. When she had first brought Greta to the Mariposa, she had appreciated its elegance and sobriety. Now it was only a place where people didn't always get better.

She went outside and walked to the parking lot to get her car. It might be just the placebo effect – surely it was too soon for the pill to take effect – but she felt the tiredness wear off and her body gradually free itself of all the dross it had accumulated.

As she joined the stream of traffic leaving the city headed towards Palisades Parkway, she went over the events that had brought her to this point in the investigation and in her life.

The previous day, when Father McKean had told her his secret, contravening one of the strictest rules of his ministry, she had felt both anxious and excited. On the one hand, there was her responsibility towards all those innocent people who were in imminent danger, the same responsibility that had finally convinced the priest to turn to her. On the other hand there was the desire to spare him the consequences of a decision that must have caused him enormous pain.

Michael McKean's work was too important. The young people he took care of loved him and they, and all those who might come to Joy in the future, needed to know that he would always be there for them.

It was after lunch with the kids, during which she had laughed and joked with Sundance, who seemed completely new in body and mind, that the call had come from the clinic. Dr Savine had informed her, with all the tact the news demanded, that Greta's condition was changing rapidly and that they must be prepared for the worst at any moment. She had gone back to the table, trying not to let any of the anguish she felt inside show, but she hadn't been able to deceive Sundance's acute and sensitive eye.

'What's the matter, Vunny? Is something wrong?'

'Nothing, darling. A few problems at work. You know what those rascals are like, they just don't like getting arrested.'

She had deliberately used the word rascals because it was a word that had always made Sundance laugh when she was little. But in spite of Vivien's attempts to downplay things, her niece hadn't been completely convinced, and for the rest of lunch she had continued looking at her, aware of her grim expression and watery eyes.

Before leaving, she had taken Father McKean aside and told him that Sundance's mother was getting worse, and that once she left there she would go up to Cresskill, to the clinic. They agreed that he would put up a notice in church that afternoon, announcing an unscheduled confession for Thursday: he would be in the confessional from early the following afternoon. If the man did not show up then, they would speak again on the phone on Friday, the day when he usually heard confession at the church of Saint John the Baptist in Manhattan, and work out a new plan of action.

During the journey, Vivien confronted the hardest test. She had to talk to Bellew and get as much as she could from him without giving anything away. She hoped that the esteem her chief had for her was great enough to allow her what she asked.

The captain picked up after the second ring. His voice sounded tired. 'Bellew.'

'Hi, Alan, it's Vivien.'

'Did you go to Williamsburg?'

Frank and direct as always. Now with an added anxiety that wouldn't take much to turn to neurosis.

'Yes. But I didn't get anything from the apartment. Our fake Wendell Johnson really was like a phantom, even at home.'

The captain didn't need to curse. His silence was eloquent enough.

'But I have another lead,' Vivien went on, 'and I think this is the big one, if we're lucky.'

'What do you mean?'

'I think it'll get us the man who's detonating the bombs.'

An incredulous voice in her ear. 'Do you mean that? How did you find it?'

'Alan, you have to trust me on this. I can't tell you anything else.'

The captain changed the subject. Vivian knew him well. She knew it was only to give him time to think.

'Is Wade still with you?'

If he had expected to hear a greeting from Russell over the speakerphone, Vivien's reply took him by surprise. 'No, he decided to give up.'

'Are you sure he won't say anything?'

'Yes.'

I'm not sure of anything, when it comes to that man. More than that, he's not sure about me any more . . .

But now wasn't the time to talk about him, let alone think about him. The captain had taken Russell's bowing out as a good sign. And his batteries seemed newly recharged at the thought of an impending arrest.

'So what do I have to do? Above all, what do you want to do?'

'You have to put the police in the Bronx on alert. They need to be ready on a coded wavelength from two o'clock tomorrow afternoon, waiting for my orders.'

The captain's reply was blunt. 'You know a request like that is a one-way ticket, don't you? The commissioner's on my back, and I can't get him off. If we move on this and don't get a result, I'm going to have a lot of explaining to do. And heads are sure to roll. Our heads.'

'I'm aware of that. But it's the only thing we can do. The only chance we have to stop him.'

'All right. I hope you know what you're doing.'

'So do I. Thanks, Alan.'

The captain hung up and she was alone.

And now she was returning to New York with a presence in the car that would gradually fade with time.

She crossed the George Washington Bridge and drove on until she got to Webster Avenue. Here she turned left, heading for Laconia Street, where the 47th Precinct was situated. She parked her car outside the building. All around her uniformed officers sat in their cars, waiting. As soon as she got out of the Volvo, the glass-fronted door of the precinct house opened and the captain came out with a man she didn't know in plain clothes. She and Bellew had agreed to meet here the previous evening, when she had called him before turning off—

The telephone, dammit.

It hadn't been on since then. She hadn't wanted it to ring while she was in the clinic. She knew she wouldn't get any important calls during the night. If anything happened, it would happen the following day. She had wanted to be alone with her sister, isolated from the rest of the world, for what had in fact turned out to be their last night together. And this morning, overwhelmed by Greta's death, she had forgotten to turn it on when she left Cresskill. She searched in the pockets of her jacket and took it out. She frantically turned it on, hoping there hadn't been any calls. Her hope was short lived. A number of messages about missed calls came up.

Russell.

Later, I don't have time now.

Sundance.

Later, sweetie. I don't know what to say right now, or how to say it.

Bellew.

Holy Christ, why didn't I switch on this damned phone?

Father McKean.

Damn. Damn. Damn.

The call from Father McKean had come at noon. Vivien looked at her watch. 2.15. She didn't know the reason for that call, but there was no way she could call him back: he must be in the confessional by now. If he had a penitent with him and the cellphone rang, it could be quite embarrassing. And if by some twist of fate the man they were chasing was already there, he was bound to get suspicious.

In the meantime Bellew and the other man had joined her in the parking lot. He was a fleshy man, and his physique could hardly be described as athletic, but the way he moved demonstrated that he was strong and agile.

'Vivien,' the captain said, 'where have you been hiding yourself?' Then he saw the expression on her face and his tone changed abruptly. 'I'm sorry. How's your sister?'

Vivien said nothing, hoping Doctor Savine's pill would help her, not only to stay awake, but also to hold back her tears. Her unsaid words were clearer than any speech.

Bellew put his hand on her shoulder. 'I'm sorry. I really am.'

Vivien pulled herself together. She noticed the other man's embarrassment. He had realized that something unpleasant had happened, that much was obvious, but he had no idea how to react to it. Vivien removed the awkwardness by holding out her hand.

'Detective Vivien Light. Thank you for your help.'

'Commander William Codner. It's a pleasure. I hope—'

Vivien would never know what Codner hoped, because at that moment the cellphone she was still clutching in her hand started ringing. The screen lit up, and there was Father McKean's name on the display. Vivien felt heat rise in a wave from her stomach and spread all over her body. She replied immediately, then covered the microphone of the cellphone with her finger.

She looked up at the two men. 'We're on.'

Codner made a gesture with his hand and the cars started

heading out. One came towards them and Vivien got in the front seat next to the driver. Bellew and Codner took their places in the back.

'Boys, the game has started. You have the ball, Vivien.'

'Just a minute.'

A voice she didn't know, a calm, deep voice. '. . . *and as you see, I kept my promise.*'

Then Father McKean's reply. '*But at what a price! How many lives did that madness cost?*'

Vivien moved the telephone away from her ear slightly. She grabbed the radio and gave instructions to the listening cars.

'Calling all cars. This is Detective Light. Converge on the Country Club area. Isolate the block between Tremont, Barkley, Logan and Bruckner Boulevard. I want a cordon of cars and officers keeping an eye on anyone leaving the area in a car or on foot.'

'*Madness? Were the Plagues of Egypt madness? Was the Great Flood madness?*'

Vivien felt a hand clutch her chest and her heartbeat accelerate. The man was really crazy. She heard the priest's voice, tinged with compassion, trying to speak sweet reason to someone who couldn't accept it.

'*But then Jesus came and the world changed. He taught us to forgive.*'

'*Jesus failed. You people preached his words but you didn't listen to him. You killed him . . .*'

The voice had lost its deep tone and become slightly shrill. Vivien tried to imagine the man's face in the semi-darkness of the confessional.

'*Is that why you decided to wear that green jacket? Is that why you killed so many innocent people? For revenge?*'

412

Vivien realized that Father McKean was giving her a clue, confirming his previous description. And by continuing to answer the man, he was giving her time to get there. She again lifted the radio to her mouth and spoke to the listening officers.

'The suspect is a tall, dark-haired male Caucasian wearing a green military-style jacket. He may be armed and dangerous. I repeat: he may be armed and very dangerous.'

The man confirmed the accuracy of that description with his next words, murmured with the bitterness of hate and spelled out like a death sentence. '*Revenge and justice came together this time. And human lives don't matter to me, just as they've never mattered to you people.*'

Michael McKean's voice again. '*But don't you feel the holiness of this place? Can't you find the peace you seek right here, in this church dedicated to Saint John the Baptist, the man who in his modesty declared himself unworthy to baptise Christ?*'

Vivien felt her strength fail her. Saint John the Baptist? That was why Father McKean had called her. He'd wanted to inform her that for some reason he wouldn't be at Saint Benedict but had brought his weekly visit to Saint John forward by one day.

She screamed her defeat at the roof of the car. 'He's not there! Dammit, he's not there!'

She heard Bellew's startled voice behind her. 'What do you mean? What's happening?'

She silenced him with a gesture.

'*Holiness is in the end. That is why I shall not rest on Sunday. And the next time, the stars will disappear and all who dwell beneath them.*'

'*What does that mean? I don't understand.*'

413

The voice again, self-confident, low, threatening. '*You don't have to understand. You just have to wait.*'

Another pause. And in that pause Vivien saw more people die, heard their screams in the blast of the explosion, saw them burning in the fire that immediately engulfed them. And felt herself dying with them.

The voice continued to lay out its insane threat. '*This is my power. This is my duty. This is my will.*'

Another pause. Then the true madness.

'*I am God.*'

Vivien had reached out a hand to the radio and switched to the usual Manhattan police frequency. She repeated the message she had previously transmitted, but with modifications.

'Calling all cars. This is Detective Vivien Light of the 13th Precinct. Proceed as quickly as possible to the Fashion District and surround the block between 31st and 32nd Streets and Seventh and Eighth Avenues. The suspect is a male Caucasian, tall with dark hair. He is wearing a green military jacket. He may be armed and is very dangerous. Contact me as soon as you have anything.'

From the cellphone came the subdued voice of Father McKean. 'Vivien, are you there?'

'Yes.'

'He's gone.'

'Thanks. You were great. I'll call you later.'

Vivien collapsed back in her seat. She made a disheartened gesture to the driver. 'You can stop. There's no hurry now.'

As the driver pulled over, the captain put his head between the front seats, so that he could look Vivien in the face. 'What's happening? Who was that on the phone?'

Vivien turned to look at him. 'I can't tell you. The only thing I can tell you is that we have to wait now. And hope.'

Bellew sat back down. He had realized that something had gone wrong, even though he didn't know what. Vivien knew how her chief must be feeling right now, because it couldn't be so very different from how she felt. In the car, nobody had the courage to speak.

A voice came over the radio. 'Officer Mantin from Midtown South here. We stopped an individual answering to the description and wearing a green military-style jacket.'

Vivien felt relief wash over her like a wave. 'Great, boys. Where are you?'

'At the corner of 31st and Seventh.'

'Take him to your precinct house. We'll be right there.'

Vivien made a gesture to the driver, who moved the car away from the kerb. A hand came from the back to rest on Vivien's shoulder.

'Great work, detective.'

That compliment lost all meaning the next moment. Another voice came over the radio, bringing confusion and despair back into the car.

'Car 31 here, from Midtown South. This is Officer Jeff Cantoni. We also stopped a guy answering your description.'

They didn't have time to wonder what was happening because a third voice now drowned out everything else.

'Officer Webber here. I'm on Sixth Avenue at the corner of 32nd Street. There's a veteran's parade going on. There must be two thousand of them, all wearing green military jackets.'

Vivien closed her eyes and covered her face with her hands, taking refuge in a darkness in which it seemed the sun would never rise again, and allowed herself to cry only when she and that darkness had become one.

CHAPTER 35

Vivien emerged from the elevator and slowly walked along the corridor.

When she reached the door, she took the keys from her pocket and inserted them in the keyhole. As soon as she had given the lock a first turn, the door opposite opened and Judith appeared. She was holding one of her cats in her arms.

'Hello there. You finally came back.'

Vivien's mood at that moment didn't allow for intruders. 'Hello, Judith. I'm sorry, I'm in a great hurry.'

'Don't you want a coffee?'

'No. Not now, thanks.'

The old woman looked at her for a moment with a mixture of commiseration and reprimand. 'What can you expect from someone who thinks only of tips?'

She closed the door in Vivien's face with a self-satisfied expression. The lock clicked shut, isolating her and her four-legged friends. At any other time, the woman's eccentricity would have moved and amused Vivien. But right now, she had no room for any feelings that weren't anger, disappointment and regret. For herself, for Greta, for Sundance. For Father McKean. For all the people that madman had allowed to live before he unleashed another inferno.

After their failure had been confirmed, Bellew had been

silent for a long time, afraid even to look at her. They both knew what would happen. By the next day, the whole of the NYPD would know about the fiasco. As the captain had predicted, the commissioner would demand explanations – and maybe resignations.

Vivien was ready to hand over her gun and her shield if she was asked to. She had done the best she could, but it had all gone belly up. It was the fault of chance, but above all it was her fault, her carelessness. She hadn't remembered to turn on a damned phone in time. The fact that it had happened when her sister had just died was no excuse. She was a police officer and her personal needs and feelings had to take second place in a case like this. She hadn't been able to do that, and she was ready to take the consequences.

But if other people died, she would have to live with the consequences for ever.

She walked into the apartment of a sick, desperate man who for years had gone by the name of Wendell Johnson. She found the same bare surroundings, the same sense of hopeless solitude. The grey light coming in through the window made everything seem flat, drab, devoid of life and hope.

She wandered through the apartment, waiting for it to speak to her.

She didn't even know what she was looking for, but she knew there was something unexplored here, like a suggestion whispered in her ear that she hadn't been able to understand or decipher. She just had to calm down and forget all the rest if she wanted to remember what it was. She moved the one chair from the table into the middle of the kitchen, sat down with her legs apart and her arms resting on the rough fabric of her jeans, and looked around.

The telephone rang in the pocket of her jacket.

Instinctively, she felt like turning it off without even looking to see who the call was from. Then, with a sigh, took the call. She heard Russell's excited voice.

'Vivien, at last. It's Russell. I found him.'

The line was not very good and Vivien couldn't hear him terribly well. 'Calm down. Speak slowly. Who did you find?'

Russell started enunciating the words clearly. And at last Vivien understood what he was talking about. 'The real name of the man who passed himself off as Wendell Johnson all those years was Matt Corey. He was born in Chillicothe, in Ohio. And he had a son. I have his name and his photograph.'

'Have you gone crazy? How did you manage that?'

'It's a long story. Where are you now?'

'In Wen—' She broke off. She decided to give Russell the benefit of the doubt, until she had proof of the contrary. 'In Matt Corey's apartment, on Broadway, in Williamsburg. And you?'

'I landed at La Guardia fifteen minutes ago. Right now I'm on the Brooklyn Expressway, travelling south. I'll be with you in ten minutes.'

'Okay. Come as fast as you can. I'll wait here.'

She tried to sit down again, but she had the feeling that her legs would soon start to bump together from sheer nervousness and she wouldn't be able to sit still.

She stood up and took a few steps around an apartment she knew by heart now. Russell had succeeded where she had failed. She noticed that there was no anger or envy in her. Just relief and admiration for what he had managed to do. She didn't feel humiliated. And she immediately realized why. It was because he wasn't just any man, he was Russell. The worm started gnawing at her again, heedless of her impatience. You felt pleasure at someone else's success only when you loved them. And she realized that she was completely in thrall to that man. She was sure that sooner or later she would get him out of her head, but it would take a lot of time and a lot of effort.

She hoped, with a touch of self-mockery, that looking for a new job would keep her sufficiently busy. She went into the bedroom, switched on the light and for the umpteenth time looked around that apartment.

It hit her at the speed of light, the speed of thought.

No pictures on the walls . . .

When she had been with Richard, her former boyfriend, she had learned all about artists. He was an architect, but he was also a reasonable painter. The many pictures hanging in their apartment demonstrated that. But what they also demonstrated was the natural narcissism all artists seemed to possess. Often in inverse proportion to their talent. What seemed strange to her was that this man, this Matt Corey, had done all those drawings and over the years had somehow avoided the temptation to put even one of them up on the wall.

Unless . . .

A couple of steps, and she stood in front of the rack. She took the big grey folder from the lower shelf, opened it, and went quickly through the drawings done on the unusual medium of transparent plastic . . .

* * *

Constellation of Karen, Constellation of Beauty, Constellation of the End . . .

. . . until she found the one she was looking for. The bell rang just as she was taking it out of the pile. She placed the drawing on the rough wooden surface and went to open the door, hoping it wasn't Judith with more complaints. But it was

419

Russell, looking dishevelled, with a couple of days' growth of beard, his hair unkempt and his clothes crumpled. In his right hand he held an object that looked like a rolled-up poster.

She thought two things simultaneously: that he was very handsome and that she was a fool.

She took him by the arm and pulled him into the apartment before the door opposite could open. 'Come inside.'

Vivien closed the door again immediately, the noise of the lock covering Russell's excited voice.

'I have something to show you—'

'Just a minute. First check something for me.'

She went back into the bedroom, followed by a puzzled-looking Russell. She picked up the plastic sheet with its blue surround, on which the artist had drawn what according to him was The Constellation of Wrath. The drawing consisted of a series of white dots supplemented here and there with little red dots.

As Russell looked on curiously, she went to the map of New York hanging on the wall and placed the drawing over it. They matched perfectly. But whereas the white dots appeared to be placed at random, some lost in the river or the sea, the red dots were all on dry land and had specific geographical locations.

In a low voice, Vivien said to herself, 'It's a memorandum.'

Still holding the drawing against the map, Vivien turned her head towards Russell, who was now standing beside her. He was starting to understand, even though he had no idea how Vivien had got there.

'This Matt Corey had no artistic ambitions. He knew perfectly well he didn't have any talent. That's why he didn't display a single drawing. The only reason he did them was to conceal this map. I'm sure the red dots correspond to all the places where he hid the bombs.'

She moved the plastic sheet away, and when she looked again at the map of the city, she could feel herself turn white. She was unable to restrain an anguished cry.

'Oh, my God!'

Vivien hoped she was wrong. But when she again placed the plastic sheet over the map, her impression was confirmed. She checked it again and again, running her finger over the sheet, going so close to it, she was almost touching the wall.

'There are bombs at Joy.'

'What's Joy?'

'Not now. We have to go. Straight away.'

'But I—'

'You can tell me on the way. Right now, there isn't a minute to lose.'

Vivien was already at the door. She held it open until Russell joined her.

'Hurry up. Code RFL.'

As they waited for the elevator, Vivienne felt more lucid than she'd ever felt in her life. She didn't know if it was the situation, or the pill Dr Savine had given her. Right now, she didn't care. She tried to remember the exact words the man in the green jacket had said in the confessional.

Holiness is in the end. That is why I shall not rest on Sunday . . .

That meant that the next attack was planned for the following Sunday. That gave her a little breathing space, if her theory about the drawing proved correct. But where Joy was concerned, she couldn't afford to run any risks. It had to be evacuated as quickly as possible. She didn't want to lose her sister and her niece in one day.

They went out on the street and ran to the car. She heard

Russell panting behind her. He seemed to be physically exhausted. He would have time to rest during the journey to the Bronx, Vivien thought.

She tried to call Father McKean but his telephone was off. She wondered why. He must surely have got back to Joy from Saint John's by now. Maybe after what he had been through in the confessional he didn't want the telephone to be anything but an inanimate object buried deep in his pocket. She tried calling John Kortighan's number, but it just kept ringing.

As she drove along the streets as fast as the traffic allowed, Vivien turned to Russell, who was gripping the strap above the window with his right hand. Driving, at that moment, was a simple animal fact, a question of habitual gestures, of nerves and reflexes. Curiosity was one of the few human traits remaining to her.

'So what did you find?'

'Don't you think you should concentrate on your driving right now?'

'I can drive and listen at the same time.'

Russell tried to summarize the story as best he could. 'I can't really explain exactly how I did it, but I managed to discover the name Matt Corey. He was the Little Boss in the photograph we saw at Hornell. He fought alongside Wendell Johnson in Vietnam. For years, Matt Corey was believed dead, whereas in fact he'd assumed his friend's identity.'

Vivien asked the question that interested her the most. 'What about the son?'

'He's not in Chillicothe any more. His name is Manuel Swanson. I don't know where he is now. But he used to have artistic ambitions.' He lifted the rolled-up poster he was holding in his left hand. 'And I managed to get hold of one of his posters.'

422

'Show me.'

All the while he had been speaking, Russell hadn't taken his eyes off the road. The Volvo was weaving in and out of the other cars, some of which had slowed down and pulled over to let them pass.

'Are you crazy? We're going at almost a hundred miles an hour. We'll crash and there'll be a pile up.'

Vivien raised her voice. 'Show me, I said.'

Maybe she'd raised her voice too much. She had done that once before and regretted it.

Reluctantly, Russell unrolled the poster. Vivien threw it a glance, her eyes drawn instinctively to the words in red block capitals below the photograph:

THE FANTASTIC
MISTER ME

She went back to concentrating on her driving. It wasn't until they hit a stretch without other vehicles that she looked again, this time at the photograph. And her heart gave such a strong thump, she was sure that a second one would break it.

She couldn't stop now – she had to keep driving. She found herself murmuring an invocation. 'Oh, God. Oh, God. Oh, God.'

Russell rolled up the poster and threw it on the back seat. In spite of the noise, he heard it falling to the floor behind his seat.

'What's the matter, Vivien? What's going on? Do you want to tell me where we're going?'

Vivien's only reply was to increase speed, pushing the accelerator as hard as she could. They had just left the bridge over the Hutchinson River behind them, and the car was now proceeding along Route 95 with all the speed its engine allowed.

To relieve the anxiety that was tearing her chest apart, Vivien had decided to satisfy Russell's curiosity. She still hoped and prayed she was wrong, even though she knew she wasn't.

'Joy is a community for drug addicts. My niece is there, my sister's daughter. My sister who died last night. And there are bombs there.'

Now that she had finally given vent to her anguish, Vivien felt the tears coming. There was a knot in her throat and her voice cracked. She wiped her eyes with the back of her hand.

'Damn.'

Russell did not ask for any further explanation. To clear her head, Vivien took refuge in her bitterness about life. Afterwards, when it was all over, she knew this anger would turn to poison, if she couldn't get rid of it. But right now she needed it, because it had become her strength.

When they got to Burr Avenue, Vivien slowed down and removed the flashing lamp. She didn't want to arrive in a blaze of lights and sirens. She threw a glance at Russell. He was sitting in silence, unafraid, but not wanting to trespass on what for now was a space reserved for her. She appreciated that. He was a man who could speak well but knew when it was right to keep quiet.

They turned onto the unpaved road that led to Joy. She did not drive the Volvo right into the parking lot as she usually did. Instead, she pulled up on the right, in a lay-by hidden from sight by a group of cypresses.

Vivien got out of the car, and Russell did the same.

'Wait here.'

'No way.'

When she saw that he was determined and that nothing in

the world would persuade him to stay by the car, Vivian resigned herself. She took out her gun and made sure there was a round in the chamber. It was a habitual gesture for her, one that meant security, but it made a shadow fall over Russell's face. She put it back in the holster.

'Stay behind me.'

Vivien approached the house by a different route. Making their way through the bushes and hugging the edge of the garden, they reached the front of the building, and seeing that familiar facade Vivien felt a pang of anguish. She had brought her niece here full of confidence. And now this house where so many kids were finding a new hope in life could be transformed at any moment into a place of death. She walked faster, while remaining as cautious as ever. Near the house were two kids sitting on a bench. Vivien saw that they were Jubilee Manson and her niece.

Keeping in the shadow of the bushes, she leaned out and waved an arm to attract their attention. As soon as she had it, she put her index finger in front of her mouth to silence them.

The two kids got up and came to her. Her imperious gesture and her attitude made Sundance instinctively lower her voice. 'What is it? What's happening?'

'Shut up and listen. Behave normally and do as I tell you.'

Sundance realized immediately that this was no joke.

'Do what I tell you, both of you. Get everyone together and get as far away from the building as possible. Do you understand? As far away as possible.'

'OK.'

'Where's Father McKean?'

Sundance pointed to the attic. 'In his room, with John.'

'Oh, no!'

As if to reinforce that instinctive cry, there suddenly came from the house the unmistakable sound of a gunshot. Vivien leaped to her feet.

'Go. Run as fast as you can.'

Vivien ran quickly to the house. Russell followed her. She could hear their steps crunching on the gravel, and at that moment it was an unbearable noise. She went in through the glass-fronted door and found a group of kids looking up at the top of the stairs, where the shot had come from.

Stunned faces. Curious faces. Faces scared at seeing her come in with a gun. Even though they knew her, Vivien thought it best to identify herself in a way that would inspire confidence in them.

'Police. I'm dealing with this. All of you, out and away from the house. Now!'

The kids didn't need to be asked twice. They ran out, with terrified faces. Vivien hoped that Sundance, who was still outside, would have the strength and charisma to calm them down and lead them to safety.

She headed up the stairs, keeping the gun pointed in front of her.

Russell was behind her. Russell was with her.

Step by step they got to the second floor, where the kids' rooms were. There was no one on the landing. They must all have been outside, otherwise she would have found some of them drawn by the sound of the gunshot. She looked out the window and saw a group of kids running along the road and disappearing from view.

The relief did not make her drop her guard.

She listened. No voice, no moaning. Only the echo of that shot seemed to linger like a living presence in the stairwell. Vivien carried on up the final flight of stairs to the attic. At the top, they could see an open door.

As silent as cats, they reached the top landing. Vivien stood for a moment with her back against the wall. She took a deep breath and slipped inside the room with her gun aimed.

What she saw filled her with horror and made her react in an instant. Father McKean was lying on the floor with a gunshot wound in the middle of his forehead. His open eyes stared up at the ceiling as if dazed. Under his head a pool of blood was spreading over the floor. John was sitting on a stool, looking at him with empty eyes, clutching a pistol in his hand.

'Throw the gun away. Now.'

Vivien had shouted instinctively, but John was clearly in shock. He did not look as if he was going to react, or even as if he was able to do so. In spite of this, Vivien tightened her grip on the stock of her gun.

'Throw the gun away, John. Now.'

The man looked down at the hand clutching the revolver, as if he had only just realized that he was holding it. Then his fingers opened and the weapon fell to the floor. Vivien kicked it away.

John looked up at her with tear-filled eyes. His voice was a moan. 'We'll say it was me. That's what we'll do. We'll say it was me.'

Vivien took the handcuffs from her belt and put them around his wrists, immobilizing him with his arms behind his back. Only then did she allow herself to breathe.

Russell was standing in the doorway, looking at the body lying on the floor in its pool of blood. Vivien wondered if he was here at this moment, or reliving some scene from his past. She gave him the time to recover.

John was sitting on the stool, looking down at the floor, still murmuring his incomprehensible litany. Vivien did not think there would be any unexpected moves from him. She became aware of the place where she was. An austere room with no concessions to vanity except for a Van Gogh poster on the wall.

And on the floor, next to the closet, an open suitcase.

From the wide-open lid, three things stuck out: a thick, dog-eared brown envelope, a photograph album and a green military jacket.

It was only now that she realized that the TV set was on. A freeze-frame was up on the screen. She saw Russell come in, take the remote control from the desk and restart the old video recorder. The figures on the screen began moving again. The image was so grainy, it might well be a conversion to VHS of an old Super8. And along with the image came the voice.

Vivien stared at the screen, sick at heart.

Sitting in the middle of the stage in a small theatre, motionless under the lights, in front of a crowded auditorium, was a ventriloquist. He was young, but not so young as to be unrecognizable. On his knees he held a puppet, about three feet high. The puppet was of an elderly man in a white tunic, with long snowy white hair and a beard of the same colour.

Michael McKean turned to the puppet and asked him a question in an impatient tone. 'But why won't you tell me who you are?'

The puppet replied in a calm, deep voice, 'Haven't you guessed yet? You really are stupid, boy.'

Then, moved by the ventriloquist's skilled hand, he turned his head towards the auditorium to savour the audience's laughter. He was silent for a moment, raising his thick eyebrows over his blue glass eyes in an unnatural manner.

Finally he said the words the whole audience was waiting for.

'I am God.'

CHAPTER 36

'And when we got to Joy, we saw that John, Father McKean's right-hand man, had killed him. That's all we know for the moment.'

Vivien finished her account and shared the silence of the other people in the room. Some already knew the story, had gone through it stage by stage through her words and felt the bitter taste of confirmation in their mouths. Some had heard it for the first time from beginning to end, and couldn't remove the incredulity from their faces.

It was 7 a.m. The morning light came in through the window and threw a pattern on the floor.

They were all exhausted.

Present in the mayor's office in City Hall, apart from the mayor himself, were Police Commissioner Joby Willard, Captain Alan Bellew, Vivien, Russell and Doctor Albert Grosso, a psychologist chosen by Gollemberg as a consultant to the investigation, who had been hurriedly summoned to take care of John Kortighan in his confused state.

Given what Joy had in its walls, they had all agreed that it was impossible for the kids to spend the night there. They had been entrusted to the care of the community's outside helpers and accommodated temporarily in a hotel in the Bronx that had agreed to take them in.

She had given Sundance a kiss, reserving the right to put off to the following day the news of her mother's death. As she watched them get in the bus, it had struck Vivien that it would take a lot of time and effort before they forgot. She hoped that none of them lost their way as they confronted this new test.

Once the initial crime screen investigation was over, and Michael McKean's body had been removed and his killer taken away in handcuffs, a car had brought Vivien and Russell to City Hall where they had arrived almost simultaneously with the captain and where Mayor Gollemberg was waiting for them.

First of all he had made sure that the danger of other explosions had been neutralized.

Bellew had explained that the bomb disposal experts had rendered the remote control that set off the explosions unusable and that, thanks to both the letter found in Father McKean's possession and the map – the latter a brilliant intuition of Vivien's – they now had a complete list of the buildings that had been mined. The clearance was scheduled to begin in a few hours.

Then Vivien had told the story in all its complexity and absurdity, right up to its dramatic conclusion.

At this point, Dr Grosso, a man in his mid-fifties who was the exact opposite of the stereotypical psychiatrist, realized that it was his turn. He got to his feet and began walking around the room, speaking in a calm voice that held everyone's attention from the first words.

'Based on what I've heard, I can hazard a diagnosis, though I reserve the right to modify it after I've had a closer look at the case. Unfortunately, not being able to talk directly to the person concerned, I have to rely on the testimony, which is why I suspect we'll never be able to do anything other than hypothesize.'

He stroked his moustache, trying to express himself in terms that everyone could understand.

'From what I've heard, I think Father McKean was severely disturbed. Firstly he had a split personality, and whenever his other persona, the man in the green jacket, entered him, he stopped being himself. To be clearer, when he put on that green jacket, he wasn't pretending, he wasn't playing a part like an actor, he really became a different man. But when that man left him, no memory remained. I'm sure his anguish at all those deaths was genuine. That's proved by the fact that he decided to contravene one of the most important dogmas of his Church and violate the secrecy of the confessional if it would lead to the arrest of the culprit and the end of the attacks.'

Dr Grosso leaned on the desk and looked around. Maybe this was the way he acted when he lectured at the university.

'This kind of syndrome is often accompanied by epilepsy. Let's be clear what we mean by that word. I'm not talking about the disease we're all familiar with, in other words, the eyes rolling up, the foaming at the mouth, the convulsions. Epilepsy sometimes presents itself in very different forms. During the attacks, the person affected may have hallucinations. So it isn't unlikely that at such moments, Father McKean actually saw his own alter ego. The fact that he described him proves that. And at the same time it's the proof of what I said earlier, that he was completely unaware of what was happening to him.'

He gave a shrug of his shoulders by way of introduction to what he next said.

'The fact that he had a gift as a ventriloquist, and that in his

431

youth he actually performed professionally, merely confirms this theory. There is often an identification between the ventriloquist and his puppet, at least where there's some kind of predisposition. But as the puppet's appeal to the public is the true source of the ventriloquist's success, the ventriloquist may begin to feel envy or even aversion towards his puppet. A colleague of mine is treating a patient who was convinced that his puppet was having an affair with his wife.'

He smiled, but without mirth.

'I realize that saying such things, may raise a smile. But I beg you to believe me that in a mental hospital they are far from uncommon.'

He moved away from the desk and again began pacing the room.

'As for this John Kortighan, I think he was completely under the spell of Father McKean. He didn't so much idealize him as idolize him. When he realized who he was and what he was doing, all he could do was strike down his idol. When I spoke with him, he actually suggested I tell everyone that he was responsible for the attacks, so that Father McKean's good name and the memory of all the important things he had done in his life should remain intact. As you can see, the human mind is—'

The telephone on the mayor's desk rang.

Gollemberg lifted the receiver. 'Hello?'

He listened for a moment, without changing expression.

'Good morning, sir. Yes, it's all over. I can confirm that the city is no longer at risk. There are other explosive devices, but we've located them and are rendering them harmless.'

There was a reply at the other end, which the mayor appeared to accept with pleasure.

'Thank you, sir. I'll make sure you get a detailed report of this whole crazy business as soon as possible. That's as soon as we've understood it.'

He listened again.

'Yes, I can confirm that. Vivien Light.'

He smiled, presumably at something the other person was saying.

'Of course, sir.'

The mayor looked up: 'It's for you' – to her surprise held out the receiver to her.

Vivien lifted the receiver to her ear as if it was an unfamiliar object she had never touched before. 'Hello?'

The voice she heard at the other end was one of the best known in the world.

'Hello, Miss Light. My name's Stuart Bredford. They tell me I'm the President of the United States.'

Vivien resisted the impulse to stand to attention but couldn't restrain her emotion. 'It's an honour to speak with you, sir.'

'The honour's all mine. Before anything else, allow me to express my condolences on the loss of your sister. When a loved one dies, it's as if part of us disappears with them. The gap can never really be filled. I know the two of you were close.'

'Yes, sir. Very close.'

Vivien wondered how he had found out about Greta's death. Then she reminded himself that he was the President of the United States and that he could probably find out about anything or anyone in a few minutes.

'All the more credit to you. Even though you were grieving, you still managed to see this investigation through to its conclusion and in the process saved hundreds of innocent people from certain death.'

'I did my job, sir.'

'And I thank you for that, personally and on behalf of all those people. Now I'm the one who has a job to do.'

A pause.

'First of all, I guarantee you that, in spite of what's happened, Joy won't close. As of now, I'm making that a special commitment. You have the president's word.'

Vivien remembered the bewildered faces of the kids as they climbed in the bus taking them away. Knowing they would still have a home filled her heart with peace.

'That's wonderful, sir. Those young people will be happy.'

'And as far as you're concerned, there's something I'd like to ask you.'

'Go ahead, sir.'

A small pause, perhaps for reflection.

'Are you free on the Fourth of July?'

'I beg your pardon, sir?'

'It's my intention to propose you for the Congressional Gold Medal. It will be conferred here in Washington on the Fourth of July. Do you think you could keep that date free?'

Vivien smiled as if the president could see her. 'I'll cancel all my other engagements right away.'

'Good. You're a great person, Vivien.'

'You, too, sir.'

'I'm going to be president for another four years. You, fortunately, will stay the way you are for the rest of your life. I'll see you soon.'

'Thank you, sir.'

The voice disappeared and Vivien stood for a few moments at the desk, not knowing what to say or do. She put the receiver down and looked around. She read curiosity on the faces of those present. And she had no desire to satisfy it.

This was her moment she had no intention of sharing it with anybody.

A knock at the door came to the aid of her decision.

The mayor turned in that direction. 'Come in.'

A man of about thirty appeared in the doorway. In his hand was a newspaper.

'What is it, Trent?'

'There's something you ought to see, Mr Mayor.'

Gollemberg gestured, and Trent approached the desk. On it he placed a copy of the *New York Times*. The mayor looked at it briefly, then picked it up and turned it so that everyone in the room could see it.

'What's the meaning of this?'

Vivien, like all the others, stared open mouthed.

The front page was entirely taken up with a huge headline.

THE TRUE STORY OF A FALSE NAME
by Russell Wade

Beneath it were two photographs, quite sharp despite the limitations of newspaper reproduction. The first showed a young man holding a big black cat. In the second John Kortighan, his face turned slightly away from the camera, was sitting on a stool, clutching a gun, and staring with empty, absent eyes at a point somewhere to his right.

Everyone present turned to look at Russell, who as usual had chosen the chair furthest from the centre of the action. Feeling their eyes on him, he assumed an innocent expression.

'We had an agreement, didn't we?'

Vivien found herself smiling. It was true, of course. He was within his rights, and nobody at this point could accuse him of breaking his word. All the same, looking at that front page, she was puzzled by one thing. She decided to satisfy her curiosity.

'Russell, there's something I'd like to know.'

'Go ahead.'

'How did you manage to get that shot of John, if in all the time we were together I never saw you with a camera in your hand?'

Russell stood up and went to the desk. 'There's something I inherited from my brother. He taught me how and when to use it.'

He put a hand in his pocket and took it out, fist closed. Then he held out his arm. When he opened his fingers and allowed everyone to see what he had in his hand, Vivien could barely stop herself laughing. There on his palm was a miniature camera.

The True Story of a
False Name

It was raining at my mother's funeral and Vivien held my hand.

As I heard the rain beating down on the umbrella, I saw the coffin enter the grave in the small cemetery in Brooklyn where my grandparents are already buried, and felt sorry that I'd never really known Greta Light. But I think I'll make up for that in time, thanks to the memory of all the words we said to each other and the games we played and the happy moments we shared. Even though I tried to ruin everything, I'll be able to get through with the help of my aunt, who's an incredible woman, and a strong woman, in spite of the tears she was crying – but then everyone cries at the thought of death.

The priest talked about dust and earth and resurrection.

When I saw him, and heard those words, I thought about Father McKean and everything he'd meant to me and others like me. It was terrible to find out what was behind those eyes and what he was capable of doing, terrible to discover how evil can even reach places you'd think it could never reach.

They explained to me that his conscious mind wasn't responsible for his actions, but only that part of him that was in the grip of something wicked that he had no control over.

As if there are two different souls inside one body.

That wasn't hard to accept. It was easy to understand, because I've felt it myself.

I saw that sick part go down into the grave together with the body of Greta Light, my mother. Two corruptible parts, destined to return to the earth and turn back to dust. She and Father McKean, their true, living essences, will always be close to me and the person I will become. As I looked at Vivien's eyes, I realized, through the grief and the tears, that I had glimpsed the right path.

My father didn't come to the funeral.

He phoned me and said he was on the other side of the world and couldn't get back in time. Once, I would have missed him. I might even have cried. Now I have more important things to cry about.

I have a family. And he's chosen not to be part of it.

When it was all over and the people were already walking away, I stood there in the rain with Vunny in front of the freshly moved earth that smelled of musk and rebirth.

After a while she turned her head, and I saw where she was looking.

Standing there in the rain was a tall man, without a hat or an umbrella, but wearing a dark raincoat. I recognized him straight away. It was Russell Wade, the guy who followed the case with her and is publishing a series of articles in the *New York Times* called 'The True Story of a False Name'.

He used to appear in the papers because he'd been involved in some pretty dubious things. Now he seems to have found a way to turn everything around. That means that anything can change, when you least expect it and if you really want it. Vivien gave me the umbrella to hold and I saw her walk towards him in the driving rain.

They talked for a while and then he walked away. As he was going, I saw my aunt stand there watching him.

When she came back, I saw a new kind of sadness in her eyes, different from her sadness over Mother's death.

I squeezed her hand and she understood. I'm sure that sooner or later we'll talk.

Now I'm here, still at Joy, sitting in the garden, and the sky is clear of rain. In front of me is a stretch of water reflecting the sun. It seems like a good omen. I've understood many things in this place, in the simplest possible way. I've learned them day by day. While I was trying to understand the guys I was living with, I think I started to know myself.

I've discovered that the community isn't going to close, thanks to the government taking an interest. Even though Vivien has suggested I go live with her, I've decided that I'll stay here in future, and lend a hand, if they want it. I don't need Joy any more but I like to think Joy needs me.

My name is Sundance Green and tomorrow I'll be eighteen.

I press the button on the intercom and my secretary replies with her usual efficiency.

'Yes, Mr Wade?'

'Hold my calls for the next quarter of an hour.'

'Of course, Mr Wade.'

'No, make that half an hour.'

'Yes, Mr Wade. Enjoy your reading.'

There's a hint of amusement in her voice. I think she knows why I've taken this time. After all, she was the one who brought in the copy of the *New York Times* that's now lying in front of me on the desk. On the front page there's a headline so big you could see it from a plane.

The True Story of a False Name – Part Three.

But what interests me most is the name of the writer.

I start reading the article and it takes me a couple of columns to realize that it's damned good. I'm so surprised that I reserve the right to feel proud for a second time. Russell has the ability to draw the reader in and not let go of him. Of course, the story's a pretty gripping one anyway, but I must say he tells it brilliantly.

The light on the intercom comes on and my secretary's voice takes me by surprise.

'Mr Wade—'

'What is it? I told you I didn't want to be disturbed.'

'Your son's here.'

'Send him in.'

I slip the copy of the newspaper into my desk drawer. If anyone asked, I'd say I did it in order not to embarrass my son.

I'd be lying.

I really did it in order not to embarrass myself. I hate feeling embarrassed. It's a feeling I've sometimes spent hundreds of thousands of dollars to avoid.

After a couple of moments, Russell comes in. He looks calm and rested. He's wearing decent clothes and has even shaved.

'Hi, Dad.'

'Hello, Russell. I must congratulate you. You seem to have become a celebrity. And I'm sure it'll make you a whole lot of money.'

He shrugs. 'There are some things in life that money can't buy.'

I reply with a similar gesture. 'I'm sure there are, but I'm not very familiar with them. In my life I've always dealt with the other things.'

He sits down facing me and looks me in the eyes. It's a nice feeling.

'Enough of the two-bit philosophizing,' I say. 'What can I do for you?'

'I'm here to thank you. And I'm also here on business.'

I wait for him to continue. In spite of everything, my son has always had the ability to arouse my curiosity. Not to mention the ability to make me lose my temper like no one else.

'Without your help, I'd never have achieved the results I did. I'll be eternally grateful to you for that.'

I'm very pleased to hear these words. I'd never have imagined that one day I'd hear them from Russell's mouth. But I'm still curious.

'And what kind of business do you have with me?'

'You have something of mine that I'd like to buy back.'

At last I understand, and I can't help smiling. I open the desk drawer and from under the newspaper take out the contract he signed in return for my involvement. I place it on the desk, halfway between the two of us. 'Are you referring to this?'

'Yes. That's the one.'

I sit back in my chair and look him straight in the eyes. 'I'm sorry, son. But as you just said, there are some things money can't buy.'

He smiles, unexpectedly. 'But I don't intend to offer you money.'

'Really? What would you like to pay me with?'

He puts his hand in his pocket and takes out a small grey plastic object. He shows it to me and I see it's a digital tape recorder. 'With this.'

Experience has taught me to remain impassive. Even now I manage to do so. Problem is, he knows all about this ability of mine.

'What's that, if you don't mind my asking?'

I've asked the question in order to gain time, but if I haven't gone weak in the head all of a sudden, I know perfectly well what it is and what it's been used for.

He confirms it. 'It's a recorder containing the phone calls you made to the general. This tiny thing in return for that contract.'

'You'd never have the guts to use it against me.'

'Wouldn't I? Try me. I can see it already.' He moves his hand in front of him, in a gesture indicating a banner headline. 'A true story of corruption.'

I love chess. One of its rules is that when you're beaten you give credit to your opponent. Mentally I take the king and lay it down on the board. Then I take the contract from the desk. With a theatrical gesture, I tear it into tiny pieces and drop it in the wastepaper basket.

'It's done. Your commitment is cancelled.'

Russell stands up and puts the tape recorder down in front of me. 'I knew we'd come to an agreement.'

'That was blackmail.'

He looks at me with an amused expression. 'Of course it was.'

Russell checks the time. I see he's wearing a cheap Swatch. He must have sold the gold watch I gave him.

'I have to go. Larry King's waiting to interview me.'

Knowing him, it might be a joke. But given his sudden fame I wouldn't be surprised if it was true.

'Bye, Dad.'

'Goodbye. I can't say it was a pleasure.'

He walks to the door. His steps are noiseless on the carpet. So is the door when he opens it. I stop him as he's about to go out.

'Russell . . .'

He turns his face to me, that face everyone says is the image of mine.

'Yes?'

'One of these days, if you'd like to, you could come to lunch at the house. I think your mother would be very pleased to see you.'

He looks at me with eyes I'll have to become familiar with

in future. He takes a moment to reply. 'I'd like that. I'd like it very much.'

Then he leaves the room.

I sit there for a moment, thinking. In my life I've always been a businessman. Today I think I made a good deal. Then I reach out my hand to the recorder and press the button, ready to listen to the recording.

It hits me immediately. I always thought my son was a lousy poker player. But maybe he's one of those people who have the ability to learn from their mistakes.

The tape is blank.

There's not a damned thing on it.

I get up and go to the window. Below me is New York, one of the many cities I've conquered in my life. Today it seems to me a little more precious. An amusing thought crosses my mind.

My son, Russell Wade, is a great journalist and a great son of a bitch.

I think he got that second aspect of his character from me.

I'm in Boston, in the cemetery where my brother is buried. I'm inside the family vault, which has been welcoming the remains of the Wades for many years. The stone is white marble, like all the others. Robert smiles at me from his ceramic photograph, on which his face will never age.

We're more or less the same age now.

Today I had lunch with my family. I'd forgotten how big and luxurious their house was. The domestics when they saw me come in gave me the kind of looks Lazarus must have had after he had risen from the dead. There were even a few of them who'd never seen me in person. Only Henry, who walked with me to meet my mother and my father, squeezed my arm as he opened the door and stood aside to let me pass.

Then he whispered a few words. 'The true story of a false name. Nice work, Mr Russell.

At lunch, in that mansion where I grew up and shared so many things with Robert and my parents, things were a bit awkward after being away all those years. All that silence and all those harsh words couldn't be wiped out in a moment just by an effort of goodwill. But the food was excellent and we talked as we hadn't done for a long time.

Over coffee, my father mentioned something he had heard.

He said several people had talked about my name in connection with the Pulitzer. When he added that this time nobody would take it away from me, he smiled. My mother smiled, too, and I was finally able to breathe.

I acted as if nothing unusual had been said, and stared down at the dark liquid steaming in my cup.

I remembered the call I had made on my way back from Chillicothe. I called the *New York Times*, gave my name and asked to be put through to Wayne Constance. Many years earlier, in my brother's time, he had been in charge of the foreign desk. Now he was the editor of the whole damned paper.

Over the phone, his voice had sounded just the way I remembered it. 'Hi, Russell. What can I do for you?'

A touch of coldness. Suspicion. Curiosity.

I hadn't expected anything different. I knew I didn't deserve anything different.

'I can do something for you, Wayne. I have a real scoop on my hands.'

'Oh, yes? What's it about?'

A little less coldness. A bit more curiosity. Plus a hint of irony. The same suspicion.

'For the moment I can't tell you. The only thing I can tell you is that you can have the exclusive, if you want it.'

He took a moment to reply. 'Russell, don't you think you've disgraced yourself enough in the last few years?'

I knew the best response to that was to tell him he was right. 'Absolutely. But this time it's different.'

'Who can guarantee me that?'

'Nobody. But you'll see me and look at what I bring you.'

'Why are you so sure?'

'Two reasons. The first is that you're as curious as a

448

polecat. The second is that you'd never miss an opportunity to disgrace me even more.'

He laughed as if I had cracked a joke. We both knew perfectly well it was the truth.

'Russell, if you waste my time, I'll tell security to throw you out the window and I'll make sure personally they've done it.'

'You're a great man, Wayne.'

'Your brother was a great man. In his memory I'll take a look at what you have.'

I never heard from him again until after that night at Joy, the night when everyone's certainties had been overturned to give way to the vast emptiness of all the things we didn't know.

As we were waiting for the police to arrive and make their initial investigations, I went looking for a room with a computer and an Internet connection. When I found it, I shut myself away and drafted the first article. I managed to get it all down, as if someone behind me was dictating the words, as if I had always owned that story, as if I'd lived it a thousand times and told it just as often.

Then I emailed and sent it to the paper.

The rest is well known.

Two weeks have gone by since Vivien's sister's funeral. Two weeks since the last time I saw her, the last time we talked. Since that moment I've been on a merry-go-round that's been moving so fast. Now it's time for that merry-go-round to stop, because I still feel an emptiness that the lights of the TV studios and the interviews and my photograph on the front page, this time without any shame, can't fill. This whole crazy business has taught me that words left unexpressed are sometimes more dangerous and more damaging than those we scream at the top of our voice. It's taught me that sometimes the only way not to run risks is to take risks. And that the only way not to have debts is not to incur them.

Or to pay them.

And that's exactly what I'll do as soon as I get back to New York.

That's why I'm standing here by my brother's grave, looking at his face smiling back at me. I return that smile, hoping he can see it. Then I tell him something I've been dreaming of telling him for years.

'I made it, Robert.'

Then I turn and walk away.

Now we're both free.

The elevator reaches my floor and as soon as the sliding doors open I get a surprise. On the wall facing the elevator, stuck to the wall with transparent adhesive tape, is a photograph.

I go closer to get a proper look at it.

The photograph shows me, in profile, in Bellew's office, with an absorbed expression, my face slightly shaded by my hair. The shot has caught me in a moment of reflection, and captured to perfection the doubts and the sense of uselessness I was feeling at that moment.

I turn my head and on the wall to my left, just above the bell, is another photograph. I take it in my hand and by the light on the landing look closely.

I'm in this one as well.

In the living room of Lester Johnson's house in Hornell. My eyes are circled with fatigue but they have a determined expression, as I look at the photograph of Wendell Johnson and Matt Corey in Vietnam. I remember that moment well. It was a moment when everything seemed lost and yet suddenly hope was reborn.

The third photograph is attached to the middle of the door.

Me again, in the apartment in Williamsburg, studying the drawings in the folder for the first time. When I didn't yet know that they weren't bad works of art but the ingenious way a man had found to draw a map of his own madness. I remember my mood at that moment. I wasn't aware of my expression.

At this point I realize my door is ajar. I push the handle and the door opens with a squeak.

On the wall facing the entrance is another photograph.

In the dim light coming from outside and filtering into the darkness of the apartment, I can't quite make it out. I assume it's another picture of me.

The light comes on in the corridor. I take a step inside, more curious than worried.

To my right, in the middle of the living room, is Russell. He smiles and makes a comical gesture with his hands. 'Will I be arrested for breaking and entering?'

I pray to God that he doesn't make me say something stupid. Instead of which, before God has time to intervene, I manage it all by myself. 'How did you get in?'

He shows me the palm of his left hand. There's a bunch of keys in it.

'With the spare keys. I never gave them back to you. At least I can't be accused of forcing my way in.'

I go to him and look him in the eyes. I can't believe it but he's looking at me as I would have liked him to look at me from the first moment that I saw him. He moves aside and points to the table. I turn my eyes and see that it's laid for two, with a white linen tablecloth and china plates and silverware and a lighted candle in the middle.

'I did promise you dinner, remember?'

Maybe he doesn't know he's already won. Or else he does know and just wants to drive home his advantage. Either way, I have no intention of running away. I don't know what kind of expression I have on my face but, confused as I am, I still think it's a crime not to have a photograph of it.

Russell approaches the table and points to the food. 'Here it is. Prepared by my father's favourite chef. We have lobster, oysters, caviar and a whole lot of other things whose names I can't remember.' With an elegant gesture he indicates a bottle cooling in an ice bucket. 'For the fish course, we have the best champagne.' Then he picks up a bottle of red wine with a colourful label. 'And for the rest, Il Matto, a magnificent Italian wine.'

I go to him and throw my arms around his neck.

While I kiss him, I feel that everything is passing and everything is arriving at the same moment. That everything exists and nothing exists only because I'm kissing him. And when I feel him return my kiss, I think I would die without him.

I free myself for a moment. Only for a moment because that's all I can bear. 'Let's go to bed.'

'What about dinner?'

'To hell with dinner.'

He smiles. He smiles against my lips. 'The door's still open.'

'To hell with the door.'

We get to the bedroom and for a time that seems infinite I feel foolish and stupid and sluttish and beautiful and loved and adored and I command and implore and obey. At last his body is lying next to mine and there's a soft light beyond the curtains and his breathing is calm as he sleeps. Then I get out of bed, put on my bathrobe and go to the window. I let my gaze, at last without anxiety and without fear, move beyond the barrier of the glass.

Outside, heedless of the lights, heedless of human beings, a light wind is blowing upriver.

Maybe it's pursuing something or maybe it's being pursued by something.

But it's pleasant to stand here for a few moments and listen to it passing, rustling in the trees. It's a cool breeze, the kind that dries the tears of men and stops the angels from crying.

And at last I can sleep.

ACKNOWLEDGEMENTS

Reaching the end of a novel is like saying goodbye to a friend: it always leaves you feeling a bit empty. Fortunately, along the way you get a chance to see old friends again and make new ones. So I would like to thank:

– Dr Mary Elacqua of Rensselaer, along with Wonder Janet and Super Tony, her delightful parents, for welcoming me at Christmas as if I was family

– Pietro Bartocci, her inimitable husband, the only person in the world who can snore even when he's awake and conduct business at the same time

– Rosanna Capurso, the brilliant New York architect, with her fiery red hair and her equally warm sense of friendship

– Franco di Mare, almost a brother to me, whose suggestions were crucial in drawing a portrait of a war reporter. If the portrait was convincing, the merit is obviously all mine. If it wasn't, the fault is all his

– Ernest Amabile, who conveyed to me as a man the things he saw and experienced in Vietnam as a boy

– Antonio Monda for making me feel like an Italian intellectual in New York

– Antonio Carlucci for sharing his experience with me and helping me discover a fantastic restaurant

– Claudio Nobis and Elena Croce, for offering me hospitality and books

– Ivan Genasi and Silvia Dell'Orto, for sharing with me the arrival of a stork from the Ikea store in Brooklyn

– Rosaria Carnevale, who apart from supplying me with fresh bread during my stay in New York, really is an excellent bank president

– Zef, who apart from being a friend really is the manager of a building on 29th Street

– Claudia Peterson, who really is a vet, and her husband Roby Facini, for lending me the story of Waltz, their unusual three-legged cat

– Carlo Medori, who has made cynicism his pastime and affection his essence

– Detective Michael Medina of the 13th Precinct of the New York Police Department, for his kind assistance at a difficult moment

– Don Antonio Mazzi, for his advice on matters relating to the priesthood. And for being in a way, with his rehabilitation communities, the inspiration for part of this story and the chief character in a wonderful adventure

– Dr Elda Feyles, anatomopathologist at the Civic Hospital of Asti and Doctor Vittorio Montano, neurologist at the same institution, for their scientific advice during the writing of this novel.

Last but not least I am obliged, though with infinite pleasure, to return yet again to my little work team, composed of people who, after all this time, face me with an alternative:

either they're not yet fed up with me

or if they are, they're amazingly good at pretending they aren't.

In both cases they deserve your applause:

– the buccaneering Alessandro Dalai, to make him understand that there's a difference between grapnel and grappa

– the crystalline Cristina Dalai, to make her continue

undaunted to replace the glasses I regularly break

– the encyclopaedic Francesco Colombo, my incomparable editor, because, luckily for him and for me, he has one more brain and one fewer Bentley

– the Cheguevaristic Stefano Travagli who, like Oscar Wilde, knows the importance of being Ernest

– the elegiac Mara Scanavino, a sublime art director, so that, in her highly creative way, she can succeed in putting everything through the mill of colour

– the Pythagorean Antonella Fassi, because he dances in the hearts of us authors with the same lightfootedness as he dances on our writings

– the glittering Alessandra Santangelo and Chiara Codeluppi, my invaluable Press Sisters, who can turn their chests into shields and ramparts.

And along with them all the guys at the Baldini Castoldi Dalai publishing house, who always make me feel like a great writer, even though the jury is still out on that one.

To them I add my agent, the science-fictional Piergiorgio Nicolazzini, because he welcomed as a true friend my alien arrival on his planet.

As in the usual formula, the characters in this story, apart from Waltz, are imaginary and any resemblance to actual people is purely coincidental.

Anyone who has read this novel will have realized that there is nothing autobiographical about the title. For anyone who hasn't and suspects there might be, I'll leave that assumption intact, as it does me a great deal of honour.

Having said that, I take my leave with a bow and a flourish of my plumed hat.

natural colour 38.34

proscription sentence of death or banishment 8.25

proselyte convert 205.10

protegé *French* one who is under the protection or care of another 178.13, 230.41, 230.42

protocol legal document 172.1

prove demonstrate, establish as true 142.33, 143.14

proven *Scots* established or demonstrated to be true 28.41

prut, prutt expression of scorn or defiance 128.7, 139.39

pshaw disparaging exclamation 138.20, 210.12, 224.36, 231.29

public short for public house 35.12, 35.39, 36.29

pu'd *Scots* pulled 48.24

pudding-eater Englishman, consumer of different kinds of sweet or savoury boiled puddings 182.18 (see note)

pugilistic relating to fighting with the fists 129.15, 129.34, 144.17

puir *Scots* poor 40.24 etc.

puling whining 236.30

punch drink usually composed of spirits, lemon, sugar and spices 174.22, 175.3, 211.41

punctilio trifling point of conduct, formality 143.14

pund *Scots* pound 41.18, 41.29

purlieus disreputable quarter, mean streets about a main thoroughfare 231.20

purpy *Scots* water-purpie, brooklime, medicinal and culinary herb 51.21

pursuer *Scots law* plaintiff 20.14

put *Gaelic English* but 47.35 etc.

quaigh *Scots* shallow, bowl-shaped drinking-cup 91.8 etc.

quality social rank 7.24

quarry *hunting* object of chase, prey 25.18

quart two pints, quarter gallon (3.6 litres) 152.19

quartering coats of arms marshalled to denote a family's alliances 24.22

quarter-master officer responsible for providing quarters for soldiers 250.36

quarter-staff pole six to eight feet long (2 metres) used in warfare and sport 188.24

quean *Scots* bold woman, hussy 123.24, 161.27

quha *Scots* who 23.22 (see note)

quhile *Scots* while 24.7

quhilk *Scots* which 23.30 etc.

quhom *Scots* whom 24.9

quick-match quick-burning match used for firing cannon 221.17

quizzing making fun of, ridiculing 13.26

quondam former 14.40, 16.23, 133.34

quoth said 67.32

quotha said he 136.37

raff low, worthless fellow 135.24

raillery good-humoured ridicule, banter 3.31, 286.23

rajah *Hindi* king, prince, Hindu title of nobility 252.6

rajahpoot (rajput) *Hindi* member of a Hindu warrior people in North India 155.33, 199.38

rap very small or worthless coin 213.42

rasp implement for making a noise by rubbing a ring on ribbed metal 58.6 (see note)

rationale rational basis, reasoned explanation 222.13

rattan switch or stick made of rattan, palm growing chiefly in the East Indies 216.38

ratten *Scots* rat 42.18

reason satisfaction, recompense 132.2

receipt recipe 46.37, 54.12

recketh cares, heeds 247.29

reckoning bill 43.34

recur return in thought or memory 62.9

reel *Scots* lively dance for couples facing each other 188.9

regale gratify, entertain 40.38, 70.29

reiving *Scots* despoiling, robbing 43.17

removit *Scots* removed 23.22

rencounter encounter, duel 245.22, 249.16

reprehension censure, reproof 36.43

reprobate person who has fallen from grace or from religion, one lost in sin 217.4

reprobated censured, condemned 25.27

resenting expressing resentment by an act of revenge 211.17

reserving with the reservation 45.19

resetting *Scots* sheltering, giving protection to 24.36

reticule woman's small bag, workbag 148.20

revêche *French* cross, cantankerous 39.14

revolve ponder, turn over in the mind 213.16

ribaldry obscenity, scurrilous jesting 212.33, 217.2

riband ribbon 200.34

riding traversing on horseback 64.39, 195.26

rigging-tree *Scots* ridge-beam of a roof 41.10

ring circle formed for boxers 129.12 etc.

rokelay *Scots* short cloak worn by women 180.19

roll rapid, uniform sounds producing a continuous reverberation 279.3

rood measure of land 72.36

roof *Scots* ceiling of a room 39.32

roof-tree main beam or ridge of a roof 91.10

room place 146.2

rose-leaf rose-petal 287.28

round bout in a boxing-match 129.11

roy *Gaelic ruadh* red, red-haired 7.23, 78.6, 126.19

rubber number of games at cards, the last of which is played to determine the winner when the parties are equal 157.20

rudas *Scots* ugly, witch-like 123.24

runt *Scots* ox or cow for fattening and slaughter 135.10

rupee *Urdu* the monetary unit of India 199.2, 265.25, 270.20

ryal *Scots* royal 23.28

'Sdeath *oath* contraction of God's death 149.2

sa *Scots* so 23.20

sabre cavalry sword having a curved edge specially adapted for cutting 129.25 etc.

sacring marking the moment of consecration 118.34, 119.7

sae *Scots* so 41.36 etc.

sahib, saib *Urdu* respectful title used by Indians addressing a European 272.24, 272.37; also

affixed to Indian titles or names 281.3

sailing-master officer in charge of the navigation of a vessel 69.4

sain *Scots* bless 111.9, 111.40

sair *Scots* sore 140.13

saloon large public room 59.9, 59.16, 59.19, 60.35

sapient *noun* person remarkable for wisdom 127.7

salam (salaam) *Arabic* the salutation 'peace (be upon you)' 276.11; ceremonious obeisance consisting in India of a low bowing of the head and body with the palm of the right hand placed on the forehead 260.30

salts see note to 159.11

sang *Scots* song 54.9

sanguine optimistic 202.19, 203.3

sasine *Scots law* legal document which testifies to the lawful possession of property 152.17

Sassenach *Scots from Gaelic* Saxon, English, lowland Scots 88.41, 92.20

sate sat 4.21 etc.

saturnine gloomy 57.10, 202.19

saul *Scots* soul 135.12

saw maxim, proverb 199.43

Saxon lowland Scot, Englishman 49.17 (see note) etc.; lowland, English 77.41 etc.

scabbard sheath for a dagger or sword 128.22, 280.31

scheik (sheikh) *Arabic* head of a Muslim religious order 274.39, 275.38

scimitar short, curved, single-edged sword used especially by the Turks and Persians 274.9

scourge whip, lash 108.12 etc., cause of calamity, disease causing many deaths 222.32

scourged flogged 92.21, 92.21

scratch line across a boxing-ring 136.31 (see note), 137.25

screech-owl name for the barn owl, from its discordant cry, supposed to be of evil omen 262.20

scunner *Scots* shudder indicating aversion or dislike 175.15

scutcheon escutcheon, coat of arms, shield 41.35

sea-chest seaman's box for his personal property 213.2, 238.36

seal signet engraved with the heraldic bearing of the owner 210.7, 210.13, 210.21; something which confirms 173.30

seannachie *Gaelic seanachaidh* professional recounter of history, genealogy and legends 67.23, 93.26

second assistant 245.10

sea-pie meat and vegetable dish with a pastry crust 211.39

self-devotion devoting oneself, giving one's life 108.21

seignior *Portuguese senhor*, title of address for a man 173.10

selt *Gaelic English* sold 139.32

seneschal steward 35.35

seraglio *from Turkish via Italian* part of a Muslim house or palace in which wives and concubines are secluded 282.9

serve satisfy 140.12

settled *Scots adjective* composed 74.41

settlement *law* act of settling property upon a person 200.30

sexagenarian person sixty years old 13.26

shafts arrows 129.24

shairman *Gaelic English* chairman, carrier of a sedan chair 47.18

shambles meat market, abattoir 106.26, 124.32

shawl *Persian and Urdu* oblong piece of material made from the hair of the Tibetan goat, worn in the East and imported into Europe 229.18 etc.

she *Gaelic English* I 131.42

shelled removed as from a shell 16.25

shentleman *Gaelic English* gentleman 47.26, 48.17, 48.24, 54.26

sherbet *Turkish and Persian* cooling drink of the East made with fruit juice, sugar and water 248.17

sheriff *Scots* legal officer who performs judicial and administrative duties 48.16

sheriff-officer *Scots* official who carries out the warrants of a sheriff 47.33 (see note)

shibboleth word or sound whose pronunciation is used as a test for detecting foreigners 130.2 (see note)

shieling *Scots* rough hut 89.37

shilling coin worth twelve pence (5p) 22.6 etc.

shooting-pony pony trained to withstand fire 286.16

shouldna *Scots* should not 191.7

show agricultural show 30.11

shudge *Gaelic English* judge 132.6, 136.24

shuttle instrument used in weaving for passing the thread of the weft across the cloth between the threads of the warp 38.32

sibyl woman of antiquity reputed to possess powers of prophecy and divination 120.9, 127.23

sic *Scots* such 23.37 etc.

siclike *Scots* such like 40.32, 47.33

sidier *Gaelic saighdear* soldier 78.6, 85.33

signal *adjective* striking 139.17

siller *Scots* silver, money 46.42 etc.

simple plant or herb used medicinally 97.29

since ago 141.43

sindry *Scots* sundry 24.1

sipahee (sepoy) *Persian and Urdu* Indian employed as a soldier in a British army 270.24, 270.27

sirdar *Urdu* in India military leader, officer 265.13 etc.

siren *Classical mythology* one of the fabulous creatures part woman, part bird who lured sailors to destruction by their singing 28.21

skene-dhu *Gaelic sgian dubh* black knife 125.13, 128.12, 139.30

skirl *Scots* make a shrill noise, cry 41.7, 163.12

slough muddy ground, mire, bog 31.41, 77.12

sma' *Scots* small 41.37

smack single-masted sailing vessel for coastal use 16.42

smock-frocks loose-fitting garments of coarse cloth worn by English labourers 140.32

smoking driving at speed 32.8

sneeshing *Scots* snuff 135.28

snood *Scots* ribbon worn round the hair by young unmarried women 49.14, 49.17

snuff-mull *Scots* snuff-box 126.35

snuffing trimming the wick of a candle to make it burn more brightly 181.19

snug in a state of ease and quiet enjoyment 22.13

sod turf 74.3, 84.20, 135.41

solecism ungrammatical use of language, violation of the rules 153.17

something *Scots adverb* somewhat, a little 133.13, 134.9

soporific tending to induce sleep 97.36

sorrel chestnut-coloured horse 50.43

souple *Scots* supple 191.10

Southlander inhabitant of the lowlands or south of Scotland 129.37

southrons *Scots* southerners, English 24.28

sowar *Urdu* in Anglo-Indian use, native horseman 269.18

sowarree (sowarry) *Urdu* mounted attendants of a person of high rank, cavalcade 278.31

spaewife *Scots* female fortune-teller 127.4, 128.36

spellit *Scots* spelled 23.20

spindle instrument used in spinning to twist the fibres into thread 80.43, 81.1

spinnage spinach 174.17

spiog *Gaelic spòg* leg, foot 125.32

spirted spurted 284.17

spontoon half-pike carried by infantry officers 59.30 (see note)

sporran *Gaelic sporan* purse 48.18 etc.

sprack *Scots* lively, animated, alert 129.18

stage-coach coach running between specified stages taking paying passengers 29.23

stamach *Scots* stomach 47.19

stand *Scots* complete set, outfit 58.16

stane *Scots* stone 41.10, 41.38, 49.11

start *Scots* leap 130.39 (see note)

stays underbodice stiffened to give shape to the figure, corset 156.10

stiletto short dagger 143.41

stilt handle 23.39

stirk *Scots* young bullock 87.34

stock farm animals 131.29

stot *Scots* bullock in its second year or more 129.41, 132.1

strain melody, tune 232.20

strath *Scots* broad river valley 97.23, 118.37

strathspey slowish Scottish dance, danced in couples 188.8

stucco-work plaster moulded for decorative effect 33.27

sublunary existing beneath the moon, earthly, temporal 176.11

subpoena'd *law* summoned, served with a writ 147.7

subsisted *transitive verb* provided sustenance for, supported 130.37

succession estate, inheritance 155.42

sugar-plum sweet 287.23

sulphur highly inflammable chemical, associated in popular belief with the fires of hell 233.1

sultaun (sultan) *from Arabic via French* sovereign or chief ruler of a Muslim country 51.34, 248.31

summat *Scots* something 135.15

supple *Scots* stout stick 128.33

supporters *heraldry* figures on either side of the shield in a coat of arms 38.33

surgeon doctor, general practitioner 159.42

surplice loose white garment worn by episcopalian clergy 154.30

surtout overcoat 20.31

swart black, dusky 57.29

sweepit *Scots* swept 40.5

swivel short for swivel-gun, small gun mounted on a swivel so as to turn horizontally in any direction 278.42

syne *Scots* since 43.18

tabatière *French* snuff-box 63.17

tacksman *Scots* tenant, especially a relative of the landowner acting as chief tenant 82.20 (see note)

tail long piece of land jutting out from a larger piece 49.3 (see note)

taishataragh *Gaelic taibhsearachd* second sight 127.39

tak *Scots* take 48.17 etc.

taken *Scots* bewitched 127.12

tale counting 246.41

tallow animal fat, used especially for making candles and soap 200.36

tamarind *Arabic* tree whose pods contain an acid pulp used in medicine and cookery 246.10

tangs *Scots* tongs 48.25

tank *Portuguese from an Eastern original* in India pool, reservoir or cistern for the storage of water 280.12, 280.38

tantivy sound of galloping or of a horn 218.25

tap-room room in a tavern where liquor is on tap 138.27

tartan woollen cloth checkered in different colours worn by highlanders 49.10 etc.

Tartarian from Tartary 247.10 (see note)

tatoo (tattoo) *Hindi* native-bred Indian pony 270.30

tauld *Scots* told 49.10

teak *Portuguese from a South Indian original* hard, durable wood used for houses and ship-building 269.7

tee'd *golf* placed on the ground ready for driving off 150.30

teedling *Scots* humming, or singing a tune without words or so softly that the words are scarcely heard 46.14

teinds *Scots* tithes, ecclesiastical dues 28.31 (see note)

tell'd *Scots* told 42.30, 42.33

Telinga *Hindustani* in Anglo-Indian usage Indian soldier disciplined and dressed in European fashion; sepoy 272.38 (see note)

tenement building of three or more storeys divided into flats 49.27

tenor course, drift, way of proceeding 21.39, 78.42, 121.29, 122.20

term-day day appointed for payment, especially the four annual Scottish quarter-days 42.39

thae *Scots* those 39.15, 161.27

thane *Scottish history* person holding land of the king, Scottish lord 189.42, 192.16

thaness female thane (Scott's invention) 189.42

themsells *Scots* themselves 39.16

thirlage *Scots law* legal restriction whereby lands were thirled, or tied to a particular mill for the grinding of grain 154.42

threep *Scots* insist, assert against opposition 163.12

thrift *Scots* work, industry 39.12, 41.15

thrum *Scots adjective* made of waste or ends of thread 71.15

tiara raised headdress worn in the east and varying according to the rank of the wearer, kind of turban 250.2

tight *Scots* neat, smart, carefully dressed 46.12

till't *Scots* to it 19.8

tilting jousting, engaging in combat on horseback 59.26

tip *slang* give 135.36

toady flatter, attend with servility 251.41

toilette dressing-table 59.41, process of dressing 60.3

tom-tom *Hindustani* Indian hand-beaten drum 279.4

tope *Tamil* clump, plantation of trees, especially a mango grove 276.41

toper hard drinker 212.10

topping *colloquial* excellent 126.6

topsmen *Scots* chief man in charge of a drove of cattle, head drover 124.28

toustie *Scots* testy, irascible 36.3

town-clerk person in charge of the legal business of a town 168.39 etc.

townfit *Scots* lower end of a town or village, town-foot 159.11

townhead, town-head upper end of a town or village 159.10, 182.10

town-house town hall 190.3

toy *Scots* cap worn by elderly women with a back flap reaching the shoulders 161.19

track *Scots* tract 82.21

traffic trade, bargain 125.20, 140.29, 262.27

trafficker trader, merchant 199.25

trafficking trading, dealing 164.22

travailed suffered childbirth 230.15

trepanned swindled, ensnared 213.7, 224.30

trew *Scots* believe 45.28

triad set of three lines 44.27

trinketing secret negotiation, underhand dealing, 164.22

troat *Gaelic English* throat 48.17

trolling singing jovially 140.33

troth truth; abbreviation of by my troth, an asseveration or assertion of truth 174.30, 184.21, 191.9

tryste *Scots* market especially for the sale of livestock, fair 136.15, 140.18

tuft clump 45.3

turf-fire fire of peat or turf cut as fuel 141.34

turnkey one who has charge of the keys of a prison, jailer 214.42

turnpike road on which the user pays

a toll 124.39, 206.7; (of a staircase) spiral 60.5

turn-up casual boxing contest, fight with the fists 136.20

tush exclamation of impatience or disparagement 88.16, 136.42

tussle contest, scuffle 135.41, 138.2

tutelar protecting, guardian 240.43

twa *Scots* two 40.27 etc.

twopenny *Scots* weak ale or beer sold at twopence a Scots pint (1.7 litres) 134.41

t'ye *Scots* to you 175.2, 175.2

tyned *Scots* wasted 123.25

Ulla (Allah) *Arabic* name of the Deity among Muslims 269.27

umph exclamation expressive of doubt or dissatisfaction 46.20, 65.19, 67.13

unconscientious careless, unscrupulous 264.12

untimely unusually late or early 122.5

unwonted unaccustomed 81.38, 134.4

unwontedly unusually 59.5

usquebaugh *Gaelic uisge-beatha* whisky 46.36, 70.40, 84.43

vailed lowered, yielded 201.8

vakeel *Urdu* agent, envoy, ambassador 268.8 etc.

valet-de-chambre *French* man-servant, personal servant 58.14

valet-de-place *French* guide to show strangers round a locality 69.39

valziant *Scots* valiant 23.24

vapouring acting in a pretentious manner 174.31

vaward vanguard 56.10

veamos *Spanish* let us see 52.17 (see note)

venial pardonable 286.15

vermint obnoxious or troublesome person 48.19

vested secured, assigned 173.6, 208.9

vicarage *Scots* teinds or tithes for the support of the vicar of a parish 28.31 (see note)

vicinage vicinity 59.15

victuals food, provisions 215.15

victualled supplied with food 125.9

vidette mounted sentry placed in advance of a military force as a look-out 269.20

vizard mask 3.8, 3.18, 3.29, 163.27

vizier high official or viceroy in the Turkish empire 273.37

voluptuary *adjective* given to luxurious and sensual pleasures 277.25

wa' *Scots* wall 41.10

wad *Scots* would 35.42

wadna *Scots* would not 36.2, 73.18

wae *Scots* woe 140.13

walth *Scots* wealth 35.23

walthier *Scots* wealthier 25.16

wan *Scots* won 42.23

wanchancy *Scots wansonsy*, mischievous, treacherous 139.37

ware *Scots* goods, cash 42.24

wared *Scots* spent, wasted 48.20

wark *Scots* work 40.27, 47.25

warld *Scots* world 40.24

wasna *Scots* was not 184.5, 184.31

wattled made of interwoven branches of pliable wood 104.32

weal good, prosperity 77.18, 127.25, 217.11

wean *Scots* child 40.19, 40.32, 169.29, 175.39

web piece of woven fabric 38.32

wee *Scots* little 36.3

weel *Scots* well 23.20 etc.

weigh *nautical* heave up an anchor before sailing 229.3

well-looked *Scots* good looking, handsome 131.25

werena *Scots* were not 40.39, 49.9

westlandman man from the west, here Dumfriesshire 128.29

wet-nurse woman hired to suckle and nurse another woman's child 163.38, 168.14

wha *Scots* who 36.11 etc.

whare *Scots* where 45.28

wheen *Scots* few, a number 140.2

whin *Scots* few, a number 48.18

whilk *Scots* which 47.25

whilst while 29.27 etc.

whipper-in huntsman's assistant who keeps hounds from straying with a whip 122.37, 286.39

whipper-snapper diminutive and insignificant person, especially a sprightly and impertinent young person 182.27

whisk whist 22.13

wi' *Scots* with 35.22 etc.

wicket small gate in or beside a larger one, for pedestrians 57.4, 7.11

wife old woman of humble rank 169.32

wildfire furious, destructive fire, often caused by lightning 221.17

winna *Scots* will not 36.10, 40.15, 41.30, 140.17

winterers *Scots* animals kept for fattening over the winter 132.1

wires *Scots* knitting needles made of wire 54.18

wolf-burd *Scots* wolf-cub 111.7, 112.7

woof threads crossing from side to side of a web, woven fabric 288.2

wont *noun* custom 71.5, 74.24, 122.7, 134.43

wont *adjective* accustomed, used 50.39, 145.24

work *noun* sewing 175.1

work *verb* knit 50.21

work-basket sewing-basket 150.18, 154.2

wot know 134.43, 136.38

wraith apparition of a person living or dead, ghost 139.28

wrang *Scots* wrong 135.12, 140.22

wranged *Scots* wronged 135.29, 140.3, 175.27

wrapping-gown night-gown 18.20

writing-chamber *Scots* lawyer's office 149.6

writt writ, scripture 23.34

wunna *Scots* will not 140.12

yaud *Scots* old, worn-out horse 23.40

ye *Scots* you 19.5 etc.

yea yes 67.32

yeoman countryman 129.24, 130.25 (see note), 141.23

yeomanly with the qualities of a countryman 200.26

yin *Scots* one 191.19

yon *Scots demonstrative adjective* that (one) over there, yonder 73.25 etc.

yoursell *Scots* yourself 47.26, 184.5

zenana *Persian and Hindustani* part of a house in which the women of a family were secluded; also the wives and concubines so secluded, harem 263.18, 265.21, 266.9, 282.7

PENGUIN ⓟ CLASSICS

The Classics Publisher

'Penguin Classics, one of the world's greatest series' JOHN KEEGAN

'I have never been disappointed with the Penguin Classics. All I have read is a model of academic seriousness and provides the essential information to fully enjoy the master works that appear in its catalogue' MARIO VARGAS LLOSA

'Penguin and Classics are words that go together like horse and carriage or Mercedes and Benz. When I was a university teacher I always prescribed Penguin editions of classic novels for my courses: they have the best introductions, the most reliable notes, and the most carefully edited texts' DAVID LODGE

'Growing up in Bombay, expensive hardback books were beyond my means, but I could indulge my passion for reading at the roadside bookstalls that were well stocked with all the Penguin paperbacks ... Sometimes I would choose a book just because I was attracted by the cover, but so reliable was the Penguin imprimatur that I was never once disappointed by the contents.

Such access certainly broadened the scope of my reading, and perhaps it's no coincidence that so many Merchant Ivory films have been adapted from great novels, or that those novels are published by Penguin' ISMAIL MERCHANT

'You can't write, read, or live fully in the present without knowing the literature of the past. Penguin Classics opens the door to a treasure house of pure pleasure, books that have never been bettered, which are read again and again with increased delight' JOHN MORTIMER

CLICK ON A CLASSIC
www.penguinclassics.com
The world's greatest literature at your fingertips

Constantly updated information on over 1600 titles, from Icelandic sagas to ancient Indian epics, Russian drama to Italian romance, American greats to African masterpieces

•

The latest news on recent additions to the list, updated editions and specially commissioned translations

•

Original scholarly essays by leading writers: Elaine Showalter on Zola, Laurie R. King on Arthur Conan Doyle, Frank Kermode on Shakespeare, Lisa Appignanesi on Tolstoy

•

A wealth of background material, including biographies of every classic author from Aristotle to Zamyatin, plot synopses, readers' and teachers' guides, useful web links

•

Online desk and examination copy assistance for academics

•

Trivia quizzes, competitions, giveaways, news on forthcoming screen adaptations

•

eBooks available to download

READ MORE IN PENGUIN

In every corner of the world, on every subject under the sun, Penguin represents quality and variety – the very best in publishing today.

For complete information about books available from Penguin – including Puffins and Penguin Classics – and how to order them, write to us at the appropriate address below. Please note that for copyright reasons the selection of books varies from country to country.

In the United Kingdom: *Please write to* Dept EP, Penguin Books Ltd, Bath Road, Harmondsworth, West Drayton, Middlesex UB7 0DA

In the United States: *Please write to* Consumer Services, Penguin Putnam Inc., 405 Murray Hill Parkway, East Rutherford, New Jersey 07073-2136. *VISA and MasterCard holders call 1-800-631-8571 to order Penguin titles*

In Canada: *Please write to* Penguin Books Canada Ltd, 10 Alcorn Avenue, Suite 300, Toronto, Ontario M4V 3B2

In Australia: *Please write to* Penguin Books Australia Ltd, 487 Maroondah Highway, Ringwood, Victoria 3134

In New Zealand: *Please write to* Penguin Books (NZ) Ltd, Private Bag 102902, North Shore Mail Centre, Auckland 10

In India: *Please write to* Penguin Books India Pvt Ltd, 11, Community Centre, Panchsheel Park, New Delhi 110017

In the Netherlands: *Please write to* Penguin Books Netherlands bv, Postbus 3507, NL-1001 AH Amsterdam

In Germany: *Please write to* Penguin Books Deutschland GmbH, Metzlerstrasse 26, 60594 Frankfurt am Main

In Spain: *Please write to* Penguin Books S. A., Bravo Murillo 19, 1°B, 28015 Madrid

In Italy: *Please write to* Penguin Italia s.r.l., Via Vittoria Emanuele 45 1a, 20094 Corsico, Milano

In France: *Please write to* Penguin France, 12, Rue Prosper Ferradou, 31700 Blagnac

In Japan: *Please write to* Penguin Books Japan Ltd, Iidabashi KM-Bldg, 2-23-9 Koraku, Bunkyo-Ku, Tokyo 112-0004

In South Africa: *Please write to* Penguin Books South Africa (Pty) Ltd, P.O. Box 751093, Gardenview, 2047 Johannesburg

Sagas of Warrior-Poets

A famous poet and fighter spends an illicit night with a woman he failed to marry long ago. Her husband has no choice but to seek redress...

All the Icelandic sagas portray a world well aware of the power of words: to praise, to blame, to curse and to taunt. Yet these five stories are unusual in putting a skald, or poet, centre stage and building the plot around his travels to seek fame, his doomed love for a married woman and his hostilities against her menfolk.

Although the mainly thirteenth-century authors drew on semi-historical traditions about people and events over two centuries before, they portrayed vivid and enduring scenes of everyday life in the farmsteads of windswept Iceland – making hay, hunting seals, rounding up sheep and struggling through blizzards. Most of the poet-heroes are notably difficult characters, whose restless energy threatens the peace of their communities, and whose own faults, as much as fate, bar them from happiness. Full of fights, invective and voyaging, these sagas also deploy their terse prose and intricate verse to explore human motive and behaviour in non-aristocratic society, and as such they are almost unique in the medieval literature of Europe.

Edited with an introduction by DIANA WHALEY

EDGAR ALLEN POE

The Fall of the House of Usher and Other Writings

'And much of Madness and more of Sin
And Horror the Soul of the Plot'

This selection of Poe's critical writings, short fiction and poetry demonstrates his intense interest in aesthetic issues, and the astonishing power and imagination with which he probed the darkest corners of the human mind. 'The Fall of the House of Usher' describes the final hours of a family tormented by tragedy and the legacy of the past. In 'The Tell Tale Heart', a murderer's insane delusions threaten to betray him, while stories such as 'The Pit and the Pendulum' and 'The Cask of Amontillado' explore extreme states of decadence, fear and hate. These works display Poe's startling ability to build suspense with almost nightmarish intensity.

David Galloway's introduction re-examines the myths surrounding Poe's life and reputation. This edition includes a new chronology and further reading.

'The most original genius that America has produced'
ALFRED, LORD TENNYSON

'Poe has entered our popular consciousness as no other American writer' *The New York Times Book Review*

Edited with an introduction by DAVID GALLOWAY